3-13-09

FICTION

Border Lass

AMANDA SCOTT

Border Lass

FOREVER

NEW YORK   BOSTON

Book design by Giorgetta Bell McRee
Cover design by Claire Brown

Forever
Hachette Book Group USA
237 Park Avenue
New York, NY 10017
Visit our Web site at www.HachetteBookGroupUSA.com

ISBN-13: 978-0-7394-9943-6

Forever is an imprint of Grand Central Publishing.
The Forever name and logo is a trademark of Hachette Book Group USA, Inc.

Printed in the United States of America

*To Julie and Pat
for all you have given to each other.
And to Tanner, just for being Tanner.*

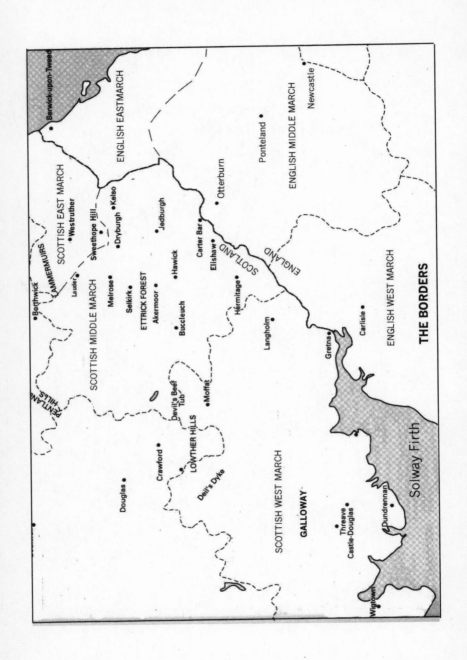

THE BORDERS

Berwick-upon-Tweed

SCOTTISH EAST MARCH

ENGLISH EASTMARCH

ENGLISH MIDDLE MARCH

Newcastle

Ponteland

Otterburn

Westruther

Sweethope Hill

Dryburgh • Kelso

Jedburgh

Carter Bar

Elishaw

LAMMERMUIRS

Lauder

Borthwick

SCOTTISH MIDDLE MARCH

Melrose

Selkirk

ETTRICK FOREST

Akermoor

Buccleuch

Hawick

Hermitage

Langholm

SCOTLAND

ENGLAND

ENGLISH WEST MARCH

Carlisle

Gretna

PENTLAND HILLS

Devil's Beef Tub

Moffat

Crawford

LOWTHER HILLS

Deil's Dyke

Douglas

SCOTTISH WEST MARCH

GALLOWAY

Threave
Castle-Douglas

Dundrennan

Solway Firth

Wigtown

Author's Note

For readers who appreciate some basic information straightaway, I include the following definitions and pronunciation guide:

Buccleuch = Buck LOO (or, as my resident phonics purist insists, Buh-CLOO)

Hawick = HOYK

"Himself," where it appears capitalized in this book, refers to Buccleuch. (Note: It could also refer to Douglas if spoken by his adherents. In general, when such a reference is made, the speaker is referring to the chief of his clan or kindred.)

Scone Abbey = Scoon Abbey

Sir John Edmonstone of that Ilk = Sir John Edmonstone of Edmonstone

The Douglas = the Earl of Douglas

Prologue

─◦─

Dunfermline Abbey, Scotland, 1389

He had been watching her most of the day.

In such a vast, merry crowd as the one gathered along the snow-covered shore of Loch Fitty, north of Dunfermline Abbey and its nearby royal palace, it was easy for him to watch the lass without drawing attention to himself.

At a rough guess, nearly a thousand people had come to enjoy the festivities preceding a Yuletide wedding in the abbey of the Earl of Douglas's eldest son to Margaret Stewart, daughter of the heir to Scotland's throne.

The lass he watched wore a long, hooded cloak of sable-trimmed, claret-colored velvet over a violet-and-black-striped silk skirt and bodice. He noted that a few dark tendrils had escaped the colorful beaded netting that confined her hair. And when she snatched up her skirts to leap out of the way of a snowball, he saw sable-trimmed winter boots that covered her legs to her knees.

She had drawn his gaze from the first moment he saw her. But had anyone asked why, he'd have had trouble explaining. He might have said that her figure, rosy cheeks, and wide grin reminded him of his mother. But surely, no man felt drawn to a woman because of a slight, doubtless wholly imagined, maternal resemblance. In his view, a man simply responded to an attraction. He did not try to explain it.

Although the lass's figure was rounder and more buxom than fashion decreed, he thought she looked as if she'd be a cozy armful, the kind of woman with whom a man could find comfort. She was clearly merry and fun-loving, and although many might condemn her present lack of dignity, he did not.

Winter-crisp air or rouge had turned her full lips as red as her cheeks. Her dark eyes sparkled as she laughed, then ducked another snowball that someone had hurled and scooped up one of her own to fling back.

Seeing hers fly straight to its target, he frowned when he recognized a young courtier who had been shamelessly flirting with her an hour earlier.

As experienced as he was himself in the art of dalliance, he had easily read her behavior then as well-practiced but meaningless flirtation. She did not care a rap for the lad but was enjoying herself nonetheless.

The young man's behavior seemed less playful, mayhap even predatory.

Despite that, the watcher was pleased to see her delight.

When she had arrived midmorning with the princess Isabel Stewart's party, a wariness in the lass's demeanor had done more to draw his attention than the simple elegance of her dress. In his twenty-five years, he had trained many dogs and horses, and had stalked deer. He'd spent much time in the woods, too, where he liked to sit quietly for no better reason than to see what he might see.

Such experience had stirred him to think the unruly crowd intimidated her, as a pack of wolves might intimidate a young doe that wandered naïvely into its midst.

He decided that was why he had kept an eye on her and had even begun to feel this odd sense of protectiveness toward her.

Most eyes focused on Princess Isabel, the young, beautiful, but still grieving widow of James, second Earl of Douglas, killed sixteen months before, during the victorious Battle of Otterburn. No one knew all the facts of his death, but the princess suspected murder and never hesitated to say so.

Others dismissed her suspicions as the imaginings of a mind distraught with grief, and the Douglases had hastily remarried her to one of their wealthier vassals. But she refused to live with her new husband, and the watcher doubted that the man wielded any influence over her. The princess had a mind of her own.

He'd never met her, but he had met her younger sister, Gelis, whose husband, Sir William Douglas, Laird of Nithsdale, was a longtime friend. Will was organizing an expedition to Prussia, to join a crusade, and since the Borders had been at peace for over a year, the watcher had decided to go with him, to search for new adventures.

Shifting his gaze from Isabel to scan the rest of her large party, he saw two Douglas knights he knew and his cousin, Sir Walter Scott, who had recently become Laird of Buccleuch.

The watcher's gaze shifted back to the fascinating lass, whose merriment had changed to wariness again. She looked as if she watched for someone in particular.

When another lady walked up behind her and touched her arm she started, then smiled with relief.

From the strong resemblance between the two, he guessed they were sisters. Then Buccleuch joined them and slipped a possessive arm around the other woman. Such an intimate gesture told the watcher she must be his lady wife.

The watcher moved away then, because Buccleuch would recognize him and might motion him over to introduce him. Much as he would have liked the introduction, he did not want to draw attention to himself just yet.

Even so, he could not resist returning a half hour later to watch her again.

Buccleuch had moved on with his lady, and the lass stood near a roaring fire, chatting with another of Isabel's ladies. Not far from them, children toasted bannocks and mutton collops at the flames.

Then, abruptly, a well-dressed man strode up to the two, caught the lass by an arm, and swung her to face him.

The watcher moved nearer, frowning.

The lass tried to pull away, but the man held her and put his face close to hers. Clearly berating her, he gave her arm a shake to punctuate his words.

The watcher stepped nearer, hesitant, thinking the man must be a kinsman of hers, one who had right and reason to speak so sharply to her.

But she resisted as if he were ordering her to do something against her will. She was growing angry, perhaps frightened.

The man shook a finger at her.

When she stepped back, he followed, emphasizing his

words with his pointing finger, thumping her chest with it as he might an obstinate lad's.

The watcher's focus narrowed until he saw only the offensive finger.

A few long strides carried him within reach.

Grabbing the lout by an arm, just as the lout had grabbed her, he swung him and slammed a blow to his jaw powerful enough to send him to the ground and keep him quiet for a few minutes, at least.

Seeing the lass clap both hands to her mouth, looking half astonished and half frightened, he swept off his plumed cap, bowed with a smile, and said lightly, "I trust that churl will trouble you no further, my lady. You should keep clear of such men."

She avoided his gaze as she murmured unsteadily, "Should I?"

"Aye, and with respect, I'd suggest that you rejoin the princess now and keep near her lest he try to accost you again."

She looked at him then, revealing a pair of long-lashed, melting hazel-green eyes as she said in a surprisingly low, delightfully musical voice, "You should not have struck him, sir. But I own, it was wonderful to see him bested for once."

"He looks somewhat familiar, my lady. I'm curious as to his name."

Dryly, she said, "He is Simon Murray, sir, my elder brother."

"Is he, indeed? I trust you'll forgive me then if I don't linger till he wakens."

Her lips twitched with amusement, but she nodded.

As he turned away, he saw the princess approaching.

"Who was that?" he heard her ask the lass.

"I don't know," she said. "But he laid Simon out with one blow, so I do wonder who he can be."

Sir Garth Napier smiled as he strode off.

It was always good to leave a woman wondering.

Chapter 1

Scone Abbey, 14 August 1390

Scotland's long-awaited Coronation Day had come at last, and a vast crowd had gathered to see what they could see. Although it might be hours yet before the ceremony ended and the newly crowned High King of Scots emerged from the abbey kirk, the teeming mass already overflowed the abbey grounds.

Scone Abbey sat on a terrace above the flat vale of the river Tay a few miles north of St. John's town of Perth. Monastic buildings lay east and west of the kirk, while to its north stood a higher mound of grassy land, known as Moot Hill.

Minutes before, John Stewart, Earl of Carrick and heir to Scotland's throne, had made his awkward way to the kirk from Abbots' House, a three-story gray-stone building that stood between the kirk and the eastern monastic buildings. While Carrick prepared for the ceremony, those privileged to witness it would take their places.

The kirk being modestly appointed and small for its ilk, only royal family members, their attendants, and higher-ranking nobility could go inside. Even so, the crowd was enormous. Nearly everyone who was anyone had come, as well as many hundreds of lesser estate or none at all.

Carrick's passage had occasioned much comment. He was thin, stooped, and pale, looked much older than his fifty years, and thanks to a kick from a horse years before, he walked with a limp. Worse, he was a man of peace and a scholar with no interest in politics. Put plainly, he was not what Scots expected their High King to be. They wanted their kings to be warriors who strode boldly and ruled decisively.

Carrick was unlikely to do either.

Movement near the largest of the eastern monastic buildings diverted the crowd's attention as a group of six splendidly attired young noblewomen emerged.

Cheers erupted when people recognized the princess Isabel Stewart, one of the few popular members of the royal family. Her late husband, James, second Earl of Douglas, had been Scotland's finest warrior, a great hero, and a man of enormous popularity. His death two years before, while leading a victorious Scottish army against a much larger English force at Otterburn, had shocked the entire country—hence the wild reaction to his tragically widowed countess.

Everyone knew she still grieved his loss and believed that murder, rather than fair battle, had taken him. That belief had strengthened with the undeniable murder in faraway Danzig of Will Douglas of Nithsdale, her sister Gelis's husband.

Not only had Will been almost as beloved a hero as the second earl, but two sudden deaths by violence of popular Douglases had also raised more suspicions than those of their princess wives. Yet few men dared voice the grow-

ing suspicion that someone was efficiently eliminating
any threat the royal Stewarts might face from the more
powerful Douglases, or from anyone else for that matter.

The crowd had been watching for Isabel, because word
had spread that the new sovereign and his wife were staying in Abbots' House, and lesser members of his family in
the eastern monastic buildings. The Austen Canons who
normally inhabited those Spartan quarters, and the Abbot
of Scone, had moved in with their brethren in the western
buildings for the duration of the coronation activities.

Although Scone Abbey was of great importance to the
country, it was not as grand as Dunfermline in Fife or
Scone's sister house, Dundrennan, in the Borders. But
Scone had served as capital of the ancient Pictish king-
dom, and therein lay its importance to the Scottish people
and the reason their coronations took place there.

The princess Isabel and her five ladies walked two by
two. Isabel walked with seventeen-year-old Lady Amalie
Murray, whose neatly coiffed raven tresses, hazel-green
eyes, and buxom figure provided a pleasing contrast to
the princess's fair, slender, blue-eyed beauty. Their gowns
contrasted well, too, Isabel in pale primrose yellow satin
trimmed with ermine, and the lady Amalie in leaf-green
and pink silk with wide embroidered bands of edging.
Isabel waved occasionally to the cheering crowd, but the
other ladies paid them scant heed, chatting instead among
themselves.

"'Tis a strange business, this, Isabel," the lady Amalie
said as her gaze moved warily over the raucous crowd.
"When we arrived two days ago, all was fun and feasting.
Then yesterday we attended a state funeral—although
his grace, your father, has been dead now for a full three
months. Then, more feasting after the funeral, and now,

on the third day, we are finally to crown the new King of Scots."

"In fact, 'tis my brother Fife who crowns him," Isabel said with familiar bitterness. "As we have seen, all must be as Fife ordains. Even the name the new King must take is Fife's own Sunday name of Robert. Thus, John Stewart, Earl of Carrick, is to become Robert the Third, because Fife declares that we cannot have a king named John without reminding people that John Balliol tried to steal the crown, even though that event happened years ago. If Carrick were to remain John, Fife says, he would have to be John the Second, which would give too much import to the usurper Balliol. Fife says *that* would undermine the line of Robert the Bruce."

"But to make such decisions is the Earl of Fife's duty, is it not?" Amalie said, still searching the crowd. "He *is* now Governor of the Realm, after all."

"Aye, so he still calls himself," Isabel said. "The truth is that his grace, my father, appointed Fife Governor because Father believed himself too old and infirm to rule properly. But in May, when he died, Fife's right to the position of Governor died with him. Sithee, he held it only at the King's pleasure."

"When others said as much, Fife insisted that the right remained with him until we buried the old King and crowned a new one," Amalie reminded her. "Moreover, besides being Earl of Fife, he is also Earl of Menteith. So the right to act as coroner today is reserved to him by tradition, is it not?"

"Nay, that is but the way he chooses to interpret that tradition. The right to act as coroner lies with his wife's family, the MacDuffs, not with the earldom he assumed by marrying her. A MacDuff has placed the crown on the head of every new King of Scots since ancient times—until today."

That Fife's version differed from others' did not surprise Amalie. He was not, in her experience, a man whose word one accepted without corroboration. Nearly everyone she knew distrusted him, save her brother Simon.

Simon admired Fife and had served him loyally for nearly eight years while, in effect, Fife had ruled Scotland. With the King less and less able to rule and Carrick uninterested, Fife had steadily acquired more and more power.

Isabel was frowning, which made her look older than her twenty-four years. With her fair hair and flawless skin, she was strikingly beautiful. But she had once been merry, forthright, and carefree. Since her beloved first husband's death, she had lost much of the vivacity that had set her apart from other beautiful noblewomen.

As their party passed Abbots' House to approach the kirk entrance, Amalie's searching gaze lit at last on an older couple near the stone steps to the kirk porch.

"Faith, Isabel, my parents are waiting for me," she muttered as she slowed to let the princess walk ahead of her.

A pair of stalwart knights preceded them, and because Amalie had been watching for her parents, she was sure that neither Sir Iagan nor Lady Murray had yet seen her. But they could not miss her if she walked up the steps right past them, as she would have to do to enter the kirk with Isabel.

"You cannot avoid them much longer," Isabel said over her shoulder with one of her rare smiles. "They mean you no harm, after all."

"I fear they may have found a husband for me," Amalie said. "I've told them I don't want one, but now that Buccleuch has succeeded to his father's title and estates, I'm sure my mother will have persuaded my father that he can make an advantageous alliance for me just as he did for Meg. Faith, but Simon said as much eight months ago at Yuletide. He said that being good-sister to a man as powerful as Buccleuch will make up for all my faults. I've avoided seeing any of my family again until now only because, since then, you have rarely stayed any-where longer than a fortnight."

"You've few faults that I can see," Isabel said. "I've told you myself that I know of more than one eligible young man who'd welcome you as his bride."

"Well, I don't want a young man or any other sort," Amalie said. Isabel had been kind enough to provide a sanctuary when she had needed one. But Isabel did *not* know all there was to know about her, and Amalie did not intend to tell her.

Instead, she said, "I'd like to slip away for a short time if you will permit it. I'll rejoin you as soon as they go in-side." When Isabel looked about to protest, she added, "I shan't be long, truly. Now that Carrick has gone in, they won't stay outside much longer, because my mother will *not* want to end up at the back of the kirk."

"Very well, but don't let them see you," Isabel said. "I'd not be amazed if your mother stopped me and de-manded to know where I'd sent you."

Amalie shook her head, letting her amusement show. Although Lady Murray was a controlling woman, she would never behave so improperly as to demand anything of the princess. But Amalie understood why Isabel had suggested she might.

Despite the princess's own sorrows, she paid close

heed to the members of her household and could always make a worried or unhappy one smile.

Peeping between the brawny pair that led their party, Amalie saw her mother still looking about. Perhaps, she thought, Lady Murray was only trying to spot one of her other offspring or Buccleuch, but she could not make herself believe it.

Sir Walter Scott of Buccleuch would be with other powerful barons invited to take part in the ceremony. Lady Murray would know that Meg was not there, due to advanced pregnancy, and that Simon was probably with Fife. Nor would her ladyship be looking for her younger son, Tom. She was looking for Amalie.

Shrubbery and tall beech trees surrounded Abbots' House, and Amalie snatched the first opportunity to slip behind a wide tree trunk. She meant to wait there until the coast was clear, but as she looked nervously about, she saw Tom Murray striding straight toward her with some of his friends.

Although he had not seen her, if she stayed where she was he soon would. Her overskirt and gloves were green and might blend in, but her tunic was pink and boasted wide bands of green trim embroidered with gold and silver thread.

Quickly wending her way through shrubbery and along a gravel path, she came to the steps of Abbots' House and saw that the front door stood ajar.

Aware that Carrick and his party were staying there, she was sure that some servants must still be inside. But she suspected that if she went around the side of the building, she would look more furtive than if she just walked in.

However, if she went boldly up the steps with her back

to the crowd, a chance observer might easily mistake her for one of Carrick's many sisters. Should anyone challenge her, she could just say she was looking for Isabel or one of the other princesses—not Gelis. Like Meg, Gelis was pregnant and had not come.

Having thus decided her course, Amalie hurried up the steps. Once through the open doorway, she closed the door just enough to conceal herself from view.

The dim entry hall was no more than a spacious anteroom with a stairway at her right to a railed gallery above. Doubtless, service areas lay beyond a door she could discern in the dark corner under the stairs. The walls ahead and to her left revealed three other doors, all shut.

As she hesitated, uncertain where to go and unable to know if any nearby room was unoccupied, heavy footsteps approaching the stair-corner door made the decision for her. Snatching up her skirts, she ran silently up the stairs, hoping to find a window from which she might see if her parents had entered the kirk.

At the landing, she saw that the gallery continued around two more sides of the stairwell, providing access to several more closed doors. Window embrasures at each end of the landing provided light, but neither one would overlook the kirk.

Opposite her, another, narrower flight of stairs led up to the next floor. She would have to open one of two doors on that side to find a suitable window, and when she did, she would be in view of anyone coming down those stairs.

As she considered her choice, to her shock, she heard a male voice inside the room to her left. Something about the voice seemed familiar.

Stepping nearer, she put an ear close to the door and

heard a second voice say with perfect clarity, "In troth, if we give him sufficient cause, he is likely enough to co-operate, but one cannot trust the man from one moment to the next. 'Twould suit me better not to have to concern myself with him at all."

"Sakes, sir," the first voice muttered. "Is it murder you seek?"

Amalie leaned closer.

"I did not say—"

Without the slightest warning, a large, gloved hand clapped tight across her mouth and nose as a strong arm swept her off her feet and away from the door.

Terrified and disoriented, she could not see her captor's face, but his grip was like a vise clamping her against a hard, muscular body. Her struggles did no good as he strode around the gallery, bearing her as if she were a featherweight and moving as silently as he had when he'd crept up behind her.

She kicked and squirmed until she realized that if she drew attention, she might find herself in worse trouble. Since she suspected that one of the voices might have been Simon's, and since Simon was not a man who would look kindly on a sister secretly listening to a private con-versation—especially one about murder—she decided that, for the present, she might be safer where she was.

Still, she had no way to know if the man who had caught her was friend or foe. Judging by the ease with which he carried her, he might be as large and strong as Jock's Wee Tammy, her huge and therefore misnamed friend at Scott's Hall who often served as Buccleuch's squire, as well as captain of his fighting tail.

It occurred to her, too, that to have been creeping about Abbots' House as he had, the man had to be either Carrick's own attendant on watch for intruders, or an intruder himself. As she was telling herself she hoped he was the latter, she realized that such an intruder might well throttle her to ensure her silence.

Why, she wondered, had she darted into the house at all? How could she do such a silly thing just to avoid a confrontation with her mother? Then a vision of that formidable dame appeared, and she knew she would do it again in an instant.

To her astonishment, her captor headed right to the second flight of stairs and then up the stairs themselves.

She tried to pull her face far enough away from his hand to draw a deep breath, but he only pressed harder. Wondering what he would do if she bit him, she tried kicking again, hit one silk-shod foot against a bruisingly hard wooden railing, and remembered she did *not* want to attract attention.

Shock and terror had eased to worry and annoyance that now were shifting back to fear, so she told herself sternly that, whoever he was, he would not dare to harm her. Even if he did not know who her father was or that her good-brother was the powerful Scott of Buccleuch, he would have to be daft to harm a member of a royal household at Scone Abbey on Coronation Day.

Slightly reassured, she began to relax just as they reached a tall, heavy, ornately carved door.

Breath tickled her ear as a deep voice murmured, "I'm going to take my hand from your mouth to open this door. If you make a sound, you may endanger both our lives. Nod if you agree to keep silent."

She nodded, telling herself she would scream Abbots' House to rubble if she wanted to, that no one could expect her to keep her word under such circumstances.

But when he took his hand away and continued to hold her off her feet with one arm as easily as he had with two, she decided to keep quiet until she got a good look at him and could judge what manner of man he was. All she knew so far was that he was one who could creep up on a person and carry her off as easily as he might a small child—all without making enough noise for anyone else to hear.

The chamber they entered astonished her further, because colorful arras cloths decked the walls, and a thick blue-and-red carpet covered much of the floor. Forest-green velvet curtains with golden ties and tassels draped the windows as well as a large bed in the near corner to their right.

"Faith," she muttered when he set her on her feet and moved to shut the door, "what is this place? Surely, this is not the lord abbot's own bedchamber!"

"Aye, although doubtless the abbot does not boast carpets to walk upon," her captor said. "At present it serves as Carrick's chamber, which means, in a very short time, it will be that of his grace, the King of Scots." Then, in a tone harsh enough to raise the hairs on the back of her neck, he added, "Now, Lady Amalie, tell me, if you please, just what the devil you were doing, listening outside that door."

Turning at last from her fascination with the bed to see his face, she gasped.

~

Sir Garth Napier, newly a baron and properly styled Lord of Westruther, saw her lips part and heard her gasp, but she did not immediately burst into speech.

She was stunned to see him, though. He could easily tell that much from her expression and the quickening movement of her impressive breasts.

"Who are you?" she demanded. "And how did you learn my name?"

"As you'd told me your brother's name, yours was not difficult to come by."

She was looking past him, doubtless at the door. "We should *not* be in here."

"No one will come here for at least an hour," he said. "But someone is sure to miss you in the kirk. You should be with the princess Isabel, should you not?"

She nodded, saying earnestly, "I must go to her at once."

"Not until you tell me why you were listening at that door."

Her gaze met his searchingly, as if she would measure the strength of his resolve. Evidently, she saw that he meant to have an answer, because she gave a soft little sigh of resignation. Her breasts were downright tantalizing.

She said, "I did not mean to listen."

"Don't lie to me," he said, wrenching his gaze back to her face and fixing a stern look on his own. "You had your ear right against that door."

"Aye, but I came up only to find a window that looked onto the kirk steps."

Recognizing a diversionary attempt, he said, "Lass, I'm not a patient man."

"No man is patient," she retorted. "But I don't even know you, because you did not tell me your name before. You just walked away."

His patience had evaporated, and he wanted to shake

her. "My name would mean nowt to you. *What* did you hear?"

She glowered at him like an angry child. He'd have wagered his recent inheritance that she was preparing to lie again.

"You had better tell me the truth," he warned her.

Shrugging, she said, "I could not hear their words. They spoke too quietly."

"They?"

"I heard two voices through the door before you snatched me off my feet. I could not hear what they said, though. Nor do I know why I should tell you even if I'd heard every word."

"I think you did hear every word," he said. "Just what do you think would have happened if I'd just opened that door and pushed you inside?"

She bit her lower lip but rallied quickly. "Why did you not?"

He was in no more hurry to explain his actions than she was to explain hers. And he was not about to give her the satisfaction of hearing he'd followed her into Abbots' House out of nothing more than the same curiosity she had stirred in him from the moment he'd laid eyes on her at Dunfermline. No man of sense would knowingly hand a woman a weapon of such magnitude.

Having seen her slip away from the princess and nip boldly into Abbots' House as if she had every right—instead of no right at all—to do so had awakened the strong protective instinct that had leapt to life at seeing Simon Murray stab her in the chest with one damnably stiffened finger.

The plain fact was that Garth had followed without thought of consequence, and had stepped across the threshold to see her skirts whisking out of sight up the stairs. Voices from beyond them suggested others nearby—doubtless Carrick's servants or some of the abbot's, assisting Carrick's people. At all events, he had not hesitated more than that second or two before hurrying after her.

He had been careful not to announce his presence by being heavy footed, but neither had he taken particular care to remain utterly silent. He knew he would have heard such an approach as his, had he been sneaking about as she had.

But so intent had she been on those murmurs supposedly too slight to be intelligible that she had not noticed him until he'd grabbed her. Even then, she had had enough sense not to draw the attention of the men in that room.

Had she seen them go into the house? Had she followed them, intending to hear what they said to each other? That thought gave him chills.

He told himself that the most likely people to be talking in that room—possibly the abbot's own reception chamber—were servants. Anyone else entering it for privy conversation would have to be of equal rank to the house's chief resident to dare usurp one of his privy chambers for such a talk.

But the present chief resident was not the Abbot of Scone.

Moreover, everyone had seen Carrick and his attendants making their slow progress to the abbey kirk. And most could deduce that the private chambers in Abbots' House would be empty for an hour or two until the new sovereign's chamberlain returned to assure that all was still in order for his grace's comfort.

In fact, only one man would consider himself equal to

that newly crowned King and thus rightfully entitled to usurp his grace's chamber to his own use. And if the lass had purposefully listened to the Earl of Fife, now Governor of the Realm, speaking with a minion—or, worse, to another noble—she ought to be soundly skelped for such folly.

The thought of the consequences to her, had Fife caught her in the act, sent icy fear racing through him. But instead of chilling him, it ignited his temper.

He said grimly, "Do you know the penalty you'd face if I were to report what you were doing? Had the people in that room been only two of the abbot's servants, it would be bad enough—"

"They were not servants," she said. Then, clearly realizing that silence would have been wiser, she clapped her own neatly gloved hand over her mouth.

"How do you know they were not?" he demanded, clenching his fists to keep from shaking her.

"I . . . I don't," she said. "They didn't sound like servants."

"Then you must have heard words, lass. You could not otherwise be so sure. If they were not servants, you'd best pray they never learn you were outside that door. Consider who else might enter a room intended for use only by the man who will shortly become King of Scots. I can think of only one person."

The roses in her cheeks paled so quickly he feared she would faint. Again he had to restrain himself, this time to avoid offering a hand to steady her.

The same instinct that had served him well in battle and tiltyard warned him not to touch her again—not yet. Whether it arose from a sense of self-preservation or a suspicion that her stubbornness would only increase if she recognized his concern he did not know. But when that instinct stirred, he obeyed it.

"I'll accept that you did not recognize their voices," he said. "But you did hear what they said. If you are wise, you will tell me what it was." Putting steel in his voice, he added, "For your own safety, lass. If they learn that you were there—"

"How could they?"

"Anyone might have seen you come in. I did."

Still, she hesitated.

His hands were fairly itching to shake the truth out of her when, out of the silence, he heard a distant, dull thud.

He held up a hand to warn her to keep silent.

"What?"

"Hush." He moved silently to the door and put his ear against it. A moment later, he straightened and said, "Two men, going downstairs."

"There are windows overlooking the front. We can see who they are."

"Don't be daft," he snapped. "Someone—servant or otherwise—may be watching from those windows. We've both taken too much risk just by coming inside. The sooner we are out of here, the better I shall like it."

"Coward. If you really wanted to know, you'd go and look."

Narrowing his eyes, letting both his temper and his tension show, he said, "If you know what's good for you, you will keep such opinions to yourself. I've a good mind to tell your brother Simon I found you in here, listening at doors."

The remaining color drained from her face. "You . . . you wouldn't!"

"Don't count on that," he said, praying she would believe him. "I'll be here all day and for the Queen's coronation tomorrow. If you have any wits at all, you'll come to your senses and tell me the truth before we both leave Scone."

He waited, hoping she would tell him at once. But he had taken her measure, whether he liked it or not, and he was not surprised when she kept silent.

"One thing more," he said. "If you won't tell me, then pray have the good sense not to tell anyone else. You cannot possibly know whom to trust."

"I trust no one," she said bluntly. "Are we just going to walk out together?"

"We are."

"Then you'd better tell me your name, sir, lest someone see us together. It will hardly redound to my credit, or yours, if I cannot name you to anyone in my family or the princess's household who may see us together."

"I suspect that anyone who'd wonder at it has gone into the kirk," he said.

"Are you so ashamed of your name?" she asked. "I should think you'd be proud of it. I do recognize a knightly girdle when I see one, after all, and yours is similar to the one my good-brother, Buccleuch, wears on such occasions."

"If you hoped to startle me by announcing your kinship to Buccleuch, you'd have done better to consider what his opinion would be of your behavior here. I warrant I can describe it for you if you cannot imagine it for yourself."

When she nibbled her lower lip again, he knew he had made his point. But then she said, "So you know Buccleuch. Must I ask *him* to tell me your name?"

He did not want to explain himself to Buccleuch any

more than she did, so accepting defeat, he said, "My name is Garth Napier." That was not all there was to it now, but she had deduced his knighthood, and he saw no reason to reveal more.

"I hope, *Sir* Garth Napier, that you don't mean to escort me into the kirk and all the way to Isabel in front of everyone else in there."

"Nay, lass," he said, suppressing a smile at the reaction that would stir. "You'll have to walk that path alone."

She wouldn't like that any better, but she had no choice.

Chapter 2

Amalie walked with Sir Garth downstairs, outside, and along the winding path to the abbey kirk without incident. As they wended their way through the crowd, she saw that the prelates, officers of state, and other powerful lords, all in their festive robes, had gathered at the front of the kirk, ready to take their part in the procession. Buccleuch was somewhere among them and would likely see them and ask questions later. But she could not worry about that now.

Onlookers crowded them, making her extraordinarily aware of the tall, broad-shouldered, athletic looking knight beside her. With her hand resting on his muscular forearm, she noted its steadiness and recalled with awe his strength and the ease with which he had carried her. No one had carried her since she was a child, and Sir Garth Napier had done it as if she still were one.

Although she had seen him well enough to recognize him in the abbot's chamber, the light there had not been good. At Dunfermline, she'd had little time to note his

features and had seen only a stalwart man of fierce demeanor. Now, knowing he would vanish again and she
might never have another chance, she wanted to get a
good look at him. But their relative positions made it
difficult.

She had seen that his face was a long oval, deeply
tanned, and his cheekbones and the line of his brow were
strongly chiseled. She noted now that his heavily lashed
blue eyes sat deep under eyebrows a shade or two darker
than his sun-streaked brown hair. His nose was aquiline,
his mouth a straight line, for his lips pressed thin as he
guided her deftly through the crowd to the kirk porch.
His chin was firm with a cleft in the middle, and she had
a notion he might be as stubborn as she was. Her eyes
were almost level with his shoulder. Her head would just
fit beneath his chin.

A boyish lock of hair had tumbled onto his forehead,
and despite the fact that he was a head taller than she and
she dared look up at him now only through her lashes in
quick, darting glances, she saw how strikingly blue his
eyes were. She looked away, hoping he would not de-
tect her curiosity. She could not decide what to make of
him, but she was sure she had never met another man like
him.

He wore a doublet of dark-blue miniver-trimmed
velvet and fashionable silk hose with one leg of striped
blue-and-white, the other a plain dark blue—clothing of
a nobleman of means. The wide knightly girdle of silver
and bronze medallions linked round his hips held a long
dirk with a jeweled hilt in a fine leather sheath. He did
not wear a sword, because one did not attend the King's
coronation so armed.

Despite the constant murmur of the steadily increasing

crowd as folks made way for them, she could hear the sheath make creaking noises as it shifted against the silver belt and wondered again at how silently he had crept up on her earlier.

His gaze shifted alertly right and left as they approached the steps, and then, before she could look away, it locked with hers and held it easily.

He grinned, and she noted flashing white teeth and the slash of a dimple near the left corner of his mouth. Heat flooded her cheeks and elsewhere within her.

Still walking as fast as the crowd would allow, he bent nearer, twinkling.

"What is it, lass?" he asked. "These folks care only about seeing the great lords and the King when he comes. They are paying us no heed."

"You *know* what it is," she muttered, glad he was no longer so stern but wishing he would not treat her lightly, either. What if he joked with his friends later, bragged that he had caught her so easily? "I cannot forget where we just were. How do you manage to walk through them all as if there were naught amiss in what we did? Buccleuch is here somewhere, and others who know me. What if they—"

"Forget that for now," he said, still smiling as if he flirted with her. "Whether of high or low estate, we are all less likely to question folks who behave as if they have every right to do what they are doing. Confidence often wins the day when one holds no other weapon. Now, lass, smile and hold your head high, for here we are."

Then, surprising her, he put his right hand over hers on his forearm and gave it a squeeze, murmuring, "Pretend you are her grace, the new Queen." With that, he released her and reached for the door, sweeping a bow as he opened it for her.

The chanting of monks in their transept stalls spilled forth with an accompanying buzz of murmurs from the congregation.

The ceremony had not yet begun. Still, the chamber was crowded and Amalie had no idea where Isabel's party would be, so her first inclination was to turn tail and flee rather than draw more attention to herself.

"Your grace," her companion murmured as he stepped back, head still low.

His words and attitude tickled her sense of humor, and she flashed a smile that he could not see with his head still down. Swallowing, she faced forward again, raised her chin, and crossed the threshold. After that, it proved easy, because Sir Duncan Forrest, one of Isabel's knights, approached her at once.

"This way, if you please, Lady Amalie," he said. "I'm to take you forward."

"Thank you," she said with a smile and a surge of relief.

A green-carpeted aisle stretched up the center of the nave between rows of people standing or kneeling on prayer stools, but Sir Duncan guided Amalie to the narrow colonnade on the south side and escorted her forward to the second row.

Instead of the last stool in that row, which, as the youngest of the princess's ladies, Amalie had expected to be hers, Isabel patted the one next to her own.

Nodding thanks to Sir Duncan, and doing her best not to trip over or step on any toes, she eased her way past Lady Sibylla, who smiled at her, Lady Susan, who did not, and the two older ladies, Nancy and Averil, to the place beside Isabel.

"Did you elude them, then?" the princess asked archly without bothering to lower her voice. Not that it mattered. The monks still chanted, and the additional buzz suggested that nearly everyone else was involved in private conversation.

It took Amalie a moment to remember eluding her parents, but then she said, "Oh, yes, thank heaven. I just pray that my mother did not see me slip away."

"Nay, she did not, or she'd have said something as I passed," Isabel said with a mischievous smile. "She has small respect for the blood royal, your mother.

"Nay, nay," she added when Amalie moved to protest. "I ken fine that she means no offense. 'Tis naught but the pride she has in her own ancient lineage, and she is hardly alone in that. Many others look upon us Stewarts as upstarts. She'd have had no satisfaction from me today, although I own, the woman does frighten me witless. Does anyone *ever* go contrary to her wishes?"

Grateful not to have to answer more questions about her absence, long though it must have seemed, Amalie said, "Scarcely anyone dares. Simon is less submissive than the rest of us, and my father sometimes reveals a stubborn streak. But neither Meg nor I have stood up to her, unless one counts my unwillingness to go home. Mother did not press me to return, though. She suggested it only once, just before you invited me to join your household, but that was all. Simon did say I should go home at Yuletide, but that was when we were at Dunfermline."

Remembering what else had happened there, and feeling herself flush at the memory, she added hastily, "Mother understood why I wanted to live with you. I did expect a summons from her after Simon told me to go home, but she sent none."

"You knew that she and your father would be here, though," Isabel said. "You told me so, and of course, nearly every noble family *is* here because most think it treasonous not to be. 'Tis only natural they would want to see you. I'm only surprised they did not look for you before now."

"They did not attend his grace's funeral, so they must not have arrived until late yesterday, and they most likely stayed with Murray cousins in town, so this morning was their first opportunity to look for me here. But Mother had that look of determination she gets when she has made up her mind to something."

"Which is why you suspect she has a plan for you," Isabel said, nodding. "But it is time that you think of marriage, my dear. If you fear they may try to force you to wed someone against your will, recall that Scottish law forbids that."

Amalie allowed herself an inward sigh. Isabel barely knew Lady Murray and stood in awe of her. It ought to take little thought for her to understand how difficult it was for a daughter of Lady Murray's to oppose her.

She was trying to think how she could phrase the point tactfully when Isabel said, "Here comes Annabella now. They must be about to begin."

With no more fanfare than a low drum roll to silence the audience, Annabella Drummond, Countess of Carrick and later to be Queen of Scots, walked up the aisle alone, followed by two men-at-arms bearing the Stewart and Drummond banners. A chair of state awaited her at the front on the north side of the aisle, and when she reached it, she sat without further ceremony, facing the altar.

"She ought to have walked in with John," Isabel muttered. "It is unfair to make her wait a full day for her own coronation. Few will pay it any heed, but of course, that is why Fife insisted on the delay, to belittle her position as Queen."

Amalie wondered if others had heard Isabel. But despite the drum roll, the monks continued their chanting and the congregation its murmuring. Beside her, Lady Averil gave no sign of hearing. But she was devoted to Isabel and would not condemn anything she said.

The chanting ceased at last, the doors opened with a trumpet blare, and a choir of twenty small boys entered, two by two, singing their way to choir stalls in the north transept opposite the monks.

Acolytes followed, swinging censers and preceding the Lord Abbot of Scone and a train of bishops, abbots, and priors. Wearing their finest canonicals and robes, they proceeded to seats arranged in the chancel, flanking the high altar.

Before it, the throne sat on a low dais behind a table draped in white linen.

The choir fell silent, and pipes played in the invited barons. As Buccleuch passed, looking splendidly dignified in his long robe, his gaze caught Amalie's, and she knew he had watched for her.

He and the other invited barons proceeded to the chancel steps, where they took places on either side.

Next, after a crash of cymbals, came the earls, who went up the steps and sat on chairs in front of the prelates on the north side of the chancel.

A royal fanfare of trumpets announced the Lyon King of Arms and the officers of state. First of these was twelve-year-old David Stewart, Carrick's heir and soon to be Earl of Carrick and High Steward of the land.

He wore cloth-of-gold and strode boldly and alone to the chancel, to take his place before the prelates on the south side. Other officers of state joined him there.

With a more prolonged fanfare, Bishop Trail of St. Andrews, premier clergyman of the realm, led Carrick himself in, flanked by his constable with the sword of state and his marischal with the royal scepter.

Behind them, looking severe and wearing fine, gold-trimmed black velvet, came the dark, lean figure of the Earl of Fife and Menteith, carrying a red velvet cushion that bore the crown of Scotland.

Carrick wore white velvet, the color of purity, but Amalie thought it a pity that Fife presented a much more powerful appearance. With his grace's white hair and beard, the white velvet made him look more like a ghost than a king. He limped beside Bishop Trail to the chancel and took his place, not on the throne but on a plain chair opposite Annabella.

The Abbot of Scone began the coronation mass. He and the monarch-to-be took Communion together afterward, and then the abbot gestured to Bishop Trail, who raised Carrick to his feet and administered the oath.

Having sworn in a voice Amalie could barely hear to be father to the people of Scotland, to keep the country's peace as far as God would allow, to forbid and put down evil, crime, and felony in all degrees, and to show righteousness and mercy in all judgments in the name of God Almighty, Carrick stood silently while Bishop Trail anointed his head and brow with holy oil "in the name of the Father, Son, and Holy Ghost, amen."

A din of cheering erupted as the choir burst into song.

Soon the cheering congregation was singing with them, and when the hymn ended, Bishop Trail guided his charge to the front of the chancel and said in a ringing voice, "I present to you the Lord's anointed, your liege lord and undoubted High King of Scots!"

More cheers erupted, along with shouts of "God save the King!"

Looking dazed by the din, the new King started when the Lord Chamberlain approached to drape him in the royal robe. Then Bishop Trail led him to the throne, where the constable presented the sword of state. Sitting to accept the scepter, the King held it in his left hand and gazed vaguely out at the still cheering audience.

At last, the Earl of Fife stepped forward with the crown on its red cushion. Handing the cushion to a minion, Fife took up the crown of Robert the Bruce, splendidly made from the spoils of Bannockburn, and placed it on his brother's head. Stepping back, he gave a slight nod but said nothing and did not kneel.

Amalie heard a sound like a growl from her left and darted a look at Isabel, to see her glowering at the scene before them. Trumpets played a fanfare and the choir broke into another hymn. Again the congregation joined in.

When the music ended, before anyone spoke, young David Stewart strode forward, ignoring the black look of disapproval on his uncle's face as he did.

Facing the throne, David dropped to one knee and, head bowed, held out both hands to his father. The congregation fell instantly, totally silent.

Looking astonished but more human than he had since entering the church, the King extended his right hand, and the boy took it between his in the traditional gesture of fealty. Still kneeling, he swore his oath of fealty in a voice clear enough to carry to the back of the church. When he finished, the congregation cheered him.

Fife continued to glower.

"Look at him," Isabel muttered loudly enough for Amalie to hear. "He's as furious as he can be."

Amalie saw that much for herself and wondered at the youngster's daring. She had heard that he was impetuous and headstrong, but she had seen him only two or three times and could not imagine anyone so young challenging the Governor of the Realm. Fife intimidated most full-grown men.

Others had seen Fife's fury, because the church fell silent again.

Fife waited only until David stepped back, then moved to take the King by an arm, brusquely gesturing to the marischal and constable to take the sword and scepter as his grace rose. Motioning then for the royal standard bearer to precede them, Fife accompanied the King to the door and outside without so much as pausing at Annabella's chair.

Hurriedly, everyone else followed them.

Outside, onlookers joined the procession to Moot Hill. Men carried the throne out and put it on top of the hill, and the King gratefully sat down again.

The crowd quickly fell silent as Fife bent, scooped up a handful of previously loosened dirt, and put it in his grace's hand.

The ladies of Princess Isabel's party were near enough to hear him say, "I, Robert of Fife, give you the land of Scotland. I will aid you to hold it."

Amalie's throat seemed to close, stopping her breath.

She shut her eyes, unsure if that voice was the same one she had heard on the other side of the door.

Turning to the crowd, Fife said a bit more loudly, "I, Robert, Governor of the Realm of Scotland, give you your new-crowned King."

She still could not be sure. Opening her eyes, she gazed speculatively at him.

The huge crowd screamed its approval as Isabel muttered her fury. "They don't even understand that he is declaring that he *gave* John the crown. 'Twas bad enough to force him to take the name Robert, but this is *too* much!"

The Lyon King of Arms stepped forward. Trumpets blew for silence, and just as the ancient Celtic seanachies of old had done, the Lyon King began to recite the King's kinship to those ancient kings. "Behold the High King of Scots, *Ard Righ Albannach*," he intoned. "Robert, son of Robert, son of Robert, son of Marjorie, daughter of Robert, son of Robert . . ."

When he finished, the first among the earls present stepped forward and dropped to a knee to swear his fealty. Other earls followed in order of precedence, then lesser nobles, down to those holding the largest baronies. Even the least of barons had to swear fealty, but not everyone need do so on Coronation Day.

At last, with a sigh of relief, Isabel said, "We can ease our way out of this throng now, I think." With a brilliant smile, she turned and looked directly at the people just behind her, who quickly made way for her.

Amalie had been about to suggest that they look for one or both of the knights who served Isabel to make way for her, but Sir Duncan and Sir Kenneth had lost sight of them as they hurried to follow her and the procession to Moot Hill.

The ladies emerged from the crowd without incident and headed for the abbey park below Moot Hill, where fires had been burning since sunrise to prepare meats for the coronation feast. Trestle tables sat in the shade of tall beech trees, and Amalie saw Isabel's knights and others guarding tables draped with white linen, clearly intended for the royal family and the most powerful lords of the realm, and their guests. Other, plain wooden trestles were available for lesser nobility, and the rest of the mob would look after themselves. Food was plentiful for everyone.

As Amalie followed Isabel with her other ladies toward one of the tables set apart for the royal family and their noble attendants, her gaze roamed freely.

Only after disappointment stirred did she realize she was seeking someone in particular, and not any member of her family or Isabel's.

Sir Garth Napier took the King's soft right hand between his own two now bared and calloused ones, and felt as if he held something fragile.

Perhaps because Robert the Third, as one must now think of him, did not suit Garth's notion of a king any better than that of most Scots, he was unprepared for the surge of emotion he felt as he gently held that hand to promise his fealty.

The powerful feelings that swept through him banished the words he had so carefully memorized, making him fear he would fail to perform his duty to the King on behalf of his own people. As it was, the people of

Westruther scarcely knew him anymore. Thanks to his duties as a knight of the realm, he had barely set eyes on the place since his father's death nearly a year before.

The previous baron's steward had served in that office since before Garth's birth and was a trustworthy man who understood commitment to duty. He supervised the Westruther estates so efficiently that, for years, Garth had paid them little heed.

Kneeling now before his King, the gratitude he felt for his birthright and the rush of pride he felt in Westruther were far greater than anything he had imagined he might feel. But at the same time, the humility he felt was overwhelming.

Awareness that he carried the requisite bit of Westruther dirt in his boot, thoughtfully sent him by his steward, gave him no courage. Instead, it was nearly the last straw, making him wonder if he could ever measure up to the men who had preceded him, and as competently fulfill all the responsibilities of his new position.

Looking up with an aching throat, he encountered a gentle, understanding smile. As if a spell had broken, the words flowed easily, his voice calm and firm:

"I, Garth Napier, Lord of Westruther in Lothian, do swear fealty for that barony, which I hold and do claim to hold of your grace, the High King of Scots, for myself and my heirs, heritably. Loyally will I do unto you the services due unto you and your heirs from said estates, God helping, now and to the end of my days."

Falling silent, his head bowed again, he heard the King say quietly, "One feels your sincerity, Lord Westruther, and comprehends your just emotion. Scotland is blessed to have the loyalty of such men as you, and the support of your kindred."

Warmth surged into Garth's cheeks. Embarrassed by his blushes, he said simply, "I thank you, your grace."

He stood then, conscious of a grim scowl on the dark, lean face of the Earl of Fife, standing behind the King to his right, and the beaming smile of young David Stewart, now High Steward of Scotland and the new Earl of Carrick.

Stepping aside for the next man, Garth drew his gloves back on and went down the hill, seeking friendly faces and idly wondering where the lass had gone.

Not until he emerged from the crowd did he spy her near a linen-draped table with Isabel's other four ladies and Isabel herself.

As he watched the women, he sensed their impatience. Doubtless, they were hungry; yet no one could sit, let alone eat, until the fealty ceremonies had ended. It would not be long now, though. The line behind him had been short.

Twenty minutes later, the Lyon King of Arms announced in stentorian tones that the High King of Scots invited everyone to join him for feasting in the park below. Garth had been thinking of trying to coax the lass away from her little group of ladies long enough to have another talk with her. But as he braced himself to let the flood of hungry humanity sweep past, he realized he would find no opportunity for further discourse before darkness, if then. Her duty to the princess must come first. Also, as a maiden, she was unlikely to wander off alone in such a crowd.

The noisy, teeming throng still pressed close around him when a voice from behind muttered, "Himself would ha' discourse wi' ye anon, m'lord Westruther. Ye're to make yourself available to him at first opportunity."

Garth turned, got a look at the man who had spoken, and recognized him as servant to another to whom he owed his duty. Clearly, any choice of activity would not be his to make until later.

He was about to turn when, in thinning numbers from the hilltop, he spied the Governor of the Realm striding toward him. Fife had cast off his robe but was just as commanding in a gold-trimmed black velvet doublet and black silk hose. Even the man's shoes and cap were black. Noting Fife's purposeful look as he approached, Garth bowed and waited for him to speak.

"You may rise, Westruther," Fife said, surprisingly affable.

"Thank you, my lord," Garth said. "How may I serve you?"

"Such an offer gratifies me," Fife said. "We have not yet enjoyed the pleasure of your presence at Stirling, I believe, since your father's untimely death. Thus, I take this opportunity to extend my condolences to you, your lady mother, and others in your family. I cannot help but wonder, however, if the late Lord Westruther would have been as quick as you were to swear fealty to the new King. As I recall, he kept his distance from the royal court."

Keeping tight rein on his grumbling temper, Garth said, "My father was ever loyal to the Crown, my lord." Knowing that the late Lord Westruther had kept his distance from Fife rather than from the late King, and pleased that he managed not to place any awkward emphasis on "Crown," Garth added, "I assure you that his actions, had he lived to see this day, would have mirrored mine exactly."

"Mayhap you are right," Fife said. "At all events, as

soon as your many duties at Westruther and elsewhere permit, we would see you at Stirling."

"I thank you again, sir," Garth said, taking care not to commit himself.

With a slight nod, Fife passed him and continued downhill, leaving Garth to wonder if he had just received what amounted to a royal command.

Amalie had tried to devote herself to the princess Isabel as they waited to eat but also seized every opportunity to scan the crowd, insisting—if only to herself—that she hoped to see her parents or brothers before any of them could confront her.

As it was, she spied Sir Garth halfway down the hill, talking with Fife.

Grimacing, she wondered what the man was doing amid barons and other nobility swearing fealty. She wondered even more if he was Fife's man and might tell the earl she had been eavesdropping on a conversation in the royal chamber of Abbots' House. That last thought gave her chills.

Turning away, she saw her parents, her thirteen-year-old sister, Rosalie, and her brother Simon, still some distance away but heading toward her. Fighting an impulse to run away as fast as she could and as far as she could, she made herself wait for them, determined not to let them intimidate her.

"Do you remember what I said?" Isabel asked, stepping to her side.

"Faith, madam, I have all I can do just to keep my wits about me."

"Aye, well, do not forget that they cannot *force* you to marry anyone," Isabel said. "Hold firm if that is what they want, and mayhap I can aid you."

Grateful but doubting that anyone who had already admitted fear of Lady Murray could help her in the situation she saw looming ahead of her, Amalie watched with a smile that was more cynical than appreciative as Isabel melted back into the crowd that waited for the King, leaving her to face her family alone.

Deciding that she wanted no one else in the princess's party to overhear her conversation with her family, she went to meet them.

Rosalie ran ahead of the others to hug her, but Lady Murray, a stout dame with a piercing eye, fashionably plucked eyebrows, and an elegant gown of tawny figured silk, was the first to speak. "Where have you been hiding yourself, Amalie? Surely you knew we would be looking for you."

"I serve the princess, madam," Amalie said, straightening but leaving a hand affectionately on Rosalie's shoulder. Pleased to think she had her voice under control, she added, "I knew I would see you here after the coronation, and since I surmised that you and my lord father must be staying in Perth—"

"Of course we are, and we assumed you would be doing so as well. But as we arrived in Perth only yestereve, we did not learn until then that the royal family and their attendants all have chambers here at Scone. Even so, I'd have thought that only the princess's most *senior* ladies would attend her here today."

"She asked us all to stay near her," Amalie said. Turning to her father, a thickset man of medium height, graying hair, and trim beard, who had honored the occasion by wearing his most elegant suit of clothes, she said, "You look very fine today, sir."

"Aye, lass," he agreed. "Ye look gey splendid, too. That pink-and-green dress becomes ye well, and I see ye're wearing the wee gold pin I gave ye on your bodice."

"It is my favorite piece of jewelry," she told him, fingering the engraved circlet.

She would have liked to ignore Simon, standing beside him. But although she disliked Simon intensely, she generally took care not to anger him. "You are looking well, too, Simon." Glancing toward the royal table, she added, "I can stay but a few minutes, for they will begin to serve the high table soon."

Lady Murray said, "We shall have plenty of time to talk later, dearling, because you will be coming home with us."

At these words, Rosalie looked beseechingly at Amalie, but Amalie ignored her, sternly suppressing a surge of guilt as she exclaimed, "Home! But why?"

"Because your father desires it. He is arranging a fine marriage for you."

"But I don't want to marry," Amalie said. Hearing the shrill tremor in her voice, she drew a steadying breath. "I do not intend ever to accept a husband, madam," she said more calmly. "I thought I had made that plain."

"You will do as our lord father bids you," Simon said. "As Meg did."

"I am not Meg," Amalie retorted, thinking he was beginning to look just as black-tempered as the Earl of Fife, albeit more colorfully garbed. "Nor need I marry if I do not want to, Simon. Scottish law—"

"What can *you* know of Scottish law?" Simon demanded, adding, "Not that it matters a whit what you think you know. You are not of full age and will therefore obey our father's command."

Forcing herself to remain calm, Amalie said, "The King and Queen are taking their places, so I must go."

Then, as much to her surprise as to anyone else's, she turned and walked away. If anyone tried to call her back, she did not hear them. In truth, the teeming crowd that threatened to obscure her view ahead, and her own angry thoughts, were each loud enough to drown out any single voice.

Trying to keep her eyes focused on the royal table, she stormed through the crowd unimpeded, thanks to those who saw her coming and warned others, until a startlingly strong grip on her upper left arm unexpectedly jerked her to a halt.

Whirling angrily in the assumption that no one but one of her brothers would dare to grab her so, she flashed up her right hand, only to pause and gape in shock.

Raising his eyebrows, Sir Garth said, "I don't advise smacking me, lass. I've a fearsome temper, and striking me is the surest way I know to stir it."

Chapter 3

Still holding Lady Amalie's arm, Garth read the indecision in her face. Her hand remained poised to strike, and she looked angry enough. But he was confident that she would not dare. The roses in her cheeks were splendidly afire, though.

With a sigh, she lowered her hand.

"That's better," he said.

"Pray, release me, sir. People are staring."

"Aye, sure; they want to see what will happen if you're daft enough to strike someone so much larger than you are," he said. He knew he was baiting her and was not certain why. He still held her arm, loosely.

She met his gaze, her beautiful, thickly lashed hazel eyes narrowing. He could still see green and gold flecks glittering in their irises.

She said, "Surely, they are more curious about why you grabbed me as you did. Moreover, I just left my brother Simon. If he should see you . . ."

"He'd be wiser to keep his distance, don't you think?"

Grimacing, she said nonetheless tartly, "I cannot say what he would do. But if you mean to stand here, holding on to me, you will draw notice from more than just my brothers or my father."

Realizing he might draw Fife's attention, or that of other members of the royal family—the lass did serve a princess, after all—Garth released her.

"Thank you," she said. "Why did you stop me?"

He smiled, remembering. "You looked so angry and so heedless of your direction. I thought I should stop you before you crashed into someone."

Realizing he was giving away more about himself than he was learning about her, he paused, trying to think. But he wanted only to touch her again.

"Why should you care what I look like or where I go?" she asked.

He considered himself a plainspoken man. But such a direct question from a female he barely knew derailed his feeble attempt to arrange his thoughts. Several answers occurred to him but not one he could repeat to her.

Feeling defensive, he said, "Why are you angry? It cannot be my fault, because you were set to strike any-one. Has someone said something he should not?"

"I cannot imagine how that is any concern of yours," she said. "But if you mean to continue this conversation, pray escort me to the princess as we talk. She will wonder what has become of me. And if I *have* gone the wrong way, 'tis because I can scarcely see the right one through all these people."

Able to see over the heads of most of the crowd, he saw that the princess had taken her seat. Her other ladies were receiving platters and baskets from gillies to pre-sent for her selection. Although Isabel looked well cared for, he understood that she or one of her attendants would soon wonder why the lady Amalie was not helping, and might well condemn her tardiness.

"I'll take you to her, my lady, but I would like an answer to my question. Who or what has upset you so?"

Her chin came up, and she gazed steadily at him. "You seem to think it is your right to quiz me whenever you like, sir. But you wield no authority over me."

"Do I not? I would remind you that as the only person aware that you put yourself in grave danger today, I must have some right to—"

"Are you daft?" she demanded. "Do you dare to speak of that here, or was that a threat to report it elsewhere? Recall that the explanation of *your* presence would defy credulity unless the man I heard is the same one I just saw talking to you."

He hesitated, because two men had spoken to him as he'd left Moot Hill. Deciding she was likely to have recognized only Fife, and glad she'd had the sense not to name him even if no one in the teeming crowd was paying them heed, he said, "He approached me to say he hopes to see me at Stirling soon because—"

"So you *are* friends with him," she said, frowning. "That is odd, I think, because my brother Simon serves him. And that man thinks well enough of Simon to entrust him with duties he does not entrust to others. How is it that, if you are *that* man's friend, you dared to knock Simon down as you did at Dunfermline?"

"Because I did not know Simon then," Garth said hastily. Realizing how that must sound, he added, "Sakes, but I still don't. Moreover, I doubt he'd recognize me even face to face. I struck him because he was annoying you and I don't like men who bully women. If you recall, I grabbed him from behind, swung him around, and knocked him down before he could possibly have seen me."

"But if he *should* learn who you are . . ." She peeped up at him from under her heavy lashes.

He said dryly, "Are you suggesting that you might tell him?"

Indignation banished the hopeful look. "Nay, I would not! I'm glad you hit him. But others there may have told him."

"If he knew then, nowt came of it. And if he finds out, I doubt he'll complain. I'm *not* Fife's friend, lass, but that incident won't add to Simon's credit with him."

"I suppose not," she said as they drew near the royal table. "I see the princess now, sir," she added with greater dignity. "Thank you for seeing me safely back."

"It was a pleasure, my lady," he replied on the same note. Less formally, he said, "Isabel stays for the Queen's coronation, does she not?"

"Of course, but we leave for Sweethope Hill House after the feasting."

"The Queen's feast also takes place here in the park, I expect."

"It does, aye," she said. "But if you mean to accost me again as you did just now, sir, I warn you I shall *not* leave Isabel's side."

He swept his cap from his head and bowed. "That must be as you will it, my lady. But it is not wise to keep your friends always at a distance."

"Are you my friend, Sir Garth? I have learned that one should rarely trust what any man says."

Checking the anger that always ignited at hearing his integrity questioned, he held her somber gaze and said evenly, "You can trust my word—always."

Without looking away, she said, "In my experience, a man is *most* dangerous when he declares himself trustworthy. Good day to you, sir."

With that, she turned and walked away, leaving him to stare after her. Only then did he realize that she still had not told him who or what had made her so angry.

⁓

As Amalie rejoined the other women and performed her part in attending the princess, she hoped her feelings did not show in her face. But she feared they might.

She knew people were watching. They were always watching her—Isabel's other ladies, if no one else—to see if she shirked her duties or did anything wrong.

Long since, she had discovered that such was the way of women in groups. Even so, the ladies who served Isabel were more agreeable than many serving other members of the extensive royal family.

Isabel, generally sunny-tempered herself, detested discord and quickly stifled it when it occurred. But some of her ladies attacked subtly, and Amalie knew that Isabel's sitting by her at the coronation would have upset at least one of them.

Not only were the others all of higher rank than Amalie, but she was also the youngest. Also, Isabel had invited her to join her household out of friendship.

The two had met during an attempted seizure of Hermitage Castle, a Border stronghold of the Earls of Douglas. Isabel's husband James Douglas had been not only the second earl but also kin to the Scotts of Buccleuch, because Wat Scott's mother was a Douglas. With that kin-

ship and the few years separating them in age, Isabel and
Amalie had soon become good friends.

The princess tended to talk with her as she might talk
with a trusted sister rather than as she did with others. She
had frankly admitted that she rarely allowed herself such
openness with her other ladies, fearing that one of them
might betray a confidence if doing so could benefit the
woman or her family.

Amalie had taken that comment to heart, knowing that
her own mother would want her to pass on any tidbits that
could serve the Murrays. That Isabel trusted her despite
also knowing Lady Murray just made her trust a more
precious gift, and one Amalie would never betray.

The princess had discussed many things with her, including her belief that her husband James had been murdered. At first Isabel had shared that opinion with all who
would listen, but she had soon come to realize that few
people agreed with her. Most dismissed what she said or
even feared for her sanity.

Amalie listened sympathetically and had trouble stifling anger when others spoke pityingly of Isabel and her
"insistence on perpetrating such a falsehood." But she understood other people's need to remember James simply
as a great hero.

Neither she nor the princess had been at Otterburn, of
course. Nor had she been with Isabel to receive the tragic
news of James's death. But she had heard how lovingly
Isabel always spoke of him and could easily imagine how
devastating the news had been for her and how much Isabel needed to know the truth.

Grown men all over Scotland had wept, for James had
been a popular leader as well as their finest warrior. Even
his greatest English rival had called him a hero.

Glancing at the princess, sitting now between the new Queen and another princess, Amalie saw that despite Isabel's smiles and cheerful comments, in moments of repose, her continuing sorrow revealed itself.

Isabel saw her and smiled, reminding her that it was not just sanctuary that the princess had offered her when she had needed it but also real friendship.

Having acquired no facts of her own about James's death, Amalie knew only what Isabel had told her and what little she had gleaned by listening when others spoke of the tragedy. But she knew the princess was not a fool or a madwoman.

If Isabel said it was murder, she had good reason, just as she had reason to think the most likely one to have ordered . . .

A chill shot through her before the thought completed itself: If Sir Garth Napier was right about who had been speaking in that room at Abbots' House, that same person had just ordered another murder.

She wished she could hear Fife's voice again under like circumstances. The few sentences he had spoken on Moot Hill had just not been enough for her to be certain.

Still, she ought to tell someone what she'd heard. But who would believe her, and how much about her own actions would she have to reveal before anyone would?

⁓

Garth watched until she bent to speak with Isabel. Then, telling himself he had no good reason to go on watching her, and calling himself a fool for concerning himself with her at all, he decided to eat before keeping his appointment.

He scanned the numerous trestle tables, letting his gaze rest briefly on that occupied by the Douglas lords before he located the table he sought. Moving then to one of the fires, he thanked those men who noted his knightly girdle, nodded respectfully, and stood aside for him. Accepting a trencher piled high with sliced beef, he found bread and a mug of ale, then made his way to the table in question.

"Room for one more?" he asked the man at its head.

Sir Walter Scott, Laird of Buccleuch, looked up with a grin and gestured to a space beside him on his bench. "Sit yourself down, cousin. I saw you waiting earlier to swear fealty to his grace and wondered where you'd got to since."

At twenty-six, Wat was two years older, and of a slimmer, lankier build. He also had hazel eyes rather than blue ones, but they shared a look of near kinsmen.

To the other nobles gathered there, three or four of whom were with their lady wives, Buccleuch said, "Some of you may not know my cousin, Garth Napier, who won his spurs at Otterburn. He has been out of the country for some months, so you will forgive us if we speak privately for a short time."

"Where is your lady, Wat?" Garth asked as he swung a leg over the bench to take the proffered seat. "I have yet to meet her, after all."

"'Tis no one's fault but your own that you have not," Buccleuch said. "I married Meg before Otterburn, after all."

"Aye, sure, I heard about that," Garth said, grinning but knowing better than to tease his cousin about certain amusing details of that marriage. "As *you* know, the wedding was over long before I learned of it. And soon afterward, we headed to Otterburn. Then, after James died and Archie became Earl of Douglas, he sent to ask me to serve him in Galloway, at Threave Castle. One does not refuse to serve the most powerful lord in the Borders at his family seat. Nor did I want to. Also, Fife had just declared himself, rather than Archie, Chief Warden of the Marches."

"Aye, sure," Wat said. He did not comment on Fife, although Garth was sure he felt as bitter as most Borderers did about Fife's assuming a title traditionally reserved to the Earls of Douglas. "Archie did you great honor, Gar."

"He did, so I was with him at Threave for nearly thirteen months, until Yuletide last year. But after young Archie married Carrick's daughter, I followed Will Douglas of Nithsdale to Prussia. As Scotland was at peace with England by then, he had decided to search for adventure with the Teutonic Knights."

"I know that your father died whilst you were away," Wat said. "I was sorry to hear of it. That his death came so suddenly must have hurt you sorely."

"You'd know. My lord uncle died just two months before I left with Will."

"Aye, but my father's wounds from Otterburn never healed right and caused him much suffering. I own, it was a relief to us all when death took him at last."

"My father was hale and hearty when I left," Garth said. "He was sick only a few days, though, and I did not learn about his death until we brought Will home."

"*That* was a dreadful thing," Wat said. Glancing around and lowering his voice, he added, "Were you with him when they killed him?"

"I came upon it afterward, too late to aid him," Garth said.

"He was dead then?"

"It was horrible," Garth said, choosing his words. Despite his complete trust in Buccleuch, he did not know some of the others near enough to overhear. "Telling Archie that we'd let his son die in a street brawl was worst of all."

Buccleuch frowned. "I'd not want to face Archie the Grim after such a tragedy, myself. Despite being born a bastard, Will grew to be one of Scotland's finest warriors, married a princess, and was Archie's favorite son. No one ever doubted Archie's love for him, or ever will."

"Archie doesn't blame me or Will's other men," Garth said. "He has treated me only with kindness, even to offering me leave to look after things at Westruther. I tell you that only because I'd intended to accept and then visit Scott's Hall to meet your Meg and admire that wee son of yours. As it is, though, I've not even seen my sister, Joan. I'd hoped to see her and her husband here."

"They *are* here somewhere," Wat said. "Crosier walked into the kirk with me. I'd expected them to sup with me, too, but they had already agreed to eat with his parents. I'm surprised you didn't see him during the ceremonies."

"I didn't go into the kirk," Garth said, seeing no reason to mention that, thanks to his intriguing adventure before the coronation, he'd barely noticed the lairds.

He was congratulating himself that Buccleuch apparently had not seen him escort the lady Amalie through the crowd when Buccleuch said, "I wondered why you took the lass to the door but did not take her in. Doubtless you will explain."

Garth had no doubt that his cousin's well-known protective instincts would extend to his good-sister, so he said only, "She had got separated from the princess Isabel, but a knight—one of Isabel's, I expect—was just inside, waiting for her."

"I see," Buccleuch said, and Garth relaxed. Having no desire to stir his cousin's notoriously uncertain temper, he was grateful when Wat went on to relay other, unrelated news about their family.

Still, he would have to take care not to stir Wat's curiosity by showing too much interest in the lady Amalie or Wat would demand to know his intentions toward her. To admit that he did not intend to marry for years yet would hardly be an acceptable response.

The two men chatted about family and desultory matters until Garth, who had been keeping one eye on the Douglas table, saw that the people there were preparing to depart. Shortly thereafter, the man who had spoken to him on the hillside beckoned, and he excused himself to Buccleuch.

~~~

From the table near the royal party where she had joined other attendants, Amalie watched Isabel, alert for the least sign that she needed anything.

In the midst of her own family, Isabel was struggling to look cheerful. Despite her efforts, Amalie decided long before the royal family finished eating that its members had little if any liking for one another.

She had never before seen so many of them together in one place. Anyone watching could see that Fife had nothing to say to any of the others.

It was likewise plain that the King would rather have been anywhere else. He murmured occasionally to the Queen, who sat beside him, but otherwise he kept so still that Amalie wondered if he ate anything or was even aware of the boisterous crowd just a few yards away, celebrating his accession to the throne.

He paid no heed to the clearing of a broad, grassy area in front of the royal table, or to the large fire laid in a rock ring there. Nor did any juggler, tumbler, bear-leader, or musician stir a blink of royal interest.

The rest of the crowd, still happily gorging themselves, noisily cheered the entertainers' antics and shouted suggestions to the musicians for tunes to play.

Darkness was falling and men were lighting torches at the fire before Amalie finished her meal. With nothing to do for the princess, she watched the crowd in the increasing glow of firelight, seeking faces she recognized and one in particular.

So intent was her search for that one person that, as the royal party readied itself to depart, Sir Iagan Murray approached unnoticed until he spoke her name.

"Sir!" she exclaimed, getting quickly to her feet.

"'Tis good to see ye, lass," he said. "I trust I see ye well."

"Aye, sir," she replied. "I am content in my service to Isabel. And tomorrow we return to Sweethope Hill. I vow, sir, we shall all be thankful to be home at last."

"But your home is at Elishaw," he said, frowning. "And your lady mother and I have decided ye should return. In troth, she fears ye might resist the notion, but she's that determined— That is to say," he went on hastily, "I've missed ye sorely and hope ye'll bide with us again till ye marry. Sithee, ye've been away now for nigh onto two years, daughter."

Amalie looked him in the eye. As a child, she had found his customary bluster frightening, but that was no longer the case. "Forgive me, sir, but in that two years' time you've said not one word about missing me until today. I was at Scott's Hall for nearly six months after Meg's wedding before Isabel invited me to bide with her."

"'Twas not that we didna miss ye, lass," he said, looking uncomfortable. "I just had more important matters to attend. After Douglas's death, when Fife tried and failed to take Hermitage Castle, he was angry that he'd failed. Your brothers were angry, too, aye. So, although your mam wanted ye to come home then, I thought ye'd be safer at the Hall till everything settled down. But then . . ." He shrugged. "Time passes gey fast, Amalie."

His memory of events seemed distorted to one who had been at Hermitage with Isabel—then Countess of Douglas—when Fife's men, including the two Murray brothers, had tried and failed to take the castle. But Amalie knew that trying to correct Sir Iagan's recollections would irritate him, and thus do her no good.

"I cannot return to Elishaw yet, sir," she said calmly. "Isabel will need me more than ever at Sweethope Hill. It is a big house, and although they've done much to make it more habitable whilst we've been away, there will be much still to do."

He frowned more heavily, and she knew she had stirred his temper, but she refused to look away or back down. She did *not* want to go home.

Grimacing, his voice clearly under tight control, he said, "I ken fine what ye're thinking, lassie, and I'll no say ye're mistaken. Your mam ought no to have flung this marriage at ye yet that she and Simon have in mind for ye."

"I suspect it was Simon's notion," she said bitterly.

"It was, aye, but Simon is heir to Elishaw and just trying to look after our interests. Moreover, I cannot deny 'tis a good notion. The man has nae estate of his own yet, but he's a knight with connections of the highest order. Sakes, I should think ye may even have met him, because—"

"Whether I know him or not, sir, I don't want to marry anyone. I have said that before, and you should know that I don't say things I do not mean."

"I do, lass, but when I tell ye who it is, 'tis gey likely ye'll change your mind, for he is a fine-looking chap, as well, Simon says. And, if ye dinna ken him ye soon will, because he'll be going into east Lothian, to Lauder wi'—"

"I don't care," Amalie said fiercely. "I won't marry anyone—ever—not to please you or my mother, and *certainly* not to please Simon. I'm sorry if I seem rude or disobedient, sir, but I do have the right to refuse, do I not?" Fearing he might erupt in fury, she added hastily, "Isabel said that I do."

"Aye, ye do," he said with visible reluctance. "If I had me own priest at Elishaw, likely I could force your obedience. But for all that your mam says . . ."

When he paused, clearly realizing it would do him no good to tell her what her mother had said, Amalie said dryly, "I can imagine what she has said, sir. But please believe me when I say that *no one* will persuade me."

"Then ye've nae need to fear paying us a visit, lassie. If ye'll come, I'll swear to see that nae one presses ye to wed."

She knew he meant well, but she also knew that after ten minutes with Lady Murray, his resolve would crumble. For that matter, despite her own determination, she was not sure she could hold out any better against her formidable mother.

"I'm sorry, sir," she said. "Isabel is ready to go now, so I must go as well."

He looked long at her, and then to her relief, he kissed her and walked away.

⁓

Inside Abbots' House a short time later, Simon Murray faced the Governor of the Realm in the upstairs chamber that the latter had taken for his own use.

Tall, like nearly all the Stewarts, but darker and thinner, Fife was sharp of mind and still fit despite being nearly fifty years of age. Simon knew that he was politically astute and utterly ruthless when acquiring power for himself.

Fife enjoyed the trappings of power, and the room they were in was small by comparison with those he customarily occupied at Stirling or Edinburgh Castle. However, the finer rooms in Abbots' House being more appropriate for the new King of Scots, Simon knew that Fife had had no choice.

That the Governor of the Realm should take rooms in Perth as lesser folk had, nearly two and a half miles from the King, was unthinkable with so many at hand who might try to influence his grace. Therefore, Fife had let everyone know from the first that he would also be staying at Abbots' House.

Fife dismissed the servant with whom he had been speaking when Simon entered. Only after the door had shut behind the man did the Governor say in his customary, soft-spoken way, "What news have you brought me?"

"None of any use, my lord," Simon admitted. "I'd hoped my father might persuade her. But apparently, the princess told her she can legally refuse to marry."

"Isabel really *must* learn not to meddle," Fife said. "She begins to annoy me. But I will deal with her, and you must deal with your sister. You do support me in this endeavor, do you not?"

"I do, sir," Simon assured him.

"It is important that I develop strong connections in the Borders, in particular with those who control fortresses there. I want to persuade such men that it behooves them to make clear their staunch loyalty to me."

"I should think, sir, that now that you have the Earl of Douglas in your camp, the rest of the Border lords will submit quickly."

"Don't be a fool," Fife said testily. "Archie the Grim is a Douglas first. Whilst he's the best of that scurrilous lot and knows Scotland needs my strong hand to guide it, he is hardly in my camp. At present, he believes I'm the best man to rule, so he supports me as Governor. But he will do so only until he disagrees with me."

"Surely, my lord—"

"The Douglas power that has long irritated us has weakened since the death of the second earl, and I mean to see it grow weaker yet. It does this country no good constantly to be at the mercy of factions that thirst for war instead of peace."

"I agree, sir, but I do not understand how that makes marrying my sister to Sir Harald Boyd so important to us."

"I reward my supporters well, Simon, as you know and

will continue to know for as long as you do support me. But your father supports no one."

"He believes that remaining neutral protects our land, and so it has, sir."

"He succeeds only in irritating everyone thereby, on both sides," Fife said grimly. "Your family owns a large estate, and it will do him good to provide your sister with a proper dowry, including a sizeable piece of land. Having earned his spurs, Boyd is entitled to such, and he will be loyal to me."

Simon nodded, wondering if Fife had forgotten that he, Simon, was heir to that land. Fife could easily have granted the new knight land from his own holdings or those of the Crown, which now amounted to the same thing. Such holdings had steadily and considerably multiplied over the past several years.

As if reading his thoughts, Fife added, "I'll see you generously rewarded, of course, when you succeed your father."

The cynical voice that lived in Simon's head muttered that since Fife was acquiring land as fast as he could, to think he would give up any when he could force someone else to do so *had* been foolish. Still, as heir to Elishaw, Simon's attitude toward sharing even a piece of it with Boyd was not enthusiastic.

"I'll expect to hear soon that you have forced your sister's submission," Fife said. "I have already told Boyd that he can expect the marriage negotiations to proceed quickly, so do *not* disappoint me, Simon."

"No, sir. It shall be as you desire."

Furious with his sister, Simon decided as he left Abbots' House that he had no choice now but to force the issue.

Chapter 4

The henchman who had beckoned to Garth led him through the crowd to stables near the western monastic buildings, where knights and noblemen had stabled or penned their horses.

Although the crowd in the park had barely thinned, many men were shouting for mounts. At his guide's urging, Garth grabbed a passing gillie and gave him a coin to fetch his horse. "Make haste, lad, and I'll have another for you."

"Aye, sir. I ken fine that the Douglas be riding."

Finding his guide still at his side, Garth said, "Do you take me to his lordship, or should I go alone?"

"We'll do neither, an it please ye, sir," the man said quietly. "He aims to discover ye as if by chance."

Garth nodded, his curiosity urging him to ask why. Experience warned him though that Archie the Grim would choose what to tell him, and when.

Accordingly, he practiced patience as he nodded to acquaintances but encouraged none to stop for conversation. Not only would the gillie expect to find him where he'd left him when he brought his horse, but it would also be easier for Douglas to find him if he stayed in one place. When he realized that his erstwhile guide had melted into the crowd, he knew he had judged the situation correctly.

Minutes later, hearing his name shouted in stentorian tones, he turned to see the earl striding toward him as other men stepped quickly out of his path.

Archie the Grim, known far and wide as the Black Douglas because of his dark complexion and darker eyes, was an inch or two shorter than Garth. His black hair, worn long and free in the fashion of his youth, had acquired flecks of silver but was still darker than that of most dark-haired men who could boast of living sixty years, as he had. His figure was long-limbed and lanky, his shoulders stooped with age, but his manner was brisk, and he wore his great power with easy assurance.

Looking sternly sober, as always, he put out his right hand and gripped Garth's firmly as he clapped him on the back with his left. "'Tis glad I am to see you, lad," he said. "How have you been keeping yourself?"

"Well, my lord, I thank you," Garth said.

"I warrant you must be heading back to Perth now, as I am."

"I am, aye."

"Then you'll ride with me for a time."

Minutes later, Garth was riding beside Archie at the head of Archie's large fighting tail. Archie considered it a measure of his importance that he rarely traveled with fewer than a hundred men, and despite the lack of housing for large retinues in Perth, Garth knew that Archie would think a smaller one unreasonable.

He also knew from experience that the Douglas rode fast. Archie and his men nearly always thundered across the countryside with banners waving, even in darkness. After all, few Borderers minded riding at night. Their ponies were nimble and used to long distances. Therefore, fast travel was common to Border life.

Tonight, though, Archie kept his mount to a near walk. When he signed brusquely to his tail to fall well behind, Garth realized their conversation would be strictly private and hoped he had not done anything to draw Archie's ire.

"I've had news," the earl said bluntly. "But first, have you learned aught that we did not know before?"

"Very little, my lord," Garth admitted. "I had thought I'd tracked our quarry to his lair, because I met one of Will's men from Danzig, who told me Ben Haldane had taken service with Sir John Edmonstone of that Ilk."

"Our Isabel's so-unsatisfactory new husband," Douglas said. "Aye, well, I agreed to that arrangement, and sithee, Edmonstone was a crusader himself, so he might take a man claiming a like past into his household without question."

"Aye, but no one at Edmonstone knew aught of Haldane," Garth said.

"I ken fine that I've asked you before," Archie said, shooting him a look from under dark, bushy eyebrows. "But are you sure you heard the name right?"

"I am," Garth said, taking no offense. "Will was in great pain and near the end when I came upon him, but he recognized me. His men were chasing those of his attackers who'd run off, so I knelt to see if I could aid him. He called me by name, sir, and he gripped my hand. As clearly as I'm speaking now, he said, 'It was Haldane,

Gar. Send him to hell for me.' I found only a few men afterward who knew the name, but they all assured me that Haldane had returned to Scotland from Danzig nearly a sennight before, after a minor disagreement with Will."

"I believe all of that," Douglas said. "But you know as well I do that Will's own lads say it was English Cliffords who attacked them. They said the battle was fast and furious and Lord Clifford himself killed Will."

"I do know that, my lord. And Clifford was in Danzig when we were there. There was some tension, and the attackers who fell did wear Clifford's device, but I talked to Clifford, and he swore that the men were not his. In his favor, and although he is English, I have never heard anyone accuse him of lying."

"Nor have I," Douglas said. "But someone is lying, and I mean to learn who. I never thought to ask before, but did you tell Will's men what he had said to you?"

"Nay, for I could prove nowt. I did see a man running before I reached Will, but it was too dark to see his face. I don't even know that he was involved, other than perhaps in running away from the attack. In any event, Will's lads were so certain Clifford had done it that they would not have listened even if I *had* tried to tell them. By the time I learned that a knight named Haldane had served Will, we could do nowt in Danzig anyway. So we took Will home to you, and since then, as you know, I've been searching for Haldane."

Douglas nodded, was silent for a moment or two, and then said, "I know you can't say yet if Haldane and his men acted alone. But I don't hesitate to tell you that Isabel has placed Will's death at Fife's door, just as she did with James's."

"Could she be right, sir?"

"To my mind, such thinking is rash," Archie said. "Everyone knows that Fife was with me when Jamie died. We led a huge Scottish army from Galloway into England. Whilst James was keeping Hotspur busy in the east, in Northumberland, we harried folks all over Cumberland. Fife did not even know Jamie's battle plan."

"In fairness to her ladyship, sir, Fife did know where James would be and might have conspired with someone else to kill him," Garth said, speaking his thoughts frankly as he usually did. "That has been Fife's way in the past, has it not? Men who stand in his path often die. But he is never at hand when they do."

Archie shot him a grim look. "So people say. I've not seen it myself though, and I'll not condemn any man on rumor alone. Fife is strong, and I'd see him stronger, because I believe he is the man Scotland needs at her helm. We certainly need him more than we need that pusillanimous priests' man, Carrick. For all that we'll serve Carrick as King of Scots till he dies, he is no ruler. But bring me evidence that Fife had aught to do with murdering my son or Jamie Douglas, and I won't just revoke my support, Gar. I'll spit Fife's traitorous head on a pike at Threave."

Garth believed him, and they rode in silence until the north wall of the city of Perth loomed before them under a pale quarter moon.

Perth was one of only two walled cities in Scotland, Berwick the other, because the English had occupied both towns for extended periods from the last years of the previous century into the early years of the current one. They had built those walls and maintained them, and they had shut the city gates at night.

The gates shut no longer, and as the earl's party neared

the north gate, Archie said, "I've been thinking about what you said. It fits with other thoughts I've had lately, so I want you to go to Sweethope Hill."

Garth had no objection. Indeed, the thought of going to Sweethope Hill intrigued him, although he thought he'd neglect to mention that to Wat Scott. To Archie, he said only, "Will you share your reasons, sir?"

"Aye, sure, for 'tis why I wanted our meeting tonight to look chanceful. I've some concern, as you do, about Fife's habit of removing obstacles in his path. For the past two years, Isabel has been pricking at him about James. Thus far, Fife has ignored her. But she has stirred others to her thinking, and this of Will is bound to add fuel to any fire she has ignited."

"I've suspected Fife's involvement, myself," Garth told him. "But if you are worried about her safety, my lord, you should send her more men-at-arms."

"Nay, for if you are right, Fife will be subtle. She is his sister, and one would think that must keep her safe, but many doubt that her brother David of Strathearn died naturally. So I want someone who knows my thinking to keep an eye on her."

After a brief pause, he added, "Mayhap you can learn something to aid your search, too. You've not talked with her yet about Jamie's death, have you?"

"No, sir, for as you know, I was at Otterburn myself. His people believe his armorer failed to fasten his cuirass properly, leaving it open for any lance or dirk. Some even think the armorer stabbed him, but as the man died in a knife fight a day or two afterward, we cannot ask him. *His* killer disappeared, and many believe that he, too, is dead. Others believe he never existed and James died heroically in battle."

"'Tis all rumor then save the last," Archie said as they passed the market square at the foot of the High Street. "Everyone agrees that Jamie's death was heroic whatever its cause. But this of Will, with what you saw and what Will himself told you at the end . . . Have you shared that with anyone but me since you left Threave?"

"No, sir. I'd intended to tell Buccleuch, and I should tell him, but I have not yet done so."

"Tell him," Archie said. "Just get his word that he'll keep it to himself. Wat's word is as good as yours or my own."

"That does relieve my mind, sir. I'm not accustomed to keeping things from my cousin. Nor should I," he added, speaking as much to himself as to Archie. "Although I serve you at present, my lord, Wat is chief of my kindred," he added. "Now that I hold Westruther, I must also answer to him."

"Use your own judgment then," Archie said. "I trust you, and I trust Wat."

Garth nodded, satisfied and grateful.

"Now then, as to how we shall proceed," Archie went on, "I want to draw as little notice to your presence there as possible. Isabel always has two or three knights to serve her and keep her men-at-arms under control. I assume you mean to attend the Queen's coronation tomorrow, so I'd have you get there early and . . ."

Monday morning at Scone dawned as pleasantly as Sunday had, with puffy milk-white clouds drifting in an azure sky. In the eastern monastic building the bustle began early, because the Queen's coronation would take

place hours earlier than the King's had and take much
less time.

Feasting, such as it would be, was to follow at noon in
the abbey park.

Isabel was already receiving visitors in the prior's
study. Amalie and two of her ladies had come downstairs
with her, and the other two were still with her, along with
Sir Duncan Forrest, to keep order if necessary.

Such necessity rarely arose with Isabel. People loved
her, recognizing her as one who cared for others besides
herself. The two ladies with her were of higher rank than
Amalie and would remain with the princess while she
met with her visitors. It was rarely necessary or desired
for Amalie to stay on such occasions.

The coronation of the Queen would be interesting, but
Amalie looked forward more to the feast. In general, the
food the abbey had provided for them was paltry compared with offerings in the much grander establishments
that had housed Isabel and her ladies over the past eight
months.

The Austen Canons of Scone considered a little bread
and water enough to begin one's day—their own beginning much earlier, just after midnight, at Matins. For their
royal visitors, they did provide ale and a tart bramble jam,
however.

Amalie liked beef, or a bowl of barley porridge or
oatmeal brose, to break her fast. Bread was all very well
in its place, but in the morning she preferred food that
provided more energy. She was glad to see and smell the
cook fires for the midday feast already burning when she
stepped outside to have a look at the day.

The other ladies were already packing, so she could
spare only a few minutes. Her own things were ready, but

she would bear most of the folding and sorting of Isabel's belongings. Older, more experienced ladies—particularly the ladies Averil Anderson and Nancy Williamson, who had been with Isabel before her marriage to Jamie Douglas—would supervise and criticize everyone and every detail until all was ready for the princess and her party to leave Scone.

In the meantime, there was still the small matter of the Queen's coronation, as *small* it apparently would be.

She had at least an hour, though, before those proceedings would begin. Although she would have liked to stroll about the abbey grounds, now much less crowded than they had been the day before, she lacked enough time for that.

It worried her, though, that so few people had returned to the abbey.

Annabella Drummond was about to become Queen of Scots and should have shared her husband's coronation. To have put off her ceremony had been not only wrong of the Earl of Fife but also demeaning to Annabella. But perhaps many more people would arrive in time to help her celebrate her day properly.

In any event, Amalie could not think more about it. She had work to do, and if others thought she was shirking, someone would surely lecture her about duty.

She did not want to hear it, so she hurried in and busied herself with Isabel's packing until it was time to change her own gown for the coronation.

Knowing Isabel had returned by then and was likely dressing, Amalie washed her face, tidied her hair, and donned the simple sapphire-blue figured silk tunic and skirt she had set aside for the ceremony. With it she wore white silk hose and her favorite pale pink silk slippers.

One of the maidservants who accompanied their party
helped her tie her ribbons and garters, and adjusted her
net and caul.

"Will ye wear a cloak, my lady?" the girl asked.

"I think not, Bess," Amalie said. "It is warm enough
outside and will be stifling in the kirk." Dismissing the
girl, she joined the other ladies.

When they went outside, she saw many more com-
moners than she'd seen earlier, as well as a few who were
clearly noble. Many folks had brought children to watch
the smaller event, still a rare enough occasion to impress
most of them.

A number of children were running around, shouting
or playing games. Their shrieks and laughter diminished
as parents shouted them to order when members of the
royal family began proceeding to the kirk.

Amalie saw Buccleuch and a few Douglas lords, but
she did not see the Earl of Douglas. She saw Sir Garth,
talking with Buccleuch and a nobly dressed couple, but
she turned her head away before Garth or Buccleuch
could catch sight of her.

The ceremony was much briefer than the King's.
Bishop Trail escorted Annabella to a chair of state near
the altar, and her son David followed them. But there was
no throne, no fanfare, and no procession of lords and prelates. Few of them had returned, and those who had entered quietly to take their places in the chancel.

After a brief Lady Mass, and with no oath for her to
take, Bishop Trail made a cross on her forehead with the
holy oil and blessed her without asking her to rise.

Then, because Fife had not deigned to lend his presence to the occasion, an attendant approached the bishop,
carrying a jeweled gold tiara on a white cushion.

As Trail reached for the tiara, to everyone's surprise, the King of Scots, who had quietly taken a chair at one side of the chancel before the Queen's entrance, got awkwardly to his feet. In a quiet but nonetheless easily heard voice, he said, "Hold there, Bishop, if you will."

Limping to Trail's side, the King took the tiara from its cushion and gently placed it on Annabella's head. Then, with a loving smile, he raised her to her feet, faced the audience, and said, "I present to you my own dear lady and your Queen."

Someone shouted, "God save the Queen!"

Others echoed the cheer, the choir sang a hymn, and it was over.

The whole business took less than an hour.

"The good Lord should bless his grace's reign for that simple act of kindness alone," Isabel said tartly when they were outside again.

"It was kind of him to put the crown on her himself," Lady Averil agreed.

"Fife should roast in hell for treating Annabella so poorly," Isabel declared. "One of my visitors told me he has organized some sort of tourney today on the Inch near Perth. He calls it a celebration, but he plainly means it to show how little he makes of the Queen. I think his behavior is shameful!"

Amalie agreed but knew better than to say so. It was one thing for Isabel to criticize her brothers. It was quite another for one of her attendants to do so.

The wind had picked up and was blowing from the Firth of Forth.

Shivering, Amalie noted that the other ladies had brought cloaks, and realized that she'd have been wiser to have done so. When Isabel chose her place, Amalie excused herself, knowing it would be some time before the King and Queen joined them for the feast, and hurried back to their monastic building.

Reaching the refectory entrance, she heard a familiar voice hailing her and, with an odd leap of pleasure, turned to see Sir Garth striding toward her.

"Good day, sir," she said, deciding that he had a pleasant smile. Still, to put him in his place, she said, "I thought I warned you not to accost me here."

"Ah, but you also said you would stay with Isabel, and yet here you are, running away again." Coming right up to her and standing so close that she wanted to step back, he said gently, "I hope no one else has made you angry."

"Only the Earl of Fife," she said. "But I don't think that counts with anyone."

"It would count with me if I could do aught about it," he said.

"But you cannot," she said. "I think he treated Annabella dreadfully."

"Then we agree," he said.

"But you are his friend," she reminded him.

"So much so that I am here instead of attending his tourney."

"The Douglas did not choose to come here though. Nor did many others."

"Many are afraid of annoying Fife," he said. "Archie the Grim is not one of those, though. He had his own reasons, I warrant. Still, you must have noticed that Douglases and their allies comprise most of the nobility that did attend."

"I don't know all the Douglases," she replied. "I do know Buccleuch is one of their allies, and I saw you talking with him and two other people."

"My sister and her husband, Lord and Lady Crosier," he said.

"I see. Still I note only how few nobles are here compared to yesterday."

"Be sensible, lass. Most who came yesterday came only because failing to attend the King's coronation is tantamount to treason. Trust me when I tell you no one wants to give Fife any reason to demand his head."

"I have told you how I feel about trust, sir. Is that why *you* attended?"

Evenly, he said, "I did so because I had to swear fealty for my estates."

Amalie looked at him in surprise. He seemed too young to have estates of his own. Then she remembered that Wat Scott was not yet thirty but had acceded to his father's title, and the Buccleuch and Rankilburn estates, nearly ten months before.

Sir Garth was smiling at her hesitation as if he had read her mind when a shriek from inside the building startled both them. As Amalie turned, a second shriek sounded, this time one of laughter.

A thundering sound accompanied more laughter, and all seemed to originate from the refectory, which lay to the left of a small entry hall. The tall door to the refectory was shut, but with a quizzical frown, Garth reached past her to open it.

Their arrival went unnoticed by the boys inside. There appeared at first, to Amalie, to be a veritable horde of them, chasing each other in all directions, even down the length of the refectory table.

A second look reduced the number to perhaps a dozen.

Louder shouts from one of them alerted his friends,

and the mischief-makers scattered, the ones atop the table leaping from it with more shrieks and darting toward two other doors, one in the same wall as the entrance and the other clearly leading to the nether regions of the kitchen and service areas.

"Michael." Sir Garth did not raise his voice, but one of the small rogues fleeing from the tabletop skidded to a halt.

"Come here."

The child hesitated, not moving for a period long enough for Amalie to feel tension. She resisted the urge to look at her companion.

The little boy turned at last, revealing a cherubic face with wary, bright blue eyes beneath a mop of blond curls. "What are ye going to do to me?"

"What did I tell you to do?"

A scowl appeared, reminding Amalie forcibly of the man beside her, but the boy said defensively, "Ye ken fine what ye said. Ye said—"

"You had better begin again." The tone, still soft, chilled her.

The child's eyelashes fluttered—also blond but thick enough and long enough for her to see them easily when he gazed from underneath them at the man beside her. As she watched, the cherubic lower lip trembled.

Amalie's heart melted. She shot a glimpse at Sir Garth, tempted to intervene on the cherub's behalf, but one look at Garth's stern face silenced her.

"Well?" he said to the child.

"Ye said I should come to ye, and so I am." He took several long steps.

"Have you forgotten how to address someone to whom you owe respect?"

The mobile little mouth twitched again with annoyance, but the child quickly controlled the expression.

"Nay, then, I have not," he said soberly. "I should address ye as 'sir.' I just forgot, *sir*." He stood before them now, and looking up, he added hastily, "I *did* forget for a minute, see you, but I remember gey fine now."

A brief silence ensued, during which Amalie struggled between laughter and fear for the boy. She dared not look again at Sir Garth.

However, evidently seeing something in his expression that relieved his own immediate concern, the little boy flicked a look at Amalie and smiled dazzlingly.

Sir Garth said dryly, "My lady, little honor though he does our kindred with his behavior, this scruff is my nephew, Michael Crosier, my sister's eldest bairn."

She had already decided they must be kinsmen. The boy was politely bowing, so she said, "I am pleased to meet you, Michael Crosier."

He gave her the measuring look from under his lashes that he had given his uncle, saying, "Ye're no wroth wi' me, too, then, like Uncle Gar?"

"No, of course I am not."

His radiant smile flashed forth again, although he shot an oblique look at his uncle before he said, "Uncle Gar will no tolerate bairns who misbehave. But, sithee, the others and me, we were just larking."

"I saw that," she said, struggling not to smile.

"Aye, then ye ken fine that it were nowt."

A hand clamped firmly on her upper arm as Sir Garth said, "It has occurred to me, my lad, that you might want to explain to your father before someone else does just what you were doing here, and how it was 'nowt.'"

"Ye'll no tell him! Ye're no such a—"

When he broke off, Amalie saw with a darting glance that his tormentor had raised his eyebrows.

"Not such a what?" Garth prompted.

"Such a traitor," Michael said firmly, giving his uncle just as stern a look as the one directed at him.

"That is generally true," Garth admitted. "But you can never be sure, especially with as much feasting and drinking as goes on at affairs such as this today. I might be taken with the drink myself and let something slip."

"Ye'd never! Ye said a man who lets hisself get ale-shot is nobbut a sorry fool."

"Even so," Garth said, "it would be wise for you to present your version of events to your father before he hears another from someone else. Do you honestly think you can trust all those other lads not to wag their tongues?"

The child thought a minute and gave him another measuring look before saying, "I'll ha' to decide that for m'self, won't I?"

"You will," Garth agreed. "Fortunately, no one has yet called you a sorry fool. You'll excuse us now. I must escort Lady Amalie back to her party."

Michael made Amalie another bow. "'Tis a pleasure, m'lady."

"But he's utterly charming," she said to Sir Garth as they watched the child dash off. "You won't really give him away to his father, will you?"

"I'm no talebearer, lass, nor do I burden myself with unnecessary family matters. I've seen how one's kinsmen will bind a man to them if they can, and I require freedom to do what I do. Did you have purpose in coming here, or were you just escaping that crowd?"

"I came to fetch my cloak," she told him.

"An excellent notion. I shall await you here."

Chapter 5

⁓

Already knowing Sir Garth well enough not to argue with him, Amalie hurried upstairs, snatched up her scarlet cloak, and hurried back down again.

"Do you think Michael *will* tell his father what they were doing?" she asked as he took the cloak from her and draped it over her shoulders.

"Aye, for he's a good lad. I'll not be amazed, though, if he edits the tale somewhat to his own benefit."

"Faith, I should think that would be the only sensible course," Amalie said, imagining what would have happened to her or to her siblings had one of them ever done such a thing as to run the length of a refectory table at an abbey.

"Would you lie to protect yourself?" her companion asked bluntly.

"What a foolish question! Wouldn't anyone?"

"I was not referring to protecting your life or limbs, just to protecting yourself from well-deserved punishment."

"So did I. Wouldn't you do all you could to protect yourself from a beating?"

"I don't lie."

She stared at him. "Never?"

"Never."

She continued to stare, fascinated. "I wonder if that can be true."

"Do you doubt me?" He frowned more fiercely than he had at the boy.

"Faith, I dare not," she said. "You look as if you would throttle me."

"I don't take kindly to having my word questioned, lass."

"Then I believe you," she said. "*Truly*, I do."

She hoped he believed her, but he gazed at her steadily, looking skeptical.

Deciding a change of subject was definitely in order, she said hastily, "Why did you follow me here?"

"Because in a crowd like that one, it is unwise for a maiden to wander off by herself," he said.

"In a crowd like *that* one? 'Tis gey small compared to yesterday. I doubt that anyone here would molest me in broad daylight."

"It was broad daylight at Dunfermline," he said.

"Must you forever be throwing that day in my face? Need I remind you that your so-called molester then was my own brother?"

"That is true, and I haven't seen him here today. Doubtless, he cares more about pleasing Fife than looking after you."

"You seem to know a great deal about me, Sir Garth," she said, glad that he had not mentioned her parents' similar absence. "But I still know very little about you—other than that you have a charming nephew."

"That scamp is certainly more charming than your brother," he said with a smile. "You should have clouted him that day, you know."

"Considering that you have just been saying I should do as *you* bid me, I suspect that you and Simon are more alike than you want to believe," Amalie said. "That is just what *he* was telling me when you knocked him down."

"Then I should not have interfered," he said. "Had I not, mayhap you *would* have clouted him. I'd like to have seen that."

"Would you? I tell you frankly, sir, I enjoyed seeing you strike him down, but I'd never have a chance to do such a thing. Not only is he larger and taller than I am, but he is also much more ruthless."

"I can show you some tricks to even the match if you like."

"As tempting as that offer is, I fear I must decline," she said. "In any event, I doubt we shall see much of each other after today. Why do you smile, sir?"

"I should not," he said. "I'd be sorry if your prediction were to prove true."

She had to admit, if only to herself, that she would be sorry, too, because for once, to have a man pay her as much attention as he had made life more interesting. In general, such attention made her nervous and uncomfortable, and she could not recall any gentleman's attentions eliciting such strong feelings in her as his did.

To be sure, there had been one young man at Dunfermline who had flirted with her most enjoyably before the incident with Simon. But now she scarcely remembered

what he'd looked like, because after Sir Garth had felled
Simon . . .

Inwardly, she shuddered at the memory.

Simon had been so angry afterward that she had feared
he would accuse her of striking him. He had not, but he
had demanded that she name his assailant. When she'd
said truthfully that she hadn't the least notion, Simon had
not believed her.

He had commanded her to ride straight back to Elishaw from Dunfermline, declaring that he would escort
her there himself. He had also said, as if it had been a
compliment instead of news that horrified her, that his
father was considering a most advantageous marriage for
her.

"To another who stands well with my lord Governor,"
Simon had added.

"As if *that* would recommend *any* man to me!"

Simon had nearly slapped her then, she knew. But too
many people had been there, any one of whom might
have challenged his right to do so.

And Simon, despite his loyalty to his so-admired master, had a healthy respect for Archie the Grim. He would
not have wanted to arouse the Douglas's ire by causing
such a scene at his heir's wedding. Simon knew as well
as she did that Archie would not hesitate to deal severely
with such insult.

That thought made her wonder if Sir Garth had suffered the Douglas's wrath after knocking Simon down.

She had opened her mouth to ask him when he smiled
and said, "What is it?"

That smile was more than just pleasant. It was as
charming as his nephew's, but she ignored her reaction to
it and said bluntly, "I was just wondering if you had faced

any consequences after knocking Simon down. Did no one tell the Douglas?"

"If anyone did, Archie said nowt about it to me. I must suppose, however, that Simon had a few things to say to you."

"He demanded to know your name. But since you had not told me, I could not tell him. And no one else admitted knowing you."

"Earlier you said that he *wanted* you to obey him. Do you not always obey your brothers?"

"Does your sister obey you?"

"She is married, so I don't command her. She obeys her husband, I hope."

"That is not an answer to my question."

"Aye, well, I asked about you first. But you rarely answer my questions."

She chuckled. "I suppose I should not be so difficult. That's what Simon calls it if he does not call it my damned recalcitrance."

"Fine language from a well-bred lady," he said with a smile. But it faded as he added, "Are you going to tell me why he demanded your obedience?"

"He had taken it into his head that I ought to marry someone. It is not important, though, because I said I would not."

He raised his eyebrows. "Someone? Anyone at all, or a particular someone?"

"Simon did not say the man's name or even that he wanted to marry me. He just said he—the other man, that is—enjoyed the favor of the Governor of the Realm and that he—Simon—could easily persuade my father to accept the match."

"So Fife means to use you as a pawn in one of his games, does he?"

"I should say, rather, that it is Simon who means to do so."

"Nay, lass, 'tis Fife who decides all. His minions just obey him."

She raised her chin. "It is possible, though, that the whole idea is Simon's. It would be to his benefit, would it not, to arrange a marriage for me with someone who enjoys Fife's favor?"

He shrugged. "That may be so, but if Fife did not see considerable benefit to himself, he'd never go for the idea. And if you think Simon would arrange a marriage of that ilk without Fife's approval, I can only say it sounds most unlikely."

It did sound unlikely, she had to admit. But the thought that the Governor of the Realm might think about her, for any reason, was even worse than Simon's wanting to use her to advance his own position.

Not that she intended to cooperate with either of them, for she did not.

Gently, her companion said, "*Did* you suffer consequences afterward, lass? I'd be gey sorry if Simon hurt you because of what I did to him."

"He didn't," she said. "He did threaten to take me right home with him, but Isabel intervened. She said that, as I was the nearest of her ladies in age to her, she would miss me too much to bear, so I must stay with her. That was not even true, because Sibylla Cavers is only a year older, whilst Isabel is four-and-twenty."

"Do you not miss your home?"

"I miss my younger sister, and I miss certain things

about Elishaw," she admitted. "But I do not miss being constantly under my mother's thumb."

They were approaching the princess Isabel's party, and Amalie saw no sign yet of the King or the Queen. But the other ladies had taken their seats, and carvers were beginning to carve the meats for the royal table.

"They will serve soon," Sir Garth said. "We had better join them."

Amalie made no objection when he increased their pace, although his choice of pronoun made her wonder if he expected to hover over her while she attended to her duties. She was astonished, though, when he escorted her to the royal table and then, in response to a gesture from Isabel, took her right up to the princess.

"You are in good time, Sir Garth, which pleases me," Isabel said, smiling. "It pleases me, too, that you found our wandering Amalie and brought her back. You must be sure to thank him, my dear, for looking after you."

"Yes, madam," Amalie said, suppressing rebellion. Turning to her escort, she said, "I do thank you, sir, for seeing me safely back. Even so, I trust you will forgive me for adding that it will be pleasant not to have you constantly waylaying me in future. Such a habit could become *most* annoying."

Looking far too interested for Amalie's comfort, Isabel said, "Has he waylaid you before, then?"

Realizing that she ought to have chosen her words with more care, Amalie said, "Like many men, madam, he is certain that all females require shepherding."

"Well, I've no doubt that you can look after yourself, my dear, but you will be seeing more of him, even so. Sir Garth is joining my household to replace Sir Duncan Forrest, who must leave us as soon as we return, to attend to some private affairs."

Stifling a gasp, fearing it came as much from delight as from shock, Amalie managed to say, "How . . . how unfortunate that Sir Duncan must go! I like *him*."

Garth had been watching for her reaction and had all he could do not to smile at the emphasis she gave the word "him."

But he knew he'd better watch his step with the princess.

Isabel was amused and clearly would not object if he cultivated a friendship with the lady Amalie. But to do so would mean danger of distraction at least, because he was attracted to her as he could not recall being attracted to any woman before.

He could not have said exactly why she attracted him. She was not only unlike women who had drawn his notice before but also definitely unlike any he would someday—a day far in the future—consider taking for his wife.

The former had all been comely sorts who boldly flirted with him, were merry companions, and—married or not—expected nothing more than amusing repartee or mutual pleasuring. The wife he chose would be a beautiful noblewoman of cheerful demeanor, who would be pure of heart and mind, completely virtuous, and as constant and true as the sunrise. She would be gentle of mood, courteous, kind—and always, always obedient to his will.

He had yet to meet such a paragon, but he was certain she existed and just as certain that when the time came to marry—which would not be a day sooner than absolutely necessary—she would quietly present herself to him.

The lass trying to compose herself now was none of those things. Well, in fairness, she was virtuous insofar as anyone still a maiden must be virtuous. And she was pleasant enough looking, he supposed. Her rosy complexion was flawless, but her figure, although rounded in all the right places to make her the sort of cozy armful he most enjoyed in his bed, was not the sort to stop other men in their tracks to stare at her and envy him his good fortune. Not to mention, there was that extraordinary something about her that reminded him of his mother.

When the lass had collected her wits, excused herself to Isabel, and hurried off to attend to her duties, he accepted his dismissal with a bow and found a place at one end of a nearby knights' table. As he waited for his food, he thought more about the nagging, inexplicable resemblance that puzzled him so.

To imagine even a similarity to Lady Napier was patently absurd. His mother was never sneaky or unduly curious about other people's conversations.

The lady Amalie possessed both of those unfortunate traits.

His mother would never lie, either. The lass believed that everyone did.

His mother was, however, a comfortable woman.

Therefore, he decided, it was no more than the comfortable look of the lass. But she could hardly *be* a comfort to any man. She was saucy, disobedient, and of a nature possibly more stubborn than his own. She refused to answer plain questions and delighted in verbally dueling with him. Moreover, in his new role as knight to the princess, the lady Amalie would doubtless prove to be a damnable nuisance.

As his restless gaze found her again—accepting a platter from a gillie and passing it with a smile to one of the older ladies to offer the princess—he reminded himself that he still wanted to know all that she had overheard in Abbots' House.

He was in a better position now to pursue those details and to glean any helpful information that the princess possessed. Isabel was markedly approachable and seemed to approve of him, so he did not doubt he would soon be privy to all she knew about James Douglas's death, and Will's, as well.

He studied the knights he could see at the table, most of whom served the royal family, and wondered which two belonged to the princess's household.

Their knightly ranks were reduced, because only the King's numerous sisters and their husbands—those who had husbands—had attended the Queen's coronation. There were, nonetheless, a dozen men seated there.

Drawing the one next to him into conversation, he soon learned who the others were, but on finding that the two from Sweethope were at the other end of the table, he knew he was unlikely to discover anything of use to him before they all left Scone. Therefore, ever practical, he applied himself to his meal.

⌒

Isabel's party did not leave Scone Abbey until nearly three that afternoon and rode only as far as Stirling Castle. The twenty-six-mile ride took them across flatlands, on well-traveled tree-shaded tracks along the river Earn, and then

Allan Water. So even with a long string of sumpter ponies carrying their baggage, they made good time and arrived before nightfall.

Amalie had expected to see many others who'd attended the coronations on the road. But those who had stayed for the festivities on the Inch, two miles east of town, must still have been celebrating when the princess's party skirted Perth's western wall, because few other travelers appeared.

Isabel and her ladies spent the night in Stirling Castle, where she had rooms of her own. The men in her party found lodgings below Castle Hill, in the town.

Thanks to the steepness of the track leading up to the castle, the ponies arrived later than the women did. But the princess's people were efficient. By the time they had finished their supper, their most necessary belongings were in their rooms.

The weather stayed fine for the next two days, and the long ride from Stirling to Linlithgow, then Dalkeith, four miles south of Edinburgh, passed without incident.

The princess being eager to get home, and Douglas of Dalkeith not yet returned from Perth, they spent only one night at Dalkeith Castle.

Departing early Thursday morning, the princess's party rode on ahead of the sumpter ponies, following the ancient Lauderdale Road into the Borders.

In general, the two older ladies, Averil and Nancy, took turns riding beside the princess, leaving Amalie to ride either with the one not doing so or with one of the princess's other two ladies. She liked Lady Sibylla Cavers better than Lady Susan Lennox, who believed herself far superior in rank and was quick to take offense when Isabel was kind to Amalie. Even Susan was carefully civil though, knowing that Isabel would dismiss anyone in her service who was not.

Amalie had been riding silently beside Lady Susan for some time. But in the village of Lauder, as they passed below the high stone wall of its famous fortress, built a hundred years before to protect that important approach to Edinburgh from English invaders, Susan said, "I want a word with Sir Kenneth." As she said the words, she abruptly turned her mount out of the line of riders.

Amalie sighed, knowing that Susan, thin and lanky with a long, horsy face, and still unwed at the ripe age of five-and-thirty, harbored hopes that Sir Kenneth Maclean, an unwed knight of similar age, might be on the lookout for a wife.

Still, Amalie was glad to ride alone for a while, because she found it trying to carry on sensible conversation with a woman who made no secret of her disdain.

She would prefer to rip Susan's hair from her head and stuff it into her—

"Good afternoon, my lady. 'Tis a fine soft day, is it not?"

Giving Garth a sour look, she said, "*Must* you always sneak up on a person?"

He grinned, easing his mount alongside hers as he said, "If you think anyone can creep about whilst riding a horse like this one, you're daft!"

Lady Nancy, ahead of them, turned to look at him with strong disapproval.

". . . *if* you will pardon my saying so, my lady," he added hastily to Amalie. Lowering his voice considerably, he said, "In troth, lass, you must have been lost in thought. I hope you were deciding to tell me what I want to know."

Since she could hardly tell him what she *had* been thinking, especially when Lady Nancy might hear, she said, "Why are you not riding with the other knights?"

"Because I was riding with Maclean and Lady Susan ordered me to ride elsewhere," he said, still smiling. "I think she is laying siege to Castle Kenneth."

Unable to suppress a smile at his turn of phrase, Amalie, too, kept her voice down to say, "It has been a long one, too. But so far she has failed to breach a wall."

He chuckled. "I have observed her for only a few days, so mayhap I have much to learn about her. But she chatters enough to drive a man to distraction."

"I wonder that he allows it," Amalie said.

"Mayhap he considers it part of his duty to keep her from annoying the princess," he suggested.

"She doesn't chatter when she is with Isabel."

"Then doubtless Isabel has told her it annoys her," he said with satisfaction, as if he had proven his point.

Giving him another look, Amalie said, "It is also possible that Lady Susan is nervous when she is with Sir Kenneth, and chatters because he does not talk much himself . . . or so I have found. I think he has the wits of a stick."

" 'Tis just as well you don't like him," he said. " 'Twould be unseemly if all the princess's ladies laid siege to her defenseless knights."

"It would be daft even if they *were* defenseless," she retorted. "Isabel keeps two—soon to be three—knights with her only so she has experienced men to protect her, to lead her men-at-arms when she travels, and to keep them in order at home.

"Before James Douglas died," she added, "Isabel always rode with an armed tail of her own, because he provided one. Afterward, Fife ordered her to dismiss those men, saying it was unseemly for her to travel with so many. But Isabel did not trust Fife. She knew he just wanted her to live under his thumb at Stirling."

Realizing she might have said too much, Amalie tried to judge his reaction with another quick glance.

He was frowning, but when he caught her gaze, the frown vanished.

He said, "It is most unusual for any woman to travel with a tail that rivals that of many barons. But somehow . . ."

"Somehow it does not seem strange for Isabel," she said when he paused. "Moreover, her knights have always been loyal to her."

"I should hope so," he said, giving her a narrow look. "They serve her, after all. Therefore, they owe her their loyalty."

"Are you loyal to her, sir?"

"Aye, sure, I am," he said. " 'Twould be dishonorable to be otherwise."

"But you are friendly with Fife," Amalie said. "Mayhap you are not aware that she believes he murdered her husband."

"Lass, her husband is Sir John Edmonstone of that Ilk," he said gently.

"You know I meant James Douglas—or you should know it. It is true that Isabel has been married to Sir John for the best part of a year now. But I have seen him only twice, because she spends almost no time with him. Surely you know that when she says she means to stay at home now that the renovations there are finished, she means she will be staying at Sweethope Hill House, not at Edmonstone."

"What I know is that you have succeeded yet again in

diverting me from the subject," he said. "I want to know why you question my loyalty to the princess."

"But I told you," she protested. "Because you are friends with Fife."

"And I told you, I am *not* friends with Fife. Moreover, whatever else one may believe of him, he did not murder James Douglas. Fife was with Archie in Cumberland when James died, at least ninety miles away from him."

She regarded him scornfully. "You must know that a man does not have to be at hand to end another man's life." Leaning closer, she muttered, "You should know, too, that Fife *never* dirties his own hands."

"Sakes, did Isabel tell you that?"

"Aye, she did, and others did, as well."

"What others?"

"Why would I tell you when you are friends with him?"

"Lass, even if I *were* friends with the man, it would not lessen my loyalty to the princess whilst I serve her."

She began to protest, but he raised a hand, silencing her as he added, "Nor would I repeat aught that you say to me without your leave, to him or to anyone."

"And you never lie?"

"No."

"Well, I don't believe that, so why should I believe the rest?"

Once again, he looked as if he wanted to murder her, but she could not help that. Everyone told falsehoods from time to time. That was just plain fact.

His emotions now visibly under tight control, he said, "You can believe me when I say that Fife is not my friend, and never was. When you saw us talking, he had approached me. I explained that before."

"How did you come to join us?" she asked. "Do you know Sir Duncan Forrest? Did he send for you to replace him?"

"He did not. I know who he is. I'd heard his name at tournaments, but I made his acquaintance only Monday, as we left Scone."

"Then how came you to enter Isabel's service?"

"A mutual friend arranged it," he said, visibly uncomfortable now.

"Who?"

"That is not for me to say," he replied. "I told you I do not lie, and I will not. But neither am I obliged to answer every question you put to me."

"True enough, although I cannot imagine why you won't answer that one." She eyed him hopefully, but he remained silent. "Oh, very well then," she said. "I expect you'll be glad to learn that Sweethope is just two or three miles from here."

"I should think it is more likely to be five miles or so," he said.

"Faith, do you know Sweethope, then? Have you been there before?"

"I know Sweethope Hill lies ten miles from Lauder and rises above Eden Water," he said. "I also know we've traveled no more than half that distance."

"Isabel did say it was ten miles from Lauder," she admitted. "But how would you know that? Did she tell you, too?"

"She did not need to. Sithee, my home lies near Lauderdale. I've known about Sweethope Hill since I was a bairn, before Jamie Douglas settled that estate on the princess when he married her. The place suffered a good deal of damage, though, during the last English invasion and in English raids before that."

"Aye, and Isabel told me the Douglases were annoyed when James settled Sweethope on her, because they thought he should keep all the Douglas estates. But doubtless, he expected everything they both had to go to their son one day," she added. "If he'd ever had time to sire a son."

"He had time to sire many sons," Sir Garth said. "He just kept so busy that he never stayed long enough in one place to be sure of siring one. In any event, that is how I know that Sweethope is ten miles from Lauder."

"It is also ten miles from Melrose Abbey," she said. "And you may be sure that if we are going to stay long at Sweethope we will visit the abbey often."

"Because James Douglas is buried there," he said.

She nodded.

"Before then, lass, you must tell me what you know," he said, still speaking quietly but in a tone that told her he meant what he said.

"I've already told you all I can," she said, looking straight ahead. "I did not hear what they were saying."

"You lied about that, though. And lying helps no one."

"Giving information to the wrong person helps no one, either," she retorted.

"I wish you could bring yourself to trust me," he said with a sigh.

"I told you, I trust no man."

"Sakes, but who can have hurt you so, to bring you to such a state?"

She could not answer, although just hearing the question brought tears to her eyes. Fortunately, Lady Susan rejoined them, ending for Amalie the need to think of an answer to his question that would not tax her own emotions even more.

He fell back to ride with Sir Kenneth, and the rest of the journey passed in a fog as Amalie fought the images that kept rising to trouble her mind.

She would not remember. She could not. When they rode into the stableyard at Sweethope Hill, she swung her off leg over to dismount by herself as a handsome man appeared from the nearby stable and strode to meet the princess.

"Good day, madam," he said with a bow to Isabel. "You were expecting me, I believe, from Edmonstone. I am Harald Boyd, and wholly at your service."

Garth studied the newcomer, noting as he did that the lass was studying him, too. However, Boyd seemed to have focused all his attention on the princess, who greeted him politely but without enthusiasm. Clearly, Garth thought, if the Douglas did not choose her knights, she preferred to choose them for herself.

He had little time to think about Boyd though, because gillies were attending to the horses. And Sir Kenneth Maclean was issuing a string of orders.

A man and woman who were clearly the princess's housekeeper and steward had hurried out to meet her. Soon, they, too, were issuing orders.

Thereafter, a bustle of activity took place that lasted until they had all had their supper and were too tired to do anything more. By then Garth had oriented himself to the large house and its environs.

After finding his bedchamber in the north wing, where male guests were housed, he learned that his duties pertained generally to training the men-at-arms to meet any trouble that might arise and to protect the princess and her ladies.

It had been a long five days since Scone, and everyone was tired. As they relaxed in the great hall after dinner, he met Amalie's sleepy gaze. His cock stirred, and the image of Buccleuch loomed in his mind's eye, glowering at him.

Smiling back at the lass, he banished his cousin from his thoughts.

Chapter 6

⌒

The Danzig night, damply overcast, was as dark as the devil's dungeon.

He heard men singing lustily in a tavern up ahead, sounding so merry that he felt an urge to step in and have a mug of ale with them. But tension gripped him at the thought. He had to keep searching.

Fortunately, the ambient glow from the tavern's tiny front window let him see his way well enough to avoid stepping off the graveled footpath into the noisome drainage ditch flowing beside it. Such ditches guided the whole town's drainage downhill to the German Sea.

Heaven alone knew where Will and the four lads with him had gone. He felt as if he ought to know, and as if he'd been searching for an age, rather than just an hour or so. Danzig, although a busy seaport, was not so large that it should take hours to search. He would look inside the tavern, but then he must go on.

As that thought struck, he heard cries up ahead and

the tavern door opened, spilling more light onto the foot-path. He heard footsteps running toward him.

"Vandals!" a man's voice roared. "Murderers! Run!"

A short, solid-looking woman stepped from the tavern and, turning toward the shouter, shrieked, "Was ist los?"

"Räubers, mit messern! Mörders! Ausreissen!"

He understood perfectly, for the shouter had simply expanded on what he had yelled before: "Robbers with knives, murderers! Run for your lives!"

The woman from the tavern stood where she was, gawking.

As he ran past her toward the noise at the bottom of the street, the woman jumped back into the doorway. The man who had shouted the warning leapt across the ditch into the empty roadway and kept going.

A backward glance revealed no further sign of him.

Hearing a clash of swords, he drew his from the sheath on his back.

He could see shadowy figures ahead now, engaged in fierce battle. As he ran, he saw two of them fall. The others scattered, one set chasing the other.

Knowing before he reached the intersection that a second road lay perpendicular to the one he was on, he saw that the second road led over a bridge to his right and disappeared into blackness. There was more light to his left, where the road ran down to the sea, enough for him to see two running figures.

He would have run after them had a groan not reached his ears.

The first body he came to showed no sign of life. The man's throat had been cut. Although a stranger, he bore a Douglas device on the sleeve of his light mail. A second man, also dead, sported a different device, identifying him as an Englishman loyal to Lord Clifford.

Hearing another groan, he moved onto the bridge to an area deep in shadow and found what, from the start of his search, he had feared he would find.

Bending, carefully feeling his way to one muscular, mail-clad shoulder, he said urgently, "Will, is that you? Speak to me, man!"

"Gar . . ." The recumbent figure moved a hand, tried to lift it.

Shouting for help, he dropped to both knees beside Will Douglas and gripped that hand, a hand he remembered as strong and firm of grip.

No longer was it so. It rested limply in his.

"Bring a torch, someone!" Then, uncertain if he had shouted in English or German, he shouted again in both languages and with equal fluency, bellowing epithets in both when he heard no response.

All the while, and oddly in much better light, he searched for Will's wounds but could find none. There was no blood to stanch, no opening in what was suddenly full and heavy armor rather than light mail. But he had been sure . . .

"Haldane," Will murmured. "Ben Haldane, Gar. Find the bastard and send him to . . ." He gasped, something gurgled in his throat, and he said no more.

Tears streamed down Garth's cheeks. . . .

The tears were still there, and his throat still ached with sorrow when he awoke at Sweethope Hill in the tiny chamber that was temporarily his own.

Unable to remain in bed any longer while his mind reeled with scenes of Danzig and his soul ached from the memories they stirred, he got up. Dressing quickly in breeks, boots, and a leather jack, he splashed cold water on his face from the washstand ewer without bothering to fill the basin. Then, after drying briskly with a rough towel, he went outside to fill his lungs with bracingly chilly morning air.

Gray dawn had banished the stars, but a half moon rode high above the dark western horizon. The eastern sky was lighter but showed no other sign of sunrise.

He strolled to the stableyard through a garden evidently providing kitchen produce although hedged with thorny roses. The scents riding the air were familiar from his childhood, reminding him of his mother's garden until he neared the horse pond where odors of the stables and the chicken yard beyond them began to prevail.

He would not take his own horse out, not after a four-and-a-half-day journey. Although they had rested a full night at Linlithgow and again at Dalkeith, his mount needed more rest. But the princess's stable could easily provide a fresh horse.

Inside, he found Angus Graham, the stable master, whom he had met the day before, busy with harness and tack. Middle-aged and whit-leather tough, Angus greeted him with respect but without obsequiousness, clearly knowing his own worth.

Returning the greeting, Garth said, "I am glad to find you here, because I'd like a fresh horse if you have one, for a morning ride."

"Bless ye, sir, we've no lack o' horses. As for being up, I'm always awake well afore Prime and back in my bed of an evening soon after Vespers. As for that, two o' me lads have been away already this past half hour and more."

"Two of your grooms?"

"Aye, sure."

Garth had expected to be first out by at least an hour or so. "Who took them out, Angus? Surely, none of the ladies can be riding so early."

"Aye, well, they are, though. Leastways, the lady Amalie—"

"Where did she go?" Garth demanded, not waiting to hear who else had gone with her. Collecting his wits when the stable master frowned, he said more calmly, "Being newly charged with the ladies' safety, and Lady Amalie being the youngest, I am concerned, Angus. Does she often ride out so early?"

"The princess has stayed here only a night or two afore now, sir, for she were having the place put in better order, which took nearly a year's time. So I canna say what her young ladyship's normal practice may be. But I *can* tell ye I ha' seen none o' them afore now ride out the morning after a days-long journey."

"Saddle that horse for me," Garth said. "And show me which way she went."

Without argument Angus obeyed, and Garth rode out of the yard feeling much the same tension he had felt throughout his dream. He knew he would not relax until he saw for himself that no Border raiders on their way to or from a raid had decided to enjoy some sport with her. If any had, two grooms could not stop them.

Amalie breathed in the fresh air and savored the peace of the low, tree-dotted hills around her. The two grooms trailing behind had chatted at first, then fallen silent. The only noises now were the low, rhythmic croaks of bullfrogs in a nearby pond and the muted clip-clop of their three horses on the grassy hillside.

A mile earlier, they had forded Eden Water, splashing across it and easily negotiating the pebbles, sand, and gravel deposits that formed its sloping banks. Less than a mile ahead, the much larger river Tweed wended its way through the low hills.

Sweethope House sat on its gentle hillside two miles behind her, and she was in no hurry to return. After a sennight of feminine chatter, forced civility, and constant awareness of social necessities, the almost forgotten sense of peace and freedom that accompanied an early morning ride was intoxicating.

Isabel would not mind if she was late returning, because Isabel also enjoyed her own company and understood Amalie's need for occasional solitude.

Today she needed solitude to think.

The meadowland ahead provided a view between two large thickets of hazel mixed with willow and aspen all the way to the river. To the west, woods of oak, elm, and hornbeam trees blocked her view of a river bend. To the east, hills and meadow shrubbery provided other obstructions. But straight ahead, through a dip in the landscape, the river beckoned. She responded by urging her horse to go faster.

When she heard hoofbeats closing the distance behind her, she paid no heed. It was the grooms' duty to keep their eyes on her and follow where she went.

The sun was barely peeping over the eastern hills, and she could hear the first blackbirds and song thrushes calling to each other in the woods. The pleasure of being there as they began their day delighted her.

The hoofbeats grew louder, a single horse now. The

lads must be racing, and if the nearer one did not take care, he would fly past her.

A little startled to catch a glimpse of his mount's head very near to her right, she glanced back to see Sir Garth Napier on a fine-looking bay, matching pace with her. Kicking her gray and leaning forward, she raced on, but he kept up easily, moving up beside her as they pounded down the gentle slope toward the water.

When he held out a hand, signaling her to slow down, she had already begun to ease back and tighten rein. She knew better than to gallop any horse right up to the water's edge.

Only when she looked back to see how far behind them her grooms had fallen, and could not see them at all, did a shiver of apprehension tickle her spine.

Controlling her expression and tone with the ease of long practice, she said, "What have you done with my lads, sir?"

"I sent them home," he said. "You are perfectly safe with me."

"Am I? I'll expect you to have more care for my reputation if you mean to go on serving the princess. She would not approve of any knight riding alone with one of her ladies, let alone a knight who ordered her grooms away."

He had the grace to look rueful. "Is that why you ride with two lads, my lady—so as not to be alone with just one? I should think you'd be safer if you rode with one groom and one or two of the other ladies instead."

"Perhaps so, sir, but being always with one or two of the other ladies grows tiresome. As for riding with two grooms, I just prefer it." At that, she pulled off her right glove, put two fingers in her mouth, and produced a shrieking whistle.

Sir Garth looked astonished, but as she had expected, her grooms emerged at once from the woods midway down the hillside.

"What the devil?" he exclaimed. "I told them to go home!"

"Aye, sure, but I've told them never to leave me alone, no matter what orders anyone else gives them. And Isabel pays them well to obey me."

To her surprise, he smiled and said, "In troth, lass, I was feeling guilty for sending them away. I did it without thinking because I wanted to talk to you where no one else would overhear us."

"To browbeat me into telling you what you want to know, I expect."

For a moment he looked bewildered, as if that thought had not crossed his mind. Then he shook his head, rueful again. "I don't suppose you'll believe I did not intend to do that, so I won't bother denying it," he said. "But I hope you *will* believe that I'm glad they did not ride all the way back to Sweethope Hill."

She could not bring herself to say she believed every word he'd said, or tell him that his thoughts registered on his face clearly enough for her to read them.

To admit the first would not be at all good for his character. Nor would it be right to let him to imagine even briefly that he had persuaded her that he always told the truth. One truth did not mean anything of the sort.

"I will acquit you of following me to bully me . . . unless—" She looked narrowly at him. "You are not going to be one of those tiresome men who are forever preaching that women ought never to do as they like, are you?"

"Do you expect me to promise that I'll never advise you to do other than as you choose? Because if that is your object, you will fail to achieve it."

"Then you *will* be tiresome. I feel sorry for your daughters."

"If I had any daughters, I would doubtless keep them close to home, but you are not my daughter. And I should look like a fool if I ordered you back to Sweethope after trying to send your grooms away just to talk with you."

"You certainly don't *approve* of my behavior," she said.

~~~

Garth had all he could do not to grin at that statement. Approval or disapproval had nothing to do with the matter.

"I don't approve of listening at doors," he said, trying to sound stern and knowing he'd failed. "Certainly not at the doors of dangerous people. As to your ride this morning, I have no right to give you orders without first knowing what the princess expects of me, and of you. Moreover, I do understand your impulse to ride. The Tweed is a beautiful river, and this part of it is particularly so."

She looked into his eyes as if she would see into his mind. "Did you truly want to talk privately with me?"

"I did, aye," he admitted, glancing at the two grooms, who had tactfully reined in some distance away.

"They won't trouble us," she said. "We can ride along the riverbank if you like. It is flat on top, even through the trees, so we can ride side by side there."

"I've never ridden along this particular stretch of the Tweed," he said. "I fished a good stretch of it near Melrose during my childhood, though. I have kinsmen there and spent a month with them every summer until I was twelve."

"What did you want to talk about?"

The blunt question—just the sort he liked to ask, himself—caught him off guard, making him feel uncharacteristically tongue-tied. He had wanted to talk to her again, and when the stableman said she had ridden out, the urge to follow had been overwhelming. His primary reason had been to protect her, but he'd also felt an unusual impulse to tell her about his dream. Now he couldn't imagine why.

He glanced at her, searching for a response that would explain his earlier words without baring as much of himself as a description of his dream might.

"You do keep popping up, and it is still gey early," she said. "Are you sure you did not tell someone to wake you if I left Sweethope Hill?"

"Nay, lass, I ken fine that I've no right to do that unless Isabel commands it. In troth, I woke early because I'd had a bad dream."

"A nightmare?" Her expression revealed instant sympathy. "Bad dreams are horrid, but I've never before heard a grown man admit to having one."

Wondering if her sympathy indicated that she, too, suffered from nightmares, he said, "I doubt there is a man alive—anyone who has seen battle, at all events—who has *not* had them. Most men just keep such things to themselves."

"But not you?"

He smiled. "I had decided to keep this one to myself."

Without consulting her, he'd turned west along the

riverbank so they would keep the rising sun behind them. She had not commented on his choice, and she remained silent now, her gaze fixed on the track ahead. His sister or mother would have urged him to go on, to explain why he would have kept the dream to himself, and then either would have pressed him to tell her exactly what it was about.

He would have resisted their efforts strongly, even angrily.

Memory of his dream stirred, the images of the dark Danzig streets returning in a rush as they so frequently had ever since the dreadful night.

"I was with Will Douglas when he died," he said.

She was still gazing ahead, but he saw her catch her lower lip between her teeth, hold it for a moment, then let it go before she looked at him.

"I see," she said. "How awful that must have been."

"Awful is one way to describe it," he said.

"Your nightmare, was it about his death?"

He nodded. "It is nearly always the same, and yet each time it differs somehow from the reality."

"Do the differences disturb you?" She looked as if the answer to that question mattered to her more than one might expect.

"Aye, they do," he admitted. He was watching her more closely now than he had been. He noticed the little nod she gave before she spoke again.

"Why?" she asked.

"Because they are things that did not happen. I probably should not describe such a grisly scene to a gently bred lady, but perhaps I can—"

"You can tell me just what you saw if you like," she

said. "I promise I shall not faint or otherwise embarrass you."

That made him chuckle. "Lass, I don't think you could embarrass me if you tried, but I hope you're right about not fainting. I'd as lief you not fall off that pony."

She smiled. "Border women do not fall off their ponies, sir."

"Never?"

"Does Isabel's sister, the princess Gelis, know you were with Sir William when he died?" she asked, forcing him back to the subject at hand.

"Nay," he admitted.

"She would want to hear it, I think," she said. "Mayhap I am only expressing how I would feel in a like circumstance, though. Gelis may not feel the same way."

"I heard that she has barely spoken since she learned of Will's death."

"His death devastated her, and she is in an advanced state of pregnancy. Isabel says Gelis fears for the baby, does not want to lose it, too. So she does not speak of Sir William and refuses to let Isabel rant to her about how his murder is just like James's death and was likely ordered by the same person."

"Isabel said that to her?"

"Aye, so Gelis said that if she could not keep such evil thoughts from her mind, she should at least not spill them from her tongue. She reminded her that his own men had said it was the result of a dispute he'd had with Lord Clifford."

"His men did say that," Garth agreed. "Over some land, they said."

"Were you not one of his men?"

"I was his friend and fellow knight," Garth said.

"Shortly after the wedding at Dunfermline, I followed him to Königsberg, in Prussia, to seek adventure. Will had heard that an order called the Teutonic Knights was to lead an army into Lithuania. Such expeditions still count as crusades, although the Lithuanians became Christian years ago. But when we arrived, we learned that the King of England also meant to join the Knights. He had promised to bring them a fleet of ships but not until July."

"But you went to Prussia in January?"

"Early February, and not a good season for sailing. Even so, at Will's urging, the Knights agreed to hire ships from the nearby port of Danzig and to let Will command them. Outfitting them would take a month, and as I'd no reason to linger, I spent three weeks exploring the Prussian countryside and parts of France, instead."

"Was that countryside as beautiful as it is here?"

"It was different from Scotland but just as wintry. Will was daft to go so early. He knew it, too, but said he wanted something to do that would keep his mind off . . ."

Realizing that he had no business repeating Will's reasons to anyone else, he paused to collect his wits.

She cocked her head, gave him a measuring look, and said, "Sir William was very close to James and hoped to be chosen third Earl of Douglas, did he not?"

"He knew that many had talked of it, and he would have made a good leader," he admitted. "But he was born a bastard, so . . ."

"Archie the Grim was, too," she said when he paused.

"Aye, sure, but his father was the Good Sir James Douglas of great repute."

"The one who died trying to carry the Bruce's heart to the Holy Land."

He nodded. "Also, Archie was the elder and Will's father as well."

"Principally, though, Fife wanted Archie and not Sir William," she said. "And Fife persuaded enough Douglases to support Archie to make it happen."

"Sakes, lass, you know as much about it as I do," he said.

"That comes of living with Isabel," she said. "She takes great interest in everything of Douglas that connects to Fife."

"Because she believes Fife ordered James's murder."

"Aye," she said, and nibbled her lower lip again.

They rode in silence for some minutes, until he realized that she was apparently as lost in thought as he had been.

"What are you thinking about, lass?"

She shrugged. "Naught that matters. What happened when you returned to meet Sir William and the others?"

"Will had been entrusted with some sort of diplomatic mission to the English emissary to the Teutonic Knights, and had taken rooms in Danzig. He had gone out earlier, taking four lads with him, and had not yet returned. My men were tired, and the town was quiet, so I went by myself to look for him."

"Could you ask questions in the town? Do you speak . . . German, is it not?"

"It is, aye, and although I'm not fluent, I managed well enough, thanks to my travels. That's one of the odd things about my dream, though. I spoke German as fluently as I speak broad Scot or English. I could understand it as easily, too."

She nodded. "That happens in my dreams, too. Not

languages, but things do happen differently, as you described. Have you had this dream more than once?"

"Aye, although once was enough, I can tell you." He described it for her.

When he'd finished, she said, "What else was different? Did you really see a woman come out of the tavern?"

"Aye, and the chap that shouted the warning, too. I also found two dead, but I've no idea how many ran off. It was black dark until someone fetched a torch. I did see Will's wounds then, and he was *not* wearing heavy armor."

"Did the people you saw say the same things as in your dream?"

"I think the words may have been different, but the meaning was similar. The one who shouted said robbers were attacking men and trying to kill them. I ran to help, and the shouter dashed across the road before we met, then vanished."

"Was he German?"

He hesitated. "Do you know, I had assumed he must be. But in my dream, he always shouts first in English or even Scot, then in German."

"You said Sir William named his killer. I'd venture to guess the name was not Clifford, or you'd have said so."

"It was not Clifford," he agreed.

"I won't ask you to tell me what it was," she said, surprising him.

"You are tactful, lass."

"Not at all," she said. "I just know you won't tell me."

"I will tell you that the words Will speaks in the dreams are always the same ones he spoke to me at the time. I will also tell you that he spoke only the one name and then asked that I send the villain bearing it to perdition."

"So you think it is possible that he asked you to do so for some other reason."

He had noted that she tended to make leaps of thought without establishing grounds for the leap. But as he was about to point out the error in her thinking, he realized she might not be wrong at all.

"I suppose I did fear that possibility," he admitted, thinking again of what Will had actually said. "He never actually finished his last sentence. He just said, 'and send him to . . .' I filled in the word at the end with what I was certain he meant."

"How could you be certain?"

"Sithee, we'd fought together and trained together with Jamie Douglas under the first earl, so we could almost read each other's thoughts. I'd have sworn that night he was naming his killer. But his lads said the man he named had left Danzig a sennight before—that, in fact, he had taken ship back to Scotland."

"Did Sir William *send* him back?"

"They'd had a disagreement, the lads said, but no one knew exactly whose idea it was for the fellow to leave."

"I know the reason some of the Douglases wanted Sir Will to become third earl was that he was an extraordinary soldier," she said.

"He was exceptional," Garth agreed. "Did you ever meet him?"

She shook her head.

"He was as tall as I am and as dark as Archie. He had amazing strength and carried himself like a king. Yet he was courteous and affable. In troth, he was one of the heartiest and merriest men I've known, and nearly as fine a warrior as James."

"Having admired him so, you must miss him sorely."

"Aye." Just admitting it brought an ache to his throat.

"With his skill, how could anyone have killed him so swiftly and easily?"

"The attackers took him and his lads by surprise. The two who survived said it happened so quickly they never saw their attackers' faces. It was dark as pitch, to be sure, but both sides were carrying torches to see their way, they said. During the battle, their torches rolled into the drainage ditch."

He looked to gauge the position of the rising sun, which had climbed some distance above the horizon.

She said, "I expect we ought to turn back, sir. Isabel won't mind that I've come out, but I do have duties to attend."

He nodded, and they turned their mounts, passing the grooms, who fell in behind them, keeping the same tactful distance.

They rode in silence until she said, "Why did you come to Sweethope Hill?"

"To serve the princess Isabel," he said. With a smile, he added, "I had other reasons, too, but I am not yet ready to share them."

"You seek information, I expect," she said. "Doubtless about James's death, since no one here can know aught of Sir William's."

"I suspect you think you are being clever, but I won't tell you any more. I do seek answers in another matter, though," he reminded her with a straight look.

She faced forward again, her chin rising a full inch. Since she was looking into the sun, she squinted, making her thick eyelashes flutter. Then she met his gaze again and said unexpectedly, "I have been thinking about that."

"Are you going to tell me what you have decided to do?"

"I have not decided anything except to tell you I've been giving it some thought. But do not press me further, sir. I grow gey stubborn if pressed."

"Then we'll change the subject," he said cheerfully. "What can you tell me about this fellow Harald Boyd?"

"Just that I think he may be the man my family wants me to marry."

Chapter 7

~

Amalie saw that she had surprised him again, which was pleasant, because this time she had meant to surprise him. She had not told anyone else what she suspected about Sir Harald Boyd. Even Garth would think she was mad.

He was frowning thoughtfully, and she waited, watching him. She knew he would have questions and was interested to learn what they would be.

When he looked at her, a twinkle appeared in his startlingly blue eyes.

That not being at all the reaction she'd expected, she cocked her head and waited for him to explain.

"You look like a bird dog eager to flush the first flight of the morning," he said. "I thought you said Simon did not tell you the man's name."

"That is true; he did not," she said. "But after the King's coronation, my father said I might already know the man. He also said that if I did not, I soon would. Father said he was handsome— I beg your pardon. Did you speak?"

"Nay, I snorted. Surely, you don't think that popinjay's a handsome fellow."

"I never said I did. My father said Simon had told him that, and I hope you do not think I align my judgment of men with Simon's."

He chuckled. "I suppose not."

"Just so."

"Then why do you think this Harald Boyd is your man?"

"If you would please me, *don't* refer to him as my man," she said. "I do wish you would listen to what I say and not just fix on certain things and ignore the rest. The part about my meeting him soon if I had not already done so was the critical bit, of course. My father also said the man would be coming into Lothian and hinted strongly that I'd meet him when he did. Now, do you see?"

"Sweethope Hill is in Lothian, so I suppose it is somewhat possible that this chap is the one. Still, Lothian is very large."

"Father said east Lothian," she said, remembering. "He talked of Lauder, too, which is only ten miles away, as you said yourself. He was not trying to be cryptic."

"Then why did he not just say the man would come to Sweethope?"

"Mercy, I don't know. Mayhap he did not know that." She paused, thinking.

"What?" he asked.

Meeting his gaze, she said, "In troth, I don't always know how I get from one thought to the next. Usually, if I stop to think about how a conversation went, I can see the path my thoughts took, but in this instance, I cannot. My reasoning does seem weak when I see that I put those two facts together as I did. They seem gey small."

"So they are," he agreed. "Perhaps you know other things that helped you form your deduction. If you consider what else has occurred . . ."

He looked at her as if he would watch her do just that.

"But I don't . . . Wait . . . My mother approves of the connection, so Simon must have told her things other than that the man enjoys Fife's favor. I cannot know what they might be, but my father does remain neutral in all border disputes. For years, he and my mother have done all they could to form alliances on both sides of the line. I also know the Boyds are kin to the Stewarts, but that is just Fife again."

"I expect Isabel told you they are kin."

"Aye, and Simon himself enjoys Fife's favor, because he admires Fife and believes that anyone of sense must also admire him. So, I don't see how that . . ."

"Do *you* admire Fife?" he asked. "Or has the princess persuaded you that he is evil enough to command murder?"

She grimaced. "I do believe he is capable of commanding murder. But I am still not persuaded that I can safely speak all my thoughts of him to you."

When his jaw tightened, she added, "I will admit that I do not admire him, but neither has anyone yet persuaded me that he ordered James Douglas's murder. You were at Otterburn. What is your opinion of that business?"

"I have none, lass. I was there, to be sure, but so were two thousand other Scots and eight thousand English. I was with Buccleuch—the old laird, not Wat."

"Wat was with James Douglas, I believe."

"Aye," he said. "My lads and I were with old Buccleuch in the water meadows where the Otterburn meets the Rede, and in fierce battle, too. The English horses had foundered in the mud, forcing the men to splash across the Rede, afoot."

"Is that why they lost the battle even though they had so many more men than the Scots had? Because they were afoot and the Scots were not?"

"Nay, they'd surprised us before dawn, so we were all afoot. They lost because Hotspur grew impatient and attacked with his army still strung out from Otterburn to Newcastle. And, too, their men who fled back along their line greatly exaggerated our numbers, terrifying all they told. So those men turned tail as well."

"Then you did not see James fall. Wat Scott did, you know, or nearly so. He stumbled over him where he lay grievously wounded. I thought of that when you said you had been with Will Douglas. Horrible experiences for both of you, but—"

"War *is* horrible, lass," he interjected. "But the only other choice is to let the enemy have its way with Scotland. We Borderers know what that is like."

"Aye, but not all agree that it is something to dread," she said. "My mother is English, and she believes that if Scotland became just another county of England, true peace would reign at last and bring prosperity to all."

"Surely you don't believe that."

"I don't know," she admitted. "It sounds well if one could only believe that Borderers on both sides of the line would stop raiding each other's herds, or that Scots could thrive under English rule."

"What does your father think?"

"He stays neutral because of my mother and her powerful English kinsmen. Sithee, she is cousin to the Earl of Northumberland. Family alliances on both sides have kept Elishaw Castle safe, although it lies less than three miles north of the present borderline. Also, because of the way that line can shift in times of conflict, we have ended up on the English side more than once in my own lifetime."

"So your father must agree with your mother, at least to some degree."

"My father does not often speak his mind," she said. "But I can tell he doubts that the raids and reiving will stop, or that true peace will ever come. Borderers, he is fond of saying, will always be Borderers."

"Forever is a long time, so I doubt we'll live long enough to know who is right," he said. "But I have allowed you to divert me yet again. Let us return to your continuing concern that I may be Fife's man."

"Well, you must admit, I would be foolish to discuss Sir Harald further with you if you are, or to follow your advice with regard to him."

"Then suppose we talk more about Fife, and James's death."

She regarded him suspiciously. "You could just be trying to find out from me what Isabel knows, so you can tell Fife."

He met her gaze easily and held it as he said, "I liked James, and Will was a very good friend. I want to know the truth."

Discerning no trace of that earlier jaw-tightening anger, she said, "Everyone must know by now what Isabel thinks the truth is about James *and* Will."

"I'm told, though, that she tends to see Fife's fine hand in everything."

"I cannot deny that," Amalie admitted. "She has cause, though. When her younger brother, David of Strathearn, died of mysterious causes, Fife assumed guardianship of

David's tiny heiress daughter and married her to one of his loyal vassals. So Fife now controls all of Strathearn as well as so much else. Still, and although Isabel knows Fife better than I do, she may be wrong about Will's death."

He was silent for a moment before he said, "But she could be right, too. Fife *is* a schemer. Moreover, Will was acting as some sort of ambassador to the English in Danzig. That was not a role Will had ever played before or the sort of role at which he was adept. The most likely person to have appointed him, though, is Fife."

"But what would that have had to do with Will's death?" she asked.

"He moved from Königsberg to Danzig because of it," Garth said. "That in itself might mean nowt, because the two towns lie close to each other. But the Scots were nearly all in Königsberg, so it separated him from most of his own men. That may mean a good deal, because he had only a few men with him that night."

"Many have come to believe Fife's primary goal is to rule as King of Scots and not just as Governor of the Realm," she said, thinking aloud.

"If that is so, it may explain his sending an ambassador to the English in Danzig, but it also suggests that his plotting has increased in scale and purpose. I'd suggest, therefore, that he's not troubling himself much to provide you a husband."

"So now you are saying that it is all Simon's doing," she protested. "But you told me yourself that whatever Simon wants, Fife must first approve."

"Aye, I did," he admitted. "But this Harald Boyd doesn't seem much of a fellow to me. I don't see what Fife gains by arranging such a marriage to you."

Annoyed that she had failed to make him see connections that seemed clear enough to her even if she couldn't explain them more logically, she said, "Very likely you are in the right of it and I am imagining things. Look, sir, you can see Sweethope House ahead, just through those trees beyond Eden Water."

On those words, she urged her mount to a canter, forestalling further conversation until they had forded the glacially formed tributary.

As they began to ascend the low hill to the stables, Garth said, "I hope we can talk again soon. Discussing things helps me think, and you have a quick mind."

She had been ignoring him, but now she turned to look right at him.

"And, too," he added softly, holding her gaze with a lurking twinkle in his eyes, "you still know something that I want you to tell me."

Trying to cover the warm rush of sensations that surged through her body, she said with hastily assumed dignity, "I have not yet decided that I should."

"Perhaps it will help if I tell you a tale from my childhood."

She returned a look intended to quell any expectation he might have that she would help him in any way, for any reason.

But when he shrugged and looked toward the house again, disappointment stirred. She was more interested in his childhood than she had realized.

Continued silence increased her curiosity until she muttered, "Tell me, then."

"'Tis just a small thing," he said, still looking ahead as if his interest lay only in reaching the stable. After a pause long enough to make her wonder if he expected her to beg him to tell the story, he said, "When I was nine, my father had a fine black destrier. He was a magnificent brute—powerful, vicious, and well tested in battle. Father ordered me to stay away from him, but my pony was elderly and disappointingly tame. The destrier fascinated me."

"So you defied your father and rode the destrier." She had taken enough of his measure to be sure of that much, at least.

"This is my story," he said. "I'll thank you to let me tell it in my own way."

She grinned. "I'm waiting for the good part, but if your father was as mild of temper as you seem to be . . ."

"If I've somehow given you that impression, you should perhaps recall our first meeting and reconsider it. I do have a temper, lass. In fact, I inherited it from him. The 'good part,' as *you* call it, is that he took a stiff tawse to my backside."

"It was a dangerous thing to do," she said. "It was his duty to punish you."

He grimaced, clearly remembering. "I couldn't sit for a sennight."

Grinning saucily again, she said, "He just wanted to make sure you would never try such a stunt again. But doubtless it also did you some powerful good."

"Aye, perhaps, but as soon as I could sit, I got right back on the brute."

She frowned. "What did your father do then?"

"Thrashed me again, of course, and again the next week, and the next."

"Mercy, you had no sense as a child!"

"None, but a month later, he gave me a fine horse of my own. Persistence pays, lass. You'll see. Resistance is nobbut one more obstacle for a determined man to over-

come. Remember that as you puzzle over what your decision will be."

⁓

That she did not reply came as no surprise. Garth had
noted that she crawled into a shell of silence whenever he
questioned her, but he believed she would tell eventually.
She did not seem devious, just wary.

He wondered again what had made her so.

As they rode between the thorn hedges flanking the
track and stables, he heard voices and noted that she had
heard them, too. One sounded angry, the other even and
controlled. The latter he recognized as that of Angus
Graham.

He could discern little yet of what either man said but
easily recognized the tones of a superior taking an infe-
rior to task. Not until the horses rounded a curve in the
track did he see them near the horse pond and recognize
Harald Boyd.

Boyd saw them at the same time and instantly stopped
berating the stable master, thus giving Garth a good idea
of what their discussion had concerned.

He glanced at the lass again. But if she had deduced
what he had, she gave no sign of it. He saw only a shallow
crease appear between her eyebrows.

"There you are, my lady," Boyd said, striding to meet
them and casting Garth a look of disapproval. "We were
concerned by your long absence. But the princess's man
here said you took two stout grooms along. Where are
they now?"

Wrapping herself in dignity worthy of Isabel herself,

the lass looked down her nose at him and said coolly, "How is that any concern of yours, Sir Harald?"

"Why, because Isabel will be worried, of course. It is a great part of my duty here to make sure that nothing does worry her. Here, let me help you dismount."

Garth said nothing, but as he dismounted, the intrusive Boyd held up his hands to the lass. Muscles throughout Garth's body tensed at the sight.

"Come now, allow me, my lady," Boyd coaxed audaciously.

That she let him assist her was another affront to Garth's good nature. But he stifled the reaction and waited patiently for Boyd to set her down.

Then, mildly, Garth said, "Did the princess ask you to find her ladyship?"

Boyd looked startled, as if he'd just recalled he was not alone with the lass. He recovered quickly, saying, "Nay, but when the lad here said you had ridden out to join her ladyship, and I next learned that she had gone out before dawn with only two young grooms to attend her—Where the devil are they, anyway?"

Garth gestured without looking. "They are coming now. As for that *lad* yonder, you'd best treat him with respect if you want more than common service from Isabel's stables. He is her stable master and has served her for years. I'd wager his standing is stronger with her than yours, my lad."

Boyd glowered, glanced at Amalie, and swiftly converted the look to a boyishly rueful one that made Garth want to smack him. Boyd said lightly, "I suppose I must apologize to the man then, must I not, your ladyship?"

"That is not for me to say," she said dismissively, turning away. "If Isabel *is* looking for me, I expect . . ."

"Oh, no, my lady," Boyd said. "She was looking for Sir Garth and asked me to seek him in the stables. He is to present himself to her straightaway."

"Then, come, my lady," Garth said, extending an arm. "We should both present ourselves, I expect. Where is the princess, Boyd?"

"In the wall garden with her ladies," Boyd said. "I'll take you."

"That will not be necessary," Garth said firmly. "We'll find her."

"I must change this dress first, sir," Amalie told him. "'Tis an old one I wear only for riding. I must not go to her without first tidying myself."

"Then I'll go with you into the house first," he said.

"It has been at least half an hour since she sent me to look for you," Boyd said. "I warrant she must be growing impatient, and the outer gate to the walled garden lies just there at the end of this track. I will engage to see the lady Amalie safely to the house. Indeed, I bear messages for her."

Further annoyed, Garth hesitated, but Amalie said, "Thank you for your escort, sir. Pray tell Isabel that I shall come to her as soon as I can."

He nodded and then watched with gritted teeth as the fashious slink patted the hand she placed on his proffered forearm.

A moment later, Garth was asking himself why he should care. The lass believed she could take care of herself, so he should let her. He was more concerned—or ought to be—about why the princess wanted to talk to him.

By the time he reached the indicated gate, he had remembered that he wanted to talk to Isabel. Even so, he glanced back to see that the lass and her escort had disappeared into the hedged front garden.

How was it, he wondered, that Boyd could have messages meant for her?

~~~~~

"You picked a fine morning for your ride, my lady," Sir Harald said as she set a brisk pace through the front garden. "However, one doubts that the princess encourages her ladies to ride with only grooms to protect them."

"What messages do you bring me, sir?" she asked, ignoring his tiresome comment and lifting her hand from his arm. She had nearly done so when he'd patted it but had not wanted to reveal her displeasure so blatantly then. Even now, she brushed a wisp of hair from her face as if she had raised her hand only for that.

"'Tis from your family," he said with a truly charming smile. Whatever Sir Garth thought of Boyd, her father had been right. He *was* a handsome man.

His features looked as if a master sculptor had chiseled them. His hair was dark with a slight wave, his brows straight dark slashes, tilting slightly upward over pale blue eyes. His smile was quick and boyish, reminding her of her brother Tom.

The resemblance was not a point in Boyd's favor.

"What is the message?" she asked again, more bluntly.

"Just that Sir Iagan and Lady Murray mean to stop here on their way home to Elishaw, my lady."

"If you had such a message, why did you not tell me yestereve?"

Smiling ruefully, he said, "Dare I admit that I was

so stunned by your beauty that I forgot? 'Twould be the truth, but I fear you will accuse me of flattery."

"I accuse you only of delay. When did you come by this message?"

"At Perth. That is, at the festival on the Inch *near* Perth, to celebrate her grace's coronation. Your parents and brothers were there, and when your brother Simon presented me, your parents asked me to relay the message to you. Simon suggested you might reward me for the warning. Dare I hope he was right?"

"Reward you? Sakes, what sort of reward had you or Simon in mind?"

"As you have already shown yourself to be a bold, adventurous lass, I'd hoped I might win a kiss or . . ." He shrugged, clearly leaving the options open.

Foreboding swept through her. Only if he were the man Simon expected to force her to marry would he dare speak to her so. But *what* had Simon told him?

"I thank you for the warning," she said, letting the chill she felt cool her tone as she put more distance between them. "I would be more grateful to you, though, if you would remember to address me properly. You are too familiar, sir."

"I meant no offense, my lady. Indeed, I had hoped we might become fast friends. Simon and Tom assured me that you were of a friendly nature."

"I expect they thought they were being helpful, sir," she said, fearing her brothers had told him more than that. "In fact, I prefer to choose my own friends."

"Aye, sure, lass, I understand."

She gave him a look.

Meeting it, then reacting with a clap to his head, he

said, "Sakes, but I must beg your forgiveness again, my lady."

"Just try to behave yourself, Sir Harald. This glib manner of yours does not please me. Nor will it please our royal mistress if you display it in her presence."

He bowed. "You will have no cause in future to complain, my lady. May I see you to your chamber now?" he added as they reached the steps to the house.

"This is far enough," she said, repressing a shiver. "Perhaps no one told you, but men are not allowed in this part of the house except in the entry and the hall. Some have rooms in the north wing but do not come through the house." She saw no reason to mention the north-wing door under the rear service stairs, near the door to the walled garden, or her disbelief in his ignorance of the house rules.

However, instead of taking her words as dismissal and leaving, he looked her in the eye and said in a harsher tone, "Do not think to dismiss me so abruptly, Lady Amalie. In future you may come to regret such rude behavior."

If she had needed confirmation that he was Simon's chosen husband for her, she now had it. For no other reason could she imagine a man of his stamp—and a knight of the realm, at that—addressing her so.

She said, "I do thank you for your escort, sir, but I must not tarry."

With a nod, she hurried inside and upstairs to her chamber, thanking the fates that the house was large and sprawling enough to provide each of Isabel's ladies with a small room of her own near the princess's chambers.

She did not like Harald Boyd. He was too glib, and his charm seemed false. She had thought his patting her hand too familiar a gesture, but she recalled that Sir Garth had put his hand over hers, too, at Scone. She had not thought about it then or since, other than to note at the time the warmth of his touch.

Her fear that Simon had somehow given Boyd to believe he could have his way with her still chilled her. But it infuriated her, too. If Sir Harald Boyd expected rewards, he would quickly learn his error.

Sending a silent thank-you to Isabel for assuring her that she need not marry anyone she did not want, she decided that the sooner she reminded Simon of that fact, the better it would be for everyone. She was not going to marry a man she could not trust, and she had yet to meet a man she could.

Certainly, that man was not Sir Harald Boyd. She did not trust him one bit.

She glanced back when she reached her door to be sure he had not followed her. Even if he had, surely he would not dare to come to her bedchamber.

Nevertheless, she had a bolt on her door, and she used it.

⟿

Garth found Isabel in the garden with the other ladies. Despite the early hour—for it could be no later than half past eight—the ladies Averil, Nancy, Sibylla, and Susan all sat with her on turf seats at the center of the garden in a broad patch of sunlight. A pavilion formed of vine-laden trellises stood in shade against the eastern wall. The only tribute to the hour was the blanket each lady had spread beneath her over her doubtless dewy turf seat.

"Good day to you, sir," the princess said. "I expect Sir Harald told you I wanted to speak with you."

"He did, madam. How may I serve you?"

"Let us walk for a time. My ladies will rest here." So saying, she rose gracefully to her feet. "We'll go this way, I think," she said, gesturing. "The pear trees are bearing fruit now. Mayhap you will pick some."

Nodding, he walked beside her along a path between raised beds of a long, narrow, rectangular herb garden.

"I've not taken time before to speak with you, my lord," she said when they were out of earshot of the others. "I wanted to judge what manner of man you were."

"I hope I have won your approval, madam. But, if you please, address me as Garth or Sir Garth. Whilst I'm here, I'd liefer use my knightly title."

"Many knights do prefer it, and it will draw fewer questions," she agreed with a smile. "I've not had a landed baron serving as a member of my household before."

He smiled back. "I warrant you have not."

"When Archie Douglas told me at Scone that he was sending you to replace Sir Duncan, I own it did surprise me. But then he explained that you might help me learn the truth about Jamie's death. I should tell you, though, I do not always trust the Douglas. He is friends with Fife and, I believe, wants you to prove Fife had naught to do with Jamie's death. What say you to that, sir?"

"In troth, madam, I know no more yet than you do about James Douglas's death. I have been trying to find the man who killed Will Douglas in Danzig."

"Still, you must have heard things about James's death," she insisted.

"Aye, sure, but naught that you have not also heard." He went on to relate all he had told Archie about the armorer and James's cuirass.

"No one doubts the armorer failed to fasten his cuirass

properly," he said. "But Buccleuch said the throat wound would have killed James even so."

"The armorer can tell us naught," Isabel said.

"Aye, I ken that, too," Garth said. "He is dead, killed in a dispute over nowt, his people say. I'll admit, though, men may be paid to *say* anything."

"And the man who killed the armorer is also dead," Isabel said.

"I'll not argue that. But if he is, no one admits knowing who killed him."

She looked into his face, studying it, and he thought as he had before that she was one of the most beautiful women he had ever seen. Part of her beauty lay in the fact that she did not indulge in the gestures and affectations that so many women, beautiful or not, used to draw attention to themselves.

The lady Amalie shared that trait.

Feeling guilty at the thought, he refocused his attention firmly on Isabel.

"Tell me about Will," she said quietly. "Archie said you were with him."

"I was," he said. Collecting his thoughts, he told her what had happened.

"I don't know anyone named Haldane, do you?" she said at the end.

"No, madam. The man was just a common man-at-arms, hiring himself out for the expedition, but one of Will's men did say he'd seen him at Edmonstone."

"At Edmonstone! My husband's home?"

"Aye," Garth said. "But none there had ever heard of him."

"You must ask Sir Harald Boyd," she said with a wry

look. "He came here from Edmonstone, supposedly at my husband's behest."

"You doubt his word?"

"Not his, Edmonstone's, who told me Sir Harald would be coming when I saw him briefly at Scone. But sithee, although Sir John was the Douglases' choice for me, he would not stand against Fife even to inquire as to my wishes. Sakes, Archie is Fife's friend, so why should not Edmonstone be as well?"

Garth frowned. "Forgive me, madam, but might you be seeing enemies where there are none? I don't know Boyd, but surely, to suspect Fife's hand—"

Grimacing, Isabel said, "Sir John told me he was sending one of his own knights. Now, I expect Boyd stayed at Edmonstone long enough to speak truthfully about being there. But he knows less than I do about the place. So, I suspect that my brother Fife has sent him here to spy on me. He likes to know what I'm doing."

"I am surprised that you do not send Boyd away if that is what you believe," Garth said, hoping she would do just that. That would solve Amalie's problem, too.

"Life is more agreeable if one does not infuriate one's brothers, Fife especially," she said. "It is dangerous enough to cross him, and I've done much of that these past two years, in protecting my interests from his grasping fingers."

"Sakes, madam, how did you accomplish that?"

She smiled impishly. "Chiefly by persuading my father to sign a paper and my brother Carrick—his grace now—also to sign it, giving me life interest in the properties from which James granted me income. That document also reinforced my right to my own properties, such as this one. James signed Sweethope Hill House over to me as a betrothal gift. It was ramshackle then, but I love it most dearly now."

" 'Tis a fine house with beautiful gardens," he said.

"Aye, the gardens are thriving," she agreed. "But now, tell me more about Will, because I mean to help you all I can to prove the truth."

He was willing enough to comply with that request, but the door to the house opened just then and Amalie stepped onto the stone porch, diverting his attention.

Chapter 8

⁓

Amalie loved the gardens at Sweethope Hill House. The front one, with its tall, thorny rosebushes to keep out wandering livestock, and its raised flowerbeds and wide walkways of scythed grass, was pleasant and welcoming to visitors. But the walled garden was her favorite.

She entered it through the back door of the house, located between the service stairs and the rear anteroom to the great hall. The stairs led up to the rear of the floors above and down to the kitchen. A nearby door led into the north wing, and a corridor connected the rear entryway with the front entrance hall.

As soon as Amalie stepped outside, she saw Sir Garth and Isabel strolling along a gravel path by the herb garden. Beyond them, the other ladies sat chatting in the rose ring, a sunny circle of turf-covered seats with rosebushes behind them. Pink and white roses bloomed in massive numbers on those bushes and, with the varied colors of the women's dresses, provided a colorful scene.

The garden was warm even at so early an hour, because the high stone wall protected it from the winds that frequently blew through the Vale of the Tweed. Even so, it was early for Isabel and the others to be outdoors, so Amalie decided Isabel must have wanted to talk privately with Sir Garth.

For a princess to be private with a man who was not her father, brother, or husband was not easy, but the garden afforded excellent opportunity for such discourse. Amalie wondered what they were talking about but knew better than to look overly curious. As it was, the others were already watching her.

Lady Sibylla Cavers smiled, and Amalie hurried to join them. As she arrived, Lady Susan said, "He is very handsome, is he not?"

Amalie's stomach growled. She wondered if the others had broken their fast already. She'd had a pear from the hall table before her ride, but that had been hours ago.

Lady Averil said, "You must have better things to talk about, Susan. Did you not bring your stitchery out with you?"

"No, my lady. I did not think we would be outside for so long."

"Your thoughts should concern nothing beyond your duty to the princess," Lady Averil said. "Pray, go back into the house and fetch something to occupy your hands—and your mind," she added dryly.

Susan looked at Amalie's empty hands and said, "I fear that Amalie, too, has neglected to bring her work with her, my lady. She can bear me company."

"I want to speak with Amalie. Moreover, it is not for you to decide such things, Susan. Go along now, at once."

Making her curtsy and then rolling her eyes so that

only Amalie could see her, Susan passed her without a word and went inside.

"Have I also done something I should not, my lady?" Amalie asked, taking the turf seat Susan had vacated.

"No, my dear, but that young woman is too concerned with other people's business. It is my duty to snub her."

"But you enjoy that duty, Averil," Lady Nancy said with a teasing smile. The two were of similar age and experience with the princess, so Nancy took liberties that the other ladies dared not. "Mayhap you ought to take yourself to task for that."

"No doubt," Lady Averil retorted dryly. "Being senior companion to Isabel does provide some advantage, though, and Susan's airs and affectations annoy me."

"I think we are all in accord on that subject, my lady," eighteen-year-old Sibylla agreed with a chuckle as she shifted a loose plait of dark auburn hair off her shoulder. Turning to Amalie, she said, "Did you enjoy your ride this morning?"

Taken aback, and anxiously casting a glance at Lady Averil, Amalie said warily, "I did, aye. 'Tis a fine morning and I watched the sunrise."

Lady Averil said, "I trust you took more than one groom with you, my dear."

"Aye, two, my lady."

"Then you were *very* well protected, were you not?" Lady Sibylla said with teasing glance. "I told everyone that you had gone for a ride, of course, because Isabel asked. But he *is* a handsome gentleman, just as Susan said."

"Sakes," Amalie said. "I thought she was talking about Sir Harald."

Lady Averil's gaze sharpened. "What is all this then?"

"Nowt to trouble anyone's mind," Sibylla said cheerfully. "Sir Garth also rode out, sometime after she did. But he did follow you, did he not, Amalie?"

"He did," Amalie admitted. "But my grooms never left us."

"I thought he seemed troubled when he left," Sibylla said, flicking a glance at Garth and Isabel. "My window overlooks the front garden, as you know. By the look of him, I suspected that he had suffered some sort of nightmare."

Amalie stared at her and then wished she had not when Sibylla went straight on to say, "But I see that you know about that. I hope it was not too terrifying. He has much experience of battle and death, I know. It disturbs me that evil spirits often force such men to revisit the horrors they have witnessed in their sleep."

She eyed Amalie hopefully.

"Faith, Sibylla, you don't imagine that young man can have told our Amalie about any such dream, do you?" Lady Averil demanded. "No man would do that."

Amalie bowed her head to keep the truth from showing on her face.

Lady Nancy said lightly, "Oh, indeed, Sibylla, *no* gentleman would describe a nightmare to a young lady. I warrant he rode out only for exercise and then, chancing to meet her, brought her safely home again. Very kind of him, I'm sure."

Looking up to meet Nancy's gaze, and hoping to ease the tension she felt, Amalie said quietly and in a way to include the others, "It was kind, was it not?"

Agreeing, the ladies turned to more ordinary topics, and Amalie was able to congratulate herself for deft handling of a sticky situation.

She indulged that belief until Garth and Isabel joined them, when Isabel said, "I left a basket in the hall with some threads I was sorting, Amalie. Do fetch it for me, will you? Sir Garth will escort you."

Poised on the brink of insisting that she could fetch the basket perfectly well without help, Amalie swallowed the words and stood. Noting Sibylla's knowing gaze and Lady Nancy's wide-eyed one, she strove mightily to look calm.

Isabel said casually, "There is no need to hurry. I mean to enjoy this sunshine, and I warrant neither of you has yet broken your fast."

"N-no, madam," Amalie said, avoiding Garth's eye and pretending not to see the arm he extended to her.

But he just put a hand between her shoulder blades instead and urged her forward. The firm touch of his hand there was far more disturbing than when he had placed a gloved hand over hers at Scone Abbey. His hand was bare this time and her bodice summer thin. The warmth of his touch was more evident. But her unease arose more from the fact that the warmth spread all through her, stirring sensations in other parts of her body, unfamiliar but oddly pleasant ones.

To make matters worse, they met Susan at the door. The look she gave Amalie as she hurried past could have turned water to ice.

"What is wrong with that woman?" Garth asked as he held the door for Amalie, barely waiting for Susan to get beyond earshot.

"I haven't a notion," Amalie said. "You may leave me now, sir."

"May I?" She heard laughter in his tone.

"There is naught in any of this that is funny," she said,

nearly stamping her foot. "Sibylla saw you ride out this morning. Moreover, she knows you had a nightmare, and she very nearly asked me what you had dreamed."

His eyes widened, but then he shook his head at her. "I don't believe it," he said. "How could anyone know such a thing? Is the woman a witch?"

"Well, if she is, she is a noble witch. Her father is Sir Malcolm Cavers."

"What did you tell her?"

"Not a word, because Lady Averil intervened. But when Isabel told me to go with you, she gave me the most knowing look."

"Isabel?"

"Nay, Sibylla, of course. And like it or not, witch or not, she sees things others do not and seems to know things others don't know. She has a good heart, though."

He waited, pointedly holding the door open until she entered the house. But when he guided her through the anteroom into the hall, she protested.

"I cannot believe that Isabel meant for you to stay with me," she said.

"I have a duty to protect her ladies," he said loftily.

"That may be so. And her knights may have chambers inside the house—"

"Boyd will stay in the dormer to look after the men who eat and sleep there."

"As I was saying before you interrupted me," she said between gritted teeth, "the men's chambers are in the north wing for a purpose, sir. Her knights are never supposed to be private with her ladies. If no one has explained that to you—"

"I have Isabel's permission," he said.

"Her permission! Why would she give such permission?"

"Because I requested it."

Glowering, she stepped away from his hand and faced him, hands on her hips, grateful that no servant was in the hall. With the midday meal hours away and no fire in the fireplace, none would come unless she shouted for one, or he did.

Fiercely, she said, "You had no right to ask her for such permission!"

His eyes narrowed, making her sharply aware that she was alone with him.

Forcing calm into her voice, she said, "You must have told her more than that you wanted to be alone with me."

"I told her that I believe you know certain things that might help clarify matters about which she is curious."

"The only thing that makes Isabel curious these days is her determination to learn the truth about James's death," Amalie said, feeling her calm slip away again.

He remained silent.

"Sakes, what do you think I could know about that?" she demanded. "I have heard only what Isabel herself has heard. Indeed, not as much, because I know only what Wat Scott told us both and the things that she has repeated to all of us."

"What did Harald Boyd want with you?"

"What has that got to do with anything?"

"Sakes, lass, stop trying to counter everything I say and just answer my questions. Isabel is unlikely to let this conversation go on all day."

Amalie's stomach growled again, the sound long and protesting.

Sir Garth's lips twitched, and when hers responded in

a like manner, he said, "Let's find something to eat. We shall both be more comfortable if we sit."

She turned quickly away to forestall any notion he might have of touching her again, and strode to the dais table. A basket of manchet loaves, pots of butter and quince jelly, and a ewer of water were all that remained from the others' breakfast.

She knew she could send someone to fetch sliced beef or fresh salmon, but the last thing she wanted was a hovering servant. Nor did she think Sir Garth would let one stay if she sent for one. If he had reached the point of persuading Isabel to allow his interrogation, he meant to get the answers he sought without more delay.

Accordingly, she split a manchet, slathered quince jelly lavishly on both halves, and placed them on a fresh napkin.

Garth pulled the basket to himself and, taking a roll, tore off a chunk and buttered it thickly. Popping it into his mouth, he chewed and swallowed.

"Water?" he asked as Amalie took her usual seat.

"Thank you," she said, watching him fill goblets for each of them.

"Now," he said as he moved a stool and sat facing her, "what did he want?"

"He was just being tiresome," she muttered.

He pulled the pot of butter closer and broke off another piece of his roll. "So it was not enough for him to have taken Isabel's stable master to task," he said. "He continued to rail on about your puny escort."

"Aye," she said. "Being tiresome, as I said." She broke off a chunk of her own bread and jelly and ate it hungrily.

"He seems to have taken more notice of your escort

than it warranted. Perhaps such a man may read more into such a ride than he should."

"You usually speak more plainly," she said. "Don't change your ways now."

"I'm suggesting, lass, that he might try to take advantage if you make a habit of such solitary rides."

"Thank you for your concern, sir," she said, lifting her chin. "Is there aught else you want to know?"

"You know there is," he said gently.

She grimaced. "That will teach me to resist sarcasm."

"At least tell me if you recognized either voice," he said.

"Tell me first who sent you here."

"Archie the Grim."

She blinked. "Why would you not tell me that the first time I asked you?"

"I did not know you well enough. Isabel knows that Archie sent me, but most folks do not. I'd as lief keep it that way."

"What do you know about me now that you did not know then?"

The look he gave her was indecipherable until he said, "I know you can keep a secret. Look," he went on, putting his forearms on the table and leaning toward her. "I ken fine that you find it hard to trust me, but we both need to learn whom we can trust, and I think we can help each other if you will just try."

"How?"

"I'm certain that whatever you overheard in Abbots' House was more than a simple, innocent conversation between servants."

"I told you they were not servants."

"Hush, let me finish. You also told me you could not

hear what they said. I did not believe that then, and I still don't."

"But—"

"If it were true, you'd have lost your temper with me by now and said so in such a way as to defy my continued disbelief. And, if there were no more details to impart, you would not have to decide whether to impart them to me. Therefore, the only thing tying your tongue is your continued distrust of me . . . of men in general. But I know, too, that you have said nowt to Isabel of what you overheard."

"Faith, did you ask her?"

"Nay." He said the word forcefully, but he did not give her the angry look that she expected. Instead, he sighed and looked helplessly at her.

Ignoring that look, her bread and jelly forgotten, she said, "If you did not ask her, how can you know?"

"Because she did not mention it, and she would have." He sighed again. "I'll answer your questions in more detail when I can, but I cannot reveal things Isabel said to me in confidence. You do know the subject uppermost in her mind, though."

"James."

"Aye, and Will Douglas has joined him there. I told you before that I want to learn the truth. I tell you now that my search for his killer has brought me here."

"Because you want to compare such information as you've gleaned up to now with all that Isabel has learned. You hope to find a connection."

"Aye, perhaps," he said.

She saw that there was more to it. But she knew that if she pressed him, he'd insist that she tell him all he wanted to know before he would say more to her.

The thought of telling him no longer seemed impossible, and she knew she had to tell someone. When Sir Harald had said her family would visit, she had considered confiding in her father. But the niggling detail of her initial suspicion, that the first voice she'd heard might have been Simon's, deterred her from confiding in anyone.

Sir Iagan knew from his sons' involvement in the attempt to seize Hermitage after Otterburn that Simon would do nearly anything Fife asked of him. So Sir Iagan might believe Simon was involved in another of Fife's plots. But he would not believe that any son of his was capable of murder.

Admittedly, both Simon and Tom had threatened to murder her at least once, but she could imagine Sir Iagan's reaction, or her mother's, to such an accusation. Simple, understandable sibling fury, they would say, nothing more.

"Well?" Garth said.

"I did recognize one voice," she said.

"Who?"

"Fife."

"So you knew straightaway when—"

"Don't be horrid," she said. "I may have heard him speak before, but I paid no heed if I did. So I did not know his voice well enough to recognize it through that door. I did not recognize it at all until we gathered at Moot Hill and he gave the King the land of Scotland and the people of Scotland their new-crowned King."

"But you're sure now that one of the two men you heard was Fife."

She nodded, meeting his steady gaze. "As sure as one can be, anyway."

"And the other voice?"

Amalie looked down, remembered her bread, and broke off another piece. She hoped he would think she had intended to do that when she'd looked away.

"Look at me, Molly-lass." His tone was gentle, but she reacted with strong irritation nonetheless.

"My name is Amalie, sir, not Molly. Moreover, I have *not* given you leave to use my name, nor should you."

To her further annoyance, his eyes twinkled, and she realized that he had purposely cast bait. She realized, too, that she had leapt at it like a trout to a fly.

"I just shortened your name," he said. "Friends do such things, you know, and I have not changed my mind about wanting to be friends. Do you really mind? After the way we met, it seems disingenuous to speak with such formality when we find ourselves alone."

Perhaps, she told herself, that explained why his lack of formality had not irritated her more. Sir Harald's familiarity irritated her considerably.

"Now, whose was the other voice?"

She said nothing for a moment. But he was buttering his second manchet, apparently content to leave her to her thoughts for a short time.

"I did not tell you everything Sir Harald said to me," she said.

He raised his eyebrows but continued to chew his roll.

"He is even more annoying than you are," she said. When that, too, drew no response, she sighed. "I don't know why he annoys me so much. I did think it was because he was overly familiar in his behavior, but he said no more than you have said, so it cannot have been that. All he really said was that my family will visit here on their way home from Scone. He did not say when they will come, but my mother does not approve of rapid travel, so I expect it will be a day or two yet."

"Is this another diversion, or did my question remind you of that detail?"

"I don't see how it—" But she did see only too clearly how her mind had leapt to her family from his question about that second voice.

As she met his gaze, she knew that his thoughts had followed a similar path, and that she could no longer refuse to answer. Hoping he would believe her, having no idea how to persuade him if he did not, she said, "I did think I knew that voice when first I heard it, sir. But with my ear to the door, I was *not* certain. I hope I was mistaken, but . . . but you must see that I cannot name him without being certain."

He held her gaze for a time in silence. Then he said, "I do understand your reluctance, lass, and I won't press you to name him. Just tell me what they said."

She nodded. Recognizing that his trust placed an added burden on her to be honest with him, she said, "I think Fife wanted the other man to kill someone."

Garth drew a long breath. He had exerted his patience nearly to its limit but knew he'd be a fool to reveal that now. Although she clearly believed that one of the men in her family was the other person in that room, he would not learn today which one she suspected. All three Murray men had attended the coronation.

He considered the best course to take with her. She appeared to be strong-willed and capable, even saucy from time to time. But underlying all that, he sensed something fragile that affected her ability to trust.

She reminded him of a puppy or young horse that had been mistreated. She had the same wariness, the same inclination to snap or kick. He hoped she would respond to patience in the same way, too. Still, he had to know all that she knew before he could decide if it aided him in any way.

"Who does Fife want to kill?" he asked.

When she began to shake her head, he felt his jaw tighten and drew another long breath, determined not to let his impatience show.

She detected it though, because she said, "Truly, I don't know. You snatched me away before I heard a name or anything else that might identify the man."

"It was a man, though."

"Aye, sure. Why would Fife want to kill a woman?"

"I don't know," he said. "But it may be important to know why you thought it was a man."

She frowned, thinking, and he kept silent.

"Fife said 'him,'" she said at last. "He said, 'If we give *him* enough cause, he will cooperate, but we cannot trust *him* from one minute to the next.'"

"That cannot be all he said."

"Nay. The most chilling part was when he said it would suit him better not to have to concern himself with him at all. Then the other said, 'Sakes, sir, is it murder you seek?' Fife said, 'I did not say—' And that is when you grabbed me."

"So Fife denied murder."

"Aye, he did say those words, but there was a note in his voice . . . He speaks like syrup pouring from a pitcher,

sir, all sticky sweet but smooth withal. I'd say he murmurs, but his voice carries easily. It just—"

"I know, and that is an apt description. Did he speak
that way throughout?"

"No, he sounded terser when he first spoke of the . . . the
subject of their exchange. I thought he was annoyed. At
the end, it sounded as if he'd accept the man's murder
if it served his purpose, and if reasoning proved useless."

"We must hope their target is not another Douglas,"
Garth said, mentally scanning a list of Douglases who
might annoy Fife enough to incite murder.

"It cannot be the earl," she said. "He is Fife's ally."

"Archie is his own man first," Garth said. "He will
support Fife as long as he thinks Fife should rule Scotland, because he knows his grace cannot handle the job
and does not want it. But, believe me, Archie would spit
Fife's head on a pike over the gates of Threave Castle if
he were to discover that he was responsible for or com-
plicit in James's or Will's deaths."

Amalie was not sure she could believe that Douglas would
have Fife's head for any reason. Was not the Governor the
most powerful man in the realm?

She recalled others saying the Earl of Douglas was the
most powerful. But at the time, they had been talking of
the second earl, not the third.

James Douglas could raise ten thousand men in days.
Archie had given up Tantallon Castle to Fife. Some said
he'd forfeited the Douglas stronghold on the coast east
of Edinburgh to win Fife's support and become the third
earl.

Fife's support might not have been the sole reason the Douglases had chosen Archie, but it had helped. Any number of Douglases believed as he did that Fife was the only one in the royal family strong enough to rule Scotland.

The rest of her conversation with Garth was desultory until they had eased their hunger. Then he escorted her back into the garden.

As they approached the others, he said quietly, "Your instincts about Boyd are sound, lass. Take care not to be alone with him again."

Anger stirred, but she could say nothing then. She had forgotten Isabel's basket, too, but no one mentioned it, and the ladies all soon went inside.

The rest of that day passed without incident, as did Saturday and Sunday. On Monday, Sibylla strode into the hall just before Nones, announcing as she stepped onto the dais to join the others that visitors were approaching from the north.

"Despite the sky's inclination to drip today, they fly the Murray banner, Amalie, dear," she said. To Isabel, she added, "I sent word to the kitchen, madam. Indeed, I warned them yesterday that we might have visitors today."

"How far away?" Lady Nancy asked her.

"Oh, a mile or two, I expect."

Isabel said, "You cannot have seen their banner at such distance, Sibylla."

Sibylla chuckled. "I could say its spirit wafted to me on the wind. But as dreary as it is today, if a wind stirred, it would just carry more drizzle. They sent someone ahead with the banner, of course. The rest will arrive in a half hour."

"Very well, then I expect you also told our people to put off serving us until our visitors have had time to dry themselves," Isabel said.

"I did, madam," Sibylla said with a nod. "I knew you would want to wait."

Amalie wondered if Sibylla had also learned of Garth's nightmare from someone else. Perhaps that was how she so often seemed to know things others did not.

In any event, the Murray family arrived in an impressive cavalcade with the Murray men riding at its head and Rosalie riding beside Lady Murray's horse litter.

Lady Murray's waiting woman rode at the litter's other side, and Sir Iagan's usual tail of men-at-arms followed. The morning's drizzle had eased to soggy air.

Amalie hurried with Isabel to greet them, hugging her younger sister with delight but a little surprised to find both Simon and Tom with them.

Tom leaped down to lift Rosalie from her pony.

Simon had long since made clear his belief that service to Fife was excuse enough for his part in the business at Hermitage two years before, but Tom had carefully kept out of Isabel's way since then—and Amalie's, for that matter.

Since Archie Douglas now controlled Hermitage, and since neither Fife nor any of his minions was likely to try seizing it again anytime soon, Tom doubtless hoped Isabel had forgotten by now that he'd taken part in the attempt.

Isabel had not forgotten, nor would she. But Amalie knew her well enough to know that she would politely accept him and Simon as guests in her house, while offering nothing friendlier. The princess was affable to an extent that her haughtier brothers derided as a fault. But she could be haughty, too. Indeed, Amalie knew that Isabel could change from one demeanor to the next in the blink of an eye, especially if someone angered her.

Undisturbed by the damp, Sir Iagan followed Rosalie, bowing to Isabel and hugging Amalie. She hugged him back. She had not missed him, but she enjoyed the familiar feeling of his embrace, as well as his blustery greeting and smacking kiss.

"Ye're looking well, lass," he said, as if he had not seen her just eight days before. "'Tis a fine, comfortable-looking house, this is now."

"Thank you, Sir Iagan," Isabel said. "It has taken two years to bring it to this state. But if you recall how it was when James gifted it to me, you know the work took nearly every minute of that time."

"Aye, sure, thanks to the damnable English. Bless us, but we must hope this latest truce lasts its time. Raiders do far less damage than the English army."

"They are also less likely to attack us here," she said, adding as her gaze drifted beyond him, "Welcome to Sweethope, Lady Murray. We have held dinner for you, so I warrant you will want to refresh yourselves quickly. Amalie can take you and Rosalie to her chamber and then show you the way back down to the hall."

"Thank you, madam," Lady Murray said, sweeping her a deep curtsy. "We have enjoyed the great honor of your esteemed brother, the Governor's, company these past two days. You will be pleased to hear that he is in excellent health and looking forward to seeing you *very* soon."

"Indeed," Isabel said, evincing no pleasure whatsoever in that news.

Chapter 9

~

Rosalie demanded directions to the garderobe, so Amalie turned her over to a friendly housemaid. Then, dutifully taking her mother up to her own room, she looked hastily around as she entered to be sure that neither she nor the efficient maidservant who attended her had left anything out of place. Lady Murray would take instant, censorious note of untidiness.

Surprisingly, Lady Murray condescended to compliment Amalie on her appearance, and even to approve of the little room. Speaking with uncharacteristic cheerfulness, she declared it a pleasant place indeed.

"It has a fine view of the walled garden," Amalie said with a nod toward the single, narrow, half-shuttered window.

"I warrant it does, and there is water awaiting you in this ewer," Lady Murray replied. "So I see you are well served."

"Aye, sure, we are comfortable," Amalie agreed warily.

"I am sure the princess looks after you well," Lady

Murray said. "One presumes that you have made the acquaintance of her serving knights."

"Yes, madam." Aware now of where her mother's unusual geniality would lead, she said, "As they often eat in
the hall with us, it would be odd if I had not."

Lady Murray shot her a look that might have scared
her witless as a child. Today it had no effect. Amalie was
having too much trouble concealing her fury.

She did wonder why her mother hesitated to speak her
mind, for she was not usually one to delay sharing unwelcome news.

Lady Murray had turned to dry her face, neck, and
hands with a towel. Turning back as she put it down,
she said archly, "Dare I hope you may prefer one of
those knights to the others? 'Tis said that one is especially handsome and charming. He also enjoys excellent
connections."

"Madam, forgive me, but coyness does not suit you,"
Amalie said. "If you have aught to say to me, pray say it
and have done. I have no interest in any knight, or indeed,
in any man. I thought I had made that plain."

Discarding the arch tone, Lady Murray said, "You will
do as your father bids you, Amalie, just as Meg did. And
you will do so without unseemly discussion. You will *not*
disgrace your family by continuing to be obstinate."

"No one in my family has paid me any heed these two
years past, madam. Why should your wishes now take
precedence over my own?"

"Take care, girl," Lady Murray said. "I am still your
mother, and you are not yet of age. Moreover, Sir Harald
is a close connection of—"

"—the Earl of Fife. Yes, I know. I had deduced for myself that Sir Harald is the man Simon wants me to marry.

Well, I have met Sir Harald and find him overly familiar, distastefully fond of his own conceit, and rude withal. You and Simon may proclaim his supposed virtues as you please. I will have none of him."

"I see," Lady Murray said grimly. "Then I shall say no more, and we will go down and join the others. Am I to share this tiny room with you, or are there rooms enough here to spare one for your father and me?"

"The housekeeper will have all that in hand, but he will sleep in the north wing, because male guests do. I doubt Isabel was expecting Simon or Tom, but—"

"Faith, I cannot think why she would not. They were with us at Scone. And if she did not know that the Governor was traveling to Lauder Castle from there, she should have. He is her brother, after all."

Amalie did not offer a reply to that, knowing she had pressed her luck enough already in challenging her mother at all. That she had done so must have surprised her ladyship, for it had certainly surprised Amalie.

She wondered if Sir Garth's bluntness was having an effect on her and decided she must have adopted some of it from him. She was not usually so quick to speak out. Although, she reminded herself, she had felt increasingly confident of her opinions about everything except men since the day she had left Elishaw to travel with the newly married Meg to Scott's Hall.

Rosalie entered then with Lady Murray's woman in her wake, and shortly thereafter the three Murray ladies descended to the hall.

Isabel awaited them on the dais and directed Lady Murray to the seat at her left, with Sir Iagan on her right. Amalie gratefully took her own place, offering her younger sister the one next to her, at the end of the table.

"A chamber is ready for you and Sir Iagan in the north wing," Isabel said when Lady Murray had settled herself. Casually, she added, "I warrant you will want to rest this afternoon. How long are we to enjoy your company?"

"I will stay two days, if that pleases you, Lady Edmonstone."

Isabel said quietly, "You are welcome to stay as long as you like, but I prefer to be addressed as 'madam' or 'Princess Isabel.'"

"That must certainly be as you wish, madam," Lady Murray said with a regal nod. "'Tis a pity that our princes and princesses are not treated to the same degree of dignity as their English counterparts and called 'highness.' But then men of our royal family may not even claim the title of prince, only that of earl. I consider that most unfortunate. See you, I am of English birth, myself."

"Yes, Lady Murray, I did know that."

"You may call me Annabel if it pleases you," Lady Murray said with more condescension than Isabel had ever displayed in Amalie's presence.

"Thank you," Isabel said. "Someone will show you to your chamber after we dine. Do ask for anything you want. If we have it, someone will produce it."

Lady Sibylla, sitting at Amalie's right, leaned nearer and murmured for her ear alone, "Your mother was Annabel Percy before her marriage, was she not?"

"Aye," Amalie murmured back. "She is cousin to Northumberland."

"Then why is she eyeing our newest knight so hungrily? 'Tis the expression of an eager lass eyeing a potential husband."

"Not for herself," Amalie blurted without thinking.

Sibylla gave her throaty chuckle and said, "So that's

it, is it? But what about—? Och then, never mind," she
added. "We should both know better than to speak without thinking, my dear, but I've never learned the trick of
that, myself."

"I warrant you just want to know if I've changed my
mind," Amalie said, smiling. "I have spoken often enough
of my decision to remain unwed. At present, though, my
family has other plans for me."

"Then 'tis good we have laws protecting us against unwanted marriages."

"I just hope my mother knows about those laws."

Isabel's chaplain stood to speak the grace before meat,
and as he did, Amalie saw that Garth had come in. Feeling her cheeks flush as his gaze met hers, she turned away,
hoping he could not see any added color from where he
stood and would think she was simply paying closer heed
to the chaplain's words.

She was glad to see him, but she was not looking forward to the meal.

From the hall's main entrance, Garth took in the scene before him while the chaplain finished his prayer. His gaze
lighting first on Amalie, he caught her eye and noted the
relief on her always-expressive face.

When the chaplain finished, and Isabel's carver began
to carve the haunch of mutton, Garth strode to the place
at the end of the men's side that the others had left for
him. Since it put him next to the taciturn senior knight,
Sir Kenneth Maclean, with no one on his other side, he
was content.

Sir Iagan had the place of honor at Isabel's right with

Boyd on his right. Simon was next, and his younger brother, Tom, sat between Simon and Maclean.

Although Garth took care to let his expression reveal none of his thoughts, he believed now that the lass had correctly deduced her family's intent.

There could be no other reason for Boyd to sit next to Sir Iagan. That place, by rights, belonged to Simon, so Boyd would not be there unless Sir Iagan or Simon had asked Isabel to allow it and she had agreed. As the least experienced of her knights, Boyd's proper place was below Garth on the end stool.

At Sweethope, the princess's knights and ladies dined with her on the dais unless she had too many guests. Other members of her household, except the kitchen staff, dined at a trestle table at the lower end of the hall.

Her men-at-arms ate and slept in the dormerlike building east of the stables and took their meals there as well, the hall not being large enough to contain so many. The men in Sir Iagan's tail would be taking their meal in the dormer now, and would set up an encampment for themselves that afternoon near Eden Water.

Garth was grateful for Sir Kenneth's silence. It let him hear enough of the other men's conversation to realize that Sir Iagan was trying rather unsuccessfully to learn more about Boyd's antecedents and expectations. It also let him overhear Tom Murray make two decidedly improper remarks about his sister.

From a grunt he heard after the second one, Simon had used an elbow to see that there'd be no more of them. Still, Garth knew that if he had heard them, so had Sir Kenneth and Boyd. Pondering the remarks, he recalled Amalie's distrust of men.

If young Murray lingered at Sweethope, he would learn to mind his tongue.

~~~

Amalie, too, had seen Sir Harald sit next to her father. Lady Murray had also noticed, because she said in a carrying tone, "I see that you keep a number of handsome knights in your household, madam. They must be a comfort to you."

Amalie shook her head at the platter of lamb collops a gillie offered for her selection. She could not think of her mother, Sir Harald, and food at the same time.

Ears aprick, she heard Isabel say evenly, "The Douglas provides my escort, just as his predecessor did."

"I should think your husband, Sir John Edmonstone, would do so."

"Do you?" Isabel replied. "He does presently provide one knight. But I can count on Douglas to provide as many as I need whenever I need them."

"I warrant Sir Harald Boyd is one of the more dependable ones, is he not?"

Amalie gritted her teeth as she rearranged food on her trencher.

"As to that, I cannot say," Isabel said. "He has been in my service only a short time. Did you enjoy your journey, madam? To have taken a full sennight to reach us, I imagine you visited a number of friends and kinsmen along the way."

Susan began talking to the lady Nancy then, and although they kept their voices low, Amalie could no longer hear the other conversation without straining, so she tried to apply herself to her food instead.

"You must like it here," Rosalie said.

Smiling at her, Amalie said, "I do, aye."

"Are the other ladies nice?"

"Aye, sure," she said, aware that Sibylla was certainly listening. She knew, too, that Susan was likely to over-hear anything negative. Susan always did seem to hear anything that she might construe as a slight to herself.

"Is that why you do not come home?" Rosalie asked wistfully.

Guilt washed over Amalie. She had not spared a thought for Rosalie, assuming that her younger sister continued to enjoy their father's favor and their mother's, as she had from the day of her birth. Even Simon adored Rosalie.

"Do you miss me?" Amalie asked, looking more closely at her.

"It is lonely without you. The coronation was the most exciting thing that has happened in the past two years. The rest has been deadly dull."

"Well, Scott's Hall lies farther from Elishaw than Sweethope Hill does. Mayhap now that I'm closer, I can visit you more easily, or you can visit me."

"I'd like that. I just wish we could stay longer now. But our lady mother is eager to be with Meg for her lying-in."

"Is that where you go from here? It would have been faster to go directly to Scott's Hall from Edinburgh, tak-ing the drove road through Ettrick Forest."

Rosalie flushed. "Aye, perhaps," she said, adding in a lower tone, "Mother and Simon wanted to come here first. In troth, I think Mother wanted to ride with Simon in the Governor's train. When she learned that the Governor meant to stay at Lauder and then travel through the Bor-ders —a progress, he called it—she said we should come here to visit you. She said—" Breaking off and looking rueful, Rosalie added, "But I must not repeat what she said. She told me I must not."

"Never mind, for I can imagine," Amalie said. "I have met Sir Harald. Moreover, Simon ordered me at Yuletide to begin thinking of marriage, and then our parents said at Scone that they knew just the man I should marry, so—"

"Faith, did they do all that? No one told me. But if Simon wanted you to marry Sir Harald at Yuletide, why did they not press the matter before now?"

"I do not know if he had Sir Harald in mind then, and I do not care," Amalie said, struggling to keep her voice down. "I do not mean to marry, ever. But what of you? Are there no handsome men dangling after you, dearling? You are growing to be a woman, and if all your gowns suit you as well as that one does . . ."

Rosalie grimaced. "Sithee, they are the opposite with me. Mother says I am too young, although I'm thirteen and girls marry even younger. Only think of Margaret of Strathearn, married already to Sir Patrick Graham! She is only six!"

"Mercy, that young?"

"Our lady mother said so, aye. But my father says he cannot afford to dower more than one more daughter. He said it nearly beggared him to pay Meg's dowry."

"Doubtless that will come as a surprise to Wat and Meg," Amalie said dryly, knowing that Wat had had to file a grievance against Sir Iagan before he saw any of Meg's dowry. Still, she knew that her father hated to part with his gelt, so she said, "Father just wants to keep you at home because he dotes on you. And doubtless Mother values your companionship, as well."

"That is all very well," Rosalie said. "But the only

men who pay attention to me other than Father are my
brothers."

A shiver of warning stirred along Amalie's spine.
"How . . . how much attention do Simon and Tom pay
you, dearling? Sithee, you should not spend time alone
with any man now that you are growing up so quickly,
not even brothers."

Rosalie shrugged. "I rarely see Simon because of his
duty to Fife, but Tom comes home frequently. After that
business at Hermitage, there was a fearful row—well,
after the Douglases chose their third earl—because he
demanded a fine for trying to seize the castle. And the
Border Wardens forced Father to pay Simon and Tom's
share, because Fife refused to let Simon pay and Tom
could not afford to."

"They should both be grateful that Archie did not hang
them," Amalie said tartly. "That is what they deserved for
what they did."

"Bless me," Sibylla said, startling Amalie, who in
her annoyance with her brothers had forgotten the other
young woman's excellent hearing. "Were your brothers
involved in that business, my dear? How remarkable!"

That comment making further discussion of the topic
impossible for Amalie, if not for Sibylla or Rosalie, she
firmly turned the conversation to other matters.

In Garth's opinion, the meal was overlong. The princess
rarely employed performers to entertain her, so the plentiful midday dinners and lighter evening suppers he had
taken in her company since arriving at Sweethope Hill
had been simple, friendly, and quickly over.

To be sure, this was the first time he had seen her with visitors. Clearly, she was exerting herself to be a good hostess.

Lady Murray was doing much of the talking at the women's end of the table. Sir Iagan showed interest only in Boyd's discourse or Simon's.

"Thinks much of himself, that one," Sir Kenneth muttered when Boyd's voice rose as he described some feat or other on the battlefield. No, not a feat, Garth amended silently. It was something amusing, because the others were laughing.

"I don't know him," Garth said. "Do you?"

"I know Fife knighted him, or that some vassal knight of his did—and not long since, either," Sir Kenneth said, taking care not to let his voice reach Tom Murray. "Puffed up with conceit, that lad is, and I'm none so sure he tells the truth about himself. And if he does not speak truly of himself . . ." He shrugged.

"Then likely he lies about other things, too," Garth said.

"Aye. And it sounds as if the Murrays plan to add him to the family."

Garth grimaced. "They may hope."

Sir Kenneth shot him a quizzing look from under his bushy eyebrows, but Garth said no more.

As the two were leaving the dais a short time later, to walk to the men's dormer and discuss the training sessions they were arranging, Garth heard Lady Murray say, "I am so pleased to make your acquaintance, Sir Harald. I have heard many good things about you, have I not, sir?" she added, turning to her husband.

"Och, aye," Sir Iagan said. "He's doubtless a fine fellow."

Lady Murray went on to say, "As the drizzle has
stopped, I mean to walk in the walled garden with my
daughter Amalie, Sir Harald. Perhaps you would care to
join us. I've no doubt she would like to know you better,
just as I would."

Shooting a look at Amalie, Garth saw her irritation.
But to his surprise, Sir Iagan said, "Ye'll have to take
your turn, my lady. I ken fine that ye'd talk more with the
lass, but I've scarce had a word with her yet. Amalie, lass,
if ye'd please your father, ye'll walk down with me to see
if Eden Water still teems with trout."

"You will find that it does, Sir Iagan," Isabel said with
a smile. "You may go with him, Amalie. Sir Harald, you
must report to Sir Kenneth. And, Rosalie, perhaps you
would like to join my ladies and me in a stroll round my
garden. You are welcome to join us, madam, unless you
would prefer to nap in your chamber."

"I'd best go and see that my woman has all in hand
there," Lady Murray said. "Rosalie can come with me.
You've no need to trouble yourself with her."

"I shall enjoy making her acquaintance," Isabel assured her. "Come along, Rosalie. I like to show the garden to my visitors."

Garth's gaze found Amalie's again as she gave her
father's arm a squeeze.

Relieved to see her smile, he turned back to find that
Sir Kenneth had already left the hall. He hurried to catch
up with him.

                           ⌒

"'Tis a pleasant place, this, even on such a day," Sir Iagan
said as he and Amalie strolled through the still dripping

front garden, past the horse pond, to the graveled track near the stables. The sky remained heavily overcast. The air was still.

"'Tis a perfect day for trout to rise," Amalie agreed, looking up at him and trying to judge his thoughts from his expression. She had never found that easy, despite the knack she had for reading other people.

"Sithee, your mam still wants ye to come home," he said, staring straight ahead as if he did not want to see her reaction. "Mayhap she will change her mind, though, now that she kens Sir Harald is here at Sweethope."

"I shall not change *my* mind, sir," Amalie said. "I do not mean to be disobedient or obstinate, but—"

"Now then, lass," he said, looking at her at last. "I can tell your mother has been screeching at ye, for I doubt ye think o' yourself as obstinate. I surely do not."

"She told me I am not yet of age, which is true, sir, and that I owe you my obedience. Most people would agree that that is also true."

"I must say that, having found nowt to disfavor the man, I canna think why ye've taken so strongly against him. He seems a good chap, and he's won his spurs and all. No mean feat, that is, as I can tell ye. Sakes, but it be more than either o' your brothers has done. I'd never expect it of Tom, for he's more interested in his lute and charming the ladies than in fighting. I warrant he'd have had to learn though, by choice or no, had I been a more belligerent man m'self."

"But you are not, sir."

"Nay, for by building powerful alliances on both sides o' the line, I've kept us safe enough without fighting. I did expect more of Simon, but he's a good man, and skilled with a sword. To be fair, though, with a master like Fife, who does his best to keep from the thick of battle, Simon's had no chance to win his spurs."

"No, sir," Amalie said, certain in her own mind that Simon had never sought such a chance. He thought his position with Fife sufficient to gain all he wanted.

"I warrant he'd take good care of you, lassie."

She knew he meant Sir Harald, not Simon. She knew, too, that she would have to make her opinion of the man plain to him. Accordingly, she said, "You have not heard how Sir Harald speaks to me, sir."

He looked at her, frowning so that his thick, graying eyebrows nearly met above the bridge of his nose. "What does he say?"

"He called me a bold, adventurous lass and suggested I reward him for warning me that my family was coming to visit."

"Sakes, who would have told him such a thing o' ye?"

She nearly told him, but a swift mental picture of him taking Simon to task, and the likely result to her of Simon's losing his temper, stopped the words on her tongue. Instead, she said, "It does not matter. What matters is that he had the effrontery to repeat it to me. Why do you think him a good match for me? Is he wealthy? You said he has no grand estate? If he has anything, no one has told me."

"Your marriage to him would double our connection to the royal family of Scotland, lass. One does not reject such a strong alliance."

"But Simon enjoys that alliance. Why do we need Sir Harald?"

"Because one cannot have too many such. Look at the Douglases. The Master of Douglas married his grace's eldest daughter, and if Archie has his way, young George of Angus will get the next one. James married Isabel,

Will Douglas married the princess Gelis, and . . . there's another one, aye. Let me think. Aye, sure, Douglas o' Dalkeith married the princess Egidia, daughter o' Robert the Steward. Like Douglas, the more such connections we Murrays can make, the better for us."

"But what does he offer me besides false charm and a leering eye?"

Her father grimaced. "Amalie, lass, I've told ye I'll take your side, and so I did when your mam would have pressed ye to stomach more o' his company. In troth, Simon wants land for your dowry—to give Boyd, that is. I'm no so sure about that. If ye were bound to have him, 'twould be otherwise, but as ye're not . . ."

"Does my mother know he wants our land, sir?"

"Faith, lass, I dinna ken, but I doubt Simon told her. She thinks a large estate must match Northumberland's Alnwick. Though she visited only once, she sets great store by it. Also, Elishaw has never impressed her as much as it impressed her father, so mayhap she'd see nowt amiss in giving Boyd a good-sized piece. But the value of land lies in acquiring more, not dividing it. I'm thinking I'll put my foot down."

He sounded as if he meant it. But Amalie had known him all her life and had never seen him withstand her mother when she had made up her mind to something. She was as certain as one could be that he would not stand long against her ladyship in this matter either. She was also by no means certain that, by herself, she could withstand the combined efforts of her mother and Simon to force the marriage.

They strolled down to Eden Water and far enough along its bank for Sir Iagan to reassure himself that large trout still leapt through its tumbling flow. They talked of

many things as they walked, but mostly Sir Iagan talked
of the landscape and the trout, comparing them unfavor-
ably to their counterparts at Elishaw.

As Amalie listened, her mind kept busy. If he could not
help her, she would just have to persuade Sir Harald that
he would gain nothing by pursuing her further.

Chapter 10

In time, Amalie and Sir Iagan wandered back toward the house, discovering as they drew near that a group of men-at-arms had gathered on the hillside behind the stables to practice swordsmanship and other skills. Sir Kenneth was supervising them, and Amalie looked to see who else was there.

"I see some o' my lads," Sir Iagan said. "After all these days of nowt but travel or standing about waiting for your mam to ready herself, I warrant they welcomed the chance to exercise."

Amalie did not reply, because she had found Garth. Holding a sword in one hand and a dirk in the other, he faced one of the men-at-arms. His opponent was similarly armed, and they circled warily. They wore only light mail.

She stopped, her heart leaping to her throat. Were they mad?

Her father touched her shoulder. "What is it, lass?"

"Should they not be carrying shields, wearing stouter armor?"

"Nay, for they are but practicing strokes and parries. They look gey skilled, the pair o' them," he added as Garth's opponent lunged and Garth struck a clanging blow to deflect his sword. That blow must have made the other man's teeth ring.

Reassured, Amalie let her father urge her homeward and focused her mind firmly on how to discourage Sir Harald's interest.

When they met him strolling out through the front doorway with Simon as if he had no duties to perform, she put her decision immediately into practice.

Ignoring him when he greeted them, she let her father reply.

Simon said, "Sir Harald wants to know you better, Amalie. You have my approval—aye, and Father's—to walk with him here in the front garden."

"My shoes are wet through," she said. "So, you will have to excuse me, Simon." Turning to Sir Iagan, she said with a warm smile, "I enjoyed our walk, sir. I hope you mean to stay for a few days."

"I canna do it, lass. I've been away too long as it is. Your mam will go to the Hall from here, to be with our Meg at her lying-in. I'll leave a few o' my lads to ride with her, but Tom and I depart in the morning for Elishaw. Simon leaves, too," he added, returning her smile. "He must go right back to Lauder."

Only to Lauder? She wanted to say it aloud but dared not. After Sir Iagan left, even with their mother still at Sweethope, Simon would assume all authority over his sisters. He had never hesitated to do so before, and his hand was heavy.

She knew her expression showed her disappointment, so she said, "Then I am doubly glad that you traveled this way, sir. It has been good to see you."

"I'm glad, too, lass. Run along now, though. Ye should have told me your feet were wet. Ye'll catch your death an ye're no more careful."

Smiling at him again, she slipped past Sir Harald and Simon without looking at or speaking to either of them and hurried up the stairs.

Garth had seen them pass and had noted Amalie's interest but could not dwell on it, as to do so might have cost him an arm or worse. He was glad of the chance to hone his skills, though, and the man he had chosen as his opponent was quick on his feet and dexterous.

An hour later, when Sir Kenneth called to them to stand down, Garth decided he had done enough for one afternoon. Excusing himself to Kenneth, he offered to send Boyd back to aid him if he meant to continue the session much longer.

"Nay, I'll deal with him later. These lads ken fine what they're about. Duncan Forrest was a good leader, and I can see that you're another, so we'll do without Boyd when we can. He does not concern himself with the men, and I've seen him with a sword. He's got skill, but he flourishes. A man shows much of himself in battle and nearly as much when he practices against others of like or lesser skill. He has never tested his weapon against you, I'm thinking."

"Not yet," Garth said. "I warrant the time will come, though."

"We can hope," Sir Kenneth said with a wry smile, clearly echoing Garth's own words to him at dinner.

After tidying himself, Garth looked for Isabel to see if she had commands for him. Since servants would be preparing the hall for supper by now and the princess loved the walled garden, he went directly to the garden. The ladies Nancy and Susan strolled together along one of the paths, but he saw no one else there.

Entering the house, he met a maidservant by the rear stairs and asked where everyone was. She said the ladies were drying their skirts by the hall fire.

"Brushing against yon garden shrubbery turned 'em all streaky wet, sir, but the princess said she will no change again for supper. The lads do be setting up now, sir. We'll serve in less than an hour."

Entering the hall through the nearby anteroom, he saw that nearly everyone was there, including Boyd, who stood talking with Simon and Tom Murray. Boyd's demeanor made it clear that he was acquainted with both, especially with Simon.

Sir Iagan was there, as were her ladyship and the younger lass, both chatting with Lady Averil not far from the cheerful flames on the hooded hearth.

Amalie laughed. She stood with Lady Sibylla, and as he crossed the room toward them, he saw Boyd disengage from the Murray brothers and move toward her. The feckless cush lengthened his stride as if he would beat Garth to them.

Having no wish to enter competition with Boyd over a lass he knew wanted no part of either of them, Garth altered his direction toward the fire without making it obvious, and paused beside Sir Iagan.

The older man had been staring thoughtfully at the

flames, but he turned and smiled. "I watched ye earlier on the hillside, lad. Ye've a fine arm with a sword."

"Thank you, sir. I've had a deal of practice."

"I expect ye were at Otterburn or with Fife in the west, then."

"I won my spurs at Otterburn, then traveled to Königsberg, in Prussia."

"Did ye? I have never been out o' Scotland save to visit my wife's kinsmen. Ye must tell me o' your travels."

Shifting to keep an eye on Boyd, Garth complied and had his reward when Sir Iagan invited him to continue the conversation by taking the seat next to his at supper. Simon looked surprised to find Garth in the seat he clearly considered his own to grant others, but he took it with good grace, and sat at Garth's right.

Boyd sat beside Simon. But he learned his error when Sir Kenneth usurped that seat, curtly informing Boyd that his place was at the end of the table.

Tom Murray, arriving barely before the chaplain said the grace, saved Boyd from ignominy by guessing rightly that Sir Kenneth would not give up the place to him, either. With little choice, he gestured to Boyd to stay put and took the end seat.

After supper, as they left the table, Isabel said, "Thomas, did you perchance bring your lute with you?"

"Aye, madam," Tom replied, looking taken aback.

"We would enjoy hearing you play for us, if you will. After such a dreary day, doubtless we all want to enjoy the hall's warmth and comfort a little longer."

Tom went off to fetch his lute, and the others formed small groups as they had before the meal. Servants cleared its remains and dismantled the trestle.

Garth, glancing now and again at Amalie, was amused

and then a little disturbed to see her make it a point to ignore Boyd. She did it deftly at first but grew noticeably ruder to the man as he persisted in annoying her. She finally said something to put flames in his cheeks that shot all the way to his ears.

Deciding that enough was enough and she was going about the business all wrong, perhaps dangerously so, he approached her at the next opportunity and said, "Take a turn about the room with me, my lady, if you will be so kind. I want to consult your opinion on a small matter."

He half expected her to refuse, and when she did not, he suspected that she agreed only to annoy Boyd. Having no objection to that, he smiled and said, "What has that villain done to make you treat him so badly, lass? I'm astonished that the black looks you give him have not withered him to dust where he stands."

She chuckled as she met his gaze. The hazel depths of her eyes reflected the golden light of myriad candles that lit the room.

"He deserves those looks," she said. "But I do not mean to tell you what he said, sir. That he annoyed me is enough. What did *you* want to say to me?"

"Since he was clearly annoying you, I just thought you might appreciate the chance to walk away from him," he said.

"Well, you should not have interfered," she retorted. Any semblance of humor vanished in a blink as the golden lights turned to icy glints. "I *want* that odious man to know exactly how I feel."

The surge of anger caught Amalie herself by surprise, so it took a moment to see that Sir Garth's amiable smile had shifted just as quickly to a much harder look. His well-shaped jaw had tightened, his lips had pressed together, and the dimple at the left corner of his mouth had become much more pronounced than usual.

An unfamiliar sensation shot through her, a mixture of fear or wariness and something else that touched her core. Scarcely able to breathe, but feeling a strong urge to defend herself, she fought to find the right words—hastily.

"You see," she said, "I cannot count on Father to let me stay unwed. He promises he will, but with my mother and Simon both so resolute, I doubt he can hold out. So I mean to make Sir Harald change his mind instead, about wanting me."

"All you will accomplish by snubbing a scoundrel like Boyd is to make him relish the hunt more," he said without the slightest easing of that hard look.

Raising her chin, she said, "In faith, sir, you offend me. Do you mean to say he sees me as some sort of prey to be hunted?"

"I do, aye, and it should not offend you to hear the plain truth," he said. "One would hope you might learn from it."

"Then what is that truth, sir—your truth? Explain it to me."

"'Tis a simple fact of human nature that nearly all men view women as prey, lass. That is especially true of un-married men seeking wealthy wives."

"But I am no heiress," she protested, remembering guiltily as she did what Sir Iagan had told her Boyd ex-pected to gain as part of her dowry.

"Wealth or its lack won't matter if you treat Boyd with

such disdain," he said grimly. "He will just enjoy the chase more, and want you more. When you react to him so, you challenge him, just as you would if you were to fling down a gauntlet before him. No knight could resist such a challenge."

"I would remind you," she said coldly, "that *you* are the one over whom I keep tripping. Are you defining your own motives, sir, or Sir Harald's?"

The look he gave her then was murderous enough to shoot a thrill of fear through her from tip to toe.

"Amalie, Tom is back with his lute, and our mother would speak with you."

Startled, Amalie turned to find Rosalie at her side.

"I'll come at once, aye," she said. Without daring to look at Garth again, she hurried away with her sister to Lady Murray.

The ladies Sibylla and Susan both being proficient with the lute as well, and the company knowing a number of ballads in common, the evening turned into a musical one, making for a pleasant change. Despite the entertainment, Amalie was conscious of tension, but whether it stemmed from Garth's displeasure with her or Sir Harald's continued, unwanted attention, she was not sure.

The only sure thing was that she wanted to say goodnight to them all and go to bed. But when she slept, her dreams turned nightmarish, and twice she awoke abruptly, trembling, from dreams of the old mill near Elishaw. In the second one, she had fallen onto the floor, where icy shards of scattered grain poked her painfully.

One of the lass's smooth, bare arms lay across his belly. She leaned up on the other elbow and stroked back the stray lock of hair that always tumbled onto his forehead. Then her soft lips pressed against his, sending a shock of warm desire through him. He set his hands at her narrow waist and shifted her so her body lay along the length of him, her wonderfully soft breasts flattening against his chest.

She rubbed herself against him, moaned, and eased a hand down, seeking his cock. Wrapping warm fingers around it, she eased it between her soft nether lips.

He gasped, the candlelight vanished, and black terror filled him.

He was no longer in that pleasant bed but running downhill as fast as he could, pursued by a thousand armed men through pitch darkness that threatened to stifle him like a harsh and heavy cloak.

He could not see a thing, but the need to run faster increased. When the ground disappeared beneath him and he began to fall, he screamed in terror.

The landing was surprisingly soft, springy, and strangely sticky.

He tried to pull away, to find purchase beneath him, but the stuff into which he had fallen closed around him, cocooning him with strands that felt familiar to his touch. The thought that it was a spider's web struck hard, and as he wondered what size its occupant would be . . .

Garth woke to find himself sitting bolt upright in his bed, his hands clammy and his heaving gasps so loud that he feared half the household must hear them.

The Murray men prepared to depart the next morning soon after the household broke its fast, Simon to ride back to Lauder, the others to Elishaw.

As Amalie followed them from the dais into the entry hall with her mother and sister, Tom stopped, looked back, and said, "Rosalie, would you not rather go home with our lord father and me?" To Lady Murray he added, "She will only be underfoot at the Hall, madam. What say you?"

Amalie glanced at Simon, who looked at Rosalie. "What do you want, lass?"

"I am going to see Meg's new baby," she said. "Mother promised."

"I did promise her," Lady Murray said. "It was kind of you to think of her, Thomas, but she will be busy at the Hall. Some experience of a lying-in will be good for her. She won't be present at the birthing, of course. That would be unsuitable, and Meg would not like it. But she can see her new cousin. As for being underfoot," she added with heavy humor, "do you think me unable to prevent that?"

Tom hastily assured her that he had thought only of her convenience and Rosalie's amusement. Then he hurried upstairs.

Isabel said from the great-hall doorway, "I expect you will travel to Scott's Hall by way of Melrose Abbey tomorrow, will you not, madam?"

"Of course," Lady Murray said. "Simon has sent a man ahead to warn the abbot of our coming. We will spend one night in the guesthouse there."

"Then I will ride with you, if you do not object," Isabel said. "I had thought I might go next week, but it will be pleasant to travel with friends. Moreover, it will allow you to extend your visit with Amalie."

Only then did Amalie realize that the subject of her return to Elishaw had not arisen again. She doubted that her mother or Simon had given up the idea of marrying her to Sir Harald, but apparently they had realized it could do their cause no good for Lady Murray to drag her to Scott's Hall and then home.

Her mother's next words made things clearer: "Do your knights all travel with you when you leave home, madam?"

"Sir Kenneth will stay here with enough men to look after things. Sir Harald, Sir Garth, and the other men will be more than enough for this short journey."

"It will be especially pleasant to have Sir Harald along," Lady Murray said. "I find him quite charming. I have not spoken with Sir Garth Napier, however. I look forward to making his acquaintance."

Amalie glanced at Garth, who had walked up behind the princess in time to hear her announce that he and Sir Harald would accompany her to Melrose.

A thoughtful look entered his eyes as he shifted his gaze to Amalie.

Remembering their last exchange, she lifted her chin. He might be riding with their party, but he had better understand that his advice to anyone other than Isabel was both undesirable and unnecessary.

"Do you favor Melrose Abbey over Dryburgh, madam?" Lady Murray asked as they waited for the Murray men. "I prefer the latter. Such a beautiful setting."

"Yes, it is," Isabel said. "I prefer Melrose because my lord husband did."

"You speak of James Douglas, of course," Lady Murray said. "I do recall now that he lies buried in the church-

yard there. But you have remarried," she added with a
frown. "Do you continue to visit his grave?"

"Yes, I do," Isabel said. "James Douglas was the love
of my life, and until I can discover exactly how he died,
he will not rest in peace."

"She looks gey displeased," Rosalie whispered to
Amalie.

"Hush, dearling," Amalie murmured back. "It is painful
for her to speak of him, and we must respect her grief."

"But James Douglas has been dead two whole years!"

"Rosalie, what *are* you prattling about?" Lady Murray
demanded.

"Naught of any import, madam," Rosalie said easily.
"I was just teasing Amalie. I have missed her, so pray do
not scold me."

"Go and fetch your stitching, my dearling. You were
too lazy yesterday and must be more industrious today.
You know I do not tolerate idle hands."

"Aye, madam, I'll go at once," Rosalie said, casting a
droll look at Amalie.

Amalie watched her run upstairs and heard a commo-
tion as she disappeared from sight. Sir Iagan came down
almost at once afterward, shaking his head.

"Nearly bowled me over," he said with a smile.
"That bairn has more energy than is good for any young
woman."

His tone was indulgent, and Amalie realized that her
parents both treated Rosalie much more kindly than they
had treated her or Meg, or even their brothers. Not that
they did not indulge Simon and Tom, for neither could
do wrong now, it seemed, but their parents did not treat
either of them as dotingly as they did Rosalie.

The child had been only eleven when Amalie had left

Elishaw, and in many ways she did not seem older now. But she was beginning to be a woman, and her body and features showed signs of maturity, if her personality did not.

Sir Iagan came to Amalie and placed his hands on her shoulders. "Ye've grown into a beauty, lass. Ye do me proud, and 'tis glad I am to see it."

"Thank you, sir," she said doubtfully, recalling a time when men at Elishaw and elsewhere had termed the Murray daughters three of the homeliest lasses in the Borders. They had done so, however, only until Meg married. Now that she was wife to Buccleuch, who had a quick, fiery temper, the comments had ceased.

Her father squeezed her shoulders, planted a kiss on her lips, and turned to make his bow to Isabel. "I thank ye, madam, for your hospitality and wish ye a safe journey to Melrose. Ye'll be welcome at Elishaw whenever ye choose to come to us."

"Thank you, Sir Iagan," Isabel said with a smile. "I should thank you for your daughter's companionship these past months. She is a great comfort to me."

Simon and Tom came clattering down the stairs and led the way outside.

As Amalie moved to follow, a touch on her arm stopped her, and she turned to find Sir Garth gazing somberly down at her. Heat fired her cheeks, and she had an instant desire to flee, although she could not have explained why.

Garth saw the color flood her cheeks as he said, "Art still vexed with me?"

"I . . . I thought I had vexed you," she said. Then she squeezed her eyes shut as if she wished she had not spoken.

He almost chuckled but decided that would be tactless. Instead, he said, "I did not mean to anger you. I was just uneasy, because to tease a man can be dangerous."

"I don't tease. I *want* to discourage him." She looked around, but even Isabel had gone outside. "I should go, sir. My brothers and my father are leaving."

"I know. I also heard that when your mother travels to Melrose tomorrow to stay the night there, Isabel will go, too. Simon is taking his men back to Lauder with him, and your father will spare only a few to accompany her ladyship and your sister, so the princess is likely to send some of her own men with them when they go on to Scott's Hall."

"'Tis safe enough from Melrose to Rankilburn Glen, sir. No one would interfere with them," Amalie said.

"You may be right," he said. "But Sir Kenneth told me that as the princess always travels with a large escort, she seeks to see other women as well protected. It was he who told me she will want to send some of us along to Scott's Hall."

⁓

Amalie knew he was right. Isabel had done as much before, for other female travelers. It would disturb her to allow Lady Murray and Rosalie, who had been her guests, to depart with a smaller escort than the one with which they had arrived.

She said, "I wonder if Isabel will stay longer than usual at Melrose, then."

He shook his head. "She need not. We can divide our group and still protect both parties. It is only about twenty miles to the Hall from Melrose, after all."

"Is it? I've not traveled there from here."

"We'll follow Ettrick Water, which joins the Tweed at Melrose." He hesitated, then said, "I shan't return straightaway."

"You're going away? But where?"

"To Galloway."

A wave of disappointment struck her. She would miss him. Worse, if he went away and Sir Harald stayed, the latter would prove a nuisance. And if Simon tried to force the marriage he sought, she was not sure Isabel could protect her—especially if Simon acted under Fife's direction.

"What is it, lass? Don't say you'll miss me, for I shan't believe it."

"Are you leaving for good?"

"Nay, but I've learned that Fife is to journey through the Borders, and I'll warrant Archie knows nowt of it. So I thought I'd better go myself to warn him. Sithee, Fife tried once to seize Hermitage, and Archie will want to do all he can to prevent him from making such mischief again."

Realizing he did not know that her brothers had taken part in the attempt on Hermitage, and not wanting to tell him, she said, "Fife is Chief Warden of the Borders now. Doubtless he thinks it is both his right and his duty to meet with landowners and inspect their estates."

He grinned. "That may be what is in Fife's mind, but I can tell you that few Border lords will heed his orders if Archie issues contrary ones. Archie is still Warden of the West March and still considers himself lord of all three, despite anything Fife may think to the contrary. So Archie would not thank me for keeping this news to myself. I'll be gone only a few days, though."

Amalie was silent, assuring herself that his absence would mean nothing to her, that Simon would stay at Lauder and she could easily manage Sir Harald.

Although her disappointment lingered, it eased considerably when she realized that her awareness that Garth would ride all the way to Threave Castle in Galloway to warn Archie about Fife had banished the last lingering vestige of concern that he might somehow serve Fife.

Garth watched the expressions play across her fascinating face and wondered what she was thinking. She had looked near tears when he had said he was leaving. But then she had nearly smiled, so whatever had troubled her about his departure was nowt to what had pleased her.

Thus did the lass continue to disturb his thoughts, so his dream the night before had been both prophetic and a well-deserved warning. That she attracted him was patently obvious. It was equally obvious that if he continued to respond to that attraction, he would soon find himself in the suds one way or another.

Buccleuch's image stirred in his mind's eye then. When memory of the sticky web followed, he told himself firmly that he could not allow her to divert him more now, in any event, because it was important that he get word to Archie.

He had first learned of Fife's intent soon after the Murrays arrived, and had expected the first obstacle to warning Archie to be a lack of easy access to Isabel. In his position as serving knight, it was no part of his duty to approach her, let alone to request what might be lengthy discussion with her. Then it occurred to him that, as Kenneth was to stay at Sweethope, he would take charge of the journey to Melrose.

Midway through that afternoon, as he had confidently expected, Kenneth told him that Isabel wanted to see him.

"She'll be in the garden, lad. Go to her there."

Garth found her with all of her ladies including Amalie.

"You will take charge of my escort, sir," Isabel said.

She did not ask him to walk with her, however, so to keep her from dismissing him at once, he said, "I am honored, madam. I have traveled that way often to visit my kinsmen."

"I assumed that you had," she said. "I thought, too, that you might enjoy a brief visit at the Hall, so I mean to send you and some of our men with Lady Murray and Rosalie from Melrose. You will return here as soon as you see them safely arrived and have rested your men and the horses."

"Yes, madam." He hesitated.

"Was there something you wanted to add, sir?"

"There is, aye," he said. Unable to think how to phrase his request without stirring undue curiosity among the other ladies, he was relieved when she stood and suggested that perhaps they should walk.

"What is it?" she asked when they were beyond earshot.

"Fife plans to travel through the Borders, and as he is beginning here, I'm thinking Archie kens nowt about it. I'll need a few extra days to ride and tell him."

She nodded and asked a few questions but agreed that

Archie should know of Fife's plan. As he took his leave a few minutes later, his gaze met Amalie's.

When she looked wistful, as if she had decided after all to miss him, his loins stirred, and he realized that danger definitely lurked ahead.

Chapter 11

Amalie and the princess's other ladies kept busy that afternoon and much of the evening, preparing for her to depart the next day with Lady Murray.

As it was, they did not get off until the morning was half over. But that was due as much to thick fog as to Lady Murray's strong distaste for early rising.

At last, the fog dissipated, revealing high, hazy clouds. They were soon ready and mounted—except for Lady Murray, who preferred her horse litter.

She was comfortable in it, though, and the gillie who guided her horses was one of Elishaw's own. So Amalie expected few complaints.

Seeing Sir Harald, she grimaced, realizing only then that he would take charge of seeing them back to Sweethope while Sir Garth rode on to Galloway.

She tried to persuade herself that Sir Harald's presence would give her further opportunity to discourage him. However, since she did not want to spend any time in his company, that thought just depressed her.

With the added men from Elishaw, their cavalcade was larger than usual. But they set a good pace, despite the litter, and Isabel declared that they ought to reach the abbey comfortably by midafternoon.

Amalie spent the first hour riding beside Sibylla, enjoying her sunny good humor. But neither objected when Rosalie guided her pony alongside Amalie's and said, "You won't mind if I ride with you, I hope. It grows tedious riding by our lady mother. She dozes unless the pace grows too fast to suit her. Then she scolds, as if I ought to have prevented it."

Amalie chuckled. "I doubt she scolds you often, dearling. You seem to have a knack for managing her."

"She does not require managing," Rosalie said. "I know that you and Meg chafed under her strictures, but truly, she does not say such things to me. I'm more worried that she and our lord father will not *let* me marry than that they will press me to wed a man I do not know, or one I dislike, as they did with Meggie and have been trying to do with you."

Sibylla had considerately tightened her rein to let them draw ahead and talk privately. Even so, Amalie said only, "Our parents do seem very fond of you."

"I expect so," Rosalie said with a shrug. "They rarely tell me I should not do something I might want to do, as you did. Why did you say I should not ride with any man, not even Simon or Tom? That seemed strange to me."

Realizing she had to choose her words carefully, and aware that Sibylla might well overhear them, Amalie said, "I was just noticing how pretty you are becoming, I expect. I worry that someone might try to take advantage of you. They do, you know." Remembering what Garth had said, she added, "Sithee, love, men enjoy the chase and see pretty young ladies as prey to hunt."

Rosalie grinned impishly. "But that sounds amusing, and our *brothers* would not hunt me. Moreover, I like to ride with them. Tom is always merry and makes me laugh. And Simon teaches me interesting things."

"Simon rides with you?" Amalie could not recall his ever riding with her or Meg unless the whole Murray family traveled together.

"Aye, sure, whenever he chances to be near Elishaw, he stops with us for a day or two. When he does, he takes me riding. And Tom has been helping our lord father run the estate for some months now. He is frequently too busy to ride with me, but he does whenever he can, and it gives me pleasure."

Recalling belatedly how little she had known of men, or anything else, at thirteen, Amalie said carefully, "Then you would be wise to use Simon and Tom to practice understanding men. Our father may be as helpful with that as our brothers, but you should learn to observe them all closely, Rosalie."

"What *do* you mean?"

Amalie took another tack. "You will be visiting the royal court in Edinburgh in a year or two, and houses and castles of kinsmen and friends. In such company you will meet all manner of young men, and some not so young. By learning to recognize unusual behavior in our own menfolk, you will train yourself to judge men you don't know. 'Tis much wiser than to assume that all men are as trustworthy as our father."

"Or Simon and Tom," Rosalie said thoughtfully. "I begin to understand. But they are always much the same with me, so I don't know what to look for."

"Simon has a wicked temper," Amalie said. "If you don't know that, you have been fortunate in never having stirred it. Father, too, gets angry quickly. Indeed, each of them expects always to get his own way, so I venture to suppose you have not yet crossed any of them."

"Or they just like me better than they like you," Rosalie retorted saucily.

"Rosalie—"

"Oh, don't scold," she said, laughing. "I meant only that whilst there were three of us at home, and I too young for anyone to count, you and Meg just drew their anger. You especially were accustomed to say whatever came into your head."

"Was I?" It was hard to remember being so carefree.

"Well, you did stop doing that shortly before you went away with Meg. Indeed, you grew unnaturally quiet then, I thought. But you can also be stubborn about getting your own way, so I warrant you just annoyed them more than I do."

Having said as much as she dared, and not wanting to encourage further discussion of her own habits, Amalie said, "I do tend to irritate Simon, don't I? Even so, love, it will be good practice for you to learn the signs of even the smallest changes in their moods, so that you can better judge the many young men who will pursue you from the moment they clap eyes on you."

Rosalie giggled. "Do you truly think they will?"

Amalie said sincerely, "I am sure of it."

Their route took them along the river Tweed, and although Amalie kept her eyes on the track ahead, she managed to stay aware of where Sir Harald and Garth were riding. She soon realized she would have little opportunity to snub Sir Harald, because Garth had sent him to lead the main body of men, well behind them.

Four men-at-arms preceded their party, but Isabel did not like riding through clouds of dust, so she never allowed more than that to ride ahead unless they'd had word of potential danger threatening an area she passed through.

As the knight in command, Garth rode with the forward party, and Amalie enjoyed watching how easily he controlled his mount. Occasionally, he dropped back near the princess but whether by Isabel's choice or his, she could not tell.

The ladies Averil and Nancy took turns, as usual, one riding beside Isabel while the other followed with either the lady Susan or Sibylla. Nancy was now with Susan, and Sibylla soon returned to ride three abreast with Amalie and Rosalie.

They arrived at Melrose Abbey just a little later than Isabel had expected.

Before they saw the abbey itself, on the north bank of the river Tweed just east of where it met Ettrick Water, they had skirted broad pasturelands filled with baaing, bleating sheep, and passed through orchards and across fields containing pigs or cattle. The abbey lands were extensive.

As they rode downhill across a flower-strewn meadow bright with color, Amalie gazed sadly at the charred and broken walls of the once magnificent abbey. Before its destruction, it had occupied the site for over 250 years.

Much of its stonework remained, and the monks had restored some buildings, but the sight reminded her yet again of why Scots hated the English so.

When they entered the graveled yard outside what had

once been the cloister, the abbot appeared in the doorway of the chapter house in his long, unbleached, and undyed Cistercian habit. Its hood was down, revealing his long, darkly tanned face and wispy, tonsured hair.

The damage, now that they could see into the inner precinct, was more appalling. In the old days, Isabel had told Amalie, the Cistercians had not allowed anyone within the abbey's wall. But of late, that strict rule had eased. With the wall still broken in many areas and its cloister destroyed, the inner precinct now began at the chapter house and was marked with a low stone wall of its own.

Much of its area was charred rubble, but the chapter house and other restored buildings were clearly habitable and occupied.

The restored guesthouse stood within the damaged outer wall, not far from the graveyard but some distance outside the marked precinct.

As the abbot moved with dignity to greet the princess, and Garth quickly dismounted to assist her, Rosalie looked around in dismay.

"Faith," she exclaimed. "Whatever happened here?"

Isabel glanced back as she dismounted and said, "The English burned the abbey five years ago. As you can see yonder, the villains destroyed the beautiful abbey kirk, even knocking down its walls. Its rebuilding alone, they say, will take a quarter of a century or more."

"But to have destroyed all this is sacrilege!" Rosalie protested.

The abbot said, "Aye, my lady, but all is as God wills." Returning to Isabel, he said, "Your men will camp by the river as always, princess. If they require food or other assistance, they need only ask. We want them to be comfortable."

"Thank you," Isabel said. "The plantings are coming along well this year."

The abbey fields and tidy orchards had been burned, as well. But the monks and lay brothers had soon replanted them and now, five years later, most of the trees were heavy with fruit.

Recalled from her musing by a word from Lady Averil, Amalie dismounted quickly without assistance and hurried to the guesthouse to attend to her duties.

The princess's ladies enjoyed an early supper in the hall of the guesthouse. The food that lay brothers in hoodless, undyed robes provided for them was plain but sufficient. Their own men had set up their encampment and were cooking their meal over their own fires.

After supper, as the lay brothers bore empty platters away and dismantled the trestle tables, Isabel excused herself. "You will forgive me," she said, "if I leave you now to visit the graveyard."

"May I walk with you part of the way?" Amalie asked.

"I'd enjoy your company," Isabel said, raising a hand when Susan stood, looking eager to join them. "The rest of you may amuse yourselves until I return."

"With permission, madam, Rosalie and I will retire," Lady Murray said. "We must be off in the morning, and Sir Garth has said he wants to make an early start."

Amalie made no comment then, other than to bid her mother and sister goodnight. But as she and Isabel walked along the tidy, stone-lined pathway to the graveyard, she said, "Sir Garth had better say his prayers tonight if he expects to get my lady mother off to an early start."

Isabel chuckled. "Is your mother always a lie-abed sort?"

"She did not used to be," Amalie said. "But even be-fore Meg married, she had begun to take her days in a more leisurely way. She is still quick to criticize any error, though, so I am certain she still keeps Elishaw run-ning smoothly."

"Indeed, I should think she would," Isabel agreed as they reached the little wicket gate in the low stone fence that surrounded the graveyard. "You will not want to come further with me, so I'll take leave of you here. Do not wait for me," she added. "You are safe on any grounds near the abbey. I often roam through the orchards or the meadows. The river path is pleasant, too."

The graveyard being nearer the orchards than the river, and a break in the abbey's wall inviting her to go that way, Amalie decided to walk up to the nearest one, where she soon found pear trees bearing ripe fruit.

Certain the monks would not object, she picked a ripe one, wiped it on her skirt, and bit into it. The juice ran down her chin, making her grin. With no one looking, she did not hesitate to wipe it off with her sleeve.

She wandered happily amid the trees, enjoying the peaceful evening twilight.

The moon peeked over the northeastern horizon as she was thinking she ought to return to the others. But as she turned back the way she had come, she saw that Isabel was still in the graveyard, sitting quietly on a stone bench.

Not wanting to disturb her, Amalie skirted the abbey wall instead and found a path heading toward the river. Moonlight painted the water silver, and to her right, below where the track they had followed curved around the abbey wall, small fires dotted the hillside above the riverbank.

The moon seemed to rise quickly. It was nearly full and cast enough light for her to see that her path crossed the track ahead and continued to the river.

At the intersection, she did not hesitate. She was not ready yet to give up her peaceful evening and rejoin the other women.

A soft, warm breeze blew toward her from the river. The path was smooth and well tended, the moonlight on the river magical. The low *"hoo-hoo"* of an owl, clearly calling to her, gave the increasingly dark landscape a delicious eeriness.

She fixed her eyes on the sparkling flow of water and breathed in the herbal scents of the trees and the low shrubbery along the riverbank.

A wide grassy patch between two large, shadowy clumps of trees and bushes beckoned her. She stepped off the path, already curving to follow the river's course, and walked toward the water. She could see several ducks—coots by their sounds and, by shape, at least two hooded mergansers. They floated in the moonlight as if it were day, riding the river's slow but powerful current. As she moved nearer, a large figure stepped out of the deepest shadow of the shrubbery to her left.

She opened her mouth to protest his springing up again, for although his back was to the moon and his face shadowed, she had not one second's doubt who it was.

Before she could speak, he raised a finger to his lips and then pointed.

Obligingly, she kept silent and followed the line of his pointing finger to the opposite bank, where two small deer drank peacefully from the river, their slender forelegs splayed at water's edge, their hindquarters higher on the bank.

Warm delight filled her soul as she watched them. They were beautiful, and the moonlight dappling them with silvery splashes as overhanging shrubbery moved in the soft breeze made them more so.

She waited until they had drunk their fill and vanished before she said without looking at him, "Must you keep springing up like this? It is only by God's grace that you did not frighten me witless."

"Take care, lass, lest I return a similar rebuke that you're sure to find tiresome."

She caught her lower lip between her teeth, realizing that at such an hour even the tolerant Isabel would say that she ought to be inside with the other ladies. She also sent a prayer of thanks aloft that her mother and Rosalie had retired.

"I see that I need say no more," he said. "I might do so anyway under other circumstances, but in troth, I'm glad to see you."

His words stirred something deep inside her, an odd mixture of delight and panic. Her teeth pressed harder on her lip until she realized she was hurting herself, and licked it to soothe the hurt.

He started to say more, stopped, then cleared his throat and began again. "I want to speak to the princess, but she was still in the graveyard when last I looked, and I did not want to seem to hover."

"Nay," Amalie said. "She does not like people to watch her there. I walked with her to the gate and then went for a stroll in the orchard. She told me to."

"But now you are here," he said, putting a hand on her left shoulder. His touch was gentle, but the warmth of his hand penetrated the sleeve of her tunic and seemed to continue right through the rest of her, making her feel warm all over.

"Why did you want to speak to her?" She was astonished that the question came out clearly, almost calmly, because she could scarcely think.

Part of her wanted to pull away from that hand and run from the magical moonlight and the beauty of the river, and certainly from him. But another part wanted to stay, to find out what he would do next.

"I want to kiss you," he said softly.

Garth saw her eyes widen. In the moonlight, her pupils were enormous, looking like the dark pools bards and seanachies sometimes mentioned when they recited romantic ballads. Her lips were parted and looked swollen, as if they would welcome kissing, but she looked startled, uncertain, almost frightened.

He had been astonished to see her, and his first impulse had been to stride out and confront her, even shake her for walking about all alone in the night. Did she not realize that an encampment full of lusty men sprawled nearby? Not that he or doubtless even the odious Boyd would allow such a thing to happen, but if the lass never trusted any man, what the devil had possessed her to risk it?

His right hand still rested on her left shoulder.

Even so, the thought of grabbing her, nay, touching her in any way, stirred his body to a hunger that was unlike any it had revealed before. When she'd touched that pointed little tongue of hers to her lips, he'd had all he could do not to pull her to him with both hands and kiss her senseless.

Even now, even though he knew he'd be wise to go slowly with her, he had to fight the temptation to teach her that her actions had consequences.

But his admission that he wanted to kiss her had not turned her away.

Nor did she look unwilling.

Still, the part of him that kept urging him to protect her warned him now that he could easily misstep.

These thoughts sped swiftly through his mind in the split second before he said, "I won't if you don't want me to."

Her lips parted more. Her wee tongue peeped out again.

He bent closer, looked her in the eye.

"You'll have to say aye or nay, lass. I know what I want, and if you tease me, I'll throw caution aside, but—"

She leaned forward and lightly kissed his lips.

When she would have jumped back, he stopped her simply by firming the hand that still rested on her shoulder and pulling her back. Had she resisted, he might have released her. He would never know though, because she did not.

Although her own behavior astonished her, Amalie could not have resisted had she wanted to. But the plain truth was that she did not want to. Nor did she protest or resist when his free hand came to her other shoulder and one strong arm slid around her to pull her closer to him.

He had straightened enough that she had to tilt her face up to his, but she did not mind that either. His lips were soft against hers for a brief time, then not soft at all but hungry and demanding.

She had a momentary sense of danger, a qualm that might have been distrust. But as if some fiber of her body had warned his of that qualm, the hard, muscular arm across her shoulders eased upward at the very moment she might have tried to pull away. Instead of doing so, her body relaxed, even pressed a little toward his.

He moaned softly but eased his hold more, then ended the kiss with a sigh, making her look at him in surprise and—dared she admit it, even to herself?—surging disappointment.

"What is it?" They both said the words in the same breath.

His eyes danced. "We should go."

"Is that why you sighed so heavily?"

"Nay, that was because I did not want to stop, but I recalled your lack of experience and also where we are. The good brothers would be wroth with us if they should find us here like this. The abbot might even order me to leave."

She felt a shiver up her spine, realizing that she ought never to have let him kiss her. She did not care a whit for any lay brother or even the abbot himself, because she knew that no one at Melrose would do anything to upset Isabel.

And Isabel knew her. She would know that whatever Amalie had done, she had done out of innocent foolishness. But she had also led Garth to believe she would welcome his advances and thereby had done both him and herself a vast disservice.

Men—gentlemen and noblemen—who did this sort of thing with young ladies of good family expected those ladies, or their families, to demand that they marry. Garth had annoyed her as often as he had made her laugh, but she liked him even so. And she had not been able to resist the chance to learn what it would be like to kiss him. To have done so under such circumstances, though, was unfair.

She could not marry him or anyone else.

Before her yearning to kiss him again could provide her with reason to keep silent, she said, "My behavior just now may have given you the wrong impression, sir. I will not marry you. I have not changed my mind about never marrying."

He chuckled and gave her shoulders a squeeze. "Sakes, lass, I was counting on that. God knows you have made your position clear enough on that point."

Her right hand tensed to strike, but common sense intervened before she did. Not only were his hands still on her shoulders but she was the one at fault. He had asked for permission before he had kissed her.

That made his behavior even worse. But, faith, she had kissed him first!

Nevertheless, the chill in her voice should have been perfectly audible to him when she pushed his hands from her shoulders, stepped back, and said, "If you wanted to speak to Isabel, you are too late. The moon is shining down on the entire graveyard now, and she is no longer there."

⁓

Garth was aware of the chill in her tone and the touch of injury as well. He was sorry he had hurt her, and sorry, too, when she stepped back. He had responded instinctively, recognizing the likelihood that if he disclaimed interest in more than kissing her, she would be less likely to withdraw further from him. As experienced in the chase as he was, and as skilled with skittish creatures, he knew that a touch of rejection was likely to reassure her and would not increase her apprehension.

He liked her too much to risk letting her think for more than a moment that he expected to marry her. She was amusing and interesting, even fascinating at times. And the fact that she was so determined never to marry presented a uniquely intriguing challenge. The plain fact was that he had no desire yet to entice any woman into marriage. He had been a villain to kiss her, but thankfully, he had stopped before he did anything more. Sakes, the kiss had been as innocent as a kiss could be. He had barely tasted her soft lips. They had tasted of pear juice.

"I can see that Isabel has gone in, lass," he said. "I did not intend to accost her in the graveyard, in any event, or as she returned. But the monks would frown on my entering the guesthouse without an invitation from her."

"So you want me to seek her out for you."

"If you are not too angry with me."

"I am not angry, sir. I know it was my fault as much as yours. I don't know what I was thinking, but they do say that a full moon makes people behave badly."

"The moon is past full, lass, and you did not misbehave," he said gently. "But I'd be grateful if you would find Isabel for me. I can wait outside the door, and she can invite me into that wee anteroom that serves as an entry hall for the guesthouse. The abbot will expect even a princess to have a chaperone with her whilst she talks with a man, though. So ask her if you may perform that service. I'd as lief not have to reveal my plans to anyone else."

"You never said *why* you want to speak to her. Did you not tell her in the garden that you mean to go to Threave?"

"I did, aye, but we talked in haste, and it has puzzled me how to talk to her without revealing to others that I'm acting as more than a serving knight. But if you will serve as my messenger now, and as chaperone if need be . . ." He waited.

"I can do that," she said. "But what if one of the lay brothers or monks or the abbot sees us before I get inside?"

He grinned. "Why, I shall tell them that the youngest and naughtiest of Princess Isabel's ladies apparently failed to notice that darkness had fallen and was lost in thought by the river when I came upon her there. So, performing one of my duties, I am returning her to the guesthouse with a stern warning not to do such a foolish thing again. I shall look very irked, I think, to have been put to such trouble."

"What a good thing you told me you never tell lies, sir. In troth, I am not sure what else I should call that, but I am sure—"

"The only part that might be untrue is the part about being irked, although even that will be true if you continue with that thought," he said. "I did meet you in just such a way, and if you have not realized yet that you ought not to have wandered so long or so far, Molly-lass, I can certainly make that fact plainer to you."

She grimaced. "Perhaps we should go now."

"Perhaps we should."

Still savoring pear juice, he did not trust himself to stay longer with her.

Chapter 12

⸺

Amalie was not sure if she was more annoyed with Garth or with herself, but she did not want to pursue that thought, so they walked silently to the guesthouse.

As they approached the front door, she wondered with a rush of anxiety if it might be bolted. But when he reached past her and lifted the latch, it opened easily.

"I'll wait here," he murmured. "If she's gone to bed, just come and tell me."

But Isabel was still in the guesthouse hall, sitting by the little fire with the ladies Averil, Nancy, and Sibylla.

"Bless us, Amalie, are you just coming in?" Nancy asked.

"Aye, my lady," Amalie admitted, avoiding the lady Averil's gimlet eye but sure that the older woman would have something to say to her later.

"Come and warm yourself by the fire," Sibylla said.

"Thank you, but I'm not cold." Making her curtsy to Isabel, she said, "May I trouble you for a private word, madam?"

"You may, aye," Isabel said, getting up and motioning the others to stay where they were. "Shall we go into the anteroom?"

"Please," Amalie said, stepping aside to let her go first.

In the anteroom, Isabel said quietly, "Is it Sir Garth? I know he is cousin to your good-brother and friendly to you, so mayhap he gave you a message for me."

"He did, aye," Amalie admitted. "I know I should have come in sooner—"

Isabel shook her head. "Don't worry about that now. What is the message?"

"He is on the step outside," Amalie said. "He told me you can invite him into this room if I stay with you, and that he will not mind if I hear what he has to say."

"As both Averil and Sibylla have long ears, I think it would be wiser for me to step outside to speak with him," Isabel said. "It will be wiser yet if you stay here to intercept anyone who may come looking for me."

Although Amalie could not imagine how she would stop either a determined Lady Averil or even Sibylla from doing exactly as she pleased, she nodded and watched as Isabel stepped outside and pulled the door to behind her.

Half-expecting Garth to open it again, to see if she had her ear against it, Amalie stayed away. But when he did not, she wished she'd had the nerve to listen, because he'd still not said just why he wanted to speak with Isabel.

Surely, she told herself, they had already consulted about James Douglas's death, and Will's, too, because Isabel would willingly discuss with anyone her certainty that Fife was behind both tragedies.

Just as surely, the princess knew nothing of what Amalie had overheard at Scone. Had Isabel known that Fife had discussed a possible murder plot, she would not have kept that knowledge to herself. All of her ladies would have heard about it.

What if Garth had learned something more, though, something that he believed made it his duty to tell Isabel that someone had overheard such a plot? What if he feared that Douglas or even the King was Fife's intended victim? Such a fear would certainly give him cause to ride all the way to Galloway to talk with Douglas. It would also explain his need to talk to Isabel now.

But if he did mention the plot to her, she would demand details. Specifically, she would want to know *who* had overheard that conversation at Scone.

What, Amalie wondered with increasing dread, if Garth identified her?

She took a step toward the door just as it opened and Isabel slipped back inside and shut it again.

"No one troubled you?" she said.

"Nay, you were gey quick," Amalie said, trying to read her expression.

"Mainly, he just wanted to tell me that you know why he's here and where he's going, because he'd asked you not to tell anyone and knew you'd keep silent. In any event, he said, it was *his* duty to let me know he'd told you. And so it was."

"Aye," Amalie said, struggling to hide her relief, hoping she looked as if she did not care what he did, and assuring herself that she must look as if that were the case, because it was. She didn't care, and wouldn't, no matter what he did or said.

"You look tired, my dear," Isabel said. "I am going up in a few minutes, but Averil and Nancy will look after me. You may as well go straight to bed."

"Will the lady Averil not be vexed that I was out too long?"

"I won't let her bite," Isabel said with a smile. "Sir Garth was glad to find someone he could ask to approach me. And I'm grateful to have had speech with him. The only thing I cannot like is his leaving us in Sir Harald's charge."

Amalie grimaced.

"Just so," Isabel said. "Your mother's comments and Simon's friendship with him would have made it clear that he's the man they want you to marry even if I hadn't guessed as much from the attention he pays you—and your obvious dislike. So, although Sir John sent him, Boyd is Fife's man. Do you not agree?"

"He is, aye, so mayhap you should dismiss him," Amalie said hopefully.

"I'd like to," Isabel said with a sigh. "But knowing that he serves Fife, I can watch him. If I dismiss him, my annoying brother will just be cleverer next time and send someone I'm less likely to suspect."

"It is difficult."

"Aye, so go to bed, and I'll do likewise, and tomorrow will be a new day."

⁓

Thursday morning dawned in an impenetrable blanket of fog that covered all of Melrose and doubtless, Amalie thought, dashed Garth's hopes for an early start.

In fact, none of the other ladies descended to the hall for breakfast much before Lady Murray and Rosalie appeared. The two had rested well, though, and announced themselves ready to depart as soon as they had broken their fast.

As they all ate, Amalie kept an uneasy eye on the lady Averil, but the older woman just reminded her it was her turn, and Susan's, to make the princess's bed.

By the time everyone went outside, the fog had dissipated and the sun shone brightly in a cerulean sky. Wispy haze rose from the yard, where Lady Murray's horse litter awaited her.

The men who would accompany them to Rankilburn stood ready as well.

Garth escorted her ladyship to the litter and helped Rosalie mount her pony, while one of the other men assisted Lady Murray's woman in mounting hers.

After seeing his charges settled, Garth returned to take leave of the princess.

"We are ready, madam," he said with a bow. When she nodded, he turned to Amalie and said, "Have you any messages for your sister, my lady?"

"My mother and Rosalie will say all that is necessary, sir. But I would count it a favor if you'd seek out Jock's Tammy and Sym Elliot, and give them my regards."

His eyebrows shot upward, and he said with a teasing smile, "I hope you are not setting me this task to bring Buccleuch's wrath down on me."

"They are just friends of mine. You'll be doing nothing improper."

"Indeed, I have met them both, Sir Garth," Isabel said. "Oh, and also, I have decided that you should take Sir Harald with you, so he can lead my men back to me here. It does not suit my dignity to return home with only half my usual escort, or to let my men travel without an experienced knight to lead them."

"As you wish, madam."

Just four words, but Amalie could see that the princess's decision annoyed him. He did not want Sir Harald any more than Amalie or Isabel did. But if someone had to have the horrid man, Amalie was glad it was Garth.

As he bowed again and turned away, his jaw tightened until the dimple beside his mouth showed clearly.

She glanced at the princess to see that her eyes were twinkling.

Suppressing her own relief, Amalie said, "I think he doesn't want Sir Harald."

"I can see that," Isabel replied. "Well, I don't want Sir Harald either. I have decided that I especially don't want Sir Harald in charge of our party when we return to Sweethope Hill."

Amalie wondered how anyone would prevent that, since Garth was going to Galloway, but she did not ask for clarification. She got on well with Isabel, but the princess's tolerance even for those she liked could turn in a blink to royal hauteur if one annoyed her. To question her on any point was to tread on thin ice.

In any event, Lady Murray was waving, so Amalie excused herself and went to bid her mother and Rosalie farewell. She also reminded them, as she had at breakfast, to send word of the birth as soon as it happened.

"To be sure we will," Rosalie said. "I can hardly wait to see the new bairn. Meg is certain it will be another wee laddie, but I want a niece."

"I warrant Meg and Wat will be happy with either," Amalie said.

Lady Murray said austerely, "They will accept God's will as we all must. And you, Amalie, would do well to remember that a good daughter obeys those in authority over her. She also does all she can to ensure her family's security."

"I know you mean well, madam, but my father promised me that I need not marry where I cannot be happy. I believe he meant it, too, because he also said he does not like the notion of dowering me as the Governor desires."

"Did he? We shall see about that."

"Then you approve of dowering me with a sizeable bit of Elishaw land."

"Land?" She frowned. "Do you mean to say that is what Fife expects?"

"He does, aye. I thought you knew," Amalie added mendaciously.

"I expect I did," her ladyship said. "One does not recall every detail, I fear."

Amalie left it at that and bade them farewell, satisfied that her mother had *not* known, and hoping she cared more about the land than Sir Iagan thought she did. If not, the only thing to do was pray that he would continue to hold his ground.

When Garth turned, caught her eye, and waved, she waved back. That Sir Harald also waved—and might mistakenly have believed that she had waved to him—was tiresome. But at least he was *not* staying at Melrose.

Isabel then announced to everyone that, rather than return to Sweethope with only half an escort, she would await the others' return. Sir Garth, she said, had told her they might be back as soon as Friday night but would certainly be there by Saturday midday at the latest.

The time passed slowly. The weather remained fair, and the steady murmur of the nearby river was soothing. The men hunted and fished, avoiding noisier activities that might displease their hosts. So the respite at Melrose was peaceful and—as Susan Lennox complained—downright boring.

"We might as well be cloistered nuns," Susan said Friday afternoon. "The horses must rest, so we cannot ride. The monks will not talk to us even to say good morning. And the men do not want us walking farther west than a few steps toward the Ettrick Water or farther east than the first bend in the river without a proper escort. And since, by proper, they mean several men, we'd make a spectacle."

Agreeing with her for once, Amalie could only remind her that Isabel had suggested the others might return that very night.

"Aye, sure, but even if they do, I warrant they'll want to rest their own horses longer than just overnight, and I don't like this place. It is too quiet."

Amalie knew that Susan thought Sweethope Hill House was too quiet, too. Indeed, Susan thought anyplace not teeming with eligible men was too quiet. She had once admitted that she'd joined the princess's household believing they would live at court and enjoy amusements that had been common before the old King died.

The princess detested court gatherings, although she had enjoyed them before James Douglas's death, *if* James could attend them. But Sir John Edmonstone enjoyed the rowdier ones far too much for her taste, and she enjoyed them not at all.

In any event, Isabel and her ladies had to wait until midday Saturday for the men to return. When they did, Amalie was astonished to see Garth leading them.

Sir Harald rode beside him, of course. But Sir Harald did not loom as large as he would have by himself. He would not lead the princess's party home, either.

"I bring messages for you, Lady Amalie," Garth said as he strode to meet the princess. "No bairn has arrived yet, but mayhap Princess Isabel will allow you to walk with me later so I can relay the rest of the news to you."

"Indeed, you may, sir," Isabel said as she cast Amalie a droll look. "But do stroll with me now toward the graveyard, for I have not paid my visit yet today. You must tell me how you fared and how soon we can go home to Sweethope."

"We can return this afternoon if you like, madam," he said. "The sumpter ponies are rested, because Lady Murray and Rosalie traveled with their own. And the lads' horses will do well enough if we do not push them too hard."

"There is no hurry, sir," she said. "But come now, and we will discuss it."

Amalie watched them go with a sigh. The lay brothers were setting out the midday meal, so the likelihood of enjoying a stroll of longer than five minutes or so before they sat down to it was small if one existed at all.

Lady Averil said, "Stop gawking at them, Amalie. You should be tidying yourself for dinner, not standing there like a post."

"Yes, my lady."

She hurried away, visited the garderobe, tidied herself, and hurried back downstairs, only to find that they had not yet returned. Since Isabel also wanted to visit James's grave, Amalie wondered if the lay brothers would delay dinner for her.

But Isabel had noted the time. She and Garth returned just as the bell rang for dinner, with the news that they would all depart Sunday morning after prayers.

Amalie ate silently, wondering why Garth had not

ridden to Threave. Galloway lay sixty miles away at the west end of the Borders, so she knew he had not ridden there and back in just two full days. Curiosity stirred impatience, but she managed to contain both until the ladies finished eating and Isabel sent for him.

To assuage any concern the monks or abbot might have at seeing a man and a maid walking along the river path, the princess had also sent for two of Garth's men to follow them at a discreet distance. That the men were amused to have drawn such a duty was evident, but a frown from Garth wiped the smiles off their faces.

"Why did you not go to Threave?" Amalie asked as soon as they started walking toward the river path.

"Because Boyd was with me, of course. The others would have said nowt to him about my activities. And Isabel had said she would tell him I was attending to family business if he asked about me here."

"Why did you not say the same thing to him, then?" she asked.

He gave her a look. "I told you, lass, I do not tell lies. If the business I am on is family business, it is Douglas family business and that of the princess. If Isabel were to say only what she had decided to say, even she would not be lying unless she called it Napier or Scott family business. And she wouldn't do that."

"So the Douglas will not learn about Fife's progress through the Borders?"

"I am not the only one capable of delivering that message," he said. "Your friend Jock's Wee Tammy is taking it. Don't look so surprised, swee—" He broke off with a sudden coughing spell that made her look at him in concern.

"I did not know that you knew Tammy. Are you all right, sir?"

"Aye, sure." He cleared his throat. "That I know Tam should not surprise you. Buccleuch *is* my cousin. I've visited Scott's Hall any number of times, as well as Wat's beloved peel tower in the buck's cleuch from which his title derives."

"We lived there after Meg married him," she said. "They did not remove to Scott's Hall until after his father died and Wat became Laird of Buccleuch."

"Aye, well, he agreed to send Tam to talk to Archie," Garth said. "But I needed to talk to Tam before he went, to deliver your messages to him and to Sym Elliot, who was away for the day, as well as to be sure in my own mind that Tam had my messages for Archie clear in his."

"Messages? What else besides Fife's Border progress?" she asked. Then she immediately wished she had not, sure that he would snub her curiosity.

He said, "One of Will's men told me sometime after I'd left Threave that he'd seen the chap Will named as his killer, at Edmonstone. I went there to find him, but no one there knew the name. It occurred to me that Will's man could help me find him, so I told Tam to ask Archie to bring him along when he comes."

"What is the man's name—the one you suspect?"

"Ben Haldane."

"Does the Douglas not know Haldane if Will's men now serve him?"

"Nay, because Will took on many new lads before he sailed to Königsberg. He wanted men who were as hot for adventure as he was."

They talked about Scott's Hall then until they reached the confluence of the Ettrick Water with the Tweed. The waters were turbulent there, with one flow crashing into the other, so they stood a few minutes to enjoy it. But with the two men-at-arms looking on, they had no reason to linger and soon started back.

The rest of the afternoon and evening passed quickly, and Sunday morning they departed after prayers without seeing the abbot or a monk. Two lay brothers served the ladies' breakfast, guided their prayer service, and then saw them off.

Their journey passed without incident, as did the next two days. Amalie, busy with her duties, saw little of Garth and nothing of Sir Harald, who apparently had chosen to take his meals for a time with the men-at-arms in their dormer hall.

She did encounter Sir Harald late Wednesday afternoon.

Having spent all morning and half the afternoon with Susan, inspecting the princess's winter clothing, sorting garments that needed attention from those that did not, and setting others aside for discard, Amalie had decided to reward herself for a big job well done by taking a brisk walk down to Eden Water and back.

Returning to the house through the front garden, she had shifted her thoughts to what she would wear for supper that evening. Footsteps behind made her turn with a smile, expecting to see that Garth had sprung up again.

Instead she faced Sir Harald, who returned her smile with a knowing grin and said, "Well, lass, you do look pleased to see me for once. I suppose you must have missed me these past few days. But I shall be supping with you tonight, so you should smile again."

"You are too familiar, sir, and you assume too much," she said, striving to keep her anger to herself. Life with her brothers had taught her that letting any tormentor see her anger gave that tormentor entirely too much satisfaction. She added crisply, "I thought you were one of the other ladies, that's all."

"You're a dreadful liar, lass, so don't try it with me after we're married. I'd take a switch to an untruthful wife just as I would to an untruthful serving wench."

"Now you are offensive, sir. You have no right to address me in such a manner and can do yourself no good thereby. Indeed, you make too much of what others may have told you, because my father has told me I need not marry you," she added, fervently hoping that she could count on Sir Iagan to keep his word.

Not looking at all worried, Sir Harald said, "Does he say that? I expect, then, that he will not make the final decision in this matter."

"No one else is entitled to make that decision, except me," she snapped.

"Watch your tone, lass," he said. "Sharpness does not become you, and you must be aware of your brothers' opinion of you. I doubt they will expect me to treat you with more than common civility."

A chill shot up her spine at those words, but she said grimly, "You overstep with every word you utter. Take care that I do not complain of you to the princess."

"Dare you do that? Does the princess know as much about you as I do?"

"She knows *everything* about me," Amalie declared, raising her chin but glad for once that she was not speaking the truth.

"Boyd, Sir Kenneth wants you. You should not be dallying here with her ladyship when you still have duties to perform."

Never had she been so glad to hear Garth's voice. That Harald Boyd was *not* glad to hear it was evident, which pleased her even more.

~~~~~

From the stable doorway, Garth had seen Boyd hurrying after Amalie and had followed as soon as he could without drawing undue attention to himself or to them. He had seen her turn and smile, then frown. And he had likewise noted her increasing irritation. His temper had stirred right along with hers.

Now, having banished Boyd, and glad that Kenneth had looked for him when he had, he said, "What did that feckless cush say to irk you so?"

"What is a cush? I've not heard that word before."

He grimaced, recognizing her usual diversionary attempt, but he said, "Around here, it just means a low, useless person. Now, what did he say?"

She opened her mouth as if she were about to let loose a stream of complaint but stopped before a word had left her tongue. Then, looking rueful, she said, "He just treats me with infuriating familiarity. I wanted to slap him."

"Don't do that, lass, especially if you are alone with him, as you just were."

"But ladies often slap gentlemen who forget their manners."

"If they are wise, they do so only if others are nearby and able to make the . . . uh . . . gentleman think twice about retaliating."

"You told me yourself that I should have clouted Simon, and Sir Harald is more puffed up in his own conceit than Simon could ever be."

"Sakes, what *did* Boyd say to you?"

"He called me a liar and said he'd take a switch to me after we are married if I dared to lie to him. I told him he was odious and that I'd never marry him."

"Good," he said with more heat than he had intended. "What else did he say?"

"He calls me 'lass,' instead of 'my lady,'" she said with a near growl.

Garth didn't say a word to that, but his temper eased and his lips twitched.

She looked up at him and then flushed fiery red. Defensively, she said, "Well, he does, and I don't like it when people do so who should not."

"I'll be sure to remember that," he said.

"Does that mean that you won't do it anymore?"

"No, but I'll remember that you don't like it," he said, struggling to contain his amusement. "Nay, now, that's not the way to make a proper fist." He reached for the offending, ungloved hand and found it small and warm in his own.

"You said you would show me," she reminded him, looking up from under her lashes in a way that made him want to kiss her again. Had they been anywhere but in plain sight of both the stable and the front door, he would have.

Instead, he said, "I'll show you how if you're sure, but I think I may have made an error in making such an offer. If you do strike a man, be sure you hit hard enough to discourage his behavior and don't just ignite his wrath. And don't tuck your thumb in like that," he said, using his free hand to open her fist. "You'll do more damage to your thumb that way than to your opponent."

Looking serious, she made another fist, this time with

her thumb out, and examined the result. Turning the fist
one way, then the other, she said, "I'll break my nail. For
that matter, the ones inside are sticking me."

He had not thought about the long fingernails tucked
inside her tender palms.

Making an experimental fist of his own, he could
barely feel his nails against palms calloused from riding, swordsmanship, and other things he did that, despite
gloves, hardened a man's hands. "Tuck them in closer by
making a tighter fist," he suggested. "See if that helps."

She did, and nodded. "'Tis odd, but I think it does
help. Now what?"

He held up his right hand, palm outward. "Hit that."

She did, lightly.

"Harder."

She tried again with the same result.

"Still too light," he said. "No man would feel that. You
can't hurt me, so you've no need to worry about it. Just
hit as hard as you can."

As if she hoped to make a liar of him, she pulled back
and let fly, but her aim was off, and if he had not caught
her arm, she would likely have spun right around.

He grinned at her. "You want to use more than just the
muscles in your arm. Use your shoulder, too, and fix your
gaze where you want to hit. You're swinging wildly. Do it
like this." He showed her how to jab.

She tried a few more times and began to get the way
of it.

"See this spot right here," he said, indicating the center
top of his abdomen below his ribs. "Many nerves come
together here, and you are of a satisfactory height to do
a man more damage by striking there than by aiming for

his jaw. You can aim lower, too, and try to get him in the cods, here."

He demonstrated.

She was attentive, perhaps even fascinated.

"Look at me, lass," he said.

When she did, her eyes were twinkling, and he realized what he had called her.

He shook his head. "Don't expect me to apologize."

"I won't," she said. "To be truthful, it does not infuriate me as much when you do it, although I cannot imagine why it should be any different."

"Nor I," he said. "Press yourself, just here," he said, touching himself just beneath the center of his ribcage. "Can you feel how tender that is? That's it," he said approvingly when she grimaced. "Strike there but take care, because if you strike too high, you'll hurt your hand on his ribs. And, lass, don't do this unless you can scream like a banshee at the same time and draw the attention of someone near enough to come to your aid. Otherwise, you'll only find yourself in the suds."

"I'll practice," she said, her eyes gleaming as if she could imagine herself knocking Boyd flat.

Garth decided he'd better keep a close eye on both of them for a while.

⌒

Amalie did not have a chance to try her new skill straightaway. But that night, she shut a large, well-stuffed pillow between her bedchamber door and its frame to keep the pillow at the height she estimated the bottom of Sir Harald's ribs to be. Then she practiced jabbing her target as hard as she dared until her arm grew tired. It was not satisfactory, but she thought it good practice for her aim.

Thursday and Friday announced themselves with morning fog that lingered until afternoon, and she kept busy inside both days.

On Saturday, she awoke to see dawn twilight and a still bright waning half moon in the sky outside her window. Getting up, she peered out and saw that although wisps of ground fog moved like wee ghosts through the garden, there were not enough of them to obscure the landscape.

Dressing hastily, she went downstairs and out to the stable, where, to her delight, the stable master and two grooms, anticipating her arrival, had her favorite mare already bridled for her. She rode astride and without a saddle, as most Border women did, so when the stable master made a cup with his hands, she stepped into it and let him toss her up.

Thanking him, she signed to her grooms to follow and rode out of the yard to the path that would take her across Eden Water to the river Tweed.

She soon put her mount to a gallop, enjoying the crisp morning air as it caressed her cheeks and delighting in the brief respite from duty.

When she slowed again and turned to be sure the grooms were still with her, she saw a third rider with them, and then saw the grooms turn their horses.

Although the eastern hills showed a glimmer of nearing sunrise, the land was still dark enough so that she did not immediately recognize the rider. But suspicion stirred, because Garth knew it would do him no good to order her grooms home.

When she recognized Sir Harald, she grimaced. She had not seen him in the stableyard but decided he must have been nearby. He could not have caught up with them so quickly had he needed to bridle and saddle his horse.

"I thought you'd like some company," he said lightly as he joined her.

"You were wrong," she said. Putting two fingers to her lips, she produced a shrieking whistle.

Chapter 13

Amalie wasted no time in discussion or waiting for her grooms but turned her mare back toward Sweethope Hill and urged it to a fast pace, knowing the grooms would fall in behind her. Her delight in the morning was gone, replaced with anger because Sir Harald had spoiled her ride. That he managed to keep pace with her, and seemed to taunt her by doing so, made her even angrier.

She had to slow for the track to the stables, but as soon as she rode into the yard, barely reining the mare to a full stop, she flung her leg over and slid to the ground. Tossing her reins to a gillie, she turned away from Boyd with chilly hauteur and strode toward the house.

He caught up with her just past the horse pond and stepped in front of her, saying, "Hold there, lass, I would speak with you." When she tried to pass, he caught her shoulders and forced her back to face him, so close that she could not see the house. Gripping hard, he said, "I want you to know I *never* meant to anger you so."

Carefully measuring her words rather than shrieking, she said, "Let me go."

"It's no use giving me orders, for you will never rule me or our household. I'll just show you now how easily I can make you feel pleasure and forget your anger."

Unable to free herself, she said, "Let go of me, or I'll scream."

He grinned, shook his head, and still gripping her tightly with his right hand, lowered his left, letting the back of it brush across her right breast. "See," he said, extending one finger and teasing the nipple more. "Don't you like that?"

Shocked, she stared at him in disbelief before her right hand shot up to knock his away. She struck hard. Then, instead of lowering her hand when his jerked away to the side, she swung back and slapped his face as hard as she could.

Gripping both shoulders again, he yanked her close, lowered his face to hers, and, grinning again, said, "You *do* know how to stimulate a man, lassie. But you should know that some of us demand kisses as the penal—"

His expression changed ludicrously as he released her and sailed up off his feet into the horse pond, Garth having grabbed him from behind by no more than his hair and breeks and heaved him there.

She stared in astonishment as Boyd, sputtering and splashing, struggled to stand in the slippery pond, only to slam down hard on his backside.

"I will escort you to the house, my lady," Garth said evenly.

"But that was remarkable!" she exclaimed. "I would never have thought anyone could just pick him up and throw him like that. He is nearly as big as you are. But he deserved it! I won't even tell you what he did, but I slapped him good, and you have made him even sorrier. Perhaps now he'll behave himself."

Garth said nothing. Touching her shoulder, he gestured toward the house.

Fairly dancing with delight, she kept up with his long strides on the path. "He followed me, just as you did last week," she said as they approached the steps. "And he sent my grooms back, too, just as you did. So I whistled."

"That was sensible."

"What was sensible, and what I'm *very* glad I did, was to tell those lads never to let anyone order them away from me," she said. "But *he* seems to think he has the right to do that, and when I turned back to the house, he did, too. If he thinks I would *ever* marry him after what he did then, he is quite the daftest man I've ever known."

Garth opened the door for her and urged her inside with a touch to her back.

"Where are the others?" she asked.

"They had not come down when I left the house," he said. "They may be in the hall by now, but come this way." His hand shifted to the center of her back.

Since he had to have left the house only minutes before he heaved Sir Harald into the pond, she thought the likelihood that anyone had come down yet was small. But she willingly let him escort her along the corridor to the anteroom at the end.

She was certain he was as pleased as she was and went to the anteroom to look into the garden and hall to see who, if anyone, had already come downstairs.

When he closed and locked the anteroom door, then went to the opposite door and looked into the hall, she was sure she had guessed correctly.

"Are they there?"

"Not yet," he said, shutting and bolting that door, as well.

A warning tickle touched the base of her spine.

"Why did you lock both doors?"

"Because I have something to say to you," he said. "And I do not want anyone to interrupt us whilst I'm saying it."

She opened her mouth to tell him he had no business locking himself in a room with her, but his grim expression silenced her before the words got out.

"You were a fool to slap him," he said. "I warned you not to do that."

"He made me angry when he spoiled my ride," she retorted. "Then he made me angrier by insisting that he could easily make me *forget* my anger just by giving me *pleasure*. That's what he said, 'pleasure.'"

"When I told you not to slap him, I explained that a man who has already proven he is no gentleman is likely to become infuriated if a woman slaps his face. I showed you a better way, and I told you to scream. You could also have run away from him had you hit him *where* I showed you."

"He was too close to me to do aught else," she snapped, in no mood to listen to such strictures. "He was touching me, too, in a place he had no right to touch me. I just reacted, and I just never even *thought* about screaming."

"Molly-lass, I—"

"*Don't* call me that! And *don't* say any more."

"But I—"

"Men! You are *all* horrid. I think you should all be kept in cages!"

Turning on her heel, she stomped to the door to the

corridor and reached for the bolt, but he caught her shoulder just as Sir Harald had, albeit more gently, and she reacted without thought.

Because she had reached with her right hand for the bolt, he grabbed her left shoulder, and when he turned her, her right arm still extended toward the bolt.

Something inside her snapped at the thought that he was treating her just as Boyd had, and that Garth, too, assumed he had the right to scold and command her.

Her right hand fisted tightly as she whirled, and she jabbed it forward with all her anger behind it, straight to the target, just as she had practiced and practiced.

She was too quick for him to catch her fist, but he managed to turn enough to deflect the force of her jab and to catch hold of her wrist right after she struck him.

As quick as thought, he backed two steps to the nearest bench, sat on it, and pulled her sharply facedown across his knees.

Although she struggled furiously and cried out at him, neither did her any good. He smacked her three times, hard, on the backside.

"But I just did what you told me to," she protested angrily as he released her. Scrambling awkwardly to her feet, resisting the temptation to rub the part that hurt, she said, "You *told* me I should have clouted Simon when *he* scolded me."

"I expected you to have better sense than to try it with me," he retorted. "A good thump may teach a loutish brother to mend his ways, but a woman should never clout a man just for caring about her well-being and telling her the truth."

"I told you the truth, too," she said stubbornly.

"Aye, you did, lass," he said. "I'm not denying that. I

could tell how angry you were the minute I stepped out the front door."

"I never even saw you."

"I know," he said. "When I opened the door he was passing you, and you looked at him as he stepped in front of you. Every inch of you said you were angry. I did not wait, because when he put his hands on you, I knew you'd not be strong enough to keep him from doing whatever he chose. I expected you to scream."

"I was just too angry," she admitted. "And when I get angry, I must do something. It doesn't happen often, but when it does, I have to hit something or throw something or stomp my feet. I wanted to hurt him. By heaven, I'm *still* angry!" Tears filled her eyes, making it hard to see him.

Garth saw her tears but did not react to them. He was afraid he would laugh and really infuriate her. She was definitely not a child, but she had sounded so much like an angry one that it tickled his sense of humor.

"You're laughing at me," she said with a sigh, dashing a hand across her eyes. "I warrant I deserve that, too."

"When I stopped you at the door," he said gently, "I was going to say that I ought to have taught you a few more things before letting you think you could defend yourself. I'm sorry now that I failed to do that."

She regarded him soberly, her eyes still glistening, her lower lip caught between her teeth.

"Don't look at me like that," he warned. "That can have consequences, too, and you are already angry enough with me."

"What consequences?"

"I'm afraid I'm as bad as Boyd is, lass, just as you said. When you made him angry—if I heard him properly—he wanted to punish you with kisses. I don't want to punish you anymore, but when you look at me like that, I do want to kiss you."

"Faith, you *are* just like him. As for your apology, if you were really sorry, you'd be sorry for more than just neglecting to teach me properly."

"If you are asking me to apologize for putting you over my knee, you will wait a long time for it. *All* actions have consequences, which is why one should think before acting. You did not. In troth, neither did I, but I've trained long and hard to react swiftly when attacked, and I did. It would be disingenuous to apologize for that, because given the same circumstances, I'd do it again. So I won't apologize."

She continued to gaze at him, and his own words echoed in his mind.

He touched her cheek, stroking with one finger, and when she did not react, he met her accusing gaze and said, "I know it sounds as if we reacted the same way, but we did not. I did nowt but touch your shoulder. You reacted to your own anger, not to mine. I did not deserve your attack."

She drew a breath, then reached up and took his hand from her cheek but did not let go of it. The temptation to kiss her grew stronger. He wrapped his fingers around hers, and when she did not pull away, he searched her gaze.

She licked her lips again. "I think I should—"

"Wait," he said as she paused. He'd heard noises of arrival in the hall.

"I can't wait, or I'll lose my courage," she said. "Sithee, I thought it was Simon at first, but now . . . now I don't know—"

The hall door rattled, and they heard Sibylla's voice on the other side.

"Faith, but some dolt has bolted this door on the inside," she declared. "I shall have to go round to open it."

Putting a finger to his lips, Garth reached past Amalie, opened the door, and urged her ahead of him into the corridor, shutting the door behind him.

When she would have turned toward the entry hall, doubtless to take the main stairs up to her bedchamber, he shook his head and drew her past the service stair to the door into the north wing instead.

⁓

Amalie wanted to curse Sibylla.

She did not know why she had chosen that moment to tell Garth she had thought the second man in the room with Fife at Scone had been Simon. Perhaps, she thought, she had wanted to give him something to make up for hitting him. But she had told him, however obliquely, and his mind was quick enough to grasp the gist.

She had to explain.

But as he silently closed the door between the passageway to the north wing and the corridor to the entry hall, she heard Sibylla's quick footsteps approaching and knew she dared not say a word.

Her heart pounded, and Garth was too close to her for her own comfort. Moreover, her emotions were in a turmoil the likes of which she had not known before. First, she had been pleased with herself and with Garth for besting Sir Harald as they had. Then, instead of expected praise from Garth, she had drawn censure, surprising and angering her. And then he had humiliated her.

Remembering the consequences she had suffered made her swallow hard, but she could no longer blame him for reacting as he had. Much as she would have liked to think their actions were the same and that he had been a beast to punish her, she knew he was right. She had attacked him.

She also believed he had spoken the truth about why he had grasped her shoulder. Knowing he had been about to apologize made her feel even worse.

"Sibylla's gone into the hall from the anteroom, lass," he said quietly. "But you'd better let me leave here first. Wait a few moments so I can make sure no one else is likely to intercept you, and then you can use either stairway."

"But I shouldn't stay here," she protested. "Besides, I want to tell you—"

"You'll have to tell me later," he interjected. "No one else will come into this passageway. The lads who look after Kenneth's room and mine use the outer door, never this one, and Kenneth left for the dormer before I went outside."

"But it wasn't Simon I heard. I just thought it might be before I got close."

He said quietly, "I doubt you know what you think right now, but we'll talk it all out later. Now, we must both go." With that, he put a hand under her chin, tilted her face up, and kissed her soundly on the lips.

"Loathsome," she muttered as he opened the door. "*Just* like Sir Harald."

She thought she detected a smile, but then he was

gone, shutting the door behind him. Her lips still burned from the touch of his.

Opening the door to look into the corridor a minute or two later and finding it reassuringly empty, she darted out and up the stairs to her bedchamber, where Bess, the maid who attended her, was sweeping the floor.

"I were just about to go downstairs, me lady. I didna think ye'd be back from your ride so soon."

"Prithee, fetch my gray kirtle, Bess. I can take off this skirt and tunic by myself, but I need to hurry if I'm to go down and break my fast with the others."

"Aye, me lady," the girl said, going quickly to the kist where the gray kirtle lived and pulling it out to give it a good shake.

When Amalie went back downstairs to find the others at the table, Sibylla gave her a look of amusement, making her wonder how much she had guessed. But Isabel looked surprised to see her and said, "Sibylla said you had gone for a ride."

"I got hungry," Amalie said, careful to look at neither Garth nor Sibylla.

To her relief, no one else questioned her, and conversation was desultory.

Garth left as soon as he had eaten some beef and bread and drunk a mug of ale. It seemed easier for her to breathe after that, but her emotions refused to settle.

As the day passed, whenever she remembered how abruptly he had pulled her across his knees, anger flamed again.

When she remembered his kiss, her emotions were less predictable. Anger vied with other feelings, some more physical than emotional.

During the midday meal, she ignored him as completely as she ignored Sir Harald. But when the ladies adjourned to the warm, sunny garden afterward, she seemed able to think of nothing that did not immediately lead to Garth. She even wondered if he had noticed that she was ignoring him. Did he care?

Calling herself a fool, she focused on the garment she was mending for Isabel until a gillie came to inform the princess that two riders were approaching.

"Likely, it be nobody, madam, for they carry no banner and one looks more like a lad than a full-grown man. But ye've said ye want warning when men come, and the other be one o' the biggest men I ever saw, so I thought ye'd want to know."

Amalie's gaze met Isabel's as the princess smiled. "I'm thinking you may know them," she said. "Go and see if you do, and then come tell us the news. If you don't know them, leave them to Sir Kenneth or Sir Garth and come back."

Setting aside her mending, hoping the riders were from the Hall with news of Meg's baby, Amalie shook out her skirt and hurried to the gate. Opening it, she looked into the yard, then snatched up her skirts and ran to meet them.

In the refectory hall of the men-at-arms' dormer, Garth had also received word of the visitors. He paused long enough to finish issuing orders to the men with him for the afternoon training and then went to see who had come.

As he stepped into the yard, he saw Amalie on tiptoe, her arms tight around the larger man, who gazed down fondly at her, his huge hands lightly touching her shoulders. The other one was a gawky, redheaded lad nearly as tall as she was but less than half the weight of the man she hugged so fiercely.

Garth strode to meet them, saying, "Unhand her ladyship, you ruffian!"

When all three turned toward him, looking by turn guiltily amused, wary, and annoyed, he grinned, put out his hand, and said, "Welcome to Sweethope Hill, Tam. Any other women here you'd like to hug?"

The huge man known by the unlikely name of Jock's Wee Tammy served as captain of Buccleuch's fighting tail. He returned Garth's firm handshake, but his expression turned as wary as the lad's when Amalie said indignantly, "I was hugging *him*, sir." On a challenging note, she added, "He is a *very* good friend of mine."

"Sakes, my lady, have a care," Tam said. "Ye'll be havin' 'im think—"

"You wrong me, Tam," Garth interjected. "I know you well enough to be sure you've been a good friend to her ladyship. But who is this lad with you?"

"I be another o' her good friends," the lad said, grinning at Amalie.

As Garth opened his mouth to rebuke such cheekiness, Amalie laughed and said, "You are indeed, Sym, and always will be. This is Sym Elliot," she added with a brief, cool look at Garth.

"Not Dod Elliot's youngest brother! Why, the last time I saw you—"

"I grew o' course, sir," Sym said, straightening as if he might grow more if he stretched. "I'll no be as big as Tam, but I mean to grow bigger than Dod."

There was enough meaning in the words to make

Garth smile again. As a bairn, the lad had been a sore burden to his much older brother, who had served as captain of the guard at Raven's Law, Wat Scott's beloved peel tower, and now served in the same capacity at Scott's Hall. Garth could recall more than once when Dod Elliot's displeasure had resulted in a few painful moments for young Sym.

Wat had told him about other misadventures of Sym's, many of which stemmed from the lad's unfortunate and too-frequent habit of following Dod and Dod's reiving friends whenever they had indulged in the common Border practice of raiding other men's cattle, both English and Scot.

Sym had followed them even when Wat had led them, one such time having been the raid that resulted in Wat's meeting and marrying his lady wife.

This stream of thought flashed through Garth's mind in seconds before Tam stopped it by saying quietly, "We've brought word from Threave, my l—"

"Both of you rode to Threave?" Garth interjected quickly.

"Aye, for Himself thought it would be good experience for the lad."

As Garth hid a smile at hearing his volatile cousin called simply "Himself," Sym said, "It *was* good experience, aye. But I ought to ha' stayed wi' me lady till she births her wee bairn. I swore to serve her all her days, ye ken."

"Her ladyship will do her birthing better without such a queesitive gudget at her door, asking every five minutes can he do summat for her," Tam said.

"Well, I ken a good bit about such," Sym said, glancing at Amalie.

"Take yourself off to see to our horses now and leave the conversin' to your betters," Tam said in a tone that brooked no argument.

"Aye, sure, I'll go," Sym said, giving him a look that seemed to Garth to be half remorseful, half challenging. Then the lad turned back with a flashing grin and a bow to say to Amalie, "It be good to see ye again, me lady."

"You, too, Sym," she said with a smile. "So Meg has not yet had her baby?"

"Not yet," Tam said, adding sternly, "Away wi' ye now, lad."

Sym went, and watching him, Garth said, "What did Douglas say, Tam?"

Tam looked around, but although Boyd stood in the doorway of the dormer, no one was near enough to hear them talk. When Tam still hesitated, Amalie said pointedly, "Should I leave, Tam, so you can continue your discussion privately?"

He looked at Garth.

Amused but wishing she would not continue to display her annoyance with him so blatantly, Garth said, "If you would, my lady. Tell the princess we'll have two guests overnight, but assure her they'll sleep in the dormer—the lad, at least."

"We both will, aye," Tam said. "I'd liefer stay with the lad, sir."

"I hope I'll see you again before you depart, Tammy," Amalie said. Then, without another word to Garth, she turned and walked back to the garden gate.

He watched her until Tam said, "I dinna think she'll hear us now, sir."

"No," Garth said with a sigh as he turned back to find

the larger man regarding him with a quizzical smile. "What are you grinning about?"

"The lady Amalie vexes easy," Tam said. "I do recall that about her."

"Do you, indeed?" Garth said.

"Aye, and it be nae use to take that tone wi' me, my lord. I'm no the one lookin' at ye as if ye were dust under me feet. D'ye ken how ye came to vex her?"

"I do, but I do not propose to share that with you, nor do I want to hear any more 'my lords' from you whilst you are here."

"Sakes, does her ladyship no ken who ye are?"

"She should if she's given it any thought, because she knows I swore fealty with the other barons at Scone. But I believe she thinks of me only as Sir Garth Napier, cousin to Buccleuch. I'd as lief not mention Westruther here, in any event."

"A baron actin' as servin' knight to the princess be bound to cause talk, aye."

"It would, and Isabel agrees," Garth said. "But I mean to find out who killed Will if I can, and James, too. Archie sent me here, thinking I might learn more from Isabel. I'm beginning to think I may learn more from Sir Harald Boyd instead."

"Who is he?"

"The chap who was just watching us from the dormer threshold," Garth said.

"D'ye think he killed them?"

"Sir John Edmonstone sent him, so I doubt it," Garth said. "Still, he is Fife's man, so likely Fife arranged for him to spy on Isabel, and mayhap to achieve a second purpose, as well." He did not explain about Amalie, nor did Tam ask.

Instead, Tam said, "Did ye no say Will's man told ye he'd seen this Haldane at Edmonstone, too, but that none there had heard o' the man?"

"I did, but I've discovered no other sign of him. He may be dead, come to that, so I'm watching Boyd. What better way for Fife to know what Isabel is up to than for him to send a man to join her household, just as I did?"

Tam frowned. "If ye're thinkin' this Boyd be Fife's man, why not have a talk with him—a persuasive talk, as ye might say?"

"Because knowing I can't trust him gives me an edge only until I challenge him. I can always have that talk if I need to, though. Now, what did Archie say?"

"He's that pleased that ye sent us and gey wroth wi' Fife," Tam said. "It be just as ye expected, sir. The Douglas's men in Stirling and at Scone told him Fife were ridin' to Lauder. But, sithee, there were nowt in that to unsettle him, Lauder being Fife's to control and none so far from Edinburgh."

"What does Archie mean to do?" Garth asked.

"He'll be on his way from Threave now, sir. He said ye're to meet him at Hawick midday on Tuesday. If Fife leaves Lauder meantime, the Douglas'll expect ye to ken where he's gone. Sym and I stopped at the Hall, too, long enough to glean news of our lady and to send a pair of lads on to Lauder to keep watch."

"Good, but they'd better be sharp lads," Garth said. "I'll not be pleased if they lose track of Fife or if he catches them at it and questions them."

"They'd no be pleased to be questioned, either," Tam said. "I told them to come to Sweethope Hill if they had aught to tell me, so if the Governor does catch them, they ken only that they serve Himself. I also told them that if anyone *should* ask, they must say they'd had a message for Westruther about the new bairn and were just ridin' on to Edinburgh with another for the laird's brother there."

Garth nodded. "That should keep them safe enough, I agree," he said. "Do you mean to stay and ride to Hawick with me?"

"Aye, sir," Tam said. "Himself said I should, and also to take the Douglas back to the Hall if Fife hasna left Lauder. But Douglas may just go on to Hermitage."

"If Fife hasn't left yet, Archie will go straight to Lauder," Garth predicted.

~~~~~

Amalie's curiosity was threatening to drive her daft. Having believed Tammy and Sym had come to tell her Meg had had her child, only to learn that they had come to see Garth, she felt cheated. Tammy and Sym were *her* friends.

More than that, Tam knew her deepest secret, one she had shared with no one who had not been there. But one of the few others who knew was Sym Elliot. Young Sym would never betray her on purpose, any more than Tam would, but as honest, direct, and guileless as Sym was, he had already nearly let something slip.

Just thinking about that, recalling how Tam had sent him away so abruptly, she wondered if Tammy would feel obliged to tell Garth.

Then she felt guilty, because Tam had been a particularly good friend to her. She could not believe he would betray her under any circumstances.

But what if Garth ordered him to tell him all he knew

about her? Garth was a knight of the realm, a man other men respected for that fact alone.

Would Tammy lie to him, swear he knew no more of her than Garth did?

Deciding she could not be alone with Garth again until she could be sure her own behavior would not betray her, she avoided his gaze at supper, and avoided him altogether afterward by sitting with Sibylla and engaging her in conversation.

The result of that was that Sibylla walked upstairs with her and straight into her bedchamber without so much as an invitation. At least Bess was also there.

"You may go, Bess," Sibylla said, holding the door open. "I will assist your mistress if she requires assistance."

Bess looked at Amalie, who reluctantly nodded.

Sibylla smiled in her friendly way as she shut the door behind Bess. "Don't look so wary, my dear. What you do is no business of mine, nor is it my duty to scold you. But I thought you should know that I did hear your voice when I tried that door this afternoon. I assume Sir Garth is the man who was with you. I heard him say only the one word, 'Wait,' so I cannot be sure."

Although her cheeks flamed, Amalie lifted her chin, fully intending to say she had no idea what Sibylla was talking about. But as she met her steady gaze, she found herself saying instead, "Aye, it was. Are you going to tell Lady Averil?"

"I've already said that is not my business," Sibylla reminded her. "Had it been Sir Harald, I'd strongly advise you to keep away from him, but Sir Garth will not harm you."

Amalie almost contradicted her but held her tongue.

Sibylla knew too much as it was. Instead, she said, "Sir Garth had seen Sir Harald accost me in the garden earlier. You need have no fear that I shall have aught to do with *that* man. My parents want me to marry him, but I do *not* like him, Sibylla."

"You won't marry him then. But take care to keep out of his way. He has only to enter a room to give me a bad feeling all over."

Amalie promised to be careful, and a few minutes later Sibylla left.

Amalie went to bed but did not sleep well, waking in the small hours from another dream of the old mill and its prickling, scattered grain. As a result, she arose later than usual on Sunday, but managed to make it downstairs in time for prayers.

It being her turn again to make Isabel's bed, with the lady Nancy, and having a long list of other duties to perform afterward, she scarcely gave thought to Garth or anyone else until Isabel sent for her late in the afternoon.

The princess looked somber when Amalie entered the hall, making her fear at once that she had learned of the private anteroom scene with Garth the previous day. But Isabel said only, "You have a visitor, my dear."

"Who, madam?"

"Your brother Tom. He thinks it best to tell you his news privately, and I agree, so he is waiting for you in the anteroom."

"But I don't want to speak with him privately," Amalie declared. "Pray, madam, if you already know what he means to say, can you not tell me?"

"It is his duty to tell you, but I'll go in with you if you like," Isabel said.

Amalie agreed, and they went into the anteroom to find Tom pacing. He shot Isabel a questioning look but did not object to her presence.

"What is it?" Amalie said. "Why have you come?"

With more gentleness than she might ever have expected from him, he said, "Our father is dead, lass. He died yesterday or late Friday."

Chapter 14

Amalie stared at Tom in stark disbelief. "What are you saying? How could such a thing happen? Who would kill him?"

Tom grimaced. "No one killed him, Amalie. It was plain enough when we found him that he'd fallen from his horse and hit his head on a rock."

Tears welled in her eyes, and a painful knot formed in her stomach. "How can you be so sure? He was a fine horseman! And why do you say when *you* found him? Surely, his men—"

"The lads at the gate said he got a message Friday afternoon and rode out fast, without his usual tail," Tom said. "I was away, and—"

"Doing what?" Anger stirred, and she recalled that he had acted as Simon's toady before, and that Simon acted for Fife. And, worse, that Fife had said—

Ruthlessly interrupting that unpleasant thought, she told herself fiercely that neither of her brothers would willingly help kill his own father.

"Father sent me to look into reports of English raiders near Kelso, so I spent Friday night with some of our
people there. When I got back, Jed Hay was on the gate
and told me about the message. He said Father rode out
minutes after it arrived and had not returned. W-we found
him late yestereve, so I spent much of last night in the
saddle, first getting him home and then riding from Elishaw to Jedburgh."

"But why go out without his men?" Amalie demanded.
To Isabel, she said, "Father never went out without a half
score of men-at-arms or more in his tail."

Tom shook his head. "No one knows the answer to that.
Our captain of the guard asked how many he wanted to
take and got his head bitten off for asking, he said. Father
said nowt to anyone about the contents of his message."

Struggling to control intensifying grief, not wanting to
give way to it, Amalie looked blindly at Tom, unable to
think of anything sensible to say to him.

Sir Iagan had been the only member of her family on
whose affection she could rely, casual though it had been.
Like most men, he had been reluctant to show his gentler
feelings, and his temper was uncertain at best. But she
loved him and had felt closer to him during their last visit
than she ever had before.

He had promised to stand up for her, and although she
had doubted he could succeed against her mother's argu-
ments and Simon's, he had taken her part. And now he
was gone. Tears spilled unheeded down her cheeks.

Tom said, "Princess, with respect, I would have a short
time alone with her."

Isabel said, "Amalie?"

Gathering her wits, brushing away tears, Amalie glowered at Tom. "No."

"Please, lass."

"I don't want to talk to you. I don't want to be alone with you. Rosalie—"

"Amalie, I swear to you"—he darted a glance at Isabel—"Rosalie has nowt to fear. I failed you, I admit that. But I'll not fail her. I swear I won't! And Simon dotes on her. If . . . if anything happened, he'd kill to protect her. Moreover, I . . . I just didn't know . . ." He glanced at Isabel again. "Please, I must speak plainly with you."

She hesitated, but Isabel said, "You have a duty to listen, my dear. I will be on the other side of that door. If you need me, just call out. As for you, sir," she added. "If she does call for me, you will answer for it in a way you will not like."

"She won't need you, madam, and I thank you," Tom said.

As soon as Isabel had shut the hall door behind her, he moved toward Amalie, spreading his hands when she stepped back. "I meant what I said, lass. I did not know until Simon told me today that they mean to force you to marry Boyd because he'll marry you despite your history."

"You spoke with Simon already today?"

"Aye, of course," he said. "It was my duty to tell him before anyone else. He is Murray of Elishaw now. I was up at first light to ride to Lauder, and we talked at length before I came here. Tomorrow, I'm off to Scott's Hall to tell Mother and Rosalie. I'd go at once, but with all the riding I've done, I'm nigh spent."

"I won't ride to the Hall with you."

"There is no need for that. Simon will collect you on his way to Elishaw for Father's burial. You must go home for that, though."

"Aye, I want to go," she agreed. "Are you truly sorry, Tom?"

"Aye, lass, I am. I never stopped to consider that a husband could legally return you on your wedding night because of it. I did you a great disservice."

"Does Simon agree?"

"We did not speak of it, because I did most of my thinking on the way here."

"*Will* you talk to him?"

He swallowed visibly. "I doubt it would help you avoid marrying Boyd, because Fife is the one most set on that. Simon said so. I don't think he even likes Boyd as much as he seemed to before. But he does admire Fife, and he believes strongly that it will benefit you to marry someone who enjoys Fife's favor."

"Father told me Boyd expects Elishaw land as part of my dowry."

"Simon said they'd discussed settling some of Wauchope Forest on you, aye, that section between Carlin Tooth and Catcleuch. 'Tis a pretty property and will produce a good income as long as we remain at peace. Doubtless, that is why Boyd is so eager to wed you. Also, if trouble comes again, it puts an ally between us and the border crossing at Carter Bar, which is good for us."

She sighed. "I won't marry that man, Tom, no matter what it gains us or what Simon says. Father promised to support my decision. Will you?"

"It won't help, lass. Simon is head of the family now. It is his support you need, not mine. I'll speak to him if he'll listen, but that's all I can do."

With a sigh, she said, "I'm going to rejoin Isabel now. You will sleep in the north wing, because that is where male guests sleep here. Someone will show you."

Although he looked as if he wanted to talk more, she ignored the look and went into the hall, where Isabel met her with a searching gaze and a sympathetic smile. When Tom followed, the princess motioned to a gillie and said, "We sup in an hour, sir. Meantime, the lad will take you to your room to refresh yourself."

After the two had gone, Isabel said quietly, "I'm sorry about your father, my dear. You will miss him, I know."

"Thank you, madam. Will you excuse me for a short time? I'd like to walk before we take supper."

Isabel nodded, and Amalie went outside into the walled garden.

Garth, too, had spent a busy day. Along with his duties to the men-at-arms at Sweethope Hill, he had to prepare for his journey to Hawick to meet Archie.

Earlier, he had seen more riders in the distance, approaching from the north. But there were five of them, too many to be Tam's lads riding from Lauder.

Sir Kenneth and two of their men met them and escorted their helmeted, mail-clad leader to the house. When he had gone inside, Garth returned to his duties but kept an eye on the other four as they rode into the yard.

He was amused when young Sym Elliot ran to help with their horses.

Sym came to him a quarter hour later and said with a frown, "That were Tom Murray wi' them men, sir, the lady Amalie's brother. Sithee, Tam told me I should make m'self useful whilst we're here, and he said I should tell ye now that one o' them said the lady Amalie's da's been killed."

"Sir Iagan Murray? Murdered?" Garth glanced toward the house.

Sym was shaking his head. "Nay, sir, he did fall off his horse, the man said. Sithee, I met him once, Sir Iagan. Capernicious old coof, he were, too—"

"You will keep *that* opinion to yourself," Garth warned him.

"Aye, sure," Sym said, nodding. "Him being dead and all. I expect since he were her da', she'll be sorrowful. Me lady will be, too," he added with a sigh.

He was right, Garth knew. For all Amalie's irritation at her father's choice of a husband for her, his death would hit her hard. He knew as much from his own experience. To Sym, he said, "You'll be going home soon, lad."

"Aye, and Tam did say we'd be riding wi' ye to Hawick," Sym said, looking more cheerful. "He said mayhap I'd see the Douglas there, too."

Tam strode up behind him, saying, "Here, what are ye plaguin' his lord— Ai-de-mi," he went on with a glinting look at Garth, "but ye should be findin' work to do, lad, to help out, as I told ye."

"Aye, well, I were," Sym said. "Ye also said I should come to tell 'im the lady Amalie's da' died. Sithee, I canna be in two places at once, can I?"

Leaving Tam to deal with Sym, Garth returned to his own preparations, noting as he did that Boyd was talking with one of Murray's men instead of seeing to his duties. He wished he could ask Tam to deal with Boyd, too.

Keeping an eye on him, Garth saw him frown as he turned from Murray's man and headed for the dormer. The path also took him toward the garden wall, and as he neared the dormer, the garden gate opened and Amalie stepped out.

She looked Garth's way as she pulled the gate shut. But if his presence registered with her, he could see no sign of it. He saw only sadness and perhaps a touch of emotional exhaustion.

When Boyd turned abruptly toward her, she did not see him either.

She continued to follow the pebbled path toward the stableyard.

Realizing that Boyd meant to intercept her again, Garth shoved the sumpter basket he was holding into the arms of the lad helping him and strode toward them.

Amalie's attention remained fixed on the path, and Boyd's was on Amalie, so neither saw him.

Boyd reached her before Garth could stop him, but Garth had already seen that the distance was too great to do so without breaking into a run. And he could not run without calling more attention to the pair than necessary.

Boyd spoke to her, because her head snapped up and she looked at him. But she did not react other than to nod in response to whatever he had said.

Garth lengthened his stride, and Boyd saw him.

With a slight bow to the lass, he walked away from her, and she stood where she had stopped until Garth reached her.

"I heard about Sir Iagan's death," he said. "'Tis a great loss, I know."

"It is, aye," she said. "I don't know why I came out of the garden. I wanted to walk, and I do love the garden, but it seemed so empty and lonely that . . ." She shrugged, and then said abruptly, "I just came here."

"What did that devil Boyd say to you?"

"Only what you said, or some such. He had heard, too."

"Sym said it was your brother Tom who brought the news."

"It was Tom," she said. "Sir Harald just said he was sorry and walked away."

"It must be close to suppertime," he said gently. "Mayhap you should return to the garden if that is where Isabel expects to find you."

She hesitated, and he remembered what she had said about the garden.

"Would you like me to go with you? Or are you still vexed with me?"

She looked bewildered, but her expression cleared quickly. "Yesterday morning seems so long ago, and 'vexed' is a poor description of what I felt then. But Tammy and Sym came, and now Tom, and I don't feel like the same person I was then. I cannot think, sir, but I *never* thought my father would be the one to die."

A tingling chill stirred somewhere deep within him at those words. "Sakes, lass, you aren't thinking that the conversation you overheard—"

"Don't you see? I don't know what to think. If it *was* Simon with him, then it cannot have been my father they discussed."

"But you *said* you did think it was Simon," he said.

"Nay, only that I thought at first that it might be. I tried to explain that, but you said we'd talk of it later. The fact is that I cannot be sure. I had not heard Simon's voice for months, and I first heard *that* voice through the closed door as I reached the landing. That's when I thought it sounded like Simon, but when I got closer and listened right at the door, it could have been any man, even you."

"You know it was not I."

Amusement stirred in her eyes, and he knew that for

a moment at least, he had eased her sorrow. Then she said, "I do know that much, aye. But that is all I know for certain."

"Could the voice have been Tom's?"

"Anyone's," she said again. "Wait, though. Tom was at Scone, but I saw him walking with his friends just moments before I went into Abbots' House. I don't see how he could have reached that room before I did."

"Not if you saw him outside," Garth said. "I was right behind you, after all, so I'd have seen him if you had not." It occurred to him that they were still standing in plain sight of anyone in the yard, so he said, "You should go back into the garden, lass. If you are not still furious with me, I'll walk with you."

"I barely feel anything, let alone fury," she admitted. "I expect I ought to go with Tom to the Hall tomorrow, to be with the others when they hear the awful news. But he says no, and truly . . ." She sighed.

Urging her back toward the gate with a light hand, first on her shoulder and then her back, he said, "You need not ride so far. They will go to Elishaw as soon as they hear— your mother and the lady Rosalie, that is," he added. Meg would not be traveling anywhere yet if Wat had anything to say about it.

"Tom said Simon will collect me, like a bundle or such, on his way home," she said. "I expect he'll come tomorrow, since he did not ride with Tom. Naught will happen at Elishaw, anyway, until my mother arrives. But it is still warm, so she will not delay. In any event, I shall have time to pack things to take with me."

"Do you have a maidservant to go with you?" he asked, stepping ahead to push open the gate and hold it for her.

"Nay, but Isabel will provide someone."

"I could arrange for some of our men to ride with you, too," he said. "But doubtless your brother keeps some of his own men with him whilst he serves Fife."

"I don't know," she said, waiting while he shut the gate. Then she said, "But you'll be riding to meet Douglas tomorrow, won't you? I expect you'll ride at least partway with Tom and his men, since you will go much the same way."

"I doubt we'll leave as early as he will," Garth said as they walked along the path toward the trellis pavilion. "He'll want to reach your mother as soon as he can, and I need not be in Hawick before midmorning Tuesday to meet Douglas."

"Might he not arrive earlier?"

"Nay, for Tam said he'd be at least two days behind him and traveling with a large contingent of Douglas men. I doubt Fife will leave Lauder soon anyway. He will want to know all he can about the Border strongholds he means to visit before he visits them. That is his usual way, if all I've heard these past months is true."

She nodded, and he realized she did not care a whit what Fife did, or why.

The vine-covered pavilion stood ahead of them. He would have liked to take her into it, sit her down, and let her cry herself silly if it would make her feel better. But she would not thank him for suggesting it, and he could not stay there with her for even a minute without harming her reputation if anyone saw them.

Chances were good that someone would, too. If Boyd had seen them enter the garden together, he could come in himself at any moment. And Boyd would like nothing better, Garth was sure, than to report such misbehavior.

Amalie looked both thoughtful and forlorn, and as

the pavilion would conceal them from the house unless someone stood on the roof, the temptation to take her in his arms and hold her close to comfort her became nearly overwhelming, but he was unsure that she would welcome his comforting.

She looked up at him and said, "We should go in, sir. Supper will be ready soon, and I must go up and wash my face before we eat."

He nodded and walked silently with her into the house.

Supper, always the lesser of the two primary meals, was no grander than usual despite their guest. But afterward, Tom Murray revealed that he had brought his lute along and offered to play for the princess and her ladies.

Lady Averil gave him a look that Garth could not decipher unless perhaps she thought it unsuitable entertainment after such news as Tom had brought Amalie.

But Borderers rarely indulged long in bereavement, and Stewarts were even less inclined to do so. Isabel said politely that she was sure they would all enjoy the entertainment, whereupon Lady Averil held her peace.

Tom had a pleasant voice and was an exceptionally skilled musician. But Garth noted that Amalie looked lost in her own thoughts. Then, abruptly, she stood and walked to the rear of the hall and into the anteroom.

Garth saw Sibylla exchange a look with Isabel and start to get up. But Isabel gave a slight shake of her head and, surprisingly, shifted her gaze to Garth.

When she beckoned, he went quickly. "You have a task for me, madam?"

"The lady Amalie may have gone into the garden again," Isabel said. "I do not mind if she chooses to stay away from everyone for a time. But pray, sir, see that the

gate is bolted and that she is safe. I do not know Thomas
Murray's men."

"Do you want me just to attend to the bolt, Princess?"
he asked bluntly.

"I believe you can look after whatever needs looking
after, sir, and without distressing her further. That is what
I want you to do. Sir Iagan's death has greatly distressed
her. To be sure, she may have gone upstairs and not into
the garden at all. But if she had, I think she would have
gone out the other way to the front stairway."

"I agree, madam. I'll see that she is safe."

"I know you will." Then, with a sigh, she said, "He
plays well, does he not?"

Garth shot a glance at Murray. "Tolerably well, I
suppose."

"Sir Harald seems most entertained."

"We must hope he remains so," Garth said, hoping instead that Boyd would follow him into the garden and
give him an excuse to teach him his manners.

From where she stood in the garden's open gateway, despite the rapidly dimming twilight, Amalie saw Garth
step out onto the rear steps of the house.

The sun set earlier each night, and when she had come
out, she'd opened the gate to watch it. The view then had
been astonishing, for in a streak of still-blue sky between
the western hilltops and a patchwork above them of
peach, rose, and violet clouds, the sun had nearly disappeared below the horizon. She had seen at once that the
narrow crescent moon, just south of it, would set minutes
afterward.

The stableyard was empty, and the moon's tip still peeped above the hilltops now hiding the sun. The colors in the clouds were fading fast, and she wished Garth had come out sooner to share the sunset's full beauty with her.

He was striding toward her now, and when he was near enough, he said, "What are you doing there, lass? That gate should be bolted by now."

"Come, look," she said. "The sun and moon are setting at almost the exact same time. The moon has been up all day, too, of course, but is it not unusual for them both to go down at once?"

In her experience, men who had begun scolding rarely stopped just because one wanted to direct their attention elsewhere. So she was pleasantly surprised when he looked at the still-visible moon, smiled, and said, "I don't know how unusual it may be. But I own, I have never seen it happen before."

"Mayhap it is an omen of good fortune," she said. "I must ask Sibylla. She knows all about such things."

"Does she?" His voice sounded deeper than usual.

An odd, tingling sensation streaked through her, making her look up at him.

He was watching her, and when her gaze met his, his eyes narrowed.

"Why do you look at me like that?" she asked.

"I was trying to tell if you were still sad."

"Doubtless, I shall be sad for a long time," she said. "I have not lost anyone close to me before, you see. It is the shock of it, I think. So sudden, and he was kind to me when last we spoke. He promised he would honor my decision not to marry. I did not believe him, because my mother and Simon would soon have persuaded him otherwise. But it was kind of him, don't you agree?"

"I do," he said, but a different note in his voice told her he was uncertain whether he did or not. She decided not to press him to be more forthcoming.

"With no moonlight, we'll soon not be able to see where we're going," he said. But he shut the gate and shut out most of the ambient light with it.

"I don't mind," she said. "I know the paths well. Did Isabel send you to fetch me? I'd have expected her to send Sibylla or Susan, or even Tom."

"Tom is still playing his lute. Isabel sent me to be sure the gate was bolted."

"Oh."

He stood close to her, close enough for her to smell the leathery scent of the jack he still wore over a soft white shirt.

She fell silent, and he stayed quiet, too, until she looked up at him again. "That's better," he said. "There will be starlight, despite those clouds yonder."

Chuckling at his hopeful tone, she said, "Are you suggesting that we should stay here until there are enough stars out to light our way?"

"I was just thinking that your eyes would reflect starlight even better than moonlight," he said.

"Faith, you are flirting with me! Do you say such stuff to every woman?"

"I never say such *stuff* to anyone," he said firmly.

"My dear sir, I had been coming to believe that perhaps you never do tell lies, but if that is not a huge—"

"I did not say I never flirt," he protested. "I said I never say such claptrap as that. I swear I've never made such a daft statement to any lass before. But when you asked if

I was suggesting we stay out here, the thought came into my head and I said it before I thought. By my troth, lass, I did not mean to flirt, not now."

"You always do seem to say whatever you think to me," she said, recalling one or two times when he had irked her by doing just that. Tonight it did not irk her at all. Until he had stepped out into the garden she had been feeling chilly, both inside and outside. Since then, she had warmed up considerably.

"If I were to say what I'm thinking right now, I'd ask to kiss you again," he said. "But, as you are grieving so much tonight, it would be daft—"

"The last time you asked me, I kissed you first," she said, wondering at her own daring. "This time *you* will have to decide for yourself."

Without hesitation, he put an arm around her shoulders, tilted her face up with his free hand, and claimed her lips with his own in a warm, moist kiss.

The sensations that enveloped her body were different from before, more encompassing, and they spread warmth all through her. She pressed harder against him, feeling the length of him, and feeling him stir against her.

Even then, she did not want to stop.

Nor did he, for he pressed his tongue against her lips, slipping it between them when they parted. It felt as if it belonged there. His taste was pleasant, and the sensations he stirred awoke a yearning in her that she had not known before.

She pressed her tongue against his, to see what he would do.

His right hand moved up her side to the softness of her breast. He held his hand still there, and her breath stopped as she waited expectantly for what he would do next. He kept kissing her, gently, leaving his hand where it was.

Then he straightened with a rueful smile.

"Why did you stop?" she asked, fighting her disappointment.

"Because we should go in, lass," he said gently. "It is too dark out here, and the things I'm tempted to do are too tempting. Also, you are too vulnerable right now, and therefore won't defend yourself well, I fear. We dare not stay longer."

She was reluctant to agree, so she said nothing but let him take her back inside. When they reached the anteroom, he gave her a little push and said, "You go on in by yourself. I don't want to have to explain myself to your brother."

Amalie shook her head at him but obeyed. A short time later, when Isabel recommended an early night, she agreed at once.

Garth did not sleep well that night. His dreams were full of spiderwebs again, tightening to ropes, as if every facet of his life were entangled. He awoke the next morning in a cold sweat again, certain the things he had imagined doing with the lass before he slept were haunting him, warning him of the snares that awaited men with such thoughts about a noble maiden. If he did not take great care . . .

To force the unwelcome thoughts from his head, he got up, broke his fast, and went to see what remained to do to ensure that all went smoothly during an absence the length of which he could not yet know. He reached the stableyard to find Tom Murray ready to depart with his men.

When Tom greeted him, Garth said, "You're off to the Hall, then."

"Aye, but I'm thinking I'll send two of my lads back to Elishaw to warn them that I'll be bringing my mother and sister home with me. The place looks as bad as any place would with none but men living in it for weeks, and in troth, I never thought about going on to the Hall. I just knew I had to tell Simon about my father's death. I expect I thought he'd deal with all else that needed doing. I warrant my mother won't think much of having just three of us to escort her, though."

"Speak to Buccleuch," Garth recommended. "He'll not let her return to Elishaw without an adequate escort." Seeing Tammy stroll out of the stable, he motioned him over. "This is Tam Scott, captain of Buccleuch's fighting tail. Tam, I've been telling Murray that Buccleuch will be happy to provide a proper escort for Lady Murray and her daughter on their return to Elishaw."

"Aye, sure," Tam said. "Ye've nowt to worry ye there, sir. We'll be headin' out in a few hours ourselves, bound for Hawick and the Hall, if ye'd like to wait."

"Nay, for my lady mother will be wroth enough with me that I went to break the news to my older brother before telling her," Tom said with a rueful look. "The sooner I get to her, the less likely it is that she'll toss my head in my lap."

Tammy looked quizzically at Garth.

"No," he said, understanding that Tammy was offering to ride with Tom. "I want you with me, because I may need you."

When Tom had departed, Tammy said, "D'ye foresee trouble ahead, sir?"

"I don't know yet," Garth said. He could hardly admit to Tam that he did not like Amalie's riding alone to Elishaw with her brother Simon but had not yet thought of any way to prevent it.

The likelihood was great that Simon would take the opportunity, grief or no grief, to press the marriage to Boyd. But it was certainly Simon's right—and duty, now that he was Murray of Elishaw—to arrange his sister's marriage.

Garth told himself that it was no affair of his. He could not imagine why it should disturb him so much that a young noblewoman of good family remained stubbornly opposed to doing as her family bade her. Obeying them was *her* duty.

Recalling his dream, he shook his head at himself. Even forewarned of entanglements, he seemed unable to resist poking his nose into her business.

⌒

In the hall, the ladies were breaking their fast when Isabel said, "As your brother Simon means to escort you home to Elishaw for Sir Iagan's burial, Amalie, you will want to take Bess with you. Mayhap one of the other ladies would like to accompany you, as well—Susan, perhaps, or Sibylla."

Sibylla was not there, and Susan looked rebellious, so Amalie said, "Bess will be sufficient, madam. Indeed, I do not know if Simon would . . ."

She hesitated, not wanting to say that Simon might

forbid her to take anyone else along, although that was perfectly true.

The question proved moot, though, because when Simon Murray finally arrived that afternoon, he did not come alone. The Governor of the Realm and a large body of men-at-arms accompanied him.

Chapter 15

After the long day of waiting in vain for Simon's arrival, Amalie and the other ladies had just taken their places on the hall dais for an early supper when a gillie had come running to tell the princess that a large party of men flying the royal Stewart banner were riding up the track.

Isabel had grimaced but said only to let the kitchen know she would have guests for supper, and to tell her housekeeper to prepare rooms in the north wing for the Governor and for any others in his company who might expect proper beds.

"Tell her not to concern herself if there are not enough beds, and by no means to give anyone Sir Garth's chamber," she said. "If there is not enough room, they will just have to make do. We can put some here in the hall if we must."

Lady Averil stood, saying, "You will want to change your gown, madam, before you sup with the lord Governor."

"Sit down, Averil," Isabel said. "If Fife had not the common civility to send ahead to warn me of his coming, he can expect no extraordinary welcome."

"What can he want here?" Amalie asked, remembering that Tom had said Fife was even more determined to see her wedded to Sir Harald than Simon was.

"I do not know," Isabel said. "But I warrant we will find out soon enough."

Garth saw the riders approaching, and he, too, recognized the royal Stewart banner. He, Tam, and young Sym were harnessing a sumpter pony with two large baskets that contained items he would need when he rode with the Douglas.

He had put off their departure as long as he could, and he sensed Tam's impatience to be gone. As it was, they were leaving later than he had intended.

Watching the host of riders fill the tracks to the house and stableyard, he said quietly, "Your lads at Lauder appear to have failed us, Tam."

"They'll be keepin' well out o' sight is all," Tam said. "The Governor must have made his decision gey quick to come here, or me lads would have noted all his preparations and one would have come to tell us. The lack o' such news tells me it happened on a hop. I do recognize the man with Fife, though, sir."

"Simon Murray," Garth said, nodding.

"The lady Amalie's other brother," Sym put in helpfully.

"Aye," Tam said. "If Fife be travelin' with Simon, he must mean to go on to Elishaw with him. Likely, we can tell the Douglas as much. Ye can see that these horses comin' into the yard now all be lathered. Sithee, they've pushed them hard."

"A strange way to begin a royal progress through the Borders," Garth said.

"Aye, ye'd think he'd have begun farther east anyway if he meant to keep the Douglas from learnin' of it. Elishaw be close to Hermitage, and for all that Fife calls himself Chief Warden o' the Borders, Hermitage and all be Douglas country."

"So is the rest of the Borders, to hear Archie talk," Garth said dryly.

Sym said, "Aye, sure, and most folks do agree with him, too."

"We'd like your silence more than your conversation, lad," Tam said.

"Nay, let him have his say," Garth said. "His views on the current state of the realm could be enlightening."

"Now, sir, ye'll no be wantin' to be encourag—"

"What does 'enlightening' mean?" Sym demanded suspiciously.

"It means clarifying, shedding light on, that sort of thing," Garth said, his attention focused more on the milling horsemen than on Sym. "Put plainly, it means we might learn something by listening to you."

"Ye might, aye. I ken *that* villain well enough, any road."

"Which villain is that?"

"Yon Fife is which," Sym said darkly. "He were at Hermitage two years ago. I were nobbut a bairn then, mind ye, but I ken *him* fine. He's no to be trusted, sir, nor the other brother, neither—that Tom one as left early this morning."

"I believe you," Garth said, wishing he could stay long enough to learn what was going on inside. But Archie would expect them to reach Hawick by midday, and Hawick was twenty miles away. Moreover, they had packed food to eat on the way.

To tell the others he had decided to go inside and eat his supper with the princess and her guests would be neither a popular move nor wise in itself.

As matters stood, they would have to push their horses to make Dryburgh before dusk, and there would be no moon again that night. It hovered now just above the western horizon and would vanish within the hour.

One other detail deterred him from entering the hall.

Amalie was evidently not yet fully aware of his true rank, and he thought it might be better if Fife were not the one to remind her that he was also a baron. Fife would remember him though, and he *would* address him as Westruther.

It had seemed more comfortable and perfectly logical to ignore his new title after his father died. It was easier, too, to go on being Sir Garth Napier as he looked into details of Will Douglas's death and after he came to Sweethope Hill.

Knighthoods, which one acquired only through rugged training and at the risk of one's hide, if not one's very life, drew more respect than baronies, which descended to one by birth. For that reason, knighted landowners often preferred the knightly form of address and used the barony title alone only if the barony was of considerable importance. Some men, however, did not do so even then.

Sir Iagan, although baron of Elishaw, still used his. Buccleuch did not.

Garth had to admit, though, if only to himself, that he

had chosen to remain Sir Garth Napier not only out of knightly pride but also because Lord Westruther would draw too much notice at Sweethope Hill.

Until Tam had asked him why Amalie did not know his full identity, Garth had not considered what he was doing as any form of deception, only as simplifying his life.

He had not denied who he was. He had just not shouted it from the treetops.

But now he had to consider how she would perceive the matter.

She was growing to trust him. He was as sure of that as he was that the sun would rise. She was no longer wary in his presence, and he wanted to encourage that. Also, she had let him kiss her, had even encouraged him—twice—to do so.

And as dangerous as he knew it to be, he wanted to kiss her again.

"Pull that strap tighter, Sym," he said curtly. "We've two hours of riding ahead, and you won't like repacking that basket after the pony shakes it off."

The lad obeyed without comment, and Garth had no further excuse to linger.

"Look yonder, sir, to the south," Tam said quietly.

Garth followed the direction of the other man's nod to see three horsemen approaching. "Now, who the devil— Oh, it's Boyd, doubtless just in time for his supper, too. Where's he been all day, I wonder."

"Sithee, I'll help him with his horse," Sym said with a gleam in his eyes.

Garth nodded and held up a hand to silence Tam's objection.

Sym soon returned, flipped a coin with a cheeky grin, and said, "Sir Harald said he'd rid to Kelso for Sir Kenneth. Said Sir Kenneth did order new bridle straps and rings from a currier there."

"Did he, indeed?" Garth said.

Tammy raised his eyebrows.

"One must suppose he could think of nowt else," Garth said to him.

"I'd ha' thought one o' the gillies would ha' gone for such, m'self," Sym said. "Master Wat wouldna ask a belted knight to run his errands for him."

"You are wiser than one might think, my lad," Garth said. "I trust you had sufficient wisdom not to mention that to Sir Harald."

"That grugous catwit? I'd no tell him the time o' day," Sym said, slipping his coin into his shoe. "Will we go now?"

"Aye," Garth said reluctantly as he cast one last glance at the house.

Telling himself that he could do naught to aid the lass against the combined forces of her brother and Fife, he mounted his horse and led the way downhill from the stableyard to the track that would take them a bit beyond Dryburgh that evening and eleven miles farther in the morning to Hawick.

———

Amalie would have liked to run out of the hall and upstairs to avoid both Simon and Fife, but Isabel forbade any of her ladies to leave.

"Will the Governor not expect you to welcome him properly, madam?" Lady Averil asked rather austerely.

"He comes without warning," Isabel retorted. "Let him come to me."

He did so minutes later. When he and Simon entered the hall with a third man, alarmingly garbed in priestly habit, Amalie's nerves stood on end.

Gillies and maidservants hurriedly set more places at the princess's right, where Garth, Sir Kenneth, and Sir Harald sat when all three were present.

Sibylla, beside Amalie, reached to pat her hand, three fingers of which were rhythmically tapping the table. Sibylla's touch stopped the tapping, whereupon she murmured, "Take a breath, my dear. Never provide any man the advantage of your agitation. 'Tis better to look your most serene at such times."

"Greetings, little sister," Fife said, his voice carrying easily over the several yards yet between them. "I trust we are welcome, although we must wonder when you do not show us the courtesy of sending to tell us so, or come to us yourself."

"I do not believe I was expecting you, my lord," Isabel said. "If you mean to make a long stay with us, you'd have been wiser to send word ahead."

The serene Sibylla got up abruptly, clapped one hand to her belly, the other to her mouth, and gasped, "Forgive me, madam!" Looking as if she would throw up on the spot, she added, "I would seek my chamber . . . with . . . with haste, madam!"

Isabel nodded, and Sibylla hurried out.

Amalie, although concerned for her well-being, was sorry to see her go. She had been certain the outspoken young woman would help Isabel protect her.

"We stay only overnight," Fife said, barely sparing a glance for Sibylla. "I trust so short a visit will not strain the resources of this place. It is smaller than I remember. Surely, you would find more comfort at Edmonstone, Isabel."

"I am content, sir. We were about to take our supper, but I have told my people to put it back a half hour, so that you and your companions may refresh yourselves. How many do you expect to eat and sleep here in the house?"

"Just the three of us, and my man, of course. But he will sleep on his own pallet outside my door, as usual."

"I must warn you that we rarely receive gentleman visitors here," Isabel told him. "So the north wing, where we house them, is not commodious."

"My men will camp on the hillside above Eden Water," Fife said. "Providing for the three of us and my servant will not trouble you much."

"Doubtless my housekeeper is seeing to everything. Do you expect to celebrate mass here tonight, Father?" Isabel asked the priest.

Amalie was watching Simon, who had not yet looked at her, let alone spoken. His attention remained fixed on Fife and the princess.

Fife said, "Father Laurent is my priest, who often travels with me. And you know Simon Murray, now Laird of Elishaw, of course."

"As he was a guest here just a fortnight ago, I do. How do you fare, sir?"

"Very well, madam," Simon said, bowing. "Thank you for your hospitality."

"You need not thank me, sir. We did expect your arrival earlier, because your brother Thomas told us you would collect Amalie today to take her home. As it is too late now to reach even Jedburgh, let alone Elishaw, before darkness falls, and as it is likely to be another moonless night, you must certainly stay."

"Excellent," Fife said, rubbing his hands together. "We will refresh ourselves at once. I note that your serving knights are absent, Isabel, although I suppose they must sup with you. I do not believe you have presented them to me as yet."

"Surely, you do not mean to say that you know none of them, sir," Isabel said, raising her eyebrows.

Blandly, he replied, "Sir Duncan Forrest I know to be Archie Douglas's man, and I believe I may have seen Sir Kenneth Maclean at one time or another in a tiltyard or tourney. I knighted the third of them myself, although I have not seen him now for months. My point was that you have not formally presented any of them to me or, I believe, to your husband."

"Indeed, sir?" Isabel said. "But I was told at Scone by Sir John himself that *he* was sending Sir Harald to me."

"Oh, indeed," Fife said without a blink. "I do recall now that Boyd applied to him, doubtless in a foolish belief that *my* reference would not be sufficient for you."

Knowing better than to rise to that fly, Isabel said, "Sir Duncan has returned to Galloway. But if you like, I shall present Sir Harald and Sir Kenneth to you when you return here to eat. They are both a trifle late, but with so many men arriving unexpectedly, they are doubtless very busy."

"Are you reduced to merely two, then?" A hint of sarcasm touched his voice.

"There is a third," she said. "But he left earlier for Melrose Abbey."

Amalie looked down, fearing that her surprise at the lie would give it away.

"To what purpose?" Fife asked.

"I believe that is my affair," Isabel said coolly.

He shook his head. "So you are still mourning the loss of James Douglas, I expect. It is unhealthy to extend any bereavement so, madam. You would do better to be living dutifully with your new husband."

"I did not choose my present husband, sir, as you know well. Nor did I ever promise to live with him."

"Still, if Edmonstone ordered you home, you would be bound to obey him."

"Would I? The Douglases made the arrangement. Perhaps you should discuss your concern with Archie the Grim."

"Perhaps I will, but I did not come here to quarrel with you."

"Did you not, sir? Then why have you come?"

"We will discuss that after we sup, I believe," he said. "If you will have someone show us where to refresh ourselves we will soon rejoin you."

"He is up to something horrid," Isabel said with a grimace when the men had gone. "I don't like this."

"Doubtless, his lordship is merely accompanying the lady Amalie and her brother—who has served him for many years now, after all—to honor them with his presence at their unfortunate father's burial," Lady Averil said soothingly.

"Fife never does honor to others unless he can gain something worthwhile for himself," Isabel muttered.

Amalie, nearly overwrought with tension, had deduced exactly what Fife intended from the simple fact of his arrival at Sweethope with Simon and a priest.

"He means to marry me to Sir Harald," she said into the silence that fell then.

Her declaration floated into the air and hovered there as the others stared at her. The surprising thing from her viewpoint was that she had sounded perfectly calm, as if the notion had not utterly terrified her.

Moreover, she *felt* calm, even limp. Not only had all her tension gone but every other feeling and emotion had vanished with it, as if something deep inside her had torn open and let every feeling spill right out of her. Nay, though, that was untrue. She felt cold clear through.

"You are as white as a sheet, Amalie," Susan said from her seat just the other side of the space Sibylla had left.

In a voice that did not sound at all like her own, Amalie said, "I was marveling at how calm I feel. I was so tense I could hardly breathe before I said what I was thinking, but now . . ." She paused, thinking that now it was as if she were no longer herself but watching some other hopeless person seek words to continue.

Isabel said, "Remember, they cannot force you. Even Fife must obey the law."

"Simon is Murray of Elishaw now," Amalie said, struggling to collect her wits. "He will make me obey him. Would the Governor accept less?"

"A woman *must* obey the head of her family, madam," Lady Averil said.

"Not if he tries to force a marriage on her against her will," Isabel insisted. "Even a priest must honor her refusal in such a case."

Amalie hoped she was right, but any confidence she still had was ebbing fast.

The men returned in less time than she had hoped. Sir Harald was with them and took the seat at Simon's right. Fife sat at the center next to Isabel, and Amalie wished Garth were there, although she could not imagine what he could do to help.

It was a solemn meal. The men did not converse with

the women, chatting quietly among themselves instead. Sir Kenneth did not come in to supper.

When Isabel gestured for servants to clear the table, draw the curtains, and light the candles as they did each evening after supper, Amalie thought it had been both the longest and shortest one of her life.

For one wanting to know the worst, it took far too long. For one *expecting* the worst, it was far too short. She doubted the meal had taken an hour from the time the men had sat down until she realized Isabel had finished.

Shortly thereafter, the princess turned to Fife, clearly expecting him to speak.

When he did not, she said, "Well, my lord, what now?"

"A wedding, madam," he replied without hesitation.

"Faith, sir, this is no time for a wedding," she said curtly. "Especially if you are expecting to see the lady Amalie marry when she has just lost her father."

"I understand your reluctance," he said smoothly. "But consider, if you will, that she will be traveling twenty-five miles or more with a large force of men-at-arms, to attend her father's funeral and see him buried afterward. Surely, her reputation will be better guarded if she travels as a married lady with her husband."

"Hardly cause enough for a forced marriage," Isabel protested. "If it is so dangerous for her to go under your protection and Simon's, she need not go at all."

Looking from one person to another, Amalie saw doubt everywhere except on Isabel's face. She knew the princess meant well and doubtless believed all she said, but Amalie could not make herself believe Isabel could prevail against Fife.

"This discussion is unsuitable for us to have before

such an audience, Isabel," Fife said, his tone no longer conciliatory. "Dismiss your servants."

"I will *not* allow you to force Amalie to marry a man she dislikes."

"She will do as she is bid," Fife said. "Tell her, Simon."

Simon said, "In troth, Princess, it was the wish of my lord father that she marry Sir Harald, and I mean to see that wish carried out. Amalie will do as I command, and I believe it is wisest for her to marry straightaway."

"I should think you would want to avoid even appearing to act with such unseemly haste," Isabel said. "Amalie, do you *want* to marry Sir Harald?"

"You know I do not, madam," Amalie said.

"If you are going to be obstructive, Isabel, you must leave," Fife said.

"I would remind you that Scottish law is on my side, sir, *and* that this is my house," Isabel said indignantly.

"And I would remind *you* that this is *my* realm," he said coldly. "I will allow you to leave with dignity and retire quietly to your chamber. If you refuse, I warn you, I have men in the entry hall awaiting my command. They will remove you and anyone else who tries to interfere with this wedding. Which shall it be?"

White-faced with fury, Isabel did not reply but stood up, turned to Amalie, and said, "I am abjectly sorry for this, my dear. I had no idea he had come to believe that he, instead of God Almighty, orders the entire universe."

Fife's tone did not change as he said, "Take your other women and the servants with you, Isabel. The lady Amalie will stay here."

Isabel said nothing, but the other ladies got hastily to their feet and followed as she swept from the chamber.

Most of the servants had already slipped out. Those who had not, fled with the ladies.

The door shut behind them all with a thump, leaving Amalie alone on the dais with a priest and three men determined to have their way with her.

⎯⎯⎯⌒

Never in his life had Garth been so reluctant to leave a place. He perfectly understood his duty to the Earl of Douglas, and he knew that Archie would have no sympathy for a young woman forced to marry against her will. He'd have even less for a man who tried to interfere with that wedding, especially as Archie was friendly with the most powerful of the men seeking to see it accomplished.

Garth also was sure that even if he were to ride back to Sweethope Hill, he could do nothing to stop whatever was happening there. For one man to stand alone against the Governor of the Realm and a large force of his men, not to mention the lass's own brother—now head of her family—would be utter folly.

The farther he rode, the stronger his reluctance grew. He had no idea how long Archie would want him to stay with him, or even if Archie would keep him. The summons might mean only that he wanted a report of all Garth had learned since their meeting at Scone. But Garth really did not care what Archie wanted.

The plain truth was that he had grown fond of the lady Amalie. The thought that men who ought to be protecting her were doubtless at that very moment forcing her to marry a man like Boyd grated on his very soul.

He had never before felt so helpless. What, he asked

himself, was the use of his skill with a sword, lance, or
dirk if he could do naught to help someone he cared about
as much as he was coming to care about her?

As these and other such thoughts streamed through his
head, Tam and Sym had been talking amiably. Garth had
lent about half an ear to their discussion, mostly out of ap-
preciation for Tam's patience with the cheeky Sym, who
asked endless questions about their route and location.

The lad had just demanded that Tam tell him what
villages the river Tweed flowed through. Earlier, he had
wanted to know the southernmost destination of the drove
road they'd followed before turning off it to ride along the
river's north bank.

When Tam protested the apparently unending pelter of
questions, Sym said, "And what happens to me if ye fall
off your pony and die afore we get where we're a-going,
then, eh? I should ken every road and river, should I no?
I ken them all fine for miles round Rankilburn Glen, after
all."

"Ye ken them all because ye followed Himself and the
rest of us to places ye ought never to have gone," Tam
retorted indignantly.

"Aye, well, ye'll no say it never did anyone any good,
me having that ken. Now, will ye?"

Tam sighed, evidently in agreement. And for a few
blessed moments there was silence but for the quick,
steady clip-clop of the trotting horses.

The sun was touching the horizon, and Garth knew
that after it set, they would have little more than another
hour's fading light, if that. He was about to suggest that
they urge their mounts to a faster pace when Sym said,
"Coo, who would that be now, a-riding after us like Auld
Clootie's own?"

Looking back, Garth saw the rider in the deep shadows of overhanging trees, and saw skirts and long hair flying as she rode. Reining his mount in, he narrowed his eyes. The woman was riding recklessly, taking a grave chance that she and her horse would meet disaster at any moment.

She was hatless, and her flying dark hair made him fear for a startling moment that it was Amalie. But when she emerged from the deepest shadows and dying rays of the sun glinted on her hair, they touched off coppery highlights.

In sudden dread, his mind making the sort of unreasoned leap he had once scolded Amalie for making, he wrenched his horse's head around and kicked it hard to a gallop, meeting the lady Sibylla minutes later.

"What is it, my lady?" he demanded. "What has brought you here all alone like this, and at such reckless speed?"

"I dared take no time to persuade anyone else of the need, sir," she said. "Nor could I dawdle, for the princess needs your help."

"Isabel *sent* you?"

"In a manner of speaking," Sibylla said. "I saw you in the yard before they came, so you know that Fife came with Simon of Elishaw. They mean to force her to marry Sir Harald Boyd. You must stop them, sir."

"I'd be happy to stop them if I had any notion how I might do so."

"I've been puzzling over that as I rode," she said, surprising him. "The only thing I can think of is that Fife *can*not perform the marriage ceremony himself. The priest must do it. So, if you can but think of a way to stop a priest . . ."

"If he is Fife's priest, he will do as Fife commands," he replied.

"Even so," she said. "You must think of a way. Fife has men in the entry hall, which can only mean that he is prepared to eject Isabel from the proceedings if she protests them."

"How did you manage to slip past them?"

"I ran out of the great hall, holding one hand over my mouth and the other clapped to my stomach. They did not try to stop me. In any event, I went straight upstairs, so they had no cause to try."

"So you managed to slip down the service stairs and out through the garden."

"It was easy enough. Had anyone looked down the corridor as I opened the door, he might have seen me, but their attention was on the hall, so I had little fear. I demanded a horse, and Angus brought me one. He tossed me up and said he'd fetch a pair of grooms." She shrugged. "We may meet them on our way back."

Tam and Sym had followed Garth with the sumpter pony, and as they reined in beside him, Sym gaped at Sibylla. "That were ye, a-riding like Auld Clootie?"

"Is that how I rode?" she asked him.

He nodded, gazing at her in rapt admiration.

"What is it, my lord?" Tam asked. "What has happened?"

"We're going back," Garth said. "At once."

"Ye dinna want us to ride on and tell the Douglas? He'll be expectin' us."

"He'll see us when we can get there," Garth said. "For now, I want you to follow me. I mean to ride on ahead. You keep an eye on Lady Sibylla."

"He can keep both eyes on me if he wants," Sibylla

said. "But I don't mean to dawdle, so we're all going to ride like the devil now, Sym. Can you keep up?"

"Aye, sure, m'lady," the boy replied eagerly. "That be how I always ride when I'm no burdened with older, slower folk."

Trying to collect herself, and remembering Sibylla's advice about never giving a man the advantage of her agitation, Amalie drew a deep breath and let it out. Then she drew another. Although far from serene, she did feel calmer.

She had not looked at Simon or, indeed, at any of the men.

She heard the scrape of a bench shifting but kept her head up and her gaze fixed straight ahead.

Hearing footsteps, she was certain they must be Simon's, but to her surprise, Harald Boyd stepped before her, wearing his most charming smile.

"Lass . . . my lady . . . if I have given you any cause to dislike me, I would ask your forgiveness now. I promise always to cherish you as a husband should."

Amalie did not respond. He blocked her view of the doorway to the entry hall, but she could easily imagine it. Just as easily did she imagine that Garth stood there. She could look right through Sir Harald and, with utter clarity, see Garth.

"I told you it would do no good," Boyd said. "I cannot think why she has taken such an aversion to me, but so it has been from the outset."

"You did not even try to win her over," Simon said.

"Why should it be necessary to exert himself?" Fife

asked. "The arrangement is already complete, the forth-coming settlements decided. It is a suitable marriage for the lass, and for him. No more need be said. Father, we can begin now."

"No," Amalie said, still staring right through Sir Harald.

"Amalie," Simon said sharply. "Recall whom you ad-dress and show respect."

"I mean no disrespect, Simon, but I do have every right under Scottish law to refuse to marry a man I do not want to marry. Moreover, our lord father told me that he was withdrawing his support for this marriage."

"Well, he did not tell me that," Simon said. "On the contrary, he told me he favored the match. Sir Harald is a belted knight, a man of honor, and one whom you should be proud to wed."

"I don't want him," Amalie said. "He treats me with disrespect and has from the moment we met. I want naught to do with the man, and since the princess knows that Scottish law supports my refusal, you must know it, too."

"Young woman, come and stand before me," Fife com-manded softly. When she hesitated, he said in the same soft tone, "Would you dare defy your King?"

"With respect, sir, you are not his grace the King."

"Nevertheless, I hold *all* his grace's power," Fife said. "To defy me is to defy the Crown of Scotland. Do you understand the penalty for such defiance?"

"Amalie, get up and do as he bids you," Simon snapped. "Not only do I mean to see this marriage take place but if you do not obey, I'll do whatever is necessary to force your compliance, and I will do it here and now. Do you understand me?"

"Threats of violence are unnecessary, Simon," Fife said. "Clearly, your sister does not yet understand the power I wield. You need only explain it to her."

With a nod, Simon said harshly, "To refuse his command is a form of treason, Amalie, punishable—if he chooses—by death."

Chapter 16

A shiver of fear rippled through Amalie. Recalling how easily Fife had ordered every detail of the coronation at Scone, and believing Simon, she got up.

Her knees felt unreliably weak, but she told herself that since she could not depend on anyone else in the room, she would have to deal with them all by herself. How she would do that, she did not know. She could not even think.

When the Governor gestured, she walked around the near end of the long dais table to the place he indicated in front of it, facing him.

"Now do you understand that I govern all Scotland and am not to be defied?" he asked her in that same soft, silky-smooth voice.

"Yes, my lord. But do you not have to obey the laws of Scotland?"

"Not when it does not suit me," he replied. "Father, are you ready to begin?"

"I am, sir," the priest replied. "But I must say that I

cannot approve of marrying this young woman against her will."

"Then it is as well for us that you are not the one to say what she will or will not do, is it not?" Fife said, looking sleepy. "You will stand here, beside me."

"To be sure, my lord, all must be as you command," Father Laurent said. As he obeyed, he said, "Sir Harald, come now and stand beside your intended bride."

Sir Harald stood up, and Amalie's hands curled into fists. She wanted to scream, and her feet itched to run. But she could see no escape.

Garth had urged his horse to its fastest pace, and the others soon fell far behind. Despite the lady Sibylla's intent to ride like the devil, they'd had the sumpter pony to consider, so Garth had left it all to Tam to sort out.

Sibylla might have tried to keep up with him despite the sumpter, but her horse was blowing hard. She had to have pressed the poor beast fiercely to have caught them as quickly as she had.

When Garth dismounted at last in the stableyard, his horse's sides were heaving, but one of the lads had heard the pounding hooves and came running. Garth tossed him the reins, saying, "Look after him, but don't make a stir about it."

Without awaiting a reply, he strode to the garden gate, hoping that no one had yet discovered that Sibylla had had to leave it unbolted. When it opened with its usual ease, he slipped inside. Dusk was fading to darkness, and the garden lay in shadows. But there was still enough light for anyone who looked out to see him.

The great-hall curtains were shut, and Sibylla had told him she'd seen guards only in the entry hall. Riding up the track, he had seen for himself that Fife's men were still setting up their encampment on the hillside behind the men's dormer.

None had paid the lone rider any heed.

At the postern door to the house, he remembered that if a man in the entry hall looked, he might see him moving about. Someone might also have taken the precaution of checking the premises and put a guard at the rear door.

Taking care but ready to declare himself a member of the household if necessary, he opened the door and stepped silently into the dim corridor. As he shut the door behind him, the one to the anteroom opened, and Isabel beckoned.

"We must hurry," she said as she drew him into the little chamber. "Fife is determined she shall marry Harald Boyd despite her adamant refusal, and Simon has commanded her to obey. Even the priest is willing, law or no law. I do not think she can hold out against the four of them, sir. And Fife sent everyone else away."

Garth muttered, "I have been trying to think. But in troth, madam, I do not know what I can do to stop them if you could not."

"Do you *want* to stop them?" she asked, peering closely at him.

"I do," he replied. He realized as he said the words that it had become more important to him than he had imagined to prevent them from forcing the lass into a marriage she did not want, but the situation seemed hopeless. "The lady Sibylla said we need only stop the priest, but I've *no* idea how we can do that."

"I know one thing that *may* work," she said. "But only

you can do it, and you've no time to give it much thought, because Fife just ordered the priest to get on with it. Mind you, even this tactic may fail. Moreover, if it succeeds, you will have made a dangerous enemy of my brother. But if you are willing . . ."

"I don't care about any of that. Just tell me what I must do."

As Amalie watched Sir Harald stand and move around the table toward her, she was wishing she could throw the sort of tantrum she had often thrown as a child, if only to relieve her fury. She had long since learned, however, that screaming and stamping her feet were more likely to win swift punishment than what she'd hoped to win, and she did not doubt the result would be the same now.

"My lord," the priest said to Fife, "should not her lady-ship have someone to stand up with her, another of the princess's ladies, perhaps?"

"I will stand up with her if she likes," Fife said, not moving.

Amalie gritted her teeth and glowered at Simon. To her surprise, he looked disconcerted, as if it had at last come home to him what he was forcing her to do.

"Simon?" she said softly.

"Sir Harald will be a good husband to you, and you'll live near Elishaw," he said. "All will be well, lass, you'll see. You will like having your own household."

"Go stand by her, Simon," Fife said. "You must give her away, after all."

"Don't do this, Simon," Amalie said. "I don't *want* this, and you can stop it."

"Nay, then, I cannot," he said, getting up and moving to stand at her left.

Sir Harald, in obedience to the priest's gesture, moved to her right.

When both were in place, Fife said, "You may begin now, Father."

"Very well," the priest said, turning toward Sir Harald, "Harald, if thou wilt have this woman to thy wedded wife, repeat after me . . ."

Amalie, gazing blindly at a point beyond the priest's shoulder, saw the anteroom door move. Then it opened wide, and her imagination seemed to play the same trick it had played earlier, letting her see Garth standing there.

"One moment, Father," he said as he stepped into the hall. "I believe you have left out an important question or two, have you not? Do not the laws of Holy Kirk oblige you to ask if there be any man present who knows cause or can show just impediment to this marriage? Also, as I recall the last wedding I attended, you ought to ask each of the primary participants that same question. You did not."

Clearly startled half out of his wits, the priest whipped his head around and exclaimed, "By my faith, sir, do you declare such a cause or impediment?"

"I most certainly do," Garth said. "These two cannot marry, because the lady Amalie is already married—to me."

"Don't be a damned fool, Westruther," Fife said, getting to his feet as Amalie's astonished gaze collided with Garth's.

He looked steadily at her and said, "Her ladyship *is* my wife, my lord. There is nowt you can do to alter that unless you are willing to kill me now and go on with this travesty. I'd submit, though, that you had better think before you do that, because many people in this house, who are not fond of you, will know what took place here. Moreover, the lady herself will refuse to submit willingly to Boyd as his wife. She is bold enough to hold her own with anyone, as I know to my own cost."

Amalie dampened suddenly dry lips. For a man who prided himself on always speaking the truth . . . How did he dare to tell such a great lie to the Governor of the Realm? And what would happen when Fife learned it was a lie, as he must?

"I had not heard that the lady Amalie had married," Fife said with a chilly look. "Or that you had, come to that."

"She is *not* married, not to him or to anyone," Simon declared angrily.

"Let *her* deny it then," Garth said.

Fife looked at her. "What say you, lass? Tell the truth, or I will be angry, and you do *not* want that. Art married to Sir Garth Napier, Baron of Westruther, or not?"

Amalie's hands were shaking. She gazed at Fife for a long moment and then looked up at Simon, beside her. She dared not look at Garth. Even so, she could feel him. His presence filled her mind more than that of all the other men in the room, enveloping her like a warm blanket.

Fife would hang them both when he learned the truth, but she could not say the words he demanded to hear. Not only was her mouth dry and her body quaking so that she could barely trust herself to force out sensible words, but also, if she said Garth had lied, she would have to marry Sir Harald.

"She does not deny it," Garth said, sounding as if he had expected as much.

"*I* do deny it," Fife said. "If you continue this farce, Westruther, I shall demand an examination of the lass. As her maidenhead is intact, that will prove—"

Amalie shot a look at Simon and was horrified to see his lips twitch as if the horrid threat amused him. The look vanished, but Simon astonished her further by saying firmly, "I'd certainly agree to such an examination, my lord."

"Nay, then, you will not, sir, for you no longer have that right," the priest declared. He turned to Fife. "I *can*not marry the declared wife of another man to Sir Harald, my lord. You know as well as I do that marriage by declaration alone is perfectly legal in Scotland. Sir Garth has declared himself her husband and she does not deny it. Therefore, they *are* legally married."

Amalie had all she could do not to demand instant explanation, but Fife was already speaking.

"Take her then," he said with a dismissive gesture. "See to it that she does not trouble me again. Indeed, if all she had to do was tell us she had married you, she has caused us all much unnecessary bother. You should beat her soundly for that, sir."

"I have been looking forward these past few moments to doing just that, my lord," Garth said, striding toward her with a stern look on his face.

"No," she protested. "Wait! You can't!"

"Silence, Molly-lass," Garth said, his tone warning her not to argue.

She glanced at Simon, who had opened his mouth, surely to protest Garth's declaration again. But he closed his mouth with a snap when he caught her eye, and looked down at his feet.

Fife had already turned away.

A firm hand grasped her upper arm, and before she had any idea what Garth meant to do, he picked her up and draped her facedown over his shoulder.

"Put me down!"

He ignored her, and realizing what a sight she must present to the others, she held her tongue as he carried her into the anteroom. The first thing she saw as he did was Isabel, looking unusually fearful as she tried to see past them into the great hall.

"Shut that door and bolt it, madam," Garth muttered. "Your unpredictable brother is doubtless already having second thoughts and may yet follow us."

The relief Amalie had felt at leaving the hall behind her evaporated.

"Aye, he may," Isabel said as the door shut and the bolt clicked home. "But I did manage never to tell him you were here as a serving knight, sir. So unless Boyd tells him so immediately, Fife will expect you to take her away at once. Can you not take her to Westruther or to Scott's Hall?"

"Neither lies close enough," he said. "There is no moon tonight."

"Aye, sure, I forgot. You must take her to your room then. No, wait, Fife and Simon will be sleeping in the north wing tonight."

"I'll sleep in my own room," Amalie said, trying to collect her wits. "I'm very grateful to you for rescuing me, sir, but we are *not* married and they cannot molest me upstairs. Pray, do put me down. This position is most uncomfortable."

"Keep silent, lass," Garth said. "We'll talk later, but *not* here or now when someone may break in at any moment. We have to stay at Sweethope, so we must behave like a properly wedded couple. And, since I told Fife that I mean to beat you, he must not find us bickering here. He may accept that the princess stopped us, but I must still look like an angry husband in complete control of his wife. What about her bedchamber, madam?"

"No, not there!" Amalie protested. Although she had evidently escaped marrying Sir Harald, disaster still lay ahead if Garth learned the truth about her. And, alone together, in her room . . . "My . . . my room is too small."

"She is right," Isabel said. "With the best will in the world, sir, the pair of you would never contrive to sleep or do otherwise in that tiny room."

Otherwise! There could be no otherwise, or he would find out and hand her right back to Simon! "But I can sleep there alone," Amalie said. "Then, tomorrow, after Simon and Fife leave, Sir Garth can take me to Scott's Hall. Faith, madam, you cannot mean for him to sleep with me!"

"He has the right now, my dear," Isabel said gently. "You heard the priest. You are truly married now."

"We must go somewhere, madam," Garth said urgently. "I don't want to see Fife or Simon again tonight if we can avoid it. Nor do I want her answering any questions about what happened in there."

"You are quite right, sir," Isabel said. "Clearly, you must take my bedchamber for the night. Go straight up the service stairs, and Amalie will show you where it is whilst I go back into the hall and try to divert them for a time."

"Isabel, I cannot take your bed," Amalie protested. "Where will you sleep?"

"I shall take Averil's bed, and she can take a maidservant's cot. We'll sort everything else out tomorrow after your brother and mine have gone."

"But I—" She broke off, tensing, when Garth put his free hand on her backside but relaxed when she realized he was only shifting her weight a little.

Evidently experiencing the same brief alarm that Amalie had, Isabel said, "I heard Fife's advice to you, sir, *and* your reply. Surely, you won't really . . ."

"I've no intention of harming her," Garth said evenly. "I just want to get her out of here and safely up those stairs."

"You also have your husbandly duty to perform," Isabel said with a straight look—almost, Amalie thought, as if she were reminding him.

"Have no fear, madam," he said on a much grimmer note. "I shall claim my rights thoroughly enough to ensure the outcome of any damned *examination*."

Amalie gritted her teeth to keep from shouting at them both that such an examination, horrid as it would be, could do Fife no good. Such a reaction being unthinkable in Isabel's presence, especially with Garth's hand where it was and Fife and the others just the other side of the great-hall door, she kept silent.

The hand stayed where it was as, without further ado, Garth opened the door, strode across the corridor with her over his shoulder, and went up the service stairs.

In the hall, Simon faced Fife.

"You have disappointed me, sir," Fife said sourly.

"You ought to have brought that lass to heel long before now."

"I did not know she had married, my lord."

"Faugh," Fife snarled. "I'd wager all I own that they were not married before Westruther made his declaration. Had you done as you should, she'd be Boyd's by now. But, although that event is over, all is not lost. You do have another sister."

"Rosalie?" Simon gaped at him. "She is but thirteen, my lord."

"Then she is of legal age for marrying. I would agree that she's a trifle young for my taste, or yours, but she will age. Do you object to a young one, Boyd?"

"Not in the least, my lord. Doubtless one can train a young wife more easily to her duties than an older, bolder one. Moreover, I saw the lady Rosalie when she visited here, and she is most comely. Also, one must suppose that she will enjoy the dowry promised to the lady Amalie."

Fife shifted his gaze to Simon. "She will, I trust."

"When she marries, aye," Simon said. "But I do not agree that she is old—"

"You are in no position to debate that if you wish to remain in my service, sir," Fife said coldly. "We will accompany you to Elishaw as we had planned, to attend your father's obsequies and to commiserate with your lady mother and your so-handsome little sister. You will inform them both then that it is by your wish and mine that this match *will* occur. Do I make myself plain enough?"

"With respect, my lord, what if I cannot persuade them?"

"Simon, I am being generous," Fife said. "Your family's long habit of playing Jack-o'-Both-Sides has irked many. Were I to declare you traitor, hang you, and confiscate Elishaw as a royal estate, I'll wager no one would oppose me."

"As to that, sir, surely you know—"

"I want men I can trust to defend such places, so that I need not expend national resources to do so," Fife cut in. "By installing Boyd on the part of Elishaw nearest the border crossing at Carter Bar, and keeping you at the castle, I may prevent the annoying English from crossing there again. So, are we in agreement?"

Simon remained silent, knowing he had little choice.

"I believe we do agree," Fife said, turning as the anteroom door opened again. "Ah, Isabel, my dear, I see you have returned. May I offer you some claret?"

~⁀~

As they went up the stairs, Amalie found voice enough to murmur, "Please put me down now, sir. Someone will see us."

"If a maidservant does, I want her to see what Fife saw," he replied quietly.

"But why?"

"Because it will be safer for both of us than if she could tell him we looked relieved or pleased with ourselves after playing that scene for him in the hall."

"Then you don't mean to ravish me?" she said warily. "You told Isabel—"

"I told her we would consummate our union, lass. We must."

"But I don't want to, and I doubt you would force me."

"Molly-lass, you know I won't have to force you."

She believed him, because even now the thought of what his touch could do to her stirred responses all through her body. But she could not let it happen.

If it did, it would destroy a friendship she had come to cherish and any tenderness or desire he might feel for her.

Her mother had made that clear, and Lady Murray did not lie.

At least he was not angry with her—not yet. He had also called her Molly-lass again, just as he had in the hall. She had trusted him then, and perhaps she could trust him now, but she did not understand why everyone else thought they were married. Even if they were, it would not last long.

Softly, he said, "Lost your tongue?"

Swallowing, she said, "I just don't understand why we must couple at once."

"Because until we consummate our marriage, it won't be a real marriage."

The realization struck her hard that *he* truly believed they were man and wife, and he meant to treat her accordingly.

But they had reached Isabel's bedchamber.

Alarmed that Lady Averil or one of the other ladies was about to see her slung over his shoulder like a sack of grain, she murmured hastily as Garth raised his free hand to knock, "Prithee, sir, put me down first."

"I will, aye," he said as he lifted her easily and set her on her feet. Still holding her, he looked into her eyes as he added, "I'd as lief not have to discuss all that has happened tonight with anyone else yet, so wait until—"

The door opened, and Lady Averil stood on the threshold, her eyebrows soaring upward when she saw them. "Sir Garth," she said sternly, "you know that gentlemen are not allowed in this part of the house. Amalie, I am astonished at—"

"The princess sent us, my lady," Garth said. "Amalie and I are married now, and she kindly offered us her own bedchamber for the night."

Radiating disapproval, Lady Averil looked at Amalie.

Reluctantly, she said, "Isabel did send us, my lady. She said she will share your chamber. If that is too great an imposition, then perhaps—"

"No command of hers is ever an imposition," Lady Averil said austerely. "Pray send for me, sir, if anything here is not to your liking."

"Thank you, my lady," Garth said. "I am sure we will not disturb you."

Lady Nancy was in the room, too, but when Lady Averil summoned her, she quickly emerged.

"How does Sibylla fare?" Amalie asked, remembering her sudden illness.

"I am sure it was just a temporary upset," Lady Averil said with a glance at Garth. "Good night now. We wish you both very happy, I'm sure."

"Thank you," Garth said, urging Amalie inside and shutting the door.

The princess's room was large and cool, its window shutters open to admit the soft night air. But to Amalie just then it seemed hard to breathe there. She turned to face Garth and saw, to her relief, that he looked only concerned.

"You've had quite a night, Molly-lass," he said. "But

I should tell you first of all that the lady Sibylla was not sick. She is the reason I returned when I did."

"Sibylla pretended to be sick so she could send someone to fetch you?"

"She rode after me herself. Said it would take too long to persuade anyone else that someone should. Sym Elliot says she rides like the devil, and he's right."

"She never counts cost," Amalie said, wishing she need not do so. His presence was having the same effect on her that it always did.

"Just don't be trying to emulate her," he said. "She took a great risk, riding as wildly as she did, not to mention riding out alone with all of Fife's men milling about on that hillside. I don't mean to be a harsh husband, lass, but I would react badly to such behavior on your part."

She sighed. "Are we really married, sir? I had no idea one could marry so easily, without banns or hearing a priest say the words."

"We can be married in a kirk later if you want," he said. "But we are as legally bound now as if we'd had the banns read and all."

"Can naught be done to change it?"

He hesitated. "Simon could demand an annulment. You need only tell him that you stayed silent because you did not know what it would mean to—"

"Faith, is that what it was? *I* did it?"

"We both did it. I made the declaration, and by law, if a man declares before witnesses that he is married and the woman does not deny it, the marriage is legal."

"Mercy!"

"I must tell you," he said, "I held my breath, expecting you to declare it a lie."

"But if you never lie, I'm surprised such a notion even occurred to you."

"I did not think of it," he admitted. "Isabel did."

"Isabel *told* you to lie?" She felt an odd surge of disappointment. "Is that why you did it?"

"No, lass. I would not lie for Isabel unless someone threatened her life and I required the use of such a ruse to save her."

"Did you believe my life was in danger?"

"I did not."

"Then, why did you deceive them so?"

His gaze met hers. "Because I could *not* let them force you to marry Boyd."

"That was kind of you, sir, but you must want an annulment now."

"Must I?"

"Aye, sure. You cannot tell me I am the sort of wife you seek."

"In troth, lass, I had not thought of seeking a wife yet. Still, I'll own that you do not meet the qualifications I once thought I would require."

"Of course, I don't," she said. "You are forever telling me how I ought to behave, and in the most irritating way. Doubtless you want a wife who will do as you bid without your even having to tell her."

"The lass I had designed for myself was comely, of course," he said with an air of wistful memory. "She was also pure of heart and mind, and perfectly virtuous, as well as being gentle, courteous, kind, and *always* obedient to my will."

"I don't fit any of those requirements," she said. "But she sounds tiresome."

"She would be, aye," he said. "Now, as for you, you

are certainly comely enough, and you come from a noble family, which will be important to my mother. You are often courteous. You have any number of other attributes to offer a man, and I have not the least doubt that you are entirely virtuous."

With a mournful catch in her throat, she forced herself to say lightly, "Do gentlemen always seek entirely virtuous ladies to marry?"

"Aye, sure, but you've nowt to worry you on that head. Now," he went on before she could decide how to reply, "you will want time to ready yourself for bed, and I must have a word with Tammy. I've a notion I'm not going to sleep for some time yet, so he and Sym must ride to Archie and explain my delay to him."

"You *will* have to go, though, won't you?"

"I will, because I must tell him all that has happened and confess that I've learned nowt about Will's death or James's that we did not know before. Although Isabel is sure that both were acts of murder and I *know* that Will's death was, I cannot provide Archie with any useful evidence. The details about James are debatable, and the accused armorer has died. Evidently, so has the man who may have killed the armorer. I dislike having to admit failure, but there it is."

"What will you do?"

"Archie expects to see me tomorrow midday at Hawick. If Tam and Sym ride out at first light, they should arrive in time to meet him. I'll follow when Simon, Fife, and their men have departed for Elishaw. I cannot take you with me to Archie, so I must stay here at least long enough to know you will be safe."

"Am I not to go home then?" The relief she felt stirred

instant guilt. How could any daughter but a wicked one feel relief at missing her father's burial?

"You'll not go with Simon and Fife as escorts," he said. "I think Archie wants only to know where Fife is going and if I've learned more about Will or James. If that is all, I will return late tomorrow or Wednesday. We can ride to Elishaw then together. Have you any idea how long Simon will wait to bury your father?"

"Well, it is summer, but recall that he sent Tom to fetch our mother, and I doubt he will proceed without her. She would be dreadfully angry if he did."

"As I recall, she does not travel swiftly," he said.

"No, and Tom most likely did not reach the Hall until late this afternoon. Also, he will have to arrange a proper escort for her, because . . . What?"

"I told him to leave her escort to Buccleuch to provide. And Buccleuch does *not* travel slowly. Therefore, his men are unlikely to do so either."

Amalie shook her head. "Go and talk with Tammy, sir. But do not worry about Wat. Even he cannot get my mother out of her bed before midmorning, or force her to travel more than ten miles in a day. The distance from Scott's Hall to Elishaw is more than twice that far."

He looked skeptical, but she urged him to go and have his talk with Tam.

When he had gone, she curled up on a cushioned window seat and tried to think about anything other than what he would think of her by morning. Since she could imagine only that he would end a marriage she had insisted she never wanted, it was infuriating that her eyes welled with tears at the thought.

A rap on the door gave her time to dash the tears away before Sibylla walked in. "Don't scold me for intruding," she said. "I heard Sir Garth go downstairs, and I've brought a jug of wine and two goblets. Even if you do not want any, I warrant that, after such a day as he has had, he will be grateful for some."

"He told me you rode after him to bring him back."

"Aye, I did. The sight of that priest padding in Fife's shadow like a tame cat told me what they were about. And since you have made it plain that Harald Boyd repulses you, I thought you'd rather not be forced to marry him."

"You were right, and I thank you for what you did. But Garth should not have tricked me into marrying him, either. I'll wager you've heard by now how that happened, so what am I to do, Sibylla?"

"Is it so dreadful, being married to Sir Garth?"

Tears spilled down Amalie's cheeks, and as she wiped them on her sleeve, she said, "I should *not* be crying. I never wanted to marry and he won't want to stay married, so I should just be glad he was willing to tell such a huge lie to rescue me."

"He won't seek an annulment, Amalie," Sibylla said quietly.

"You cannot know that."

"Aye, sure, I can. That man shows his feelings in every expression and gesture he makes, just as do you, my dear. I predict you will both be very happy."

"You don't know what you are talking about. He is forever correcting me, and I have ignored and defied him. That is not behavior that makes a good marriage. What's more, I lack *every* quality of the bride he hoped to marry."

"Do you?" Sibylla said dryly.

Amalie could not explain exactly what she lacked,

not to Sibylla, so she said, "Sakes, you should not even be here. Thank you for the wine, but pray do go away now and let me cry in peace."

"You won't cry, because I brought you something besides the wine," Sibylla said. Taking a small vial from her sleeve, she held it out. "Dab a little on your wrists and behind your ears before he returns. He'll like it, I promise you."

"Thank you," Amalie said. "It won't make any difference, but thank you."

"Keep that vial," Sibylla said with a grin. Then she was gone.

Chapter 17

It was dark in the garden and silent except for a few crickets chirping.

Garth's eyes quickly adjusted to the soft glow of myriad stars, and staying on the grassy verge to muffle his footsteps, he followed the white-pebbled path to the gate. Gently opening it and shutting it after himself, he crossed to the dormer, found Tammy and Sym, and took them into the dormer's entry hall to speak privately.

Cutting off their astonished exclamations at learning of his sudden marriage, and strictly adjuring both to keep the news of it to themselves, he told them what else he wanted them to do.

"Aye, sure, sir," Tam said. "We'll be off for Hawick then as soon as it grows light enough to see where we be a-goin'."

"At the screech o' dawn," Sym said, adding hopefully, "Won't we ha' to push the horses hard, even so, sir?"

"No need for that," Garth told him. "The Douglas won't look for me until midday, and you'll have at least five hours and won't be stopping at Dryburgh. So you should make it in time. If the Governor and Murray leave here early enough, I may be just a short while behind you."

Bidding them goodnight soon after that, he walked back to the garden gate, trying to imagine what lay ahead. With a half smile and a shake of his head, he pondered what he had done and wondered what demon had possessed him to do it.

Had he been a fool? His father would have said so if he had submitted to such an impulse before that gentleman breathed his last. But the late Lord Westruther had gone beyond any ability to call his son to account for his misbehavior.

Even as Garth was thanking the Fates for that, he felt a twinge of disappointment that his sire would never meet Amalie.

He smiled then, knowing that his father would have liked her the moment he clapped eyes on her. His mother might be more difficult, because he had it on the word of his sister Joan that mothers-in-law rarely liked their sons' wives, especially wives of their eldest or only sons.

But Lady Westruther was a woman of strong good sense and a ready sense of humor. Where his father would have condemned his impulsive lack of forethought or discussion, and berated him for both, her ladyship was bound to think he had got just what he deserved. She would insist that all her sympathy lay with his bride.

Crickets still chirped in the garden, but the only other sound he heard as he retraced his steps was the distant, soft whicker of a horse in its stable.

First things first, he decided, reaching the steps. Before he could introduce Amalie to his family, he had a task to complete. He could not allow his thoughts to dwell on the people he must tell, or what anyone else might think of his marriage.

As he opened the door into the corridor, his senses alerted again for voice or footstep. He continued to listen warily as he bolted the door and went up the service stairs. Most servants who used them would not know that he had Isabel's consent to be there, so any he met would point out his error. He hoped he would have a chance to explain himself before anyone raised ruckus enough to catch Fife's attention.

So far, he realized, he had been lucky.

As he approached the door behind which his bride awaited him, all thought of duty, explanations, or possible interruption vanished, leaving only anticipation of the true first duty that awaited him. His body stirred strongly, and he realized that what lay ahead had stirred his imagination and other parts of him more than once since he had met her.

He hesitated at the door when it abruptly occurred to him that he could not be sure of his welcome. She was as capable of greeting him with a well-formed fist or a basin of icy water as with a smile. But he had told her to ready herself for bed, and after all that had occurred, perhaps she had obeyed.

Renewal of doubt surged strongly as he lifted the latch. Even so, he was unprepared to see her standing fully clothed by the window with the shutters open, gazing out at the stars. She had taken off the net that confined her hair, and it hung in soft ebony waves to her waist. The gleaming tresses reflected the orange-golden glow of the candles that lit the room, producing flame-shaped highlights.

She turned and looked soberly at him as he shut the door.

"Why are you not in bed, lass?"

"We must talk," she said.

"We can talk later," he said firmly. His body had definite, other intentions now—urgent ones—and it was clamoring to fulfill them.

Telling himself it was his duty to make sure that Fife would not find her a maiden if he did manage to order an examination, he moved toward her.

Amalie eyed him, trying to gauge his mood. She wanted to talk because there were more things she wanted to know. There was also the one thing she had to tell him before he learned it for himself, but she did not know if she had the courage.

"Why does Fife call you 'Westruther'?" she asked, knowing from experience that her best course was to put him on the defensive as quickly as she could.

His grimace told her that she had succeeded, however briefly. "I don't remember if I told you that my father died whilst I was in Danzig," he said.

"No," she said. "I thought he must be dead when you told me you had sworn fealty on Moot Hill for your estates. You also told me your home is at Westruther. But Fife called you Westruther rather than Sir Garth, so yours must be a powerful barony. My father is . . . was a baron also, but although his estate is large, he counted his knighthood as the greater title."

"Many men do," Garth said. "I'm proud of mine, too, but my father, though also a knight, took the barony name as his father had. Some do, others do not. Mayhap, everyone will behave the same someday. Such things do change."

"Why did you not tell me before?"

"In troth, lass, I had not thought about it. It did occur to me, though, that you might think I'd deceived you if you heard someone address me as 'my lord' or as Westruther. I felt guilty then, so mayhap I had avoided discussing the subject. I'd told myself I kept it quiet here because a serving knight known to be a landed baron would draw unnecessary notice. That is true. Such knowledge might even give certain people notions that the princess and I . . ." He hesitated, unwilling to suggest what people were capable of suspecting.

"You need not explain that, sir," Amalie said. "People do make unfair suggestions just because she does not live with Sir John Edmonstone."

She felt guilty now, because she had known that he owned estates and was therefore most likely a baron, but she was not ready to talk about herself yet.

"What is Westruther like?" she asked.

"I'll take you to see it soon," he said. "Now that I have a wife, I expect I shall have to assume the rest of my duties and stop leaving them in my steward's hands. He'll be glad to have me home, but I must first finish what I began. Still, I could take you there after I meet with Douglas and we see your father buried."

"Will you just leave me there?"

"Not alone. My mother will be happy to show you all you want to see. Do you think you will enjoy being mistress of your own household?"

Remembering what it had been like to go with Meg to Scott's Hall, where Lady Scott had not been particularly welcoming, Amalie did not believe Lady Napier—or Westruther, if that was how she called herself—would be more so in what she would view as her own home, so she shook her head. "I'll stay here with Isabel until you get your other business sorted out. Then we can go together."

"So you are reconciled now to the notion of being my lady wife?"

She was sure her heart stopped beating for a moment. Was that what she had said? Whether she had or not, she knew it was what she yearned for. With that, her fear that he would reject her when he learned the truth increased tenfold, becoming so great that her certainty of his rejection brought tears to her eyes.

"Faith, sweetheart, don't cry," he said, reaching for her and pulling her close. "It fair makes my heart ache to see your eyes well up like that."

"Pay them no heed then," she muttered gruffly against his chest. "I cry if a kitten purrs or a gown gets wrinkled." Looking up at him with a watery little smile, she said, "I can cry at will just by thinking of something sad."

"Can you?" He raised his eyebrows, but his eyes twinkled.

"Aye, I can. It worked if my father scolded me, so it used to make my sisters want to tear out their hair to watch me. But it never fooled my mother, so I gave it up when I was about eleven. I can still do it, though, I'm sure."

"Well, it won't affect me any more than it did your mother. I can always tell real tears from those summoned forth on purpose."

"Mercy, how?"

"My sister Joan mastered the art and could fool our

father, just as you could fool yours. But, having watched her do it many times, I finally realized that when she cried over something real, I wanted to comfort her. When she was faking, I was just annoyed. Real emotion is the only kind that stirs a responsive emotion in me. The faking just set off my temper, so I'd advise you not to try it with me."

"What is Joan like, apart from that?"

He still had his hands on her shoulders, and they gripped tighter as if he'd had an impulse to shake her. He said, "Enough diversion, lass. It is time we were . . . What is that wonderful aroma?" He leaned closer, sniffing.

"I . . . I put on some of Sibylla's perfume," she said. "She lent it to me."

He bent nearer, his nose so near her ear that his breath blew a warm breeze across her neck.

Her gown was low cut, and when he sniffed lower, his chin touched the rise of a breast, tickling her with his chin stubble.

She caught his chin in one hand and tried to shift it, saying, "You will scrape me raw, sir. Have done!"

Instead of obeying, he grasped her hand and turned it to sniff her wrist. "We must get you more of this, sweetheart. I like it gey fine."

"Sibylla said you would. I wonder how she knew."

He grinned. "Don't go making up reasons, lass. I know how women's minds work. I've had nowt to do with Sibylla, so don't be thinking I have."

She could not resist the grin and smiled back, but her heart was not in it. She feared that neither of them would be smiling much longer.

His fingers moved to her bodice lacing, but he paused

and put a hand behind her head, cupping it as he brought his lips slowly to hers.

"You have the most beautiful skin, Molly-lass," he murmured, still inches away. "I want to touch you everywhere to find the softest, smoothest places."

A fluttery sort of shiver raced through her. Her body welcomed his touch as it had from the first, and his caress soothed her mind as well.

Something about him made her feel safe, although she had not the least idea why, or if she could trust her own feelings. Remembering the past, she had a disheartening notion that she would be foolish to do so.

Still, he was her husband now. He said so, the priest had said so, and both Fife and Simon had agreed. A fleeting thought of her mother flashed into her mind. But the image faded when she remembered his estates and his connection to Buccleuch. Her mother was above all things practical, and she appreciated the value of wealth and powerful connections more than almost anything else.

His lips touched hers and her body responded strongly, suspending her thoughts and any lingering resistance she might have felt. His kiss was warm but possessive as he searched and tasted her lips, licking and sucking them as if to explore every tiny crevice and find the softest place, just as he had promised.

He had said he wanted to touch her everywhere. Her body flamed at the thought, and heat surged through it to every pore.

She savored it all, marveling at his gentleness as he sent sensation after new sensation rippling through her with kisses on her mouth, her chin, her ears, her neck, even her eyes and nose. The hand on her lacing remained at rest as he tasted her.

The fingers of his other hand laced through her hair, as if he would grip her tighter and hold her where he wanted her. Even with that thought, she felt only a fierce, powerful hunger for him coursing through her.

When her body pressed toward his as if it could melt right into him, she moaned softly and wondered for a second who had done so. Then his tongue slipped between her lips, seeking softer places within, and she tasted him back.

When the fingers at her laces stirred and tugged, and she felt them growing urgent in their task, guilt stirred rather than discomfort. *Would* he be able to tell?

Her mother had assured her that a husband would know instantly if he had married a maiden, but Lady Murray had not explained *how* he would know.

With a last tug, the lacing of her bodice was undone. Still holding her head and still penetrating her mouth with his agile tongue, he dealt deftly with the tight bodice sleeves as he pushed the garment off her shoulders and arms to the floor.

Her shift and skirt remained, but he soon found the tapes for her skirt, and it slipped off to follow the bodice, leaving her in her shift.

It was thin cambric, and she stood by the open shutters. Warm though the night was, she shivered. As if he detected it and would protect her from the elements, he eased her around so that his back was to the window.

She nearly smiled. Indeed, her lips twitched, for she could feel them do so, and then his right hand, no longer occupied with her skirt, moved to caress the side of her left breast, cupping it and pressing gently into its softness.

One finger inched around to the cambric-covered nipple, brushed across it to the lace edging of her shift, then to its ties. She barely knew what he was doing before the shift parted and his warm bare hand touched her skin.

Without releasing her mouth, he picked her up and carried her to the bed, Isabel's bed, already turned back.

Amalie tensed, but he laid her down and said, "Don't move, Molly-lass. Don't move a muscle."

She could feel air rather than cambric touching most of her upper body.

"But—"

Putting a finger to her lips, he said, "Don't talk. Not yet."

He slipped off his leather jack, untied his shirt, and stripped it off, casting it to the foot of the bed so carelessly she was sure it had slipped right to the floor.

His belt and boots followed, dropped where he stood.

Then he reached to open his breeks.

She shut her eyes and, as she did, realized that he was watching her and that his gaze had fixed itself on her breasts, wholly revealed now by the gaping top of her shift. Since the garment was the gathered-at-the-neckline sort that opened to her waist when untied, she knew he enjoyed a view of more than just her breasts.

Opening her eyes and noting his expression, she knew he liked what he saw. He continued to look, so she watched him as closely while his breeks came off.

She stared then. She had seen a man rampant before but not such a man as this one. He was larger all around, for one thing. Her breath caught.

"Don't be afraid," he said softly. "I'll try not to hurt

you. But, stay, lass. Do you even know how men and women couple? Nay, of course not," he said, answering his own question. "Doubtless—"

"I do know some things," she murmured.

"Ah, good, then at least the telling won't terrify you."

"If you mean to explain," she said, "could you get into bed first and . . . and just hold me?"

"Aye, sure," he said, complying at once without snuffing a single candle.

The room that had seemed so dimly lit when they came in seemed ablaze now with light, especially when he hesitated, gazing again at her breasts. Then he slipped an arm under her shoulders and drew her close to him.

She had forgotten one little, obvious, consequence of her request, though. Her bare breasts pressed now against his hard, muscular, bare chest.

He held her so for a time before his hand came gently to cup her head again, and his lips sought hers. But he kissed gently without the hungry passion she had sensed earlier when he had explored her mouth.

"Better?" he said, relaxing back against plump pillows but still holding her close, so she now lay nearly face-down and halfway atop him, with her left cheek against his chest. A few dark hairs tickled her face and lips.

"I do feel better," she said. "But I want to ask you a question."

"You don't need permission. Ask me whatever you like."

"You told me not to talk," she reminded him.

"So I did. Dare I hope you will always be so obedient to my will?"

She swallowed. He was not making things easier, but

she had known that nothing about their night together would be easy.

"What do you want to know?" he asked.

She liked his voice, especially when he talked to her as he did now, as if they were friends. She did not want to lose his friendship. Not only did she have few friends of her own, but she cared about him and enjoyed his company.

He turned and eased up on an elbow so she slid off onto her side. Looking at her, he said with concern, "What is it, Molly-lass? Tell me."

She swallowed again and sent up a silent prayer, but she would get no help from God now. She had to tell Garth, because he would soon find out for himself, and she could not let him think that she had purposely cheated him. Surely, if a man and his bride had never been . . . had never . . .

"Is it easier to get an annulment if a man and woman *don't* couple?"

He stared at her, visibly checking whatever impatient or angry words had nearly burst from his lips. When he did speak, his voice and his patience were under control. "Don't tell me you still want one," he said. "I won't be-lieve you."

"I just—" Breaking off to lick drying lips, she tried to sit up, but he held her firmly in place.

"No, Amalie, just tell me what is wrong. Why did you ask me that?"

"Because I'm sure you will want to give me back, and if it is easier without coupling, I think we should stop."

"Not unless you tell me exactly *why* you think I'd want to give you back."

"My mother said that a man can tell if his wife is a

maiden or not. If she is not, the law says he can give her back. What if you should think I'm not?"

"Faith, Molly-lass, any man could tell by just looking at you that you've nowt in that to worry yourself. If you were the sort of lass to give favors out of wedlock, you'd not be handmaiden to the princess. Also . . . well, one only has to know you for a short time—"

"I'm not," she said, unable to listen to more.

"Not what?"

"Not a maiden," she said dismally, tears welling in her eyes.

The tears sparkled, and Garth stared at them, unable to believe what she had said. He felt nothing at all, and felt that way long enough to make him think she must be lying to give him reason to abandon her. But she had willingly responded to him—and tentatively at first, innocently, not as a woman of experience would.

But perhaps, a voice in his head countered, not the way a truly virginal woman whom no one had kissed before or who had never . . .

He shook his head, clearing it, realizing he wanted to kiss her tears away and that he felt utterly stunned. Well aware that shock could numb a man's emotions even quicker than disbelief, and feeling anger now as well, increasing anger, he said with forced calm, "Tell me what happened."

"What do you think?"

He brushed away a tear with his thumb and said, "Sweetheart, you've lived for nearly two years with a woman we both know takes great care of her reputation.

If any man out there could brag of having seduced you into granting him favors of any sort that could sully your name or hers, others would know. Certainly Isabel would, because someone would deem it a duty to tell her. She would also take note of any behavior on your part that encouraged men to take liberties."

"She let you be alone with me," Amalie said.

He frowned. He had not thought of himself as taking liberties, but of course, he had. And it was true that Isabel had encouraged him. Sakes, she had pushed him to declare the marriage. She had to have noticed before she had done it that he might be willing to marry the lass. He had scarcely had time before—or, to be truthful, the inclination—to wonder about Isabel's reasons.

Considering them now, he shook his head again. "I don't know how women think," he said. "But it would take no wizard to discern my attraction to you. Nor to note your failure to rebuff me the way you did that villain Boyd."

With a wry look that made him want to kiss her again, she said, "Sibylla said you wear your feelings on your face and in every gesture. She said that I do, too. But, although I like her, I don't always think she knows what she's talking about."

"Faith, I think she may be a witch," he said with sincerity.

"She also predicted that we'd be happy," Amalie said as another tear trickled down her cheek to her ear. She rubbed the ear. "That won't come true now."

"It won't if you don't learn to listen to your husband, my lass. I have made it as plain as I know how that I do *not* believe you encouraged any man to lie with you, so tell me what really happened."

"One did so without encouragement," she said with a catch in her voice.

Ruthlessly stifling rage that threatened to reduce him to a gibbering dafty or overwhelm him to the point of bellowing at her as he shook the name of the villain from her, he drew a long breath. Letting it out slowly, he eased far enough away from her to let him gently retie the strings of her shift.

"I knew it," she said dolefully, as she moved to turn away.

"You said you wanted to talk, sweetheart, so we are going to talk," he said, pulling her back to face him. "Now, I want a round tale, and we're not going to do anything else until I get one. I don't want you or me catching our death of cold before then, so under the covers with you unless you want to close those shutters and sit with me on that well-cushioned window seat under them."

She had not expected him to demand an explanation, and the thought of providing the gruesome facts brought the incident rushing back to her as if it had happened two hours before instead of two years.

To think that just a short time ago, he made her feel safe!

Avoiding his gaze, she said, "Is it not enough to know I am no longer a maiden, sir? Must you force me to dredge up all the details?"

He had not let go of her arm after pulling her back, and he did not release it now, but his grip was gentle. He said, "I'm your husband, Amalie. I *should* know."

"Why?"

He did not answer right away, and that surprised her as much as anything else he had done. She knew what Wat Scott would have said if Meg or she herself had ever asked him why *he* should know something. Wat asked a question and just waited silently until one gave him the answer. But if that person refused . . .

Meg had once told her that Wat believed it was his duty to know her secrets and her dreams, and her duty to confide them to him. As her husband, he said, he was responsible for her. Therefore he also insisted on being the one to decide how much she should tell him and, in return, how little he need tell her.

In truth, and despite such declarations, Meg dealt admirably with Wat, and he loved Meg. But Amalie had expected the same uncompromising attitude from Garth. That it was not forthcoming disconcerted her.

He remained silent now though, his hand still on her arm.

"You cannot tell me why you should know, can you?" she said.

"I can answer," he said quietly. "It was a reasonable question. I was just trying to think how it must have been for you to be forced, as I'm sure you must have been. It cannot be easy to talk about something like that to anyone, let alone to a man you scarcely know, despite being married to him. Yet, if you cannot talk to me about the things most important to you, I cannot be a good husband. And I'm realizing, sweetheart, that I want more than anything to be a good husband to you."

Her tears spilled over then in a veritable flood, and she cried as she had not cried since the day her world had changed from one in which she believed the only danger came from English invaders or Scottish ones, to the real world, where the greatest dangers came from the least expected people.

Both of his arms came around her then, and he held her close without saying a word, letting her tears spill across his bare skin without notice. Even when he shifted slightly to a more comfortable position, he still held her close and did not speak. One hand rubbed her gently between the shoulder blades, soothing her as if she were a weeping bairn.

She sobbed until she realized her nose was running all over him along with her tears. With an embarrassed gasp, she tried to stanch the flow and sit up.

"It's all right, sweetheart," he said then. "Cry as much as you like."

"I don't *want* to cry anymore. I'm dribbling all over you!"

"I clean up easily."

"Most men *hate* weeping women."

"I can do without most of them myself."

Her tears ceased altogether then. "What a thing to say!"

"Why? It is the truth."

"Well, you need not always speak the truth so wholeheartedly, sir. Sometimes you might try for a little tact."

"I've never really understood the difference between tact and a lie," he said. "If you want me to tell you what you *want* to hear, just ask me what I think that might be. Like as not, I'll get it wrong most of the time, not being equipped with the ability to read your mind—at least, not yet. But I'd be gey willing to try."

She tried to glower at him but knew she had not succeeded when his twinkling gaze caught hers again. "That's better," he said. "Now, tell me."

Her first instinct was to evade it again, but a stronger instinct warned that it would serve no purpose but to pit her will against his.

She knew who would win.

"I won't tell you all the details," she said. "I can't do that without reliving the whole horrid thing, and I simply won't. As it is, I still dream about it and wake up terrified and in a cold sweat."

His lips twitched then in what she thought might be sympathy, but he only nodded and said, "Tell me what you can."

The one thing she knew he would want her to tell him, she could not and would not. So she began with their ride to the old mill.

⁓

Garth had been watching her closely, but when she mentioned her dreams, she struck a respondent chord in him. After her warning that she would not tell him everything, he wondered how hard he dared press her.

Hearing that the bastard had taken her to a mill near Elishaw, he realized it had been someone she trusted. No wonder she had told him she trusted no man.

That she trusted *him* enough to tell him any of it touched him deeply. But what she would do when his resolve to know the villain's name knocked up against her stubbornness—and doubtless her fears, as well—he could not tell.

He'd do well, he decided, to listen carefully and hope she continued to reveal more than she realized. Then, when he learned the bastard's name, he'd kill him.

Chapter 18

⁓

Amalie lay quietly after telling Garth what had happened at the mill, her head resting in the hollow of his shoulder. She felt drained but still fearful. He had fallen silent again and, for once, had not expressed his thoughts or demanded more details.

He had listened.

His body had relaxed too, some time before—all of it.

He turned his head until his gaze captured hers. "I want to know his name."

"I can't tell you," she said, meaning it. That much she would keep to herself.

"I am your husband, lass. In such a thing as this, I have the right to know."

"Well, I won't tell you. You may think you can force me—"

He winced, silencing her, then drew a deep breath and let it out before he said, "You need tell me only what you want me to know. But you should consider that I will meet all the men in your family, many of their friends, and most of the men who live or work at Elishaw. I'm going to wonder about every one of them."

"I expect you will," she admitted cautiously. "But I still won't tell you."

He kept that intense, steady gaze on her for a torturous time longer, but she met it until, with a nearly indiscernible nod, he sighed.

"What?" she demanded. "Why do you look like that?"

"Because your silence has persuaded me that the number of suspects is more limited than I had thought. I can rule out the servants, for example."

With that discomfiting gaze still upon her, she could scarcely breathe.

"I think I can rule out friends of your family as well."

"How could you possibly?"

"Think, lass. You would be unlikely to protect a servant, let alone to go into a lonely mill with him. And although your father might have missed noticing one male friend or another hanging around you closely enough to ride to that mill alone with you, your mother would not. Moreover, had either of your brothers taken note of such a man, surely they would have pressed him to declare his intentions."

She could think of nothing to say to that.

"I am also fairly sure, sweetheart, that your attacker was not Simon."

"Mercy, you cannot know that. Do you pretend to read minds, like Sibylla?"

"Nay, but had Simon been the one to deflower you, he would surely know that you cannot prove yourself a maiden by examination. Yet he agreed to one."

"But, don't you see?" she protested. "Simon nearly

smiled when he said that! Sithee, I think he changed his mind about my dowry when he inherited Elishaw, because Fife insisted that a portion of the estates be part of it. Simon is not a bad man, sir. I do not like him much, but in fairness, he is years older than I am and was mostly away from home. So I scarcely know him. I think he viewed me, not as a sister—Rosalie is the only one of us who stirs fondness in him—but as an asset he could use to increase his favor with Fife. Then, when our father died—"

"So Simon *is* the one!"

"No!" Amalie exclaimed, horrified that she had led him to accuse an innocent man. "I did think he must have told Sir Harald, and thereby led him to treat me with such detestable familiarity, but Simon cannot have done that. Neither Sir Harald nor Fife mentioned it, or seemed to know that their vile examination would do them no good. And surely, if one had known, the other would have as well."

"So Simon did know you had been attacked."

"Aye," she said, remembering. "But he would not believe it was an attack. He believed it was my fault, that I was wanton and provoked it."

"Then your attacker was Tom or your father," Garth said flatly.

She could not answer. The easy speed with which he had reduced the field from a host of possibilities to two astonished her. Realizing she could not let him blame her father any more than she could let him blame Simon, she remembered that Wat Scott knew the truth and that Tammy and Sym knew things, too, and that she trusted all three to keep her dreadful secrets to themselves.

That thought made her look at him again. If she could

trust the three of them, she had been wrong to declare all men untrustworthy. As it was, Sym had nearly . . .

His brow wrinkled thoughtfully as he returned her look. She realized that his mind had taken a track much like the one hers had followed when he said quietly, "That lad, Sym Elliot. He said he knew things about bir—"

"I do have more to tell you, sir, but pray do not ask me to explain all of it now," she interjected quickly. "In return, I will tell you who it was."

"No bargain, sweetheart. It was Tom, and clearly, there were consequences. Is there a child hidden away somewhere that I ought to know about?"

Tears sprang to her eyes again. "No, my lord, there is not."

When she caught her lower lip between her teeth, doubtless to avoid saying more, or in hope of stemming her tears by biting down hard, Garth was just sorry to see the tears again. He was even sorrier she was trying to put distance between them by using the formal title. He believed her account, and he doubted that he needed to know more about the incident, although his curiosity still burned, as did his rage.

But he knew that he would be wise to dampen both.

He could not kill her brother, so he would just have to wait for nature to take its course. Such a scoundrel would surely come to an unhappy end. In the meantime, Garth could make Tom's life miserable just by telling him he knew what he had done and warning him to keep well out of his way.

For the present, he said only, "I won't press you any

more tonight, sweetheart. And if I don't get back in time to take you to Elishaw for Sir Iagan's burial, perhaps it will be just as well. I doubt that I could meet either of your brothers without wanting to punish them for all they've put you through."

She said nothing, but she did dab her eyes dry with a bit of the coverlet.

As if he had not noticed, and hoping that if he kept talking, he could ease the strain of her sorrows, he said matter-of-factly, "I must meet with Archie first. He will doubtless go at once to intercept Fife at Elishaw, but you cannot ride there with his horde of Douglases. That *would* cause a stir, even with me along. But after I talk with him, and one man he is bringing with him, I'll come back to fetch you. Then we'll go to Elishaw together if you still want to, even if it is too late for the burial."

"I don't know yet if I'll want to," she said. "What will you do about Tom?"

Realizing with distinct satisfaction that she could not imagine he would do nothing, he said with a slight smile, "I'll let him know that I know; that's all."

She tilted her head, frowning, her gaze searching his. At last, she nodded. "If that is so," she said, "I warrant we shall see little of him."

"We won't see him at all at Westruther," he said. "Now, come here to me. This is, after all, still our wedding night, and things were going well for a time, so at least your experience has not put you off sex altogether. Or has it?"

He hesitated, realizing with a jolt that such an experience might well have turned her against coupling forever.

Her smile was still watery but nonetheless real. "I thought it had," she admitted. "I thought I could not bear any man to touch me. But now I suspect I worried more that a husband would send me back to my father in disgrace than I did about what a husband might expect of me."

"You have never objected to my touching you," he said softly.

"I did once," she retorted.

He smiled then. "You said I was as loathsome as Boyd, aye. You should pay a little penance for that gibe, I think, if you will not object to my touch now."

"What sort of touch?" she asked suspiciously but without fear.

"This sort," he said, drawing her into his arms again and holding her close. "Do you think we can recall where we were before our talk?"

In response, she snuggled against him.

⁓

Amalie snuggled close, savoring his strength and his warmth for a time until her thoughts drifted back to what he had said about where they had been before. They were not exactly as they had been, because her shift was between them now. She missed the feeling of his bare skin against hers.

As if his thoughts again followed the same track as hers, his hand moved to the side of her breast and, brushing the nipple, to the ties of her shift. His fingers dealt more swiftly with them this time, but when they were loose, his hand stilled.

"Art sure, Molly-lass?"

Smiling, she pressed herself harder against him and

moved a hand to his chest, her fingers toying with the soft curly hair she found there. "I'm sure."

His touch remained gentle at first as he stroked her, warming her all over, then it grew more teasing, still gentle but sure and playful. His lips played with hers, and then his tongue teased hers and she teased back, astonished and delighted that she could feel playful with him.

His hands moved over her body, slipping her shift up and off her. And then he began caressing her with his hands and his lips, and invited her to touch him.

She learned quickly, because his responses were open and his enjoyment clear. He seemed in no hurry, content to let her explore him as he found more ways to let her know how delighted he was with her.

After a time, she realized that he had begun to tease her senses more and more, to the point of torment. It was pleasant torment, but before long her hunger for him grew unbearable. His hands and lips moved lower then until one hand gently touched her between the legs and began to tease her there.

She gasped.

"If you want me to stop, tell me," he said. "I don't want to hurt you or do aught that you do not like."

"Do as you please," she said. "But for mercy's sake, don't stop now."

She thought she heard him chuckle low in his throat. Then he took her hand and moved it to himself, silently urging her to take hold of him.

Without a qualm, she did, rubbing herself against him until he said, "Lass, I cannot hold out much longer. I want to be inside you."

"I want you there, too," she said, guiding him.

He was gentle until he could be gentle no longer, but

she met every thrust. She had not known what an agreeable thing coupling could be.

When they lay back, sated at last, he said, "You are mine now, sweetheart, in every way. I would defy anyone to say otherwise."

"Aye, sir, and you are mine," she said. The deep satisfaction she felt at those words astonished her.

⁓

Webbed in chains and shackled to a damp stone wall in pitch darkness, as if in a dungeon so deep that light could not penetrate, he hung from his shackles. But he felt no pain even when he shook them, trying unsuccessfully to break free.

If there was a floor below or a ceiling above, he had no sense of either, only of the web. Then a tiny white dot appeared in the distance like a pinprick in the blackness. It began slowly to grow into a circle of light, and as it grew, shapes formed inside until he could discern blue sky, puffy white clouds, and Amalie.

She wore the claret-colored velvet cloak she'd worn when he first saw her, and she stood atop a high, sheer cliff. A breeze stirred her flowing hair and her skirts. As the circle grew, he saw that the cliff rose far above a river valley, perhaps the Dale of the Tweed, although he knew of no cliff so high in all the Borders.

She turned her head until she seemed to see him, and smiled. Her smile froze as the wind blew harder, then harder, until she was leaning tensely back against it.

It continued to strengthen even then until worry filled him, and fear. Then helpless terror enveloped him as the wind scooped her up and blew her off the cliff.

Garth awoke with a gasp, shaking, to see Amalie by the window in a pale blue, silky-looking robe somewhat too long for her. She gazed out at what was either early dawn or a later, overcast morning. It did not matter to him which it was. He was just glad to be awake and out of his chains, and to see her safe.

"Good morning," he said huskily.

She turned with a smile. "It is going to be a fine day when the sun comes up," she said. "Tam and Sym rode out a short while ago."

"Then they should make Dryburgh in two hours or so, and Hawick by noon," he said. "You were not thinking of going downstairs to break your fast, were you?"

"I had not even thought about dressing yet," she said. "I found this robe of Isabel's in that kist by the bed, but I don't know if anyone has told Bess that I am in here, or if Bess would dare to enter whilst you are with me."

"I think we will ask them to bring us food here," he said. "I'd as lief not subject either of us to more of Fife's company yet, or your brother Simon's."

"I'll put my head out then and see if I can find some-one," she said.

"There is no hurry," he told her.

"Are you not going to get up?"

"I would rather get to know my wife better," he said. "Come here."

Her eyes danced. "And if I do not?"

"Then I will get up and fetch you. But doubtless you will shriek if I do, and the lady Averil will rush in to see who is attacking you."

She chuckled. "I think I would rather she did not come in." With that, she slipped the robe off her shoulders and walked smiling to the bed.

He held the covers back as his cock stirred to welcome her.

⁓

An hour later, Amalie stirred sleepily on hearing a solid click. Coming wide awake, realizing it was the door latch, she looked first to see that Garth was covered and then at the door as Bess peeped around it.

"Be ye awake then, mistress?" the maid murmured. "Princess Isabel said I should tell ye that if ye like, she'll ha' someone bring food up for the pair o' ye."

Her eyes shifted toward Garth and widened when he turned over and sat up.

"Sakes," he said. "What is the hour?"

"Nigh onto Terce, sir," Bess said. "Me lord Fife and Simon Murray be near ready to go. The princess said to ask ye did ye want to bid them farewell, m'lady."

"No, Bess," Amalie said. "I shall see them both again soon, so I mean to be lazy this morning. Prithee, do tell the princess we will gratefully accept her offer of food to break our fast and will be downstairs shortly afterward."

"Aye, m'lady, I'll tell her. The lady Sibylla were asking after ye, too."

"Thank you, Bess," Garth said.

With another startled glance at him, the maid fled.

"I did not expect to fall asleep again," Amalie said.

"Nor I," he agreed, smiling lazily. "You must have worn me out."

She felt heat rush to her cheeks, remembering. Somehow, things she had hitherto thought about only with embarrassment and fear seemed natural, even fun with him.

He made her feel desirable and beautiful, and his body fascinated her.

He encouraged her to explore him while he explored her. And although she felt quite daring in some of the things she had done to and with him, he seemed to delight in all they did. He had even revealed some secrets of her own body to her.

Remembering that he had to ride to Hawick to meet Archie Douglas, she put aside thoughts of more sex play, and got out of bed. As she slipped Isabel's robe back on, she hoped Bess would remember to bring her some fresh clothes.

Garth got up and swiftly donned the clothing he had taken off the night before. "I must go to my chamber and fetch the things I mean to take with me, lass," he said. "I'll be only a few minutes, though, if your brother and Fife are safely in the hall or in the stableyard." He was gone on the words, leaving her alone.

Bess returned before he did, bearing a tray with a basket of rolls, butter, jelly, two mugs, and a pitcher of ale. "It be all cold food, m'lady," she said as she set it carefully on a side table. "The princess did say, though, that she'd send someone up with a platter o' warm sliced beef, too. Shall I fetch your clothes to ye here?"

"I would like them, aye, the green kirtle and tunic, I think," Amalie said, wondering what Garth would say if she offered to ride partway with him.

~

"No, sweetheart," he said when he returned. "You'd do better to stay here."

"But I'd like to go," she said. "Is aught amiss that makes you forbid it?"

"Just a nightmare in which the wind blew you away," he said with a rueful smile. "I've had others in which I fall into a web. But in this last one, I was webbed in chains and as helpless to stop the wind as I'd be to aid you with any trouble you might meet, riding back without me." Stroking her cheek, he kissed her and murmured, "I don't want anything to happen to you whilst I am away."

His concern warmed her as it always did, but she said, "Why should anything happen? I was safe here for months before you entered Isabel's service."

"Aye, well, it may not have occurred to you yet, but we made a dangerous enemy last night by blocking Fife's scheme. Whilst he is anywhere about, I want you to stay right here." He gave her a look. "Don't defy me in this, lass. I want to know that Isabel and Sir Kenneth are keeping you safe until I return."

She did not argue, and twenty minutes after Bess reported that Fife, Simon, and Sir Harald Boyd had crossed the Tweed with Fife's men, she went with Garth to the stableyard. Six men-at-arms were already mounted and waiting for him.

Nodding at them, Garth touched her cheek one more time, flicked another glance at the men, and mounted his horse without a word. Then, smiling warmly, he said, "I'll be back as soon as I can be, sweetheart."

Having a strong feeling that he had nearly warned her again to behave herself but had thought better of doing so before the other men, she said demurely, "I hope you will. But which way do you go, sir? Isabel says the best road south from here is the one through Kelso to the Jedburgh road. I think that is how Father went."

"Aye, she told me," he said, his eyes twinkling as if he knew she had read his thoughts. "If I were riding with a large party, I'd take that road. But Fife and Simon are going that way to Elishaw, so I'd liefer avoid it, and I can reach Hawick quicker by riding south from Dryburgh Abbey. The tracks we'll take are rougher than drove roads, but I'll have only these few lads with me. We'll travel swiftly enough."

She knew he could not travel swiftly enough to suit her.

She missed him the moment he was out of sight, and her mood was sober when she joined the other ladies in the hall. That each was aware of her marriage, and that not all were happy about it, did not surprise her.

Lady Susan shot her numerous, narrowed-eyed looks as they attended their duties, but Amalie ignored her. Lady Averil remained her usual, placid, well-bred self. If she disapproved, Isabel's heartfelt approval had silenced her, but Averil would not lavish good wishes on one of her charges in any event.

Lady Nancy, however, did not hesitate to express her delight.

"So romantic, my dear, and such a surprise to us all," she said, beaming. "But *when* did you marry him? I vow I heard not one word of such an astonishing event. Very remiss of you it was not to tell us all and let us celebrate with you."

Feeling trapped, Amalie looked around for Isabel, hoping she might intervene. But it was Sibylla who, clearly overhearing despite being some distance away, said with a chuckle, "My dear lady, you should spare the poor child's blushes. You *must* know that she did but obey her husband."

"Oh, to be sure," Lady Nancy said, nodding. "Forgive me, my dear."

Assuring her ladyship that she took no offense, Amalie drew Sibylla to the lower end of the hall on the pretext of needing her assistance to slip new covers on the cushions in the window embrasures. When they were alone there, she said, "How did you dare to say such a thing to her?"

Sibylla grinned. "You would hardly have thanked me had I explained that it was a marriage by declaration to protect you from a forced one, now would you?"

"Faith, Sibylla, you *are* a witch!"

Sibylla shook her head. "Nay, my dear, nowt o' the sort. I just have quick ears and many friends who confide in me."

"Friends?"

"Aye, sure, this household abounds with maidservants, outdoor gillies, stable lads, gardeners, men-at-arms, and so forth. I grew up in such a household, sithee, albeit not a royal one. But I soon learned that it behooves one to make friends with one's people if one does not want gossip spread about. Surely, you have noted how most folks ignore their servants, treat them like fence posts or other necessities, and say whatever they like in front of them. Moreover, even when one's people are not right there in the room, they listen."

"They do?" Amalie could not imagine servants listening at Elishaw's doors. Her mother would never allow it. Remembering her own behavior at Abbots' House, she knew she was blushing and, lest Sibylla read her mind, said hastily, "I am sure my lady mother would never keep a snooping servant."

Sibylla laughed again. "They don't have to snoop, my dear. Nor do I. We have only to keep our ears aprick. So I heard exactly how your marriage occurred. Oh, but do not fret that I shall prattle of it to anyone else, for I won't."

"I would never think such a thing," Amalie said.

"Well, I would not blame you if you did. But there is something else I learned that you should know and perhaps share with Sir Garth—mayhap with your lady mother, as well, if she can still exert influence over Simon."

"Mercy, what did you hear?"

"That villain Fife," Sibylla muttered, lowering her voice—although, unlike most people, without looking about to see if anyone might hear her. "Evidently, he told Simon that if that so-delightful henchman of his cannot have *you*, he is to have the lady Rosalie. I should not interfere, I warrant, but I think her too young for such a creature. Moreover, I doubt the news pleases you or will please your mother."

"Sakes," Amalie exclaimed, "'tis Simon it will displease! He would never agree to such a union. He could not! She is only in her thirteenth year."

"Apparently, Fife declared her to be of legal age for marrying, and indeed, she is, you know. Moreover, Fife declares himself the law of Scotland. So even if she were not old enough, recall that only a few months ago, when his brother David of Strathearn died, Fife arranged for David's little heiress to marry one of Fife's own vassals. And she is younger than Rosalie."

Several thoughts struck Amalie at once—so fast that she could barely take them in—but one stood above all the others.

"Faith, Sibylla, Fife means to have Elishaw!"

"To be sure, he does," Sibylla agreed. "It is a border fortress that has stayed neutral in nearly every conflict. 'Tis only logical that Fife would want to force it to support Scotland. But he controls it now, does he not? Simon is Fife's man."

Amalie stared at her and felt an almost physical shift in her mind as pieces rapidly fell into place. "I . . . I must go," she said, turning blindly away.

"Where?" Sibylla demanded.

"I must think and . . . and tidy Isabel's bedchamber," Amalie said. "Forgive me, and pray tell Isabel I will explain my absence later, but I must do this, Sibylla."

Realizing how odd that must sound, and knowing that the midday meal must be nearly ready to serve, she repeated hastily, "I simply *must* think."

Sibylla did not utter a word of protest as Amalie hurried away and up the stairs, first to Isabel's bedchamber to be sure all was tidy there. Then, seeing that Bess had put everything to rights, she hurried to her own chamber and found it reassuringly empty.

She did not send for Bess but quickly changed to her riding dress.

Then, containing her soul in patience until she heard the bell that summoned the princess's attendants to the great hall and sent men-at-arms and outdoor servants to the dormer dining hall, she picked up her whip and went down the front stairs slowly and warily, praying she would not meet anyone.

Slipping out through the front door, she took the outer track past the garden hedge to avoid passing before the hall windows, and went on to the stable.

Addressing the only lad she saw, she ordered him to bring out her favorite mount. When he said he would also let her two grooms know she was riding out, she did not object. They would not hinder her, and in truth, she did not want to ride all the way to Elishaw alone. Moreover, if she *did* object, she had a feeling she would discover that Garth or one of the other knights, perhaps even Sir Harald, had given strict orders that none of the ladies was to ride out alone.

Waiting for her horse, she paced impatiently and stared at the ground, letting her thoughts flow as they would. When she turned to find a shadow right in front of her, she looked up, startled, to see Sibylla with her eyebrows raised and a knowing smile on her face.

"Where are we going?" she asked mildly.

Chapter 19

As Sibylla raised a hand to hurry the two grooms, just then emerging from the dormer, Amalie said fiercely, "You cannot go with me!"

"Certainly, I can," Sibylla replied. "I suppose I could keep you from going, for that matter. I need only tell Isabel what you are about. But in troth, I am curious to discover how you mean to—"

She broke off as the first groom reached them, to say with a smile, "Fetch my horse as well as the lady Amalie's and, pray, make haste. You will both ride with us, of course." When they had hurried off, she said, "How *do* you think you can stop the all-powerful Fife, my dear?"

"I don't know, but I must do this," Amalie said. "He will kill Simon."

"How dreadful! But I thought you did not like Simon."

"I don't! But he is my brother, Sibylla. And Elishaw is his, not Fife's."

"But he is Fife's own man," Sibylla protested. "Why should Fife kill him?"

"I can't explain it exactly," Amalie admitted. "Oh, I do know you cannot possibly understand, but—"

"Faith, Amalie, who *would* understand if I do not? Have you decided how you mean to explain this start of yours to Sir Garth?"

"He will know that I—" In the face of Sibylla's wry disbelief, she broke off with a sigh. She knew as well as Sibylla evidently did that Garth would not only *not* understand but would vehemently oppose what she was about to do. Moreover, he had warned her not to defy his wishes, and she knew from experience that even when he issued such warnings lightly, it was wiser to heed them.

"Oh, very well," she admitted. "He will not like it, but I must go anyway. As it is, Simon is as good as alone with those two, and I don't trust either one of them."

The grooms came quickly with their horses, and the two women had to delay their conversation until they had all mounted and ridden out of the yard.

Amalie was silent, knowing she could not keep her stubborn, self-appointed companion from accompanying her without incurring Isabel's censure and a likely command to stay put. She also doubted that she could persuade Isabel or anyone other than Sibylla of the still-nebulous danger she believed threatened Simon.

Signing to the two grooms to fall behind, Sibylla said, "I know of no one who trusts Fife, except perhaps your brother Simon and a few others in Fife's retinue. But do not forget, my dear, Fife is now as powerful as he has always sought to be. One challenges him only at great risk to oneself."

"I do know that," Amalie said. "'Tis one reason I fear for Simon."

Sibylla nodded. "I agree that they may soon find themselves at odds over young Rosalie. And mayhap our presence at Elishaw will stay Fife's hand if he does contemplate mischief. I own, in fact, that I do not fully understand why he is making this so-called progress of his."

"He wants to flaunt his power," Amalie said.

"Aye, sure, but his doing so may just annoy folks," Sibylla said. "Borderers have been loyal to the Douglases for nearly a hundred years, since they allied with the Bruces of Annandale to free Scotland from the English oppressors. Fife is unlikely to shift that loyalty to himself, nor is the Douglas likely to allow it."

Amalie nearly said that Garth had sent for Archie, but she decided she should not discuss his business, or Archie's, with anyone else. Sibylla knew that Garth had gone somewhere. But the likelihood was that, despite her odd powers—whatever they were—she did not know *where* he had gone, or why, unless Isabel had told her.

They discussed Fife's ambitions and general behavior for some time instead and found themselves in cordial agreement as to his villainy.

Then Sibylla said casually, "What *will* you tell Sir Garth when he learns what you . . . what we are doing?"

Realizing only then that Garth might have unpleasant things to say to Sibylla as well as to herself, Amalie said, "I think he'll be too angry with me to blame you."

"You don't seem too concerned about that," Sibylla said with a twinkle.

A shudder rippled through Amalie. As much as she

might tell herself it did not matter what Garth did or said to her, it did.

Remembering that he had once complained that family members were just ties that kept a man from enjoying his freedom, she doubted he would even understand why she cared about Simon. But she cared about her family, even those who had betrayed her or refused to listen to her.

She was her mother's daughter, and her father's. Her parents had both done all they could to protect their family, people, and property without regard for the needs of other Borderers. Some had called them selfish and self-serving.

If caring for one's own folk above all others was selfish, then so be it.

To Sibylla, she said quietly, "I don't know what Garth will say or do. He can make me feel awful just by looking at me a certain way, and he does not hesitate to say what he thinks or to act on his thoughts. But he can also make me angry."

"Somehow I don't imagine you throwing things at him," Sibylla said dryly.

Despite the turn her thoughts had taken, Amalie could not help smiling. "No, I don't throw things, but I did hit him once."

"You didn't!"

"I did so."

"Dare I ask what he did?"

"You may ask," Amalie said, gathering her dignity. "I shan't tell you."

Sibylla grinned. "I don't blame you. Is he still having nightmares?"

"Mercy, I never told you he'd had *one*. And *he* certainly did not tell you."

Sibylla's grin faded. She said seriously, "You may not admit it, and he did not, but I could tell that one morning that he'd had one. Has he endured others?"

"Everyone has nightmares sometimes."

Sibylla remained silent, reminding Amalie of Wat Scott by giving her the same feeling Wat did of a willingness to wait all day if necessary. Still, she would not tell her about Garth's first nightmare, about Will's death. With a wry smile, she said, "He dreams of webs. Last night, he saw me on a cliff and could not keep me from falling off. Doubtless he will recall *that* when he learns about our trip today."

"Webs?"

"Aye," Amalie said with a sigh. "Sithee, he does not like feeling bound."

Sibylla's eyebrows rose. "Faith, is he one who thinks marriage binds a man?"

"He did tell me once that families do bind men. But he seems content enough. Should we not ride faster?" she asked, wanting to change the subject.

"Nay, for 'tis a warm day and we've a good distance to travel—four or five hours at least, even if naught goes amiss."

"How do you know? Have you ridden to Elishaw before?"

"No, I just like to collect facts. One never knows when they'll be useful."

"Aye, well," Amalie said. "Simon and Fife will have taken the Kelso road, so I was going to follow them, because with such a large group, they will be remarked wherever they go."

"An excellent plan," Sibylla agreed. "I was concerned about how long it would take us, because the moon will doubtless hide itself again tonight. It is even now drifting to the horizon. The sky is clear, though, so if something does delay us, we should still be able to see the road by starlight."

Amalie frowned. "We won't, though, because for the last few miles or so we pass through Wauchope Forest. It is not as dense as Ettrick Forest is, but starlight by itself won't serve us well there."

"Then we must take care not to meet with any delay," Sibylla said.

Amalie sent a prayer aloft then that they would reach Elishaw safely and that Garth would not murder them both for going there.

Garth and his men kept up a steady if not rapid pace and passed Dryburgh Abbey soon after midday. They stopped half an hour later to eat and rest their horses in shade by the frothy waters of a tumbling burn above Longnewton village.

After three more hours of riding, they reached the ancient town of Hawick on a high, narrow ridge of land in the angle formed by the confluence of the river Teviot and Slitrig Water. The sharp angle between the two and the steep banks of both being admirably suited for security and defense, the town had served for many years as a stronghold for Borderers in general and Douglases in particular.

To Garth's surprise, as they approached from below the stockade entrance at the town's southwest end, the only direction from which one *could* enter, he saw no sign that Archie and his army of Douglases had arrived.

Riding up the hill toward the open stockade gate, they commanded a panoramic view of approaches from the south and saw no sign of the Douglas or his usual large contingent. Knowing that Tam would wait for him at the Douglases' Black Tower just inside the gate, Garth urged his horse to a faster pace.

When he reached the tower, instead of Tam's huge, easily recognizable form pacing back and forth in front of it, he saw the equally recognizable, redheaded, and much smaller Sym Elliot.

The boy saw him at the same time and dashed toward him as Garth reined in and said, "Any word yet from the Douglas, lad?"

"Aye, he waited for some other Douglases to catch up wi' him in Langholm," Sym answered. "But he'll be here afore dark, his man said. Tam be gone, too, Sir Garth," he added hastily. "But he left me here to *tell* ye."

"Did he go to meet Archie?"

"Nay, he went afore the Douglas's man came to say he'd been delayed."

"Then—"

"Sakes, I'm a-trying to tell ye!" Sym said. "There's been murder done!"

"Murder?"

"Aye, sir, a farmer from somewheres up near the abbey did send for the monks there, 'cause this morning he found three dead men in one o' his fields."

"Very grim, I'm sure, but what has it to do with us?"

Sym grimaced. "I'm no telling it the way the monk did. One o' them was no dead yet, and he did say he came from Elishaw. Sithee, that be the lady Am—"

"I know that Elishaw is the lady Amalie's home, lad," Garth said. He recalled with a chill that Tom Murray had sent two of his men back to Elishaw to warn them that he would be bringing Lady Murray with him when he returned from Scott's Hall. So he had taken just two men with him to Scott's Hall. "What else?"

"He said four men had attacked them, and gey well armed they were, wi' swords and dirks. They didna want nowt, he said. They just cut them down."

"Anything more?"

"Aye," Sym said, grimacing. "He recognized one from Sweethope Hill. He didna ken the name, sir, but he said he'd strutted about as if he owned the place."

Garth could easily picture Boyd from the description but knew that would be useless as evidence against him. Boyd's supposed trip to Kelso would be easy to disprove if he had not gone, and thus be more useful. However, Boyd's following and attacking Tom Murray, if that was what he had done, made no sense to him.

"Is that all?" he asked Sym.

"Aye, sir. Only except that Tam rode to the Hall to tell Himself, 'cause we knew, if Tom Murray never went there, no one at the Hall would ken that Sir Iagan be dead as well. D'ye think mayhap someone murdered him, too?"

"Tom Murray said his father died in a fall from a horse," Garth told him.

"Aye, sure, but Tom Murray doesna always tell the truth," Sym said with a look so black that Garth was tempted to ask what else Tom had done.

Deciding to ask Amalie first, in case Tom's previous untruths had also concerned her, he said instead, "How long ago did Tam leave?"

Sym glanced at the sun. "Two hours, mayhap less.

He'll be getting near the Hall by now, sir. It be nobbut eleven miles, and he'll no ha' wasted his time."

"Why did the monk come here to tell you?"

"We told them when we stopped to get summat to eat at the abbey earlier that we'd be going to Hawick. Also, sithee, the dead men did say they was bound for the Hall. What be ye going to do, Sir Garth?"

Garth had been wondering that himself. That Tom Murray was dead did not stir much sympathy in him for Tom Murray, but he had a feeling the man's death was going to be a sharp blow for Amalie. Still, she was safe enough now at Sweethope Hill, and he'd be riding back himself as soon as he reported to Archie.

He had more to tell him now, but none of it answered the questions that had begun his search. He knew nothing new about James Douglas's death other than that Isabel's conviction was even stronger than Archie had led him to believe. As for Will's murder, although he knew the killer's name, the culprit still eluded him.

To Sym, he said, "Tam should be back before nightfall then. He would not expect you to return to the Hall alone."

Sym shrugged. "I've done it oft enow, sir. But he did say he'd be back as quick as he could. He didna ken if Himself would be joining the Douglas or no, sithee, on account o' the wee bairn coming. But Himself will come now, any road."

"Why is that?"

"'Cause he swore to Sir Iagan Murray when he wed our lady Meg that he'd aid the Murrays whenever they ha' need o' him. And if they dinna need him now, I'm thinking, they never will."

Garth was not as certain that Wat would see Tom's

death, or even Sir Iagan's, as cause enough to leave his wife on the point of delivering their child. But he did think Wat would ride to Hawick to see Archie. Another thought occurred to him. "Will he not escort Lady Murray home and attend her husband's burial?"

Sym's eyes twinkled. "Himself doesna hold wi' plodding all day to ride only twenty-five miles. But he may tell Tam to see to it, though," he added, frowning. "And, sithee, they may come this way, too, 'cause the Hawick road be better for her litter than the track we use to Elishaw, through the hills north o' Hermitage."

"Elishaw lies southeast of here, does it not?" Garth said.

"It does, aye. From here, I'm thinking it must be about ten miles. Ye'd take the Hobkirk road, then cut down through the hills into the forest."

"Wauchope Forest?"

"Aye. Were ye thinking o' going there yourself?"

Garth grimaced. Impulse and instinct both urged him to go, to confront Boyd and see what he could learn from the man. However, Boyd was with Fife, not to mention Fife's large contingent of men-at-arms and Simon of Elishaw. Simon had his own men at the castle and would doubtless bar the gates to him.

In any event, he had to wait for Archie and for Wat, if Wat was coming. And Tam would expect him to be there if he did return by nightfall.

"I'll wait for the others," he said. "Mayhap you can show me where the Douglas will set up his encampment."

"Aye, sure," Sym said. "He's been here afore, sithee."

"You seem to know much for a lad your age."

Sym shrugged. "I used to follow me brother and his

lads sometimes when they went a-reiving. It be good, I think, for a man to ken the land around him."

"I think so, too," Garth said, remembering his own rambles as a lad. He had known every inch of land for miles around Westruther.

Wishing he knew the land around Hawick as well, he resigned himself to patience and settled down to wait with Sym for Archie, Wat, or Tam to arrive.

The first rider to come seeking him, however, came from Sweethope Hill.

Amalie and Sibylla reached the outskirts of Wauchope Forest while the sun was still some distance above the western horizon. Both were weary from the long ride, and Amalie suspected their horses were weary, too. But they were Border bred and strong. They would carry them all the way without difficulty.

"Is there a track through the forest?" Sibylla asked as they entered the woodland, following what appeared to be a faint deer trail.

"Not from here, but I know this area," Amalie said. "We are about two or three miles from Elishaw. See those two craggy peaks yonder through the trees?" she asked, pointing. "If we head right between them, we'll soon come to the castle."

Looking toward the sun, Sibylla eyed its position skeptically. "I hope you know what you are doing. After sunset, we'll have less than an hour of light—less than that in these woods. Faith, what if they won't let us in?"

Amalie made a wry face. "I'm more worried that Simon *will* let us in and that then . . ." She shrugged, not wanting to put into words any of the unpleasant images that had been teasing her mind for the past few miles.

"What will you tell him?"

"I haven't a notion," she admitted. "Much depends on our reception. I'll wager that Fife will be nice at first, even charming. We've both seen him act so."

"Aye, we have," Sibylla said. "But his charm is wayward, and he currently has no reason to treat us well."

"He has no cause to treat *you* badly," Amalie said. "Or does he?"

"Nay, I've not crossed him—that he knows of—unless he decides I have just by accompanying you today. But if you are right about his intent, he will find us very much in the way. And when people get in his way . . ."

"Sakes, he cannot murder a whole castleful of witnesses," Amalie protested. "I just want to keep him from murdering Simon and taking Elishaw. He has done as much, after all, when he wanted other estates—or so people say."

"He cannot gain Elishaw just by murdering Simon," Sibylla said dryly. "You have two adult brothers, after all, and doubtless other close male kinsmen."

"Aye, although I'd as lief keep Fife from murdering Tom, too," Amalie muttered, thinking of a time when she'd happily have done that herself. "Moreover, many of our close kinsmen are English Percies, which may not count in Scotland."

"It would likely be a Murray, aye, who would inherit Elishaw," Sibylla said.

Conversation languished then, because Amalie fell prey to her own thoughts and Sibylla remained silent. By the time Elishaw's walls and tower hove into view, Amalie had begun to feel utterly inadequate to the task she had set herself.

Simon might just lock her in her old bedchamber and refuse to listen to a word she said to him. But what, a disturbing demon in her mind whispered, if he treated her as Garth had after she had hit him?

Instead of increasing her depression, the image of Garth grew larger and steadied her until she decided she could deal with ten Simons.

~

Garth recognized the rider as one of Sweethope's stable lads but thought idly that Isabel must have sent a message for him to relay to Douglas.

"You must have left soon after we did," he said as the lad flung himself from the saddle and threw his reins to the waiting Sym.

"Ye'd been gone a good two hours by then, sir, but the lady Sibylla said I ought to catch ye well afore nightfall, and so I have. It be a gey good thing ye told folks which way ye'd be coming."

Garth frowned as a prickle of unease stirred. "What was the hurry?"

"The lady Amalie, sir . . ." He hesitated, doubtless, Garth thought grimly, because his own fierce frown put the lad off whatever he'd been about to say.

Or because the lad feared the news would put him in a flaming temper.

"Tell 'im, ye dafty," Sym said sharply, although the other lad was years older than he was. "What be amiss then?"

Garth bit his lip, both to keep from speaking even

more sharply and to avoid smiling at Sym's taking charge as naturally as one who did so all the time.

The messenger said, "Lady Sibylla said to tell ye the lady Amalie be riding to Elishaw, Sir Garth. She said ye'd want to know as soon as I could tell ye."

Suppressing a chill of fear, he said evenly, "She was right, but surely she was mistaken about the lady Amalie, lad. She would not ride such a distance by herself. And to what purpose?"

"I dinna ken her purpose," the lad said. "But the lady Sibylla did say to tell ye that she'd be going with her, and taking two lads from the stable, as well."

"What the devil was she thinking to let her leave?" Garth demanded.

The lad's eyes widened. "I dinna ken that neither, sir. She told me what to do afore she joined the lady Amalie in the yard."

Garth pressed his lips together, unable to express his immediate thoughts either to the stable lad or to Sym Elliot.

Sym was under no such restraint. "Take yourself off now," he said. "Ye can tell them lads yonder to give ye summat to eat if ye're hungry. But go on to them afore ye say summat here to set the man right off."

As Garth got to his feet, he realized that Sym sounded exactly as Wat Scott did when he was fast losing patience.

"Where be ye a-going, sir?" Sym asked as if he already knew.

"I'm going to take my men and ride to Elishaw," Garth said. "You tell the Douglas I had pressing business and ask him to join me there as soon as he can. If Buccleuch comes, tell him the same."

"Aye, well, he'll follow straightaway, Himself will, being he's promised. The lady Amalie counts as a Murray, as much as any. My lady Meg would surely say so. But ye shouldna leave me to take your words to the Douglas. He'd heed one o' them men-at-arms o' yours afore he'd listen to me."

"He'll listen to you," Garth said firmly. "And I'll need my men."

"Likely, ye're right," Sym said, giving the men a black look. "But do any o' them ken the forest? Sithee, sir, it be full o' bracken, scrub, and treacherous bogs. Them lads dinna look like Wauchope lads to me."

"They are not. Do you mean to say you know the forest well enough to guide me and my men safely through it to Elishaw?"

"Aye, sure, *and* do it even in the dark o' night as I'll have to by the look o' things," Sym said confidently. "Sakes, but I have done it in the dark! However, ye'd best be sending one o' them others to meet the Douglas, and yet another to meet Himself and Tam, because I canna be in two places at once," he added.

Garth eyed him sternly. "You make a good argument, my lad, but you'd do well to mind your tongue unless *you* are burning to set me right off."

"Aye, well, I'll mind it then. At least ye listen to a man."

Garth summoned his men and gave them their orders. Then, noticing the lad from Sweethope, whose presence had slipped his mind, he told him to wait until the Douglas or Buccleuch arrived to give him further instructions.

"Tell them I said you should rest here in Hawick and ride back tomorrow."

The boy's eyes widened. "I could ride with ye, sir. I'm no so tired as that."

"I thank you, but no," Garth said. Having one young-ster along was more than he wanted, but Sym's argument was persuasive. It would do them no good to have to flounder their way through the forest.

"What'll ye do when we get there?" Sym asked as they rode down the hill from Hawick.

"I haven't a notion yet," Garth admitted.

"Aye, well, ye'll think o' summat afore then," Sym said. "Or I will."

⁓

Murray men-at-arms that manned the tall, sturdy gates at Elishaw opened them when Amalie shouted her name. If they looked stunned to see two unexpected women ride into the bailey, escorted only by grooms, they did not question them.

Dismounting unaided in the yard and handing her reins to a gillie she did not recognize, Amalie told him to rub the horses down well and look after them. "They have carried us a long way today," she said.

Two others came running to help him, and the gillie assured her they would see to them. As he turned away, a man-at-arms approached her.

"I trow ye'll remember me, m'lady," he said with a bow.

"Aye, sure, Jed Hay," Amalie said. "I hope you and your kinsmen are well."

"Aye, m'lady. I'll take you in, shall I? The laird has guests tonight."

"The Governor of the Realm, no less," Amalie said,

suppressing the shock she felt at the reminder that the laird now was Simon and not her father.

"And a great number of the Governor's men, aye," Jed Hay said. "Some did ride out to camp in the woods, so we'll hope they dinna set the forest afire."

"How many are inside?" Sibylla asked.

"Fifty or more, plus our own lads, mistress."

"This is the lady Sibylla Cavers, Jed," Amalie said. "I expect we ought to go upstairs to my chamber if the hall is full of men-at-arms. Pray send someone to tell the laird I've arrived and ask him to come to me when he can."

Jed Hay shook his head. "I'm to take ye straight in, m'lady," he said. "The captain o' the guard sent *me* to tell the laird that visitors were coming. And the laird said to bring them in straightaway, nae matter who they'd be."

"Then that is what you must do," Amalie said, glancing at Sibylla.

Sibylla merely nodded, and they followed Jed inside.

As they turned the last curve of the spiral stairs and approached the archway opening into the great hall, the enticing aroma of roast mutton greeted them.

The men were at supper.

Beside her, Sibylla moaned appreciatively.

"Faith, are you hungry?" Amalie murmured.

"Famished! I do hope they feed us."

A fire roared in the great hooded fireplace in the east wall near the dais, which occupied nearly the full width of the north end of the hall.

Simon sat in what had been Sir Iagan's two-elbow chair at the center of the long board, facing the archway, with Fife on his right in the place of honor.

Sir Harald Boyd sat at Fife's right with the priest at the end.

Fife looked so distinctive in his customary all-black elegance that, despite Simon's chair, an observer might think Fife the master of the castle.

Men on benches crowded both sides of two trestle tables set perpendicular to the dais. Without hesitation, Amalie walked up between them onto the dais, where she made her curtsy as she looked directly into her brother's astonished gaze.

"Good evening, Simon," she said, rising. "Good evening, Lord Fife."

She saw no reason to acknowledge Sir Harald or the priest.

"Amalie!" Simon exclaimed. "What the . . . what are you doing here?"

"I have come to attend our lord father's burial, of course. And, as you see, the lady Sibylla Cavers was kind enough to come with me."

Beside and slightly behind her, as if to let Amalie take the lead—and perhaps the greater share of blame, as well—Sibylla swept a deep but silent curtsy.

Simon glanced at Fife, then back at Amalie. "You were most unwise to travel so far without a proper escort, madam. Where is your husband?"

It was the first time anyone had addressed her as "madam," and she took a moment to savor it before she said, "My husband? Why, he has gone to meet the Douglas, of course, but they should be here shortly. I warrant you were expecting them, were you not?" Without awaiting a response, she added with a smile, "In the meantime, Simon, I do hope you mean to give us supper. It is a greater distance than I had thought from Sweethope to Elishaw. We are starving."

The notion of mentioning the Douglas had occurred to

her as she walked toward the dais. The necessity of passing among so many rough-looking men had sent her mind scrambling for images of Garth to bolster her courage, as that image had done earlier. Instead, the notion of evoking the Douglas's power and the fact of his being so near slid into her mind. The looks of astonishment on all three men's faces were all that she had hoped they might be.

Now, if only she could manage to retain her dignity, not to mention her freedom, until Sir Garth and the Douglas arrived.

Chapter 20

Garth and his men had reached the outskirts of Wauchope Forest, but the sun had set and the last rays of dusky light were rapidly fading.

"Are you sure you know the way?" Garth asked Sym. "It will be dark soon."

"Aye, sir, I ken fine how to go, but I'm still wondering what we'll do when we get there. Wi' Sir Iagan dead, how well d'ye ken the new laird?"

"Simon Murray."

"That's him, aye."

"We are barely acquainted, but I warrant he'll recognize me. Certainly Fife and Sir Harald Boyd will, if Boyd is still with Fife. And I assume he must be as he was with him when they left Sweethope Hill."

"Will Simon Murray let us in?"

Garth thought about that. He could hardly be sure that Simon's guards would open the gates to six armed men and a lad. Fife might, though. With as many as he had in his tail, and with his own man now master of Elishaw . . .

"Fife may tell him to let us in just to show he doesn't fear us," he said.

Sym made a rude noise. "That Fife be nobbut a snooling feardie. Ye should hear what they said o' him after he rode into England wi' Archie the Grim two years ago. Puffed off to everyone that he were the true leader, Fife did—*and* still does. But the man be so timorous that the only time he *did* lead, the men said, was when he led them home again—*and* at a right good clip, they said."

"Mind you don't repeat that where he may hear of it, my lad," Garth warned him. "Fife may be a physical coward, but he's a powerful one and just the sort that a wise man watches closely. He's gey ruthless and knows how to get what he wants."

"Aye, he'd liefer kill a man as stare at him," Sym said, nodding wisely. "I were just thinking, though. If we tell 'em we've come from Scott's Hall wi' a message for the new laird from his mam or me lady Meg, like as no, they'll think me lady's birthed her bairn and be fain to hear all about it."

"I won't spin such a tale to the men on the gate," Garth said.

"Coo, then I'll tell 'em and ye can keep your gob shut."

"You had better not let me catch you telling lies."

"Well, I wouldna lie to *ye*, would I? A man doesna lie to his friends."

Glancing back to see that his men had formed a single line behind them, Garth noted that the one in the lead swiftly covered a smile. A man with quick ears, then, but remembering that he could no longer claim *he* never told lies, Garth said only, "We'll see how it goes."

"But ye canna decide when we get there, 'cause ye'd need a banner and all," Sym said. "I've got a wee one, sithee. Me lady Meg made it for me, so I could show it when anyone gives me trouble."

"But you cannot fly Buccleuch's banner!"

"Nay, or Himself would skelp me to an inch o' me life, or Dod would," Sym said. "This be nobbut a wee banner wi' her badge—a Scott moon and a Murray key—to show I belong to her. I had it when I came here afore wi' messages from her."

"Did she give it to you just for that occasion, or for any time you might think you'd like to use it?"

Sym hesitated, then looked at Garth from under his lashes. "Mayhap I forgot to give it back to her after," he said. "But she never asked for it, neither."

"We'll fly it, then, since you can make some small claim to owning it," Garth said. "But if they question us, we'll say only what's true."

"Aye, sure, we can do that," Sym said. "Look yonder now, sir. Ye can see where the castle be, for they've lighted lanterns on the ramparts."

"It will be dark before we arrive, though," Garth said.

"Aye, sure, but I've eyes like me cat, sir. I'll get us there."

Garth hoped he was right, because the sense of urgency that had plagued him from the moment the messenger arrived from Sweethope Hill had not lessened.

If Fife or Simon, or that devil Boyd, dared to lay a hand on his lass . . .

Amalie's fear that Simon might order her to her bed-chamber, as he and their mother had often done when she annoyed them, had proved groundless, for when she mentioned supper, he gestured to the gillies to lay two more places.

The men in the hall had fallen silent, so that when Fife spoke as Amalie and Sibylla took their places at Simon's left, Fife did not need to raise his voice.

"Lady Westruther did say that you are the lady Sibylla Cavers, did she not?" he said in the same silken tones Amalie had heard at Scone.

"Yes, my lord," Sibylla said. "I, too, serve the princess Isabel."

"Then your father is Sir Malcolm Cavers, of Akermoor."

"That is so, my lord. As you doubtless also know, my brother Sir Hugh died at Otterburn and my godfather is the present Earl of Douglas."

Fife's lips pressed into a thin line. Although his demeanor changed in no other way, Amalie decided that he had *not* known who Sibylla's godfather was.

Amalie had not known either, and she wondered if it would prove an asset or simply ignite the coals they were stirring.

Had they done no more than bring Fife two hostages who might allow him to force Garth and the Earl of Douglas both to do his bidding?

Sym rode beside Garth, proudly holding the banner Meg Scott had given him so its device would show clearly when they drew near enough. Women who did not hold titles in their own right did not rightfully have badges, but it had been clever of Meg to give Sym a device that identified him as her messenger, and Buccleuch's.

Even that small pretense rubbed Garth wrong, but if his lass *was* inside—with two dangerous men, if not three—he would pretend and not count the cost.

They had dipped into a declivity, so he could no longer see the rampart lights. He could barely see more than the shape of his hand if he held it up, or the dense shape of the horse and rider beside him, but the boy rode confidently.

Behind them, the men were silent, so Garth heard only the padding steps of horses on dry leaves and pine needles of the forest floor, and creaking harness.

Up ahead, except for an occasional peep, chirp, or screech from one of the forest's nocturnal denizens, all was silence, too.

~

After Sibylla's declaration of her relationship to the Douglas, Amalie had struggled to conceal her own reaction, lest Fife suspect from it that Sibylla had lied to him. Amalie suspected that she had. For although it was normal to identify oneself by one's most prominent kinsmen, to the best of her recollection, Sibylla had never mentioned a kinship to Archie the Grim.

Simon had not reacted to her declaration, though, so perhaps he *had* known, although how he would have if Fife had not, Amalie could not imagine. He gestured to his carver to see to their wants, then turned to them while she was still trying to assess his demeanor and said dryly, "I trust you two enjoyed an uneventful ride."

"We did," she said. Hoping to ward off his inclination to scold, she added, "We avoided riding through Kelso and Jedburgh because we thought it wiser than showing ourselves in such populous places."

Beyond Simon, Sir Harald said, "The wisest course would have been to stay at Sweethope, lass. But doubtless your so-called husband will not mind that you've ridden here alone. You should be glad you did not marry me."

Before Amalie could retort that she was *very* glad, Simon forestalled her by saying sternly, "You will address my sister in a more civil tone, Boyd."

"Oh, to be sure," Boyd said with a dismissive gesture. "I meant no offense."

Although astonished to hear Simon take her part rather than agree with Boyd, Amalie feared he might now demand that the other man apologize. In common civility, she would have to accept, and she did *not* want to.

But Simon returned his attention to his trencher.

Fife said, "Do you perchance know *when* the Earl of Douglas expects to arrive here, Lady Westruther? Darkness is already at hand, after all."

Surprised and a bit annoyed that Fife had been first to address her by her new title, and wondering if Garth would agree that "Lady Westruther" was the correct one for her, she was silent until Sibylla nudged her with an elbow.

The Amalie said hastily, "I know only that the Douglas commanded a meeting this morning at Hawick, sir."

"When did Westruther receive that message?"

Deciding she did not want to encourage further questions, she said, "He did not tell me that, for he does not talk of such things. I am only a woman, after all."

Boyd said, "Two messengers arrived Sunday afternoon, my lord. Neither said where they sprang from, but I expect now that they must have come from Douglas. They had gone when I awoke this morning."

"Then someone has been talking out of turn," Fife said with a frown.

"Sakes, sir, you have never said that your progress through the Borders was to be kept secret," Simon said. "Doubtless many know of your intent by now. At Lauder, as I recall, it was a common topic of conversation."

Fife shook his head. "Douglas returned to Threave after the coronation. We had not been at Lauder long enough for anyone to have sent word to him and for him to have sent messengers so quickly to Westruther."

With a wry smile, Simon said, "Many watch your movements, my lord, and surely you know that word travels exceptionally fast here in the Borders. Recall that, unlike noblemen who travel with large retinues and strings of sumpter ponies, Borderers travel light and fast. Reivers ride fifty miles or more in a single night, and even if one follows the roads, Threave is but sixty miles from Lauder. You have traveled with Archie the Grim. Does *he* keep to roads or travel slowly?"

Fife pursed his lips.

Neither Amalie nor Sibylla spoke, although Amalie flicked a glance at Simon.

He was watching Fife, so she could not see his expression.

She did discern his tension.

Fife stood. "Mayhap the Douglas *is* coming tonight, although I doubt it. I should think he'd be wise enough to stay the night in Langholm or Hawick, or even at Hermitage, and not try to lead his men through this forest in pitch darkness."

"He'll carry torches if he enters the forest, sir," Boyd said. "Our men on the ramparts will see his party and give warning long before he arrives."

The tension in Simon's manner increased, but Amalie doubted if anyone else noted it. She could even sympathize with him, for he was Murray of Elishaw now. He would not look forward with anything but dismay to a conflict that might arise between entities as powerful as the Governor of the Realm and the Earl of Douglas.

She shifted her gaze back to Fife, now nodding at Boyd.

"Whether or not Douglas comes tonight, I shall ride to meet him," Fife said. "He will appreciate such a signal courtesy whether it occurs in the forest or at Hawick. I do think the latter the more likely destination, though, for doubtless he desires to accompany our progress through the Borders. I shall welcome him if that is so. It will do the nobles hereabouts much good to see us together."

"I'll ride with you then, my lord," Boyd said, also standing.

"Nay, for you must stay here to greet Lady Murray and her daughter when they arrive," Fife said. "There is business for you to attend with them and quickly. To that end, I shall leave the priest with you."

"Do you mean to go at once, sir?" Simon asked.

"I do, aye," Fife said. "Send your people to warn mine in your bailey and also those camped outside your gates that I want to be away as fast as we can. Your men can help mine prepare. Boyd, I want a word with you, so walk

downstairs with me. Good evening to you both," he added
with a curt nod to Amalie and Sibylla.

Watching them go, Amalie drew a breath, met Sibylla's
gaze, and then turned to Simon and started to speak, only
to stop at a slight shake of his head.

Realizing that the priest still sat at the table, although
all the other men in the hall had hurried after Fife, she
kept silent and reached for a roll.

Boyd hurried back into the chamber just then, telling her that whatever Fife had said to him had not taken
long.

"His lordship would have the wedding take place as
soon as your mother and sister arrive, Simon. You must
tell them at once so the priest can attend to it."

"You don't think such a course overly zealous, Boyd?
My mother is most unlikely to agree to it whilst my father
lies unburied."

"Then you must command her," Boyd said. "You are
master here, after all."

Raising one eyebrow, Simon said, "Have you met my
mother?"

Boyd shrugged. "I saw her at Sweethope Hill, of
course, but no one thought to present me. It cannot matter, though. She is just a woman."

"Even if I were to agree with that assessment, your
priest has said he will not perform a ceremony with an
unwilling bride. You might, therefore, want to consider
whether my youngest sister will *agree* to marry you."

"Sakes, man, she is thirteen. If she balks, you will
command her, too."

"I could, of course, but I don't think I will."

"Damnation, but I suspected as much, although my
lord Fife assured me that you would obey his wishes,"

Boyd said. "Fortunately, I suggested precautions, and my lord agreed to them." Drawing his sword, he shouted, "Lads, to me!"

A dozen men-at-arms rushed into the hall, weapons drawn.

⁓

"Here now, open them gates," Sym shouted imperiously to Elishaw's guards. "D'ye no see this banner, what the lady Meg made me herself? We've come to see the laird, and sithee, we be appetized and fair pinched wi' hunger, so dinna delay!"

It was as well that no one challenged them, because Garth had no idea what he might have said after that. The gates swung open, and following Sym, he and his men rode into the cobbled bailey.

As they dismounted, he quietly ordered his men to see to the horses and await events. Then to his young guide, he said dryly, "Do you call that string of blethers you were spinning out there 'telling them nobbut the truth'?"

"Aye, sure, *I'm* famished. Are ye no?"

"And the lady Meg stitched that banner with her own hands?"

"D'ye think she canna do such things?"

"That is *not* what I said."

"Aye, well, she had it made or made it herself," Sym said. "I demanded nae details from her, and nor will them mugs on the gate. Mayhap *ye* will, and then ye can say if I lied or no."

"You stay here with the men," Garth said curtly. "I'm going inside."

"Ye might think on that again," Sym said. "Look yonder."

Glancing in the direction of the lad's nod, he saw a score or more of men emerging from the main entrance. Fife was with them, and looking their way.

⟨ ⟩

Simon had leapt to his feet when the men-at-arms rushed in, but Amalie saw that he had armed himself with only his dirk, and was not surprised when he stayed where he was as he exclaimed, "Are you daft, Boyd?"

"Don't act too hastily, Simon," Boyd retorted. "Fife told me to treat you well, but he left me these men and he has given me his promise. You know he will keep it whether you live or die, and I think your little sister will quickly agree to marry me when she learns that your death will be the price of her defiance. As for your lady mother, I'll deal with her just as easily."

"Don't be so sure," Simon retorted, his temper clearly rising. "My brother, Tom, and likely Buccleuch and a large retinue will escort her. Moreover, Fife has gone, leaving you with just these dozen men against all here at Elishaw."

"I doubt you will see either your brother or Buccleuch with your lady mother," Boyd said softly. "But in that unlikely event, I shall still hold you, your ungrateful sister, and her intrusive friend as hostages. Will your mother risk all those lives to resist the will of the Governor? I doubt it. I doubt, too, that Fife's friend Archie Douglas will sacrifice his goddaughter to defy Fife's will."

"Ah, but your priest will refuse to perform a forced marriage," Simon said.

"No, he won't. Tell him, Father."

~

"Looks as if Fife's leaving," Sym said as Garth turned quickly away and bent to examine his horse's near hind hoof, praying that Fife had not seen him.

"We'll wait for him to go," he said.

"Better if we can slip by them in the tumble and get inside," Sym advised.

The lad's instincts were good, Garth realized. As large as he was himself, he rarely thought of sneaking past anyone. Still, his men could walk about without stirring alarm, and so could Sym. And, in the teeming throng, he himself might pass unnoticed as long as Fife did not look right at him. Also, if they waited for Fife and his men to mount their horses, anyone *not* mounted would draw notice at once.

Garth nodded. "I'll go," he said. "But you should stay here."

"Ye'll be more remarkable alone than with me, sir. Moreover, ye want to find the lady Amalie. Sithee, even if she's inside, she mayn't be in the hall."

"And you think you can find her more easily than I can?"

"I can, aye. And, if she's in the hall, I can find that out afore we enter it."

Garth realized that he had not seen Simon or Boyd with Fife.

"How will you do it?"

"I'll show ye, aye, but come on. They're fetching out their horses."

Accordingly, the two of them skirted the crowd of men

shouting for horses, slipped in through the entrance, and hurried up the steps.

~

"Sir Harald is right, sir," the priest told Simon. "The Governor ordered my assistance and made it clear that further defiance will cost me my life."

Amalie said bluntly, "Simon, they will kill *you* whatever you do. That is why I came here, to warn you. Sithee, sir, Fife wants Elishaw more than any marriage."

"Be silent, Amalie; don't stir the pot," Simon said. But his voice lacked the note of curt irritation it usually held when he spoke to her.

"Aye, keep silent, lass," Boyd said. "You don't know what you are prattling about. Fife values both of us equally, Simon, and counts on our aid. I've no wish to make an enemy of you, but neither will I let you stop what he has promised me."

"You hold me prisoner in my own hall, yet don't want me as your enemy?"

"Aye, although it *is* a pity you don't have your sword or we could decide this easily. You have not won your spurs, but I'm told you're a competent swordsman."

"I'll send someone to fetch my sword, and we'll find out," Simon suggested.

"I think not," Boyd said, approaching the dais. "Not yet, at all events. Lady Amalie, pray step down here to me, and do *not* defy me again. I need only one of you for my purpose. And since I doubt that the lady Sibylla bears any real kinship to Archie the Grim, she is of small use to me. However, if you defy me, I'll have two of my men seize her and see what use they can find for her upstairs."

"By heaven, sir," Simon exclaimed, "you go too far!"

"Do I? Seize the red-haired one, lads, and—"

"Leave her, you villain; I'm coming," Amalie snapped, getting hastily to her feet and hurrying round the near end of the table.

"Seize the other lass anyway," Boyd commanded when Amalie reached his side. Grabbing her arm, he yanked her hard enough against him to reveal the chain mail under his tunic and warn her that she would bear bruises from it later.

Just then a piercing whistle shrieked from the stairway. Recognizing it, she quickly thrust two fingers into her mouth and whistled back as loudly as she could.

Releasing her, Boyd whirled toward the stairs.

Amalie glanced back to see Simon draw his dirk, put his free hand on the table, and leap across it to land between Sibylla and the men approaching her.

"Stand away from her ladyship, you lot," Simon snapped just as Amalie heard Boyd exclaim, "Westruther!"

Her attention instantly diverted, she saw Garth cross the threshold with his sword drawn. In his wake, Sym Elliot followed, dirk in hand.

"Seize the lad," Boyd bellowed to his men. "The swordsman is mine!"

"Nay, he is mine!" Amalie snapped. As Boyd shifted his sword to attack Garth, she struck fast and as hard as she could.

Recalling the chain mail, she aimed high for his throat, and then, when his head snapped back, she jabbed his abdomen with her elbow for good measure.

A strong arm swept her aside then as a gleaming blade slashed upward and clanged against Boyd's, sending his sword to clatter against the nearby stone wall and fall with a vibrating crash to the floor.

"Down, sir!" Garth snapped at Boyd, setting his sword point at the man's chest. Both weapons were thrusting swords with points meant to pierce mail.

"I yield, aye," Boyd said, dropping to a knee.

As Garth put the point of his sword to Boyd's throat and told Sym to call his men, Amalie heard a horn in the distance. Then two familiar notes sounded from a second horn. She glanced at Sym, who had hesitated near the archway.

Looking back, he grinned at her and shouted, "'Tis Himself!" Then he darted away and vanished down the stairs.

The point of his sword still at Boyd's neck, Garth roared without looking away from it, "You men, if you did not recognize those horns, learn to do so! The first was the Douglas, the second Buccleuch. Put up your weapons at once."

"Sheathe your weapons, lads, and lay them on the dais table," Simon said. "There will be no more swordplay here tonight."

"There may be more trouble for them, though," Garth said grimly. "They'll face Douglas justice for invading a Border stronghold, threatening its master, and imperiling noblewomen under his protection. Moreover, Lady Amalie is Buccleuch's good-sister, and Buccleuch has sworn an oath to defend the Murrays of Elishaw."

"Westruther, *you'd* be wise to recall that if the Douglas is here, Fife has also returned," Boyd snapped. "Also, Simon is Fife's man, sworn to obey him. But you and I can settle this properly if you let me retrieve my sword."

"Properly?"

"Aye, we'll decide as knights should, in fair battle," Boyd said.

"To do that, we'd both have to be knights worthy of the name and have the same notion of 'fair,'" Garth retorted. "By your actions here and before, you have proven yourself *un*worthy."

Hearing the sound of booted feet hurrying up the stairway, Amalie bit her lip, wondering if Fife or Douglas would appear first.

To her relief, Douglas and Buccleuch entered together, accompanied by Tammy and a man she did not know, all four ushered in by a beaming Sym.

By then, Boyd's men-at-arms had yielded their weapons to Simon.

Douglas paused inside the archway and scanned the chamber, frowning darkly. "By all the saints, what happened here?" he demanded.

Beside him, the unknown man took a step forward and peered at Boyd. "That's him, my lord," he said, nodding. "That man is Ben Haldane."

⌒

Hearing the name, Garth flicked a glance at Douglas and his companion.

As he did, Boyd struck his sword aside and dove toward his own, snatching it up and leaping lithely to his feet to lunge hard at Garth.

Garth parried the stroke, but Boyd pressed harder at him, ignoring their stunned audience.

Knowing that Amalie was behind him, Garth feared making any moves in that direction until she cried from some distance to his left, "I'm away, sir!"

Immediately, he leapt backward to his right, then forward, slashing quick and hard, using both hands for his weapon and knocking Boyd's sword high again. This time, though, it did not leave the man's grasp.

"Hold! Enough!" Douglas bellowed.

Garth stepped back at once and Buccleuch moved quickly to stand by him with his own sword drawn.

"Drop that weapon," Douglas snapped to Boyd. "You will hang soon enough, but if you don't do as I say *now*, I have them spit you where you stand."

"I cannot let you do that, Archie," Fife said calmly from the archway. "That man serves me. If he has done aught to displease you, he will answer to me."

"Done *aught*? This gallous blackguard murdered my Will!"

Fife frowned. "Have you evidence of that? I find it hard to credit."

Indicating the man who had spoken earlier, Douglas said, "This is Will's own man, who was with him in Königsberg and Danzig. Will himself named Ben Haldane as his killer, and Will's man says this foul miscreant is that same Ben Haldane, for all that he may call himself otherwise."

"Nonsense, this man is Sir Harald Boyd, who has served me loyally."

Simon, who had not stirred from his position near the dais table, said in a quiet but nonetheless carrying voice, "Even so, my lord, Boyd attempted to force matters here tonight by holding me, my sister, and the lady Sibylla hostage to his will. He likewise claimed that it was by your own order that he did so."

"Did he?" Fife frowned at Boyd. "If so, he has much to answer for, certainly. Nay, do not speak, sir," he said sternly to the offender. With more intensity, he added, "I warn you, you can do yourself no good thereby. Now, what of this charge from Danzig? Did anyone *see* him commit the crime?" He looked at Garth.

"Only Will Douglas," Garth said. "Will did name him to me, however."

"He named Ben Haldane," Fife reminded everyone. "This is Harald Boyd."

"Aye, my lord," the man with Douglas said. "But I ken Ben Haldane fine, for I saw him many times up close, and this be him."

"I do *not* know you," Boyd said. "Therefore you cannot possibly know me. Sakes, but I was never *in* Danzig."

"There, you see," Fife said. "Still, I will look into this matter, and if there is anything to the crimes you believe of this man, I *will* see justice done."

"I mean to try him myself," Douglas said. "I'd see him tried fairly."

"I'm afraid not, Archie," Fife said. "I am Governor of the Realm, after all, so he is mine unless you choose to test my authority over this."

Douglas hesitated and then shook his head.

Garth shot a questioning look at Wat. Receiving a nod, he drew a breath and looked at Amalie. Well aware of the pain he was about to cause her, and likely Simon, too, he said, "There is an additional crime to consider, my lords."

"By my faith, what else?" Fife asked, sounding bored.

"Another murder and another accusation leveled at this man."

"You refer to Haldane again, I must assume."

"No, sir. This time the witness implicated Boyd himself. I'm sorry for this, my lady," he said to Amalie. "My

"Tom!" Amalie exclaimed softly. "Where is Tom? He ought to have come with you, my lord," she said to Buccleuch.

"Tom Murray is dead," Garth told Fife. "He was on his way to deliver the news of his father's death to Lady Murray at Scott's Hall when Boyd and three of his followers hunted him down. A clumsy matter it was, too, I'm afraid, because Tom Murray had two of his own lads with him. All three are dead."

Fife said with a sigh, "Then I fail to see what evidence you can—"

"One of them lived long enough to identify Boyd," Garth said. "If you need testimony to that effect, I can give you the names of the monks who heard him."

"As I said," Fife said curtly, "I will see justice done. At present, however, though I'd intended to stay here, I shall ride back to Jedburgh tonight. This place is too full to offer suitable accommodation for all of us. You will come with me, Boyd, but leave your sword here. It will be a good lesson to you."

No one suggested that they stay, but no one looked happy to see them go.

Chapter 21

⁓

"He will see justice, eh?" Douglas muttered when the men-at-arms who'd aided Boyd had hurried after Fife and the sounds of their departure faded down the stairway. "'Tis more likely that he will reward Will's murderer for his villainy."

"With respect, my lord . . ." Simon began quietly.

Amalie, still stunned by the news of Tom's death, glanced at him and saw that, for once, her always-confident brother looked uncertain.

Sibylla was watching him, too.

"What is it, Murray?" Douglas asked sourly.

"Although I warrant Boyd thinks just as you do, sir," Simon said, "I believe the Governor will keep his word to you."

Amalie agreed.

Everyone was looking at Simon now, and she saw both Wat and Sibylla nodding as if they, too, knew what he would say and agreed with him.

Douglas frowned. "Do you think he means to do away with the man then?"

"His lordship does not tolerate fools or those who act without his orders, sir, and he did not order Boyd to kill my brother. He'd have had no cause to do so."

Simon seemed to have himself under rigid control, as if he were fighting strong emotion. Although it was hard for Amalie to imagine him having emotions other than annoyance, fury, or stiff-necked pride, she thought he might be sorry about Tom's death.

She certainly was, more than she had expected to be.

Wat said thoughtfully to Douglas, "Experience does indicate that Fife will keep Boyd from speaking out if Boyd can connect him to any of this."

Sibylla nodded again.

Amalie said, "Fife will certainly see Boyd as a risk to himself. And he removes risks and obstacles. He would have removed you, Simon. I am sure of it."

Simon met her gaze but looked bewildered. "You said he would kill me, Amalie. I'm grateful that you rushed here to warn me, for I'd not have expected that of you, but Fife knows I am loyal to him."

"But don't you see? Fife wants Elishaw just as he wanted other valuable places he has seized. Mayhap you were not in danger whilst you were willing to give him part of it and force me to marry Boyd . . ." She hesitated when she saw him wince. Satisfied though that he was listening to her for once, she added, "Will Fife be as certain of your loyalty after Boyd tells him you refused to sacrifice Rosalie?"

"But you exaggerate the danger," Simon protested. "I can see that you're thinking of the Strathearn estates and that like others, who should know better, you see something fiendish in his just wanting to protect his niece's lands for his family. Even if you should prove right about that, Elishaw is not nearly the size of Strathearn."

Douglas said, "Not as vast, but Elishaw is strategically more important to our safety than Strathearn, and a considerable Border stronghold withal. Go on, lass."

Before she could, Garth said evenly, "Art sure of all this, Amalie?"

His tone disturbed her, but she met his narrowed gaze and said honestly, "I can tell you only what I thought, sir, which was that Fife might kill Simon. That did seem clear to me before I left Sweethope Hill."

"We will discuss that particular decision later," he said in that same even tone. "Explain what you meant about Fife."

"He seizes things just to control them, I think," she said slowly, trying to discern and isolate all the bits of thought that had fallen together so abruptly and sent her hotfoot here to Elishaw. "And, then too . . ."

It was hard to think with him looking at her so sternly.

". . . there is also my father's death, and Tom's," she said.

"Do you accuse Fife of *ordering* their deaths then, when Simon does not?"

"Mercy, sir, I cannot claim to know what Fife ordered or did not order," she said, aware now only of him and paying no heed to the others.

"But you did not know about Tom when you left Sweethope," he said.

That his attitude had altered the moment he'd focused his thoughts on her was only too apparent. The way he looked at her now prickled her spine.

She wanted to be alone with him, not just so she could think better and explain but also to touch him and feel him touch her.

She would have to defend her actions first, though. Recalling that at least one of them had been in direct defiance of what he had told her to do, she swallowed hard. She had not thought much about that before, but she did now.

"Go ahead, lass," Wat said, startling her. "Tell us what you did think."

Looking at him, receiving a nod of encouragement, she said, "It was just a feeling at first, I expect. But Tom's death makes me sure the feeling was right. No one who was here tonight can doubt that Boyd wanted this castle."

Simon shook his head. "He wanted Rosalie because he could not have you."

"He didn't want *me*, though. He wanted what marrying me would get him. You told Tom as much yourself, Simon—*and* that Boyd would overlook my faults," she added steadily. "Father said he didn't like Fife's having promised Boyd land as part of my dowry. He said the value of land lies in acquiring more, not dividing it."

"I'll admit I feel the same," Simon said.

"Aye, now that you've inherited Elishaw," Amalie said. "I could see it."

"I don't blame you for believing that," Simon said. "But I disliked the notion from the first. I didn't see why Fife would not give Boyd Crown land to reward his knighthood, or at least land other than what I was to inherit."

"Land that our father owned and Tom would inherit if you had died," Amalie said, thinking aloud. "The simple answer to your puzzlement is that Fife is grasping and cannot bear to give up anything he has taken for himself, which includes Crown lands. Indeed, one wonders if he would have let Boyd keep Elishaw if the man *had* succeeded in taking it. If they were willing to kill our father and Tom so that—"

"Here now, lassie, you've no real evidence to support any of that," Douglas protested. "Bless us, but you begin to sound like Isabel! Fife thought two knights defending the area near Carter Bar would mean a stronger defense, and that is all there is to it. You cannot deny that it would either, for 'tis nobbut plain truth."

Amalie's gaze met Simon's again. "Father said he would support my refusal to marry. And, sithee, he died soon after that. Moreover, tonight Boyd said that Fife would keep his promise to give him the land whether you lived or died, Simon."

"Sakes, lass," Douglas said. "Boyd could hardly do away with Simon so soon after your father's death and Tom's without all of us suspecting foul deeds."

"I doubt, however, that Boyd thought anyone would learn of his part in Tom's death," Garth said. "Had one of the victims not lived long enough to identify him, we'd know nowt of it even now."

Simon said, "I'm curious about that identification, Westruther. I note that although you've mentioned that victim's evidence twice now, you have not said that he *named* Boyd, only that he identified him. *Did* he name him?"

"Tell him," Garth said to Tam.

After a glance at Buccleuch, who nodded, Tam said, "The monks said the lad told them he knew the killer came from Sweethope Hill because he'd seen him there himself. He said the man was all arrogance, a chap who

strutted like a cockerel and dared to take the seat beside
Sir Iagan at supper when others had more right to it."

"That was Boyd," Garth said to Simon. "I was there,
too, you'll recall, and you know as well as I do that only
one man sat beside your father that day. The princess sat
to his left. Boyd was on his right, and you yourself sat on
Boyd's right."

"You did, sir," Sibylla said quietly.

"I did, aye," Simon agreed. To Amalie, he said, "Even
so, I don't see how you came to fear so much for my life
that you rode here to warn me."

"I . . . I'm not sure now, either," she admitted, avoiding
Garth's gaze. "I truly don't recall a single thought save
the one. But in view of Fife's plan for Rosalie—"

"That's another thing," Simon said. "How could you
even have known that?"

"I told her," Sibylla said, drawing Simon's astonished
gaze to herself.

Hastily, Amalie said, "I knew you'd never stomach
that, Simon, and I feared with everything in me that Fife
would kill you when you defied him. I expect there was
more to it than that. But you know how it is with me, sir,
how my thoughts just tumble over each other. Conclu-
sions often form before I *know* how they do."

"We will discuss that, too," Garth said, giving her another look of warning that his displeasure with her remained strong. To the others, he said, "It becomes clear
that we will not resolve this tonight, and I expect we will
all be the better for sleep. Our men will look after themselves, Murray, but with Fife gone, I expect you can put
Douglas, Buccleuch, and me up for the night, can you
not?"

"Aye, sure, and welcome," Simon said. "I'm sleeping

in the great chamber, because I knew my mother would insist that I should. But I've not moved her things out yet," he added dryly.

"Mercy, I should think not," Amalie said, smiling sympathetically at him. Then, realizing it was the first time she could recall smiling at Simon in years, she caught her lower lip between her teeth.

"You're right, lass," he said, smiling back. "I'd not dare move a thing. I own, though, I'd like to have watched her deal with Boyd over our Rosalie."

"Rosalie again!" Wat exclaimed. "What *is* all this business about Rosalie?"

Simon said, "I expect someone told you that Boyd expected to marry Amalie." At Wat's nod, he said, "When he could not have her, he decided to take Rosalie instead. In fairness to Boyd, that *was* Fife's idea,"

Wat chuckled, saying, "He expected Annabel Murray to agree to that?"

Amalie was not as sure as they all were that her mother would have objected. Had Boyd managed to persuade her that the connection would enhance Murray power, she feared that Rosalie would quickly have become Lady Boyd.

However, that question now being moot, she held her tongue.

Simon said, "Buccleuch, you and Douglas will be comfortable enough in my old chamber. That way, the lady Sibylla can have Tom's—"

"Sibylla will sleep with me, of course," Amalie said. "She has no maid—"

"No, she won't sleep with you," Garth interjected. "You may let her have your old room if you like, but you will share mine."

"You'd do better to share hers," Simon said, looking from one to the other. "Tom's door has a solid bolt on it if the lady Sibylla chooses to use it, and Amalie's has a curtained bed that may be large enough for the pair of you."

The discussion shifted then to Will's man, whom Douglas declared would take a pallet in the room the earl was to share with Buccleuch. "We'll not let the lad out of our sight with Fife and Boyd still so near," he added.

They focused briefly after that on servants and other such mundane details, until Simon had efficiently sorted everything out.

As he did, Amalie kept a close eye on Garth, but although she could sense his impatience, he just listened until Douglas said, "We've little left to discuss unless you learned something more from Isabel, Garth."

"Only that she'll always believe James's death was murder, sir, and that Fife ordered it to weaken Douglas power in the Borders. She may be right, too, but you asked me to find real evidence of that, and I've found none. Nor do I think we will."

"At least Boyd did not kill him," Simon said. "He was with you, my lord."

"He was, aye," Douglas agreed.

Garth went on, "I *am* sure, as you must be, my lord, that Boyd did murder Will. I also agree with Wat that Boyd won't live long even if he might only threaten to implicate Fife. I'll assume, Simon," he added, turning to that gentleman, "that *you* cannot implicate either Fife or Boyd in Will Douglas's death."

"No, I cannot," Simon said. "You have no reason to believe me, though."

"I have no reason not to," Garth said.

"You did try to seize Hermitage two years ago," Douglas growled.

"Aye, sir, under orders from my liege lord, I did," Simon admitted. "My father was as displeased about that as I am sure you must still be."

"Aye, he *was* wroth with you," Douglas said. "I saw that, myself. The true question, though, is whether we can trust you now."

Amalie looked uneasily from one to the next as the tension grew palpable.

Meeting Douglas's fierce gaze, Simon said, "I'll do nowt to oppose you, my lord. As to supporting you or continuing my father's and grandfather's policies of neutrality, I shall have to think on it and decide that course for myself."

"I'll condemn no man for thinking," Douglas said. "I've got a mind of my own, come to that. Just don't cross me, lad, and we'll get on fine."

Simon nodded but did not speak.

"The rest of you may decide to continue your conversation for hours yet," Garth said, putting a hand on Amalie's shoulder. "But I want to have a talk with my lady wife before she retires. So if you will forgive us . . ."

"Go along, the pair of you," Douglas said. "I did forget you are but newly wedded. We can talk again tomorrow if need be."

"Thank you, my lord," Garth said, adding quietly, "Now, madam wife, show me to your chamber."

Unable to read his expression, she let him take her to the archway before she said, "Sibylla must at least accompany us upstairs, sir. It is not right to leave her here alone with all these men even if the Douglas is her godfather. And I should—"

"You will show her to Tom's room, but that is all."

Surprisingly, Sibylla said, "You should come with us, my lord."

Garth had had every intention of going with them, because he did not want to let Amalie out of his sight again. Even so, he looked suspiciously at Sibylla, wondering what she hoped to accomplish.

Receiving only a warm smile in return, he held his peace, but when they reached the door to what was apparently Tom Murray's erstwhile bedchamber, Sibylla turned her warm smile on Amalie.

Producing a vial from one tight sleeve, Sibylla handed it to her, saying, "I brought some of this for you, being nearly certain that you would fail to bring the other vial. Why do you not go to your chamber now and dab some on. I want a word with Sir Garth about something else."

Amalie looked long at her but took the vial. Without quite meeting Garth's gaze, she said, "My chamber is off the next landing, sir, to your right."

Nodding but remembering that Simon had mentioned bolts, he said, "Don't lock your door, lass."

"I won't," she said. Then, with another look at Sibylla, she hurried away.

When she had gone, Sibylla said, "You have troublesome dreams, sir."

In his astonishment, he nearly issued a sharp retort, but she added calmly, "Do not blame Amalie, my lord.

I pressed her to tell me because I'd seen your face after one such. She said you dream of webs. Is that so?"

"Aye," he muttered.

"Then I should tell you . . ."

Amalie had hastily undressed to her shift, brushed her hair, cleaned her teeth, and dabbed on some of Sibylla's scent before she heard the click of the latch.

Her emotions then were as mixed as she had ever known them to be. Fear that he would still be angry warred with gladness that he had returned, and underlying all, she seethed with curiosity.

The first thing she noted when he came in was that his expression had softened. His gaze met hers at once, and he did not look away as he shut the door.

"What did Sibylla say to you?" she asked.

"She said my naughty wife had told her about my dreams."

"But I didn't! She knew! I told you that she—" She had to stop then because in two strides he had closed the distance between them and put a finger to her lips.

As usual, when he was so near and she was uncertain of his mood, she could scarcely breathe and her whole body tensed and tingled.

"I know you did not tell her about the first one, sweetheart, and that she had somehow deduced that I'd had a bad one. But you did tell her about the webs."

Although she had relaxed at hearing the endearment, she felt a strong need to defend her actions again, and although he stood very close, he had not touched her.

Needing to touch him, she reached for his hand, slid

her fingers in against his palm, wrapped them round his thumb, and held it as she said, "I couldn't tell her what you'd dreamed about Will, so I told her about the webs instead, hoping she would think it something anyone might dream."

"She did not think that," he said, his voice gentle as the hand she held closed around her fingers and his other one cupped hers to enclose it between his two.

"No, she didn't," she admitted in what sounded to her like a very small voice. "She said that doubtless you'd thought it was an omen of entanglement—"

"As I did," he said.

"Must you *always* tell the truth?" she asked wistfully.

"You know perfectly well that I can no longer claim that," he said. "Not since meeting you apparently corrupted me."

She could not deny it. Had he not felt obliged to rescue her—

"Because of you," he went on in a decidedly provocative tone, "I was even ready to let young Sym lie for me, which is a truly despicable thing as I'm sure you will agree."

"When?"

"When he and I needed to get past Elishaw's gatekeepers earlier. So, now I doubt that you will ever again take my word for anything."

"Don't be daft," she muttered gruffly. Then, rallying, she said, "I cannot think *why* Sibylla had to bring that up again about the webs, tonight of all nights."

"She had good reason," he said.

"What?"

"I'll tell you, but I have something else I want to make clear to you first."

She grimaced. "Mayhap I ought not to have come here as I did, but—"

Silencing her with his finger against her lips again, he said, "You did not persuade even Simon that his life was truly in danger, and you did not pause for an instant beforehand to *try* to think how you had reached such a conclusion. Had you done so, you might have realized that pieces were missing from your logi— Hey!"

He jerked his finger from between her teeth, put his face close to hers, and said, "Mayhap you have forgotten how I respond to attack, my lass."

She kissed him quickly and stepped as quickly back, saying, "I am not yet ready to admit I was wrong, my lord. As long as Fife and Boyd were here, there was danger. If nothing else, I saved Rosalie from having to marry that horrid man and Simon from having to defy Fife to his face. Sithee, Fife had gone before Simon said he would not let Boyd marry Rosalie."

"But Simon did say he would not allow it, and—"

"Neither do I want to fratch with you about it now," she interjected firmly. "I want to know what Sibylla said to you."

He smiled then. "Art jealous, little wife?"

She shook her head. "I have no cause to be, sir. But I *am* curious."

Still smiling, he said, "She told me the webs don't mean risk of entanglement at all—or not precisely," he amended. "Although the ropes and chains—"

"But if they don't signify entanglement—"

"She said that being caught so in a dream means that I believe I have realized my heart's desire."

For a moment, she could not speak. Then, unable to stop herself, she said, "But how would she know that?"

"She said she had friends, sweetheart, many friends, who tell her things, even things like that. She says she believes them, and . . ." He paused, looking serious.

"And what?"

"I believe it, too," he said, kissing her. "Sweetheart, I've never believed anything so firmly in my life. But if you ever again do anything so daft-brained as—"

Grabbing his ears, she kissed him hard and felt his arms go around her.

Even so, and telling herself it was the only sure way to prevent hearing any more such tiresome stuff from him, she thrust her tongue into his mouth and pressed her body against his, delighting in his quick response.

Moments later, she was in her bed without her shift, watching him strip his clothes off faster than she had thought any man could.

He wasted no time afterward, either, using his hands and lips to stir her to passion but letting her direct much of what happened between them. She learned that a man and woman could couple with the woman on top, free of restraint, and that she could tease his senses then as easily as he had teased hers.

She could even control him to some extent, stirring his passion high, and then letting it ebb by easing her efforts.

That only worked until his control of himself began to slip, when he eased her off him and himself atop her. He strove to move gently, but in stirring him, she had excited herself to new heights, and she did not want gentleness.

He filled her within and his very presence banished any lingering doubts she might still have had about such things.

Giving herself up to the delicious sensations and her own passions, she soon felt herself soaring beyond anything she had felt before. His thrusts grew faster and faster then, until she was well nigh sobbing, but not with pain. The release, when it finally came, astonished her. Moments later, his followed.

They lay back, sated and silent, for several moments until he said, "You are so beautiful, sweetheart, and have become so dear to me. The one thing I never imagined as I pictured my perfect wife was that I should fall in love with her."

"Nay," she said with a happy sigh. "'Tis difficult to love perfection, sir. I should think she'd have bored you to madness."

"Very likely. though," he added lazily, "I cannot think how I ever imagined you might be like my mother."

"Your mother!"

"Aye," he admitted. "When I first saw you, I thought you looked a cozy armful, and there was something about you then that reminded me of her."

"A cozy armful?"

"I didn't mean that part! I meant—"

"But you thought *I* looked as if *I* would be a cozy armful?"

"Aye, sure, and I was right," he said, drawing her close again and nuzzling her neck before his lips captured hers and they began all over again.

The next time they lay back together, Amalie gazed up at the ceiling over her bed, then at the bed curtains and beyond into the room itself, thinking how odd it was to be in her own bed with the man she had married.

"You know," she said quietly. "I half expected never to come home again. But now that I have, I'm glad I did."

"But this is no longer your home, sweetheart," he said gently. "Westruther is, and we must go there very soon."

"No," she said and then smiled when she felt him tense. "It is not Westruther, the place, but Westruther, the man, that is my home now. I will be content, sir, wherever you are."

Epilogue

⌁

Christmas 1390, Westruther

He never tired of watching her.

Standing in the open doorway and looking out over the snowy slope below, he paid no heed to the chilly air he was letting inside. As he watched her heave a snowball at young Michael, he recalled the day he had first seen her, and smiled.

His nieces and nephews were all pelting her now, shrieking in their delight. He heard Amalie's laughter and a shriek or two from her as well. His mother and Joan, and Joan's husband, stood nearby, watching them all fondly.

He and Amalie had settled in well and happily at Westruther. Her sister Meg's little daughter was nearly three months old now, and in a few months, he and Amalie would have a bairn of their own. Boyd no longer troubled them in any way, having—by most accounts—suffered a fatal accident on his way back to Lauder Castle.

Harsh weather had cut Fife's Border progress short before it had well begun, so he was back in Stirling. With luck, something new would turn his attention elsewhere.

He had shown them how well he protected himself, and even Archie Douglas could do nothing about that—yet.

To be sure, they had made a dangerously powerful, implacable enemy in Fife. But Garth knew that he and Amalie had powerful friends, as well, and would deal with trouble together if and as it ever came.

In the meantime, Garth thought he might lob a few snowballs himself.

He turned to pull the door shut, and when he turned back, he saw that she had noticed him. She was smiling.

She watched him stride down the hill toward her and felt the familiar sense of rightness she always felt in his presence.

One of Joan's three little girls shrieked, "Aunt Amalie, look out!"

Whirling, she dodged another snowball that Michael had flung, scooped up one of her own to fling back at him, and then turned to meet her husband.

"Happy, sweetheart?" he said, pulling her into his arms.

She nodded, snuggling against him.

From time to time, she still dreamed of the old mill, but golden sunbeams danced on the scattered grain now, Garth was the man in her dreams, and all was well.

Dear Reader,

Border Lass's heroine, Lady Amalie Murray, was a challenging but very interesting character to develop, as you might imagine. Because of her history (*Border Wedding*), I wanted her to have a big, fierce, teddy bear as her hero, and I was fortunate to find excellent examples in my son and a number of his friends.

Translating certain illustrative incidents they provided (by example) from the twenty-first century, back to the fourteenth, proved an interesting challenge, too.

Garth as hero was just fun. I had worried and stewed over his name, going through lists of Scottish names of the period, but at first nothing excited me. I came up with his surname first. It was easier, because I wanted him related to Buccleuch (Wat Scott), and the Napiers were close allies of the Scotts. Once I landed on Napier, the name Garth began to stand out on all the lists as a nice punchy-sounding first name to go with it.

I grew up with a friend named Garth, too, and that helped. Because it is the Scottish form of Gareth, one of the nicknames is Gary, which did not fit my hero at all. So the other primary nickname, Gar, is what he became to friends and family.

The business of Scottish and English titles has long fascinated me, and *Border Lass* gave me a chance to explore their evolution a little more. Knighthood was primary even after the fourteenth century, but things were definitely evolving.

To illustrate that further, I've described a number of times the annoyance that the Earl of Fife felt at not having a more notable title. That particularly annoyed him during a visit to Scotland by John of Gaunt, then the English Duke of Lancaster.

They were both younger sons of kings and both had served as longtime "temporary" rulers, yet Lancaster lorded it over Fife because the title of duke is higher than that of earl (nowadays, two levels higher).

In 1400, Fife at last became Duke of Albany (the ancient name of Scotland). His was the second Scottish dukedom created. The first was Duke of Rothesay, granted at the same time to David Stewart, Earl of Carrick and heir to the throne.

The King of Scots then offered a third dukedom, Duke of Douglas, to Archie the Grim, but Archie turned it down with contempt. What was this foolish new title compared with that of the ever great, most honorable Earldom of Douglas? He wanted no part of it.

Archie died shortly thereafter. He has long drawn the esteem of historians and the near reverence of his descendants as a fiercely able and successful Border chief, although at the time he failed to achieve the popularity of his predecessor.

Two of Archie's children, the Master of Douglas and a daughter, married members of Scotland's royal family. And, according to Britain's *Dictionary of National Biography*, by the time Archie the Grim died, the Douglases were not only the greatest power in the Borders but also "the most powerful family in Scotland."

Sir Will Douglas, Lord of Nithsdale, is a more controversial character, at least with regard to his death. The *Dictionary of National Biography* dates his death after

1392, because of a name on the Scottish Exchequer Rolls. However, Douglas sources put it in 1390. Even the *DNB* sets what it calls "the duel" with Lord Clifford in 1390. The Douglas sources say Will died then, in Danzig. From the beginning, historians and others have debated whether Lord Clifford or someone else was responsible.

I'm sure some of you are curious about the ages at which the laws of fourteenth-century Scotland considered children old enough to contract a valid marriage. According to *The Law Relating to the Formation and Annulment of Marriage and Allied Matters* by Joseph Jackson (London, 1951) and other sources, in both Scotland and England, boys could legally marry at fourteen and girls at twelve.

My primary source for Douglas history is *A History of the House of Douglas,* Volume I, by the Right Hon. Sir Herbert Maxwell (London, 1902). Another is *The Black Douglases* by Michael Brown (Scotland, 1998).

Other sources are *The Scotts of Buccleuch* by William Fraser (Edinburgh, 1878), *Steel Bonnets* by George MacDonald Fraser (New York, 1972), *The Border Reivers* by Godfrey Watson (London, 1975), *Border Raids and Reivers* by Robert Borland (Dumfries, Thomas Fraser, date unknown), and others.

As always, I'd also like to thank my terrific agents, Lucy Childs and Aaron Priest, my wonderful editor Frances Jalet-Miller, Art Director Diane Luger and artist Claire Brown for *Border Wedding*'s wonderful cover, Senior Editor and Editorial Director Amy Pierpont, Beth de Guzman, Vice President and Editor-in-Chief, and everyone else at Hachette Book Group's Grand Central Publishing (formerly Warner Books) who contributed to making this book what it is.

If you enjoyed *Border Lass*, please look for Lady Sibylla's story in the third book in this trilogy, *Border Moonlight*, at your favorite bookstore in January 2009. In the meantime, *Suas Alba!*

Sincerely,

Amanda Scott

http://home.att.net/~amandascott
amandascott@worldnet.att.net

MORE PASSION,
ADVENTURE, AND
ROMANCE ON
THE SCOTTISH BORDERS!

Please turn this page
for a preview of

Border Moonlight

Chapter 1

Scottish Borders, Spring 1391

The child's scream shattered the morning stillness.

Whipping her head toward the sound, which had come from somewhere near the river Tweed, flowing mightily a short distance away, Lady Sibylla Cavers reined in the silvery gray gelding she rode. Pushing back the sable-lined hood of her long, dark-green wool cloak, she listened, frowning.

The scream came again and seemed closer.

Spurring the gray, Sibylla rode toward the river until she saw through a break in the trees lining the riverbank a tiny, splashing figure a quarter mile to the west, moving steadily toward her, a victim of the river's powerful, sweeping spring flow.

Without hesitation, Sibylla wheeled her mount eastward and urged it to a gallop, hoping it could outrun the river to the next ford. With her hood bobbing and long, thick dark auburn plaits flying, she kept her sharp ears aprick for more screams to tell her the child still lived, and help her estimate how fast it was moving.

As her sense of urgency grew, she leaned low along the gelding's neck and urged it to go faster.

The ford she remembered was not far, if it still was a ford. She knew only what she had gleaned about the Tweed during the princess Isabel Stewart's eight-month-long residence at Sweethope Hill, but her own experience with other rivers, burns, and rills warned her that even trustworthy fords that had remained so for years had a way of vanishing in a heavy spate, and usually did so just when one needed most urgently to cross to the other side.

As a member of the princess's household, she had had few chances to explore beyond the landscape nearest Sweethope Hill House, and the Tweed lay three miles away. She knew the banks of Eden Water better, because it flowed right around the eastern base of Sweethope Hill on its way south to join the Tweed.

At present, the river was a thick, muddy brown color and carried branches, twigs, and even larger items in its grip.

She could see a long, half-submerged log in the distance, which had apparently snagged near the opposite shore just before the river bent southward. Branches with enough still-clinging dry leaves to look like spiky plumes shot out in several directions, making the log easy to see. Other objects swept right past it, as the child would if she could not intercept it.

The ford lay just ahead with sunlight gleaming on water-filled ruts of the worn track that approached it. Although the river was much higher than usual, hoofprints in the mud indicated that, not long before, horses had used the crossing.

Reining the gray to a trot and turning, half-certain she

would see nothing but churning water, she saw with profound relief that the child still splashed, albeit with less energy than before.

She heard no more screams, and the child's strength was clearly waning, so she had little time left to save it. At best, she would have only one chance.

At the ford, she urged the gray into the water. The horse was reluctant, but she was an experienced horsewoman, and she knew it was strong.

Forcing it into the swift flow, she discovered only when it was in up to its withers that the muddy water was even deeper there than she had expected. Nevertheless, the horse obeyed, leaning into the river's flow to steady itself.

Keeping firm control of it, she fixed her eyes on the child, urging the gelding forward a few more steps until the little one was coming right toward them.

When it was near enough, Sibylla resisted trying to grab one of the thin, flailing arms with her gloved hand, and grabbed clothing instead, praying that the cloth would not tear as the water fought to rip the terrified child from her grip. The river thrust hard against the horse, eddying angrily around the already skittish beast.

The child proved shockingly heavy and awkward to hold. Then, just as she thought she had a firm grip, the gelding shifted a foreleg, turning slightly eastward.

The combination of the child's water-logged weight and the river's mighty flow pulled the little one under the horse's neck and forced Sibylla to lean hard to retain her grip. Before she knew what was happening, she was in the icy water.

Long practice compelled her to hold on to the reins. But the startled horse, already struggling to return to firm ground, jerked its head up, nearly yanking the reins free. Sibylla's skirts and heavy cloak threatened to sink her, and the combined forces of the river and the child's weight were dragging her eastward with a strength impossible to resist. Worse, the child had grabbed hold of her arm and, shrieking now in its terror, tried to climb right onto her.

Sibylla let go of the reins and, submerging, used her left hand to release the clasp at the neck of her cloak as she tried desperately to keep the child's head out of the water and find footing beneath them. The water pulled one boot off, and she kicked the other away.

Although her feet briefly touched bottom as she tried to right herself and the cloak's weight vanished when the river swept it away, she could find only water under her now. Whatever had remained of the ford was behind them.

Pulse pounding, trying not to swallow the cold, muddy water, she fought to reach the surface and to keep them both afloat. But the river, determined to claim them, swept them inexorably toward the sea.

⁓

Simon, Lord of Elishaw, returning from a visit to kinsmen with his usual, modest tail of six armed men, had forded the Tweed sometime before on his way south to Elishaw. He'd also heard the screaming child and turned back at once.

By the time he and his men reached the riverbank, the screams were well east of them, but Simon easily spotted the frantically splashing child. Beyond, in the distance, he discerned through the shrubbery a lone rider racing along the opposite bank, either a woman or a man in a dark-green cloak. Whoever it was, with the river as high as it was, and the current as strong, the person would likely need help.

As Simon turned east, one of his men shouted, "There be another lad in the water yonder, m'lord!"

Glancing back to see more splashes, Simon said curtly, "You men do what you must to rescue him. I'm going after the other one. Hodge, you come with me!" he added, singling out the largest and strongest of his men.

Then, giving spur to his mount with mental thanks to God that he was riding a sure-footed horse of good speed, Simon followed the narrow, rutted track along the river-bank, watching through trees and shrubbery as well as he could in passing, to keep an eye on the child and on the lone rider ahead.

As he rode, he wondered how two children might have ended up in the river. If they had been playing on its banks, they both wanted skelping—if they lived long enough. If not . . .

Half of his mind continued to toy with possibilities, as it was wont to do when faced with any problem, but as he drew nearer, he saw that the other rider was female and realized the shrubbery had concealed her flying plaits before.

Forgetting all else, he focused his mind on how he could aid her.

She forced her mount into the river at the ford where he and his men had crossed the Tweed earlier, and he noted how nervous her horse was of the moving water and how deftly she managed it. As the thought crossed his mind, the lass leaned to grab the child racing toward her, and he saw with approval that she was wise enough to grab hold of the front of its garments rather than trying to catch one of its madly waving arms. Still, he doubted that any female would be strong enough to hold on to it in such a current.

He spurred his horse again, his vivid imagination warning him of what was bound to happen split seconds before she fell in. She had briefly slowed the child's progress at the ford, and the south-bank entry to it lay just yards away from him.

She bobbed up straightaway and still had hold of the child. But the river had both of them and moved fast enough to make him fear he'd not catch up in time, let alone get ahead of them as he must if he were to be of any help.

The woods near the river were thicker ahead where the river bent southward and then bent due east again a half mile later.

He could shorten the distance by cutting straight across the field instead of following the river. Then, *if* the two of them could avoid drowning before he got to them, and *if* his horse could avoid putting a foot in a rabbit hole or worse . . .

Sibylla held on to the child by sheer willpower. She resisted fighting the current, tried to relax a little, and put her energy into kicking and keeping her head and the child's above water as she let the river carry them.

She hoped she could keep her wits about her long enough to think what to do, but the icy water made it hard to breathe, let alone think, and although the child seemed lighter now with the water bearing them both along, she knew they did not have long to survive unless they could reach one of the riverbanks.

Being adventurous by nature, and having grown up at Akermoor Castle within a mile's distance of its own loch to the west and the Ale Water to the east, and having been blessed then with an older brother determined to teach her how to survive the commonest perils of Border life and to look after herself, she was an excellent swimmer and possessed the ability to remain calm in a crisis.

She knew she could not successfully fight the strong current but must try to work with it, so the first thing she had done was command the child to help. By shouting at it to kick harder, she managed to shift her grip to the back of its clothing near its neck, so that by floating it on its back, she could keep its head up by bending her wrist sharply and keeping her right arm straight while she paddled with her left hand. Her body had thus shifted almost onto its side, and she found it easier to kick hard while the child floated above her legs, also kicking.

Desperation had kept her going, and for a wonder, the water had pushed her skirts up nearly to her hips, enough for them to resist wrapping themselves around her legs. She was tiring fast, though, and knew she could not go on indefinitely.

She had to find something that would float, to cling to.

She could barely manage to watch where she was going, but she knew they were rapidly approaching the river bend. Without conscious effort, because of the way she held the child and because she faced the south bank of the river, she had drawn closer to it—close enough to see boulders poking their heads up out of the water. The closer she drifted, the likelier it was that they would collide with one.

Much as she wanted to feel firm ground beneath her again, she wondered if letting the river drive them into a boulder might not kill them both.

Telling herself sternly that such a collision was more likely to injure them than kill them, and that injury would be better than drowning, she tried to judge how safely she could ease them closer yet. Only then did she remember the log.

Most debris in the water consisted of branches, twigs, and other such useless stuff, none of it large enough to provide support for both of them. But, if she could grab the log, they could at least gain a respite. They might even manage to pull themselves out of the water if the log lay near enough to the shore.

She had no doubt that she would have managed the feat easily by herself, but her fierce grip on the child made everything else awkward, and exhausting. Other than telling the little one to kick and muttering as much encouragement as she could while fighting just to swim and breathe, she had had barely spoken.

The child, too, was using what energy it had to kick and Sibylla knew she dared not waste her own energy lest she need it later.

As a result, she did not even know yet which sex the child was.

It seemed to be wearing thin breeks rather than a skirt, but its fragile bone structure seemed feminine, as did its willingness to obey her. Despite the attempt to climb onto her after she fell in, one stern command to kick hard and look for something they could grab that would help them stay afloat had been enough.

That simple trust in her made Sibylla determined not to give up.

Nevertheless, she had no illusions. She had to work her way nearer the shore to have any chance at all.

When a break in the trees showed Simon he was a little ahead of the victims, he shouted at Hodge to stay near the river so he'd be at hand if they somehow managed to make it to shore before the river swept them around the bend. Then he turned his horse to cross the open field and get well ahead of them beyond the bend.

He had ridden only a short way, however, when a shrill whistle made him look back to see Hodge waving frantically. As Simon wheeled his mount, he saw Hodge dismount and disappear into the shrubbery.

Simon put his horse to its fastest pace, wrenched it to a halt near Hodge's beast, and flung himself from the saddle. Following Hodge's footprints through the shrubbery to the riverbank, he saw the big shaggy-haired Borderer trying to step onto a half-submerged log with myriad dead branches still appended to it.

Seeing the sodden, bedraggled woman clinging to one of those branches and the child clinging to the woman, Simon shouted, "Take care, Hodge, or you'll be in the river with them."

"I'll no be going aboard it, m'lord," Hodge said. "The blessed thing be so unstable I'm afeard me weight will dislodge it from whatever's keeping it near."

"Will it take my weight?" Simon asked as he drew near enough to see for himself that the log was anything but stable. It rocked like a ship at sea.

"I'm thinking I could hold it steady enough for ye," Hodge said. "Like as not, though, ye'll get a dousing."

"I won't fall in," Simon said, noting that the woman had not spoken or even tried to push away the heavy strands of muddy hair that obscured most of her face.

She was shivering, clearly using what little was left of her energy just to hang on. The child, too, looked spent, but although its arms were around the woman's neck, it seemed to have enough sense left not to choke her.

He moved up beside Hodge, who was holding a stout branch. The log looked like the upper part of a good sized tree, but the length of it was not near enough to the shore for him to step onto it. He'd have to make a leap, and the damnable thing was bound to be slippery, but if anyone could hold it steady, Hodge could.

"Mistress, pay heed to me," Simon said as he shrugged off his cloak and draped it over a nearby shrub. "I am going to step onto that log whilst my man here holds it steady. When I do, I'll take the lad from you first. Then we'll have to decide the best way to get you out safely. Can you hang on a while longer?"

"I shall have to, shall I not?" she murmured, still not looking at him.

"Have faith," he said more gently. "I won't let anything happen to you. Hold fast now, Hodge. Don't let the damnable thing get away from you when I jump."

"I've got it, sir."

The woman looked up then, her eyes widening as Simon set himself to jump. He saw that they were grayish brown, almost matching the muddy water. Her plaits and the loose strands that concealed so much of her face were a similar color, soaked through as they were. Her lips were nearly blue. Despite her bedraggled appearance, though, she seemed vaguely familiar.

He wondered if she was the children's mother and perhaps a woman from one of the estates near Elishaw.

With no more time to think of aught but getting safely onto the log, he put a hand lightly on a sturdy branch, fixed his gaze on the flattish place he'd picked as the best spot to land, and jumped.

The log was indeed slippery, but he kept his balance by grabbing a strong-looking, upright branch. Holding on to it with his left hand, he bent toward the child, saying, "Reach a hand to me, lad, so I can pull you out."

The child shook its head, clinging tighter to the woman.

"Come now, don't be foolish!" Simon said curtly. "Give me your hand."

"Obey him," the woman said quietly. "He will not hurt you or let you fall."

"Them others tried to hurt us," the child said, teeth chattering. "Sithee, they said they was just drowning puppies. But them puppies was us!"

"His lordship only wants to help us now," the woman said as calmly as before. "I'm very cold, and I know that you are, too. We must get warm."

"Come, lad," Simon said, forcing the same calm firmness into his own voice.

"Me name's Kit," the little one said. "And I'm no a lad."

Stifling his shock that anyone would throw a wee lassock like the one before him into a river to drown, Simon said in a gentler tone, "Come now, reach up to me, lassie, so I can have you out of there and help the kind woman who rescued you. You do not want her to freeze solid like a block of ice, do you?"

Biting a colorless lower lip, Kit obeyed him, and as he grasped her arm, he reminded himself to be gentle. As stick-thin as she was, he feared her arm might snap in a too-hard grip.

Balancing himself and trusting Hodge to keep the log as still as possible, he braced a knee against the upright branch and squatted, using both hands to lift the child. Despite her sodden state, she seemed feather light to him.

"There now," he said as he held her close. "Not so bad to be out, is it?"

She was silent, staring over his shoulder at the larger man beyond him.

"That's Hodge Law," he said. "He only looks like a bear. He'll be gey gentle with you. I'm going to turn now and hand you across to him."

"I've me cloak ready for her, m'lord," Hodge said, reaching to take the child as Simon leaned out as far as he could and handed her to him.

Turning back to the woman, Simon saw that she had already begun to ease her way to the end of the log. "Be gey careful, mistress," he warned. "That current is still strong and deadly."

"You need not tell me that, sir," she said in a hoarse voice. "I have been its captive for what seems like hours now."

"Not as long as that," he replied mildly. "I saw you fall in, and I warrant you were in no longer than five minutes, mayhap ten by now."

She gave him a sour look, and the sense of familiarity strengthened, but he had been wrong about her being from a tenant family. Her manner of speech indicated a considerably higher birth. In any event, he wanted her out of the water.

Hodge was trying to shift wee Kit under his own cloak without letting go of the log, and Simon realized they had no idea how long the child had been in the water before they'd heard her scream.

The log tipped precariously, and he heard the woman gasp.

"I'm coming off, Hodge. I'll hold the log now whilst you wrap that bairn up well. As thin as she is, it will be astonishing if she does not sicken from this."

"Aye, sir," Hodge said, firming his grip on the branch he held until Simon was ashore, then relinquishing it to give his full attention to warming the child.

That they had not seen the second child float by gave Simon hope that his lads had successfully plucked it from the water. It occurred to him that although Kit had said "us," revealing that the villains had thrown someone other than herself in, she did not seem concerned about the fate of her erstwhile companion.

With these thoughts teasing his mind, he kept his eyes on the woman, but she was managing deftly now that she no longer had to worry about Kit.

Fortunately, the area where the log had snagged formed a shallow inlet of sorts, where the current seemed less fiercely determined to carry away everything in its path. When she had made her way round the end of the log, Simon released it and stretched out a hand to help her out of the water.

Her exit was anything but graceful, because she had lost her shoes, the bank was nearly vertical there, and she had trouble managing her sodden skirts to avoid tripping on them. How she had swum in them, he could not imagine.

By the time he got her out, Hodge had wee Kit swaddled tight in his voluminous cloak and held Simon's cloak ready in his free hand.

Taking it from him, Simon wrapped it around the woman, pulling the fur-lined hood up to cover her head as he said, "The sooner we get you to a fire and see you both well warmed, mistress, the less likely you are to—"

He broke off in consternation as she gave him a bewildered look, turned sheet white, and fainted. Had he not been tying the strings of the cloak, she'd have fallen flat. As it was, he barely caught her before she hit the ground.

"Sakes, m'lord," Hodge said. "What are we to do now?"

Simon did not reply. He was staring at the woman in his arms.

As he'd caught her, he had scooped her up into his arms so abruptly that the hood had slipped off again and the strands of loose hair that had hidden her face fell away as well, giving him a clearer view of her than he had had before.

He'd only met her two or three times before, but he recognized her easily.

"Ye look as if ye'd seen a boggart, m'lord. D'ye ken the lass then?"

"Aye," Simon said curtly, glancing at him.

Hodge raised an eyebrow, clearly expecting further information, but Simon said no more, striding off with her toward the horses instead.

He was hardly going to tell Hodge Law, when even his

own family did not know, that just over four years before he had nearly married the woman.

~⁓

Becoming slowly aware of hoofbeats and motion, Sibylla realized she was on horseback and that someone was holding her. The hardened, muscular body behind her held her securely and moved easily with the animal he rode.

She had no doubt who it was.

Perhaps this will teach you, the next time you try to drown yourself, to do a better job of it, she told herself with a touch of amusement—doubtless born of exhaustion or perhaps incipient hysteria.

Of all the people who might have rescued her, it had to be the one man who had fiercely warned her, after she had thoroughly humiliated him, that he would someday see to it that she got her just deserts. To be sure, they had met several times in the meantime, but always in company. He had treated her with chilly civility, and she had taken good care never to find herself alone with him.

Forcing herself to stay relaxed so he would not know she had regained consciousness, she peeked through her lashes, hoping to see where they were and be able to judge how far they were from Sweethope Hill House.

But the hood of the thick woolen cloak that enwrapped her covered most of her face, so she could not see enough of the passing landscape to do her any good.

She was warm, though, warmer than by rights she ought to be after her freezing experience in the Tweed. Certainly, the cloak was not her own, though, because the river had swept hers away, doubtless forever. And her other garments—warm or not—must still be wet, because surely, she would have wakened had anyone tried to strip her clothing from her.

Still, the hood's fur lining was soft against her cheek, the smooth, loping gait of the horse was soothing, and whatever Simon Murray had threatened years ago, she knew he would keep her safe . . . until he could safely murder her.